THE FAR CORNERS
OF THE EARTH

Some other novels by Andrew Sinclair

The Breaking of Bumbo
My Friend Judas

THE ALBION TRIPTYCH
Gog
Magog
King Ludd

THE
FAR CORNERS OF
THE EARTH

a novel by

ANDREW SINCLAIR

A John Curtis Book
Hodder & Stoughton
LONDON SYDNEY AUCKLAND TORONTO

British Library Cataloguing in Publication Data

Sinclair, Andrew *1935–*
The far corners of the earth.
I. Title   II. Series
823.914 [F]

ISBN 0-340-50203-7

Published by Hodder and Stoughton,
a division of Hodder and Stoughton Ltd,
Mill Road, Dunton Green, Sevenoaks, Kent TN13 2YA.
Editorial Office: 47 Bedford Square, London WC1B 3DP.

Photoset by Rowland Phototypesetting Ltd, Bury St Edmunds, Suffolk

Printed in Great Britain by St Edmundsbury Press Ltd, Bury St Edmunds, Suffolk

To the Sinclairs and the other Highland clans
who spread to the far corners of the earth

CONTENTS

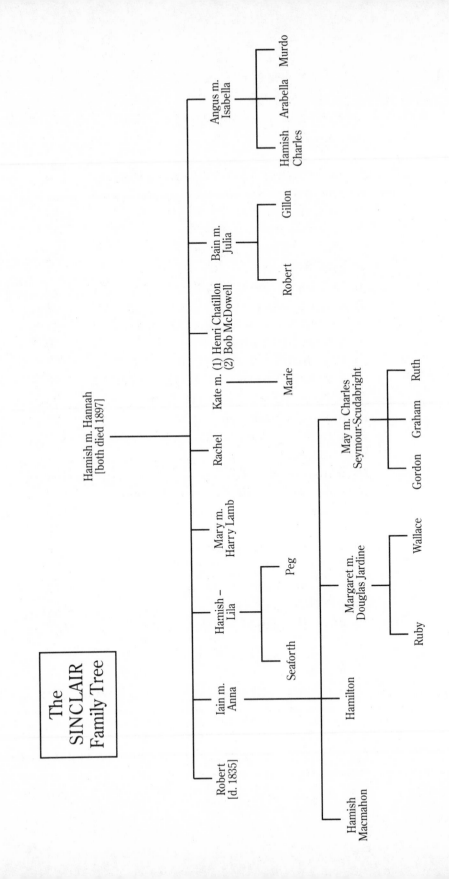

The
SINCLAIR
Family Tree

Hamish m. Hannah
[both died 1897]

Robert
[d. 1835]

Iain m.
Anna

Hamish –
Lila

Mary m.
Harry Lamb

Rachel

Kate m. (1) Henri Chatillon
(2) Bob McDowell

Bain m.
Julia

Angus m.
Isabella

Hamish Macmahon

Hamilton

Seaforth

Peg

Margaret m.
Douglas Jardine

May m. Charles
Seymour-Scudabright

Marie

Robert

Gillon

Hamish Arabella
Charles Murdo

Ruby

Wallace

Gordon Graham Ruth

PRELUDE

AN ADVANTAGE OVER SHEEP
1835

Sir John Sinclair of Ulbster looked like a giant dragonfly. Tall and erect, even in his old age, he stood in his green-and-black tartan trousers and long scarf, thrown over his scarlet jacket, with his yellow cuffs and waistband shining above his sporran. He was holding a book in his hand, his own *Analysis of the Statistical Account of Scotland*. He had stopped reading it to the Countess of Sutherland who had been widowed two years before and now sat on the sofa with her embroidery and looked to him for advice. But he was looking down from a round turret in her castle to the formal gardens which she was trying to grow on the east slope down to the shore. The straggling circles and squares of the low hedges did not seem to prosper in the sea wind. Was there any use in trying to put some sort of order on to this savage land? Sir John Sinclair put his straight nose back into his book and read on.

> The introduction of sheep must, of course, diminish the tenants in particular districts. They require a smaller number of hands to tend them than black cattle; – they can graze in places, where cattle cannot venture; – and they yield a greater produce. While it may appear a pernicious measure to drive away the people, by depriving them of their possessions, the strength of a nation cannot consist in the number of idle people which it maintains . . .

Sir John stopped reading again. His words seemed dry to him. But they were right, and he was right. He was proud of his reason and his vision. He was not a man for sentiment and cant. The countess believed in showing tenderness to her clansfolk, but with more than a million acres in the Highlands to consider, tenderness should be interpreted as a proper degree of firmness. The countess wanted his advice about what she should continue to do with her vast estate, already partially cleared for the sheep. He would be delighted to give his counsel. Such a handsome woman still, even in her old age, her stoutness only serving to emphasise her puffed and hooded eyes as bright as an osprey's above her fine beak of a nose, as she bent over her needlework, stitching in the detail of the pattern.

"I fear I am boring you, my lady."

I

"Pray, Sir John, read on, unless it bores you to read what you have written. You must already know it. But for me it is very instructional."

"What you have done is right, my lady."

"I know that," the countess said, "but it is also comforting to find a learned man of the same opinion. And a practical man. All the improvements you have done to Thurso. Those houses in Janet Street are really quite elegant, although the Scots I am afraid will never be Palladian. And that handsome temple at the end of Sinclair Street! You have left a monument to your name."

Sir John Sinclair shrugged.

"We do what we can. I have done little compared to your useful improvements. That distillery you have built at Brora – it has changed your tenants from criminals into respectable men. Instead of selling their grain to the makers of all that bog whisky, they sell it to you to make legal spirits. And you feed pigs off the spent grain from the mashing. Most laudable, dear lady –"

"I am not sure," the countess said. "We have still put half the crofters out of work with the spread of the sheep. And they leave us, they emigrate."

"Not all of them. Many become sailors or fishermen. They take to the sea, that is true, but not to leave Scotland for ever. Why, in a creek at Ulbster, a whole fishing industry has developed. The men catch the herrings, the women carry them up the steps in creels on their heads –"

"How many steps, Sir John?"

Sir John closed his eyes for a moment. He saw a vision on the back of his lids, a line of women winding and toiling up the stone steps of the deep crevasse, bowed under with heavy burdens. As they passed him at the top of the cliff's edge, they would not bob to his rank, but only glare at him in weariness and contempt. He opened his eyes to the sight of the countess stitching on her sofa.

"Three hundred and fifty steps down and the same up at Whaligoe Harbour."

"A woman can do that? How much fish does she carry?"

"Up to a hundredweight."

"Your Highland women don't seem the fair sex to me," the countess said. "Porters and climbers. Do you really think they wish to do it?"

"It is a useful employment," Sir John said confidently, as if to reassure himself. "And it is steady work. There was no profit in the crofts, herding the black cattle and growing potatoes and neeps. Men must work."

"And women too."

"And women too. So many of the families you have sent away

2

because of the sheep are all employed now in Glasgow and Greenock in the bleach-fields and the cotton-mills, which also train the children to do something useful. And there is all the building work in our growing ports and cities, and the fetching and carrying of our manufactures. Your acts have done nothing but good by encouraging people to move from a brutish life to an economic one."

"Damnation," the countess said. She had pricked her hand with her needle. Now she sucked her finger like a small girl in search of consolation. "This embroidery – it is hardly worth it. I have quite spoilt my Garden of Eden by dropping some blood on the Tree of Knowledge."

"Perhaps," Sir John suggested, "you have merely added another apple for the serpent to offer to Eve."

"I doubt if she would eat it," the countess said. "But what else can a woman do to pass the time of year in Sutherland?"

"You are doing valuable work in improvements. Your name will go down through the ages, dear lady –"

"As a benefactor? Is that what you are telling me?"

"A great benefactor. The uplifter of a whole people –"

"Then why do they resist? Why do they write such terrible things about me in *The Scotsman*? I am most pained."

"Do not be. I have dealt with this in my book."

"Then pray continue, Sir John."

The baronet turned the page to find the passage he was seeking.

The partiality in favour of former times, and attachment to the place of their nativity natural to old people, together with the indolence in which they formerly indulged, misled the Highlanders in drawing comparisons between their past and present situations. But indolence was almost the only comfort they were accustomed to enjoy. There was scarcely any variety of wretchedness to which they were not compelled to submit. They often felt what it was to want food; their scanty crops were consumed by their cattle in winter and spring; and little remained for the sustenance of themselves and their families in summer. During a great part of the year they lived wholly on milk, but sometimes they were reduced to such extremity, that they were obliged to bleed their cattle and subsist upon the blood; and even the inhabitants of the glens and valleys repaired in crowds to the shores to pick up the scanty provisions which shell-fish afforded them. They were miserably clothed, and the huts in which they lived were dirty and mean beyond expression . . .

"I have visited their huts," the countess said. "Frankly I would not put my dogs or my pigs in them."

3

"How different is their situation now!" Sir John read on. "They enjoy the necessaries, comforts, and even some of the luxuries of life in abundance. Even those who live on parish charity, feel no want . . ."

"Enough, Sir John. Shall we walk in the garden? I need the benefit of your advice about my hedges."

Sir John Sinclair bowed slightly.

"Topiary, my lady, is a speciality."

"Is that what it is called? Hedges are quite good enough for me."

A garden in the French style had been attempted outside the castle on the slope down to the sea. Carved stone parapets and steps led down to a round fountain with flowerbeds enclosed by privet and clipped bushes. There had been efforts to trim the greenery into birds and beasts, but the winds had made the foliage moult, so that a leafy pelican was as thin as a stork and a verdant elephant was without a trunk or hind legs.

"What miracles have you wrought here, my lady," Sir John managed to exclaim. "Why, Versailles in the north!"

"Stuff and nonsense," the countess said. "Nothing grows here except foul weather. Now what do I do about those hedges?" She considered a mouldy green monkey. "Do I put them out of their misery?"

"In time, in time –" Sir John said.

"In time we are all dead," the countess said, "and we two all too soon. I am viewing the miserable species now."

"They seem a little unaccommodated."

"What does that mean, sir? Plain English, if you please."

"Out of sorts, my lady. But there is a blight in the land. It is called *Phytophthora infestans*. It has attacked the potato in Ireland and may cross the Irish Sea in time."

"But these are hedges. Does it make hedges rotten too?"

"There may be a connection," Sir John said judiciously. "In diseases there is often an affinity between one illness and another."

"But if the potatoes are blighted, all my people will starve."

"No more than usual," Sir John said, "if they stay in the Highlands."

A footman came hurrying from the castle along a gravel walk which sprayed about his feet. There was something askew in him, one white stocking in a wrinkle on one knee, his wig crooked, his face purple, dust on his yellow coat.

"One simply cannot get them to wear livery," the countess complained. "They simply do not understand."

"My lady," the footman said, "there is a petition the now."

4

"There is always a petition," the countess said. "And always now. It can wait –"

"The minister came with it. It has come all the way from the Gorval."

"Is there no end to this botheration?" the countess wailed. "Is there no peace on this earth?"

"Instruct the minister to say his prayers," Sir John said to the footman, "until the countess is ready to receive him."

The footman opened his mouth, but he said nothing and turned on his heel and walked away, crunching the little stones of the path. His stocking had fallen about his ankle.

"You must stand firm," Sir John told the countess. "You must persevere."

"What can I do?"

"What you have been doing, that shall you do," Sir John said. He pointed to the far moorland on the hillside above the castle. "Look, the sheep have already improved the land. It is green now where previously it was black and barbarous. A firm persuasion will make the people go for their own good to the towns and the factories or to the sea. You know of the kelp. It did sell for twenty pounds a ton, and a man and his family may gain two pounds a week by gathering kelp for the manufacture of glass and soap."

"But my people do not want to be removed to the factories and the sea."

"Your people, my lady?" Sir John posed the question like an advocate. "When did your people last serve you?"

"At the time of the rebellion. Ninety years past, when we chased that wicked young Stuart Pretender out of the land."

"And since then, your people have not served you as soldiers for their tacks of land."

"With reluctance," the countess said angrily. "And with disobedience. I had to make threats when the recruiting officer could not sign enough of them in the Ninety-third, my regiment, against the French."

"And what was it that you said then, my lady? Those famous words of yours."

"Oh them," the countess said. "Well, they were true words about my clansmen."

Sir John smacked his lips as if on a buttered radish, and then he quoted, "They need no longer be considered a credit to Sutherland, or an advantage over sheep or any useful animal."

"I said that?"

"You did. And you brought in the sheep."

5

"Poor men," the countess said. "If they did but know their own good."

"If they did, my lady," Sir John said, "they would know you for the good countess, who removed them for the good of us all."

"If there is another famine, I shall help them."

"To emigrate, my lady. Not to move them on to another patch of land like your previous tenants. You merely sent them to another miserable glen. Charity is often the enemy of industry."

"I do not know," the countess said. "I shall be dead soon and lie beside my dear departed husband. Anyway, I have to leave the castle. My son, the second duke, wants it for his wife, Lady Harriet. Can you believe it, Sir John, as if Dunrobin was not good enough" – her hand swept in a motion towards the tall white turrets with black conical hats surrounding the fortified house – "my son is employing the man who is building the Houses of Parliament like a Gothic nightmare to rebuild this place. It will look like a gingerbread palace – something out of *The Thousand and One Nights*! It is a simple Scots castle, and we have lived here for four hundred years. And it is good enough for another four hundred years –"

"Whatever the duke does," Sir John said diplomatically, "I am sure he will do well. But he will never be remembered as well as you."

"I wish I were as sure as you are," the countess said. She turned to look out to the wrinkled grey North Sea at the end of her unkempt hedges, where sheep also grazed on the salt grass on the far side of the garden wall. "We have both done so much, Sir John. But have we done so well?"

And Sir John Sinclair was dead that same year, and the countess five years later.

I

THE WARNING OF
THE DOMINIE

1846

"I hit it."

"You lost your marley."

"I hit the plunker."

"You did not."

Angus hurled himself on Simon. It was always the same. Sinclair against Mackenzie, someone was cheating, someone was robbing, someone was raiding. Clan took on clan, and the devil and the stranger took the profit. The two boys grappled, held, twisted, tried to throw and dump and fall and wind each other. Then the big Hamish Jamie was behind his small brother, breaking his grip by holding his elbows and wrenching him loose. Then Simon Mackenzie swung a fist and blood was bright on the nose of Angus.

"Foul, Mackenzie."

The third of the Sinclair boys rushed in. Bain lashed out at Simon, only to have his blow taken on the arm of a second Mackenzie. Then the other Macs all came in, Mackay and Macdonald and Macleod, with only the Frasers aiding the Sinclairs, and the girls keening at the edges of the shinty without sticks. Then, louder, the voice of the dominie, shouting:

"Ha, you wee devils! Break it now! Or it is the strap. The rod will chastise –"

The boys split and turned to face the tall and stooped dominie in his black robe, bent like a hooded crow in judgement.

"And I will have them," he demanded. "I will have them all. Give me your bools."

He held out his clawed hand in a begging bowl of the flesh and the boys filed by, dropping in it their burned clay piggers and fired red marleys and the slate balls they called sclaiteys. The marbles filled the dominie's hand until he had to bring up his other palm to make a bigger pouch for receiving them. When the last boys had given up their treasures and the dominie's hands were heavy, he led the way back into the schoolroom and dropped the marbles under the open lid of his high desk.

"And here they will stay until you see the sin in the fighting over toys and baubles. Woe is he that shall harden his heart and raise his hand in the sight of the Lord."

For Angus, wiping the blood off his nose with his fingers, the squatting on the rough bench behind his scarred desk was worse than enduring the broken chairs in the converted tent where the Free Church minister preached to them from the Gaelic Bible on a Sabbath day. Angus could never abide the sitting for more than a minute, it was fidget, fidget all the time with him. He would rather be niffering and bartering his piggers and marleys, he wanted to spin his peerie and throw the beechwood top so its iron point struck the cluster of the other boys' tops and scattered them wild. He could watch the teetotum fall all the days of June, shouting its numbers and trading on the open face of the single dice. Or he would be after the birds, yelling at the crows that their mother was away and there was powder and lead to shoot them all, or he was calling at the cuckoo:

> I see the gowk, and the gowk sees me,
> Between the berry bush and the apple tree.

Or there would be the counting game in the ring of boys with the teller saying words that came from a time before time, words long gone with the Picts and the Druids dead in the peat bogs. What did they mean?

> Eenerty, feenerty, fickety, feg,
> El, del, Domin, egg –
> Irkie, birkie, storie, rock,
> An, tan, toose, jock –
> Black face, white trout,
> Gibbie ga – you're out.

And out of the dream that was in his head, Angus heard a voice saying: "You're out, Angus Sinclair, out of your head, you have not been listening to your dominie, what was I saying now?"

Angus felt the blush on his cheeks hotter than the blood from his nose.

"You were saying –"

"And what was it?"

"The good Lord –"

"Was it not the bad laird?"

8

"I was meaning the bad laird."

"But the Lord is good and the laird is meant to be."

"I did not hear you true, dominie."

"Then you will hear this."

And the dominie was down the space between the benches and the desks, then the flat of his hand hit Angus's ear with such a crack that the rafters shook above and a mouse fell from the roof and stunned itself on the planks of the floor. And the girls shrieked at the little thing and stood on their desks, but Hamish Jamie bent and picked it up by the tail and swung it round and threw it through the one little window under the thatch. And everybody laughed until the dominie spoke in thunder again.

"There is the wee slicket cowering timorous beastie, and now it is gone. And so shall you be gone. For the Lord giveth and the laird taketh away. The Lord gave us this glen and the growing things upon it. He gave us the fish of the river and the sea, the black cattle and the fowls of the air. But the laird says the land is his land and he will give it over to sheep, not men. He will throw down your houses and your dwelling-places. He will burn your barns and your byres. And he will send you to cut and burn the kelp weed and to till the furrows of the sea and to pass beyond it to all the corners of the earth. As he has done to Ross and Cromarty and Sutherland, in Lewis and Skye and the Western Isles, so shall he do here. We have been cleared before and now it shall be for the last time. And this school shall be a kennel for the dogs that chase the deer and the hare, and where your roofs are, there shall be ravens under the heavens."

The dominie paused in his speech as he looked round the silent children of the glen that ran down towards the sea. He saw their faces crowned with raggety hair, some round and some pinched, all pink and red with play, and he saw their poor shirts and tousled smocks, their slate pencils and torn books, one primer between each four of them. They did not seem to be afeared, but to listen, even to accept. A dry rage burned in the dominie's throat so that he coughed. This damned obedience to laird and to established minister, this bending to the law and to things as they were and should not be at all.

"When will this be?" Bain held up his hand, but he asked the question before the dominie gave him the right to speak.

"Too soon."

"I will not let them. Not the Sinclair house."

Hamish Jamie was standing and speaking, already Highland tall, more than six feet at sixteen years of age, a down of hair on his bare legs below his kilt, dyed black over the pattern on it. For who should dare to wear the old dress since it was banned after the butchering of

9

the clans by the guns of the House of Hanover at Culloden, except for the dwarf Queen at Balmoral with her German prince, all decked up in red stripes and green squares in fancy tartans like sweetie stands at the feeing market.

"*You* will stop the baillies, Hamish Jamie, and the constables and the keepers with their shotguns. And what will you use? Your bare hands and your bare feet? Or will you fall on your bare knees and ask them to spare you?"

"I will beat them."

"Then they will beat you, my boy. There are hard times to come."

The dominie looked at the stone fireplace, where no fire burned. Peats and whin-roots and pine knots and broom kindling were piled around the hearth, all brought by the pupils instead of fees. His gaze moved up to the rafters, which had been boarded over to make a loft. Other offerings were stored there, potatoes and oatmeal and salted fish for the winter months. But he would not see the cold weather here. Even by the summer, they would be gone.

"On your desks, laddies. Open the trap door. And take out from the loft all you find of the food there. You gave it to me, and I will not be needing it, and you will be wanting it. Take it down now."

As Hamish Jamie led the reaching and the scrambling into the roof, the dominie walked back to his high desk. Behind it on the wall hung a Blackie's world map, creased and stained. The little Angus had come to look at it. The dried scabs of blood on his nose were as black as the faded patches of the red British Empire that made an occasional quilt across the paper earth.

"Are we there?"

Angus stuck his finger on to the fingernail on the map that was Scotland pointing up to the north from the weight of England below.

"Aye, we are there, Angus."

"We are awful small."

"A sparrow in the sight of God is as big as an eagle. And the Scots, well you know, Angus, they have travelled all over the world. It was a Sinclair now who first went over the seas to America a century before Christopher Columbus."

"There."

Angus drew his dark finger across the dull blue paper that reduced the Atlantic Ocean to several inches wide.

"Henry Sinclair was an earl of Scotland," the dominie said, "and a prince of Norway. He brought the Orkneys and the Shetland Isles to us."

"We have our own folk there."

"And he sailed with seamen from Italy across the ocean, and he came to Canada, which he called New Scotland – Nova Scotia in the Latin."

"And do they have salmon there? And potatoes?"

"The potato comes from there. And the salmon too, Angus. The fish go there to mate and make more salmon, then they come back to our rivers."

"I like fish. My brother Iain –" The face of Angus reddened, making black smudges of his freckles.

"Where is your brother now? He is not in the school today."

"Iain is gone after the fish. We have not a one –"

"He must stay at the learning."

"He is eighteen. He is a man."

"You will never make your way in a wicked world without the learning."

With the noise of grapeshot striking the barricades, potatoes bombarded the desks and planking. Pellets and slugs and lumps bounced and scattered dried earth on to the boards. The harvest was hitting the floor.

"Will you not be careful then?" the dominie shouted. "Will you spoil the gifts of God? Get on down and take care."

Bain had come up to the dominie's desk to join his brother Angus. Both of them were now peering over the rim to contemplate the marbles trapped among the stubs of chalk and the pens and the primers. Neither boy dared to ask, but they looked up at the dominie with wide eyes. This was no day like other days. There might be a mercy in the master.

"I should not," the dominie said. "What is the matter with me? I must be daft." He scooped out a few clay marbles and put them in Bain's hand. "You can have your bools. And there will be no school more today. Get you back to your homes and to the wool cleaning. You will need to be ready for the coming of the laird's men, when they do. Get away with you."

2

TO CATCH A FISH

Iain lay on the flat rock, his left hand trailing in the narrows of the river. The water broke his arm at the wrist. Below the bent bone, his four fingers and thumb moved as thick pink weeds, waiting. The brown speckle-backed oval moved on transparent fins over the stones and stayed short of the waving lure. The mouth of the fish seemed to suck at the tips of the flesh, then it moved over the palm of Iain's hand. His skin tickled the cold scales of the trout's belly, then his forefinger and thumb jerked up into open gills and flipped the fish high in air. It arched and sparked silver and fell against Iain's free hand, which knocked it sideways up the bank, where it humped and flapped.

"Guddled you," Iain said with satisfaction.

There had been three trout guddled that morning, but Iain was set on bigger game. In the shallows of the dark pool upriver he had seen a shadow move above the stones as large as his forearm. There was a chance, a small chance, if he could chase the big fish into a tuck of the bank, he could break its head with a rock. Iain picked up the last trout, now still but gasping, and forced through its gill and mouth a dry rush that plaited it to the two other fish that he had caught that morning. And whistling "Will you not come back again" out of tune, the young giant walked up the glen towards the dark pool.

Stepping over the mosses on the roots of hazel and pine, Iain strode against the current that splashed and brawled down the vast cleft in the mountains. Through the trees, the heather was already painting the slopes of the hills in streaks of blood, while lichens scored the flanks of the black crags that trimmed the blue sky. Ahead, a belt of birches drooped their green feathery wings near Iain's hunting place, where the salmon was resting on its bed of stones.

Iain dropped his ring of trout in the crotch of a broken tree. Then he bent and worked out of the ground a boulder half the size of his head. Carrying it in both hands, he trod on wildcat's feet towards the water's edge. For a man so large, he walked as delicately as Agag of the scriptures. The sun between the branches streaked his ruddy face, for he was careful to front the light so that his shadow was cast behind him, not upon the shine of the ripples. And his slow approach had its reward. For he could see the long charcoal shape of his prey set in the sombre-bright waters against the granite stones on the bed of the corner of the pool, the big fish at ease.

For a while, the young man watched the salmon. He moved no more than a tree stump moves. Yet each half a minute, he would take one step closer to the bank, his heart in his mouth that the fish might take fright and glance aside. But the sun seemed to shower its gold upon his luck, for the salmon also swung to face the sun, so that the split rudder of its black tail was nearmost. Now Iain could take the last two paces and bend under the weight of the boulder as if bowing to a good fate.

"God speed you," he breathed and heaved the lump between his hands, up and away.

The stone flew in a lazy arch in the air and fell into the water in a spout. For a moment, Iain knew that he had missed his quarry, but then the thrash of blazing foam glittered off a stricken leaping thing, and he was plunging into the pool and slipping on the wet rocks and falling with one hand out and another bunched in a fist to knock the flying salmon further up the shallow into the bank. Iain gashed his knee and bloodied the water, but he lunged and scrabbled after the salmon, which was flailing in a flurry of spume, broken at the neck. The man clasped the fish in his arms that were thicker than the stakes that held up the nets in the waters, but the fish's head struck the man's chin in its death throe, then bucked in a last desperation on to the mosses by the pool. Crying and laughing with pain and exultation, Iain threw himself on the earth by the great fish and opened his arms and lay on his back in his glory in the light of the sun.

A black metal pipe was pointing down between his eyes. At the top of the barrel of the fowling-piece, there was the spotted face, all whinberry and oatmeal, of Donald Mackay, the chief servant of the laird, the keeper of the glen and all that swam and ran and flew in it.

"And where will you be taking that fish, Iain Sinclair?"

The young man sat up and pressed his hot forehead against the chill kiss of the muzzle of the gun.

"I took the fish, Mackay, and it is to take now where I please."

"It is the laird's fish."

"He did not take it. I did."

"It is still the laird's fish."

"And did the laird make the fish?"

"He did not make the fish. But you know it is his fish."

"I know he did not make it, and I will take it."

"You will not."

Mackay kicked the body of the salmon with his boot. It jerked again at the shock and slithered six feet along the bank into the ferns.

"That is my fish," Iain said.

Mackay raised the barrel of his gun to point at the innocent sky and shook his head.

"You are a daft laddie," he said. "You are big and bonny, that is a fact –"

Iain now rose to his height. He dwarfed the bulky figure of Donald Mackay as a heron over a cormorant.

"But you do not ken the world, Iain. If the laird put you in the sessions, you would be sent for seven years to Australia where the men and the boys go for the catching of the game."

"And you will tell him, Donald Mackay."

"I will and I will not."

"You speak like a Mackay. I will and I will not."

"I will tell him, for I have taken the oath to him and to his own which are my own. But I will not tell him until after you are gone from the glen."

"That will never be."

"It will be very soon."

"That will not be."

"Iain, Iain –" The keeper Mackay put down his gun on its wooden stock and thrust his blotched face up at the young man's. "Will you not listen? As your own mother and your father came to this glen after the coming of the sheep to the Highlands and the Isles, this is but a waiting place for them and for you. Now after the sheep, they want the moor and the forest for the deer. Not a village now, but a park for the stags. And down by the sea, they want the folk to toil at the kelp weed and hunt the silver herrings. There is no dwelling for the men now, but for the beasties. Not one at all."

"I will fight against it."

"You cannot fight your laird. You must fight for your laird."

"I will," Iain said, "if he asks me. And if he grants me the land and the river which is mine."

"He cannot ask you now. It is the English and the colours of their regiments that do the asking. It is not the chiefs and the clans that ask any more. It is for the foreigners and for the foreign wars that we are fighting. But you ken I fought the good fight at Waterloo."

"Aye," Iain said. "I ken that."

"They came at us all day, and we could not charge. First we were

near a farmhouse among the trees. And they came and we fought, and
they came on and we fought, and with bullet and with bayonet and
with claymore and with dirk we fought them away. And there were
dead men on that field, Frenchmen and our men, lying in their blood
with their arms round the one the other, and their steel still stuck in
the one the other. And there was a keening of the wounded as the sea
wind keens in the roof. And there was a blanket of the bodies as the
broom on the moor. And since that day I have never lifted hand to
man, and I will never murder my fellow creatures again."

"But you are the keeper here, Donald Mackay. You will kill the
beasties and the fish."

"Aye, but these are the living creatures God gave us for our eating
and our stay."

Iain laughed. "Then we shall eat the fish. The laird has muckle
enough to eat."

"You shall keep the fish, Iain. But it is the last fish you shall keep.
It is not for you or your folk. It is the fish of the laird of the glen."

Iain walked across to where the body of the salmon lay among the
ferns. He picked up its slippery length that had begun to ooze slime
between its scales.

"It is the fish of the Good Lord of the glen," he said. "It is so."

"Get away with you," Mackay said. "And do not you be catched
on the way home. You hide that fish, do you hear me?"

"I will stuff it down my shirt," Iain said. "And all will think I am
having a wee bairn soon."

Mackay laughed.

"You are a fine big laddie," he said. "If Boney had seen you at
Waterloo, he would have run for his life."

"You are a tolerable fine man too, Donald Mackay. Like that
Nelson, you can turn a blind eye the now."

Iain dropped the great fish in the pouch of his open shirt. Its cold
weight lay on his belly above the waist band of his drenched kilt.

"What shall we call it now?" he asked. "Mary – or Donald after his
father?"

"Get away," Mackay said, and Iain went laughing down the glen
with his salmon in his shirt and his ring of trout in his hand.

3

THE BRIGHT BUSHES

The bushes by the burn were bright with blankets and kilts and cloaks and coverings. The pine knots and the peats burning beneath the great three-legged iron cauldron filled the air with their acrid sweet incense, and the butterflies seemed like scraps of garments as they wafted from heather to broom to bracken. The soaking tubs still full of the woollen stuffs stood on their rollers, trundled from the cottages for the annual cleansing. Young women with kirtles up to their thighs were stamping on the blankets in the tubs, their eyes fearful and wanting the spying gaze of the hidden men. Mary Sinclair was waiting with a basin of hot soapy water for any peeping Thomas, and she had doused two in the morning already. Her small sisters, fair Rachel and red-headed Katie, were giggling and singing along with the women at work at the washing of the clothes.

> *They that wash on Monday*
> *Have all the week to dry –*
> *They that wash on Tuesday*
> *Are not far by –*
> *They that wash on Wednesday*
> *Are not so mean –*

Mary saw her large brother coming from the river along the burn. The wet bulge in the front of his shirt made him waddle with his bare feet splayed out to take the forward weight. His kilt was a hitched skirt, but red bloodied knees and legs like birch trees would never do for a woman with child. All the same, Mary ran towards him with her basin of suds, followed by the screaming Katie and Rachel.

> *Get away, peeper,*
> *Fly away, spy,*
> *Or you'll get a dousing,*
> *Never go dry.*

And all the while, the young women at their treading of the sodden wool in the tubs were singing:

> *They that wash on Thursday*
> *May get clothes clean –*
> *They that wash on Friday*
> *They have muckle need –*

Now the big Sarah Macdonald saw Iain coming, *ach* and she had always had her eye on him, he was certain and big enough for her, there was no gainsaying it. And she pointed and screeched and hoisted her kirtle higher to show the tops of her legs, whiter than snowbanks.

> *They that wash on Saturday*
> *Are dirty dogs indeed!*

Iain had stopped short in his tracks, faced with the shouting and the laughing of the young women and with the clothes and the blankets spread in a woollen harvest on the bushes. He turned as if to run, but Mary was upon him, throwing the soapy water up and over his red hair and the yoke of his shoulders. Rachel and Katie scampered to grab one of his knees, the gashed or the whole one. The young women sang fit to deafen a raven:

> *They that wash on Sunday*
> *Are the devil's breed!*

Iain wiped the soap from his eyes with his free hand. Then he pulled off Katie and dropped the ring of plaited trout round her neck over the flame of her hair. The little girl cried in delight and horror at her sudden necklace of fish. Then Iain reached inside his shirt and plucked out the salmon and mockingly cradled it like a baby in his arms.

> *Chin, cherry,*
> *Mouth, merry –*

As he sang, he chucked the fish under its jaws and prodded its head with his forefinger. Rachel joined in the game, pretending the salmon was a baby.

> *Nose, nappy,*
> *Cheeks, happy –*

Now the laughing Mary joined in, taking the cradled fish from Iain's arms and rocking it in hers. It might be her own little one swaddled in silver scales.

17

Eye, winkie,
Brow, brinkie,
Over the hill and far away.

Mary tossed the salmon to Sarah, who had come up from her stamping tub and was standing over from Iain, laughing in his face. She caught the fish and cradled it, then she stared at him, bold as a brass knocker.

"And is this the only bairn you are able to come with, Iain Sinclair?"

A beacon fire was brighter than the flush in Iain's face that fair dimmed the embers of his own hair. He mumbled and growled, but not a word came from him.

"The poor thing," Sarah said, dandling the slimy slithering creature. "And you with a father that dare not own to you."

Mary laughed with all the young women as Iain turned and plunged away through the bushes. His kilt snagged in thorns and was ripped open. The shrieking was so loud behind his back that it sounded in pursuit, not in glee. He gathered his kilt clumsily around his loins and ran on, mindless of the stones that were bruising his feet. He left the young women mad in their merriment at the great Iain Sinclair come to grief at the cleansing of the wool.

"Come back, come back, Iain," they cried. "We need you now. For the wringing out."

"I will wring him out," Sarah called.

"To find your ring on him," Mary said to her.

"Ach, I never did think –"

"You think of nothing but how you will get wed to our Iain –"

"I never did –" Sarah's face was now the fiery furnace that Iain's had been. "He's not a pin to me."

"Good on you," Mary said. "As if you did not spend all your day eying him like a hen at the grain."

"If you do not hush you –"

Sarah had raised her right hand from cradling the salmon, but the slighter Mary blew her a kiss.

"I did not mean it, Sarah. It is only that everybody says it. But I – not I –"

"You did say it now," Sarah said.

"Only to say, who might believe it? Our Iain and you – daft. Give me our fish."

Mary snatched the salmon from the crook of Sarah's arm, and she ran with it along the burn. Katie and Rachel went scampering after her. They left Sarah behind them, her legs planted astride, silent and angry. "You will have a bite of our Iain's salmon," Mary shouted to the treaders in the tubs. "And I will bring him back for the wringing. He has more force in him than ten of the other men." And Mary and her sisters ran away towards their home, where Iain had gone before them.

Their mother Hannah was finishing the sweeping. Cleanliness was next to godliness, all the ministers said that. But what use was it, when there were nine of them living in the cottage with its two boardings to separate the bed of the boys from the bed of the girls, and the other section beyond the planks to keep the black cows apart in the byre. The blankets, they were only cleansed once a year, and the fleas and the ticks, they hopped off the cows and the thatch, and there was scratching and itching in the winters, how could you keep a house clean now, with the bairns and the beasties under the same roof, and the fireplace in the middle of the room, so when the wind blew sorely down and the flakes from the peats were driven free, there was a black snow inside powdering away before you could catch it? God – Hannah thought – God Himself could not be so pearly-white and scoured if He lived like He made His creatures live in the glen.

The ache at her back straightened her against the handle of her birch-twig broom, and she saw Iain coming from the burn towards the house that stood topmost of them all in the clachan. Her heart swelled to see him, so big now and so small when she bore him, her Iain, her own, her first son but for Robert, and he was laid to rest before he was weaned, why did she think of the lost one before the living? She threw out her arms and smiled to see her Iain, but instead she saw the blood in a black scab on his knee, and she heard herself scolding him against her thought.

"Come here the now and let me look to that. There is hot water in the pot."

"It is not anything at all, Mother."

"That is what you say, and then there will be the poison in it, and they will take the leg off you."

Hannah pushed her son before her into the main room and sat him on the wide pine chair, where her husband Hamish sat when he was home from the field. She dipped an iron ladle in the black pot that was set over the fire, and she took out the hot water and lifted her petticoat and put its hem in the steam and knelt on the earth floor and wiped the hot linen against the hard gash on his knee. It took her a small scrubbing to soften and loosen the scab until she could staunch the red blood by the tear in his skin against the bone.

"Ach now, Mother –"

"Hush you. Did you catch a fish?"

"Four. And one great one."

"Where are they now?"

"The lassies have them."

"And what were you doing with the lassies?"

"What were they not doing with me?"

Hannah laughed with her son and stood up, leaving him to hold his finger against the wound on his knee. Then suddenly her eyes stung with the peat smoke or a tear. "Ach, you foolish boy –" She shook her head and walked away. "Were you not seen?"

"Donald Mackay saw me. But he will not tell."

"Will he not?"

"He will not. But he did say, they will be clearing our folk from the glen."

"I have heard tell that. They cannot. Already they have cleared us. Twenty-five years past, before you were born. You know the story, Iain. The countess in the castle, she was telling them to do it. God rest her soul, perhaps she was not knowing what they were doing, but they were doing it for her. We came to this glen, all the folk of the hills, the Sinclairs as your father is, and the Frasers as I am, and the Maclarens and the Macleods, the Mackays and Macdonalds and Mackenzies, and before we did not know the one the other. And they are good folk, now all the fighting is forgotten. We break bread now, and not heads. No more of that foolishness, Iain. But when we were coming to the glen, they said we will not be moving again. And what the now?"

"To send us to the sea and over the sea."

"They will not do that."

"I said that to Donald Mackay."

"They will not do that."

Now Mary was running through the doorway with the salmon in her arms, and then Katie with her necklace of three trout on a rush plait, and then Rachel, crying, "And look what we have." They praised and teased Iain, the mighty hunter. Mary found the sharp knife and took the fish outside. She slit their bellies and scraped out the guts and then ran the blade the wrong way against the lie of the scales until she had scattered around her a silver chaff. And when the fish were ready, she carried them down to the burn and washed them in the water and took them back up to the house. And so she saw her other brothers, Angus and Bain and Hamish Jamie, as they came home from the school.

Hamish also saw his three sons as they passed the field on their way home, carrying in the pouches of their kilts the potatoes taken from the rafts of the school. He himself had a small potato in his hand. It was hard and well, firmer than a boiled gull's egg. This should be a good year for that. He had hated the moving from the old hills to the lots in the glen, but there was a blessing in it. The getting of the barley and the oats and the rye was never a certain thing. Sometimes Hannah had stood in the yoke beside the cuddy all the day long, the woman beside braying beast. She had also pulled the ploughshare that he held to drive the furrow. But the new moorland given on lease and by lot was good for the potato, and there was no tacksman now to take the harvest and the rent on its way to the laird above. All was straight now, man to laird with never a middle man. And the potato was a fit brother to the porridge and the brose, the other staff of life.

"Is there no school then?" Hamish called.

"No school at all," Bain called back.

"And what is in your kilts?"

"Potatoes."

"We have enough and more."

"Dominie give them."

That was fair enough, Hamish thought. If he gave potatoes to the dominie for the learning of the boys, the dominie might give them back.

"Give them to Mother," he called.

"Aye."

As the boys went up the hill to their wood and turf croft with its thatched roof, its hump the first of all that ran down the glen to the factor's house and the established church and the blacksmith's and the tent beyond where the Free Church now was, Hamish scratched the side of the potato in his hand with his nail. A white streak appeared under the earthy skin. Water ran into the gouge. It must be wrong, the rumour from the Western Isles. The potatoes reeking like dung from the cattle beneath the field. You could never hold by the word of a man from the Isles. They were after telling stories there.

There was never a thing more for a man to do today. The two black cows were in the pasture, the turnips and the potatoes were in the ground nurtured by God's will, and in the kail-yard by the house, the gooseberries and the red currants were swelling in the sun. What did they say when they moved the men from the mountains to the glen? You Highlanders, you are born idle, you live on the black cattle, you will never lift a hand except to the whisky or the sword. And look now, we have turned our hand to the roots and the neeps, we have taken the moorland in fee and made it give us our new life. So Hamish made his way to his house in the noon of that warm and soft day.

The potatoes from the school were already boiling in the pot when Hamish came home. And the fish only needed to be steeped in the salt and steaming water to complete the meal. Mary tried to save some of the salmon for her friends at the cleansing tubs, but there was little left once the men had had their fill, big fish though it might be. There was good reason for Hannah to say grace before the unexpected feast, but Iain was graceless after the meal, for nothing Mary could plead would make him go back among the young women for the wringing. Sarah Macdonald would still be there, and she put more fear than God did in him.

So Mary took back Hamish Jamie for twisting the blankets into thick ropes to squeeze the water out of them. He was strong enough to do the work and just young enough for the women to spare his blushes. But there were too few young men in the clachan now, they were already leaving for the sea and the regiments, there were too many single women left, and they had to be bold if they were looking for a husband. "It was not like this in our time," Hamish said. "I asked for Hannah's hand, not she for mine."

4

THE CLEARING OF
THE GLEN

They came first and early in the morning to the Sinclair house, as it was topmost in the clachan of all the houses. There was the factor Hector Smith, who had come from England and knew its harsh laws and its ways. He was too red of face from the richness of his blood, but bleak eyes as dull as slate showed no life in the man. With him was a sheriff-officer and four constables, who were fondling their ash-sticks as if they were nervous about the business in hand. Angus saw them coming over the hill, and he shouted to Hannah, "Mother, mother, the men are coming."

Hannah left the pot where the hot water was boiling to make the porridge and the brose for her men and her daughters before they left for their work or their learning. She had to duck under the low door lintel and blink as the sun seared her eyes, and only then did she see the six strangers coming up to her home. She stood, legs apart, fists on her hips, confronting them. She spoke in Gaelic, the tongue of her people.

"And what would you be doing fretting honest folk before they have broken their fast?"

Hector Smith thrust a piece of paper into her hand, although he knew that she could not read it.

"Here, woman," he said in English, his native tongue.

Hannah looked at the paper.

"Angus," she said, "go on in and bring me a burning peat on the spade, and mind you do not burn yourself."

As the boy ran into the house, Hannah stepped forward and rammed the paper into the game pocket of the factor's shooting jacket.

"There's for your scrap of paper," she said. "Keep it in your own black pocket."

"You have taken the summons," the factor said. "It is against the law to return it."

He took the paper out and thrust it at Hannah again. But this time she stepped back.

"Why do you not speak," she said, "in words that God-fearing folk ken here?"

"Tell her in her bloody gibberish," the factor said, turning to one of the uneasy constables.

As the constable was explaining to Hannah the meaning of the paper, a summons to evict the Sinclairs from their house because of the termination of their lease, Angus came outside, carrying a spade before him, clasped in both of his small hands. On its iron tongue, a peat was smouldering.

"Will you take the summons now," the factor demanded and pushed the paper at Hannah.

"I will," she said. "Give it me." And she took the spade from her son's hands, and she thrust it out to take the offered summons upon the glowing peat. And slowly the paper began to crinkle and to curdle and to blacken, as the factor would not withdraw it. Then it broke into a little flame that ran along its edge and licked at the factor's fingers.

"Damn you," he cried and stuck his fingertips into his mouth to suck.

Hannah and Angus laughed. Out of the door of the house came the stooping Hamish and Iain and Hamish Jamie, all roused from their sleep. They lined up in their bulk behind Hannah, and they looked down on the constables with their ash truncheons.

"Tell them they have one quarter of an hour," the factor said, "fifteen minutes, to take their goods and their cattle from that black house before it is utterly destroyed. Tell them. And if they resist, there are dragoons waiting in Fort Augustus that will enforce the law. Tell them."

So the constable that spoke in Gaelic told Hannah and her men of the law and the force of the law. The leases had terminated on all of the glen. Some of the land had already been leased to a single southern farmer who would graze his Great Cheviot sheep on the braes, while much of the moor would make a larger deer park for the laird. There was no good in rebelling any more than there had been any good in rebelling from the clearances twenty-five years before by the countess, that had left the survivors of several different clans on their forced march to their present home. The place they had found was still not their own land, and they must leave as they could, where they would. That was the new law of Scotland.

"And for why will we go?" Hannah said.

"And to where will we go again?" Hamish said.

The constable translated to the factor, who only shook his head.

"Fourteen minutes," he said, taking a silver turnip watch from his pocket. "Fourteen minutes, and then we burn this house."

As Hamish Jamie started forward, his father caught him by the elbows and stayed his arms. "No, son," he said, "it is not the way." Then Iain moved past his mother, his fists knotted like twin boles of the Scots fir, but his mother seized him by the wrist. "Heed your father, Iain. It is not the way."

"And will you do the fighting for us, Mother?"

"Aye, they will not strike an old woman."

"They will and all."

"Twelve minutes," the factor said. "Will we have roast beef from your cattle for our dinner?"

"Clear the house," Hamish ordered. "Bear everything outside."

"Will we not fight, Father?"

"I have done with fighting," Hamish said. "I fought for the countess to keep my tack of land, and I fought against the countess when she had it taken from me. But for this new laird, I will not fight again."

"But it is our house."

"Where we are is our house," Hamish said.

"We made our house here."

"Then we will take it with us on our backs like the snail. To where there is no laird. And we will make a house there where the land is our land, and no laird will say again, 'Do this, do that, this is mine, it is not yours.'"

"I cannot," Iain said. "I cannot."

"Listen to your father," Hannah said. "He has seen good men die, and good men sent to the prison ships to Australia, all for the raising of a hand against the factor and the sheriff and the constables."

"Ten minutes," the factor said.

"Clear the house I say," Hamish said and led his sons back beneath the low door, stooping in a kind of obedience.

There was little to carry outside, for it was little they had. The iron pot and the hearthstone, the spades and the pans, the spinning-wheel and the spindle, the blankets that were cleaned on the yesterday and the boards that made up the three beds, the one for Hamish and Hannah and the one for the boys and the one for the girls, the knives and the forks and the spoons and the plates, the best shirts and the cloths and the bonnets and three pairs of shoes, the seed potatoes and the sack of oatmeal. The two black cows were driven from the byre, but the ten minutes were already gone and the constables were lighting the torches, yet the deal planking was still on the partitions and the

25

bog pine battens in the roof supporting the thatch between the birch timbers.

"Hold your hand," Hannah said. "Give us the time to take our house with us as we must go."

The constable paused, who already had his burning pitch brand in his grip. But Hector Smith said, "Proceed. We have all the village to clear. Get on with you."

"No."

Iain barred the way with outstretched arms, while Hannah began pushing the smaller boys and girls on to the thatch. "Break out the battens," she cried. "Break them out. And we will have a new house in the morning." And Hamish and Mary and Hamish Jamie began tearing the deal partitions open and throwing the planks out on to the earth.

The constable with the fiery torch stepped forward. Iain grasped the arm that held the burning brand with both of his hands. He wrenched it and wrung it as he had failed to do with the wet blankets, and the constable screamed and dropped his incendiary on the ground.

"I am hoping that I did not hurt you," Iain said.

Now the factor and the sheriff came on Iain, also the constables with their raised truncheons. But he still stood at the door of the house.

"Will you burn women? Will you put the bairns in the roof to the fire? Are you not Scotsmen?"

"You make it sore hard, man," a constable said.

"Are you not a man yourself?"

None would attack Iain at the door of his house, but only Hector Smith. He came at Iain with the riding crop that was hanging from its loop on his right wrist. He cut Iain across the nose, raising a welt of blood. Never strike a Sinclair on the face. Whether it is the shock of the unexpected, whether it is the threat of blinding the eyes, whether it is the trace of the Norse berserker in the veins, a Sinclair struck on the face is a mad bull. Iain hit and butted and kicked, he charged and hooked and lunged, and the red rage was filling his sight as he tried to break the head of Hector Smith against a rock, before the constables beat him senseless with twenty blows raining on his head from their truncheons.

In woe and anguish, Hamish stopped Hannah and Hamish Jamie from running to Iain's help until he lay still on his bloodied back. "Wait," he said. "It may be that we shall escape the gaol. He was struck the first." Then Hannah and her second son ran out to cover the body of Iain with their bodies, to stop the blows. And Hamish picked up the fallen whip of Hector Smith and broke it in two parts and tossed it aside, then he picked up Hector Smith himself and brought him to his feet and slapped his face to waken him and said, "If you ever whip my son again, Master Smith, I will surely break your neck and every bone in your poor body."

And Hector Smith was silent and shook his head and said, "Now let me go, man."

So Hamish let him go, and Hector Smith wobbled on his feet like a new-born lamb, and then he took hold of himself and told his constables, "Burn the house."

So they picked up their brands and set them on fire and put them against the thatch, where it drooped over the turf walls. And the flames ran along the reed and the straw, for it had been a dry June. And Hannah rose from the body of her eldest son and went into the house and plucked down the children from the roof, Angus and Bain and Rachel and Katie, where they had been taking down the battens and throwing them on the floor.

"We must away now," she said, "we must away. Or they will be roasting us for our own dinner."

So they gathered up the battens that they had already scattered on the earth and made their way through the smoke and under the low door. And they all stood and watched outside the flames moving up the bristles of the dark thatch as shafts of sunlight move up the bracken through a shifting cloud, and the fires met at the crest of the roof and threw up a pillar of smoke. Then the cows began to groan pitifully, while the sparks and the ashes were flying in the air, until the floating embers came down on to the deal planking and scorched the wood.

Iain was on his feet now, supported by Hamish Jamie, the mark of the whip across his face a fair testament of the reason for his rage. Hector Smith kept well shy of him, he would not go near. And Hamish said, "We will take away what is ours, or it will be consumed in the fire." So he and Hannah and the seven children bore away the few battens and the planks and the household things and the farm tools and the two black cows, and they went down the hill towards the other houses of the clachan. But the factor and the sheriff-officer and the four constables had gone before them, and Hector Smith was already giving his foul pieces of paper to the other families of the glen, and the torches were lit to set fire to the whole of the community.

As in their house, so with the other houses. The men raged and did nothing, the women shrieked and wept, the children wailed or stood in fear, then all hands went to the clearing of the goods and chattels before all was set in a blaze. The dominie came to protest and denounce, but his voice was a piping in the wind. Mewing like a cat with froth upon his lips, daft Ron Mackenzie ran at the sheriff-officer, who caught him and bound him with a rope, for Ron was touched in the head, and if that was what the rebellion was, it was sore proof that rebellion was madness. And so the people of the glen found themselves leaving their burning homes to gather in the tent that was their Free Church, to listen to their dominie and preacher tell of God's will and why He permitted the razing of the glen.

"Woe unto them that join house to house – so spake the Prophet Isaiah – that lay field to field, till there be no place; that they may be placed alone in the midst of the earth. Woe until the laird that makes of the houses of his people a waste for the sheep and a wood for the deer, so that he shall dwell in his mansion in the wilderness with strangers for his shooting companions and beasts for his sustenance. It is not your wickedness, my people, that has turned the face of the Good Lord against you. It is the wickedness of the Lords of Sutherland and the Macdonald Lords who have turned their face against the Lord God. They believe that they are the lords of His Creation. Shall they make the land of God in their image? Shall they decree that where God put His Adam and His Eve and the generations of their children to till the good earth, they shall put the beasts of the field to chew the cud and the beasts of the forest to roam and devour? Unnatural – wicked and unnatural. Just as they would not build us a church here, for well they knew that there would be a tearing down before there was a building up, as the Tower of Babel itself was torn down, so they will defy the will of the Lord and make a brae of our gardens and a ruin of our hearth and our homes."

The dominie looked down from his rough platform at the sixty people and a hundred children crowded under the low tarpaulin tent. His mouth was bitter at the injustice of a few men to their fellow creatures. By what right? There was no right any more upon earth, but he had to preach the righteousness of heaven. For there was might indeed in Scotland now, and if might was never right, there was a sore confusion in the person of the laird. He had to speak obedience and gag on the words.

"If the ways of the world are wicked, the Lord God has said so, and his Prophets have said so. But we must not do so. We must turn our eyes to the Lord and praise Him – not for this new trial and tribulation which He in His infinite wisdom has chosen for our affliction – but we must ask Him to change the hearts of the dukes and the countesses and the lords who oppress Scotland so sorely, after they have had their sonsy titles from south of the border, and after they have needed muckle rents from us to pay for their abominations in London town. And if the Lord will not change their hearts, we must go from here, where no proud laird shall harden his heart against the people, where the land is free and the birds and the beasts upon it, so that man can enjoy the fruits of the earth and the fishes of the sea without the bidding of a master. And we will heed always the word of the Good Lord, when He saith Yea and when He saith Nay, blessed be the name of the Lord."

A voice seemed to be torn from the throat of Hannah in the congregation. "And where is God the now? How will He help us?"

The dominie had no answer. But the need of the people made his thin body quiver like a flung knife.

"We shall take up this tent which is His tent. Let us follow Him, for He shall show us the way."

The dominie's words were not too soon. Already the torches were burning through the guy-ropes of the tent, as the people came out to see the destruction. Such was their fury that the constables backed away and allowed the people to undo the ropes and lay down the tent on the ground and stamp the wind out of it and roll it in a bundle and place it to drag behind a cart to pull it away behind a black ox and a cuddy yoked together in front. And behind them walked a procession of the homeless and the wanderers, the men wrapped in their plaids and wearing their bonnets and carrying their infants or their spades in their hands, the women with their scarlet shawls leading their children and driving the few cattle behind the carts, where their smallest ones rode on the household stuff piled above the planks and the battens for the homes they were to make again. But on that sad trail and trial of the people of the glen, hardly a one thought that they would find a home once more, but they would ever be on the rough road to nowhere at all, on foot without end.

The dominie knew where to take them. Five miles on over the hill, there was a ruined church with its gravestones still standing around it. Even the forces of the law would not dare desecrate the lodgings of the dead. They were in the last sanctuary, beyond the writ of law, truly at the mercy of God.

They set up their tarpaulin tent on poles among the stone arks and the marble slabs and the crosses and the urns that marked the names of those who had gone before. Here was AMY ROSS – *Rest in Peace*, there KIRSTY MACLEOD – aged two years, *Abide in God*, and there DUNCAN MACKENZIE – *God Is My Shepherd*. The sides of the shelter were protected with horsecloths and rugs and plaids, while blankets made up the compartments for each family in its sleeping. Outside, the cattle and the cuddies cropped the nettles and the long grasses between the headstones. Fires of peats cooked the porridge and boiled the few potatoes that remained. The people of the glen were safe for that night, but for that one night.

In the morning, the man from *The Scotsman* came in his frockcoat and his billycock hat. He was a writer for the journals and the newspapers as all of his trade were, ready to write of the troubles of others as long as he did not fuss himself except for the words. "My articles," he told them, "will make your terrible treatment and your foul wrongs known in all the corners of the earth."

"But will they give us back our home?" Hannah asked.

"I cannot answer for that," the writer said and wrote in his notebook things that might be praise or blame or pity or untruth. Who was to know? But for the true recording, Mary borrowed the little diamond ring that the mother of the mother of Hamish had given to Hannah on her wedding, and Mary scratched on the glass of the one standing window in the church, *Glen is a wilderness – Blow ship to the colony – Mary Sinclair*. It was the only memorial of their passing.

For they could not abide in the churchyard. They had nothing to eat, they could not eat the seed. If they were to kill a cow, they could not have the milk of it. The folk of the near clachans were fee-holders of the laird, and they were sore afraid to help the wanderers for they might lose their homes and be made to wander as well at the laird's will. People were divided from people in their fear. Then a dark and smiling man came to them. He was saying there was land on a loch by the sea, and welcome to it. They could graze their black cattle and raise their potatoes and their oats. There were herrings by the millions for the catching, there were mussels and limpets for the taking from the rocks, if all else failed. There was always the harvest of the sea. And there was the working at the kelp weed, when a man and his family might take in thirty shillings a week in the season. For those who were laborious, it was a good life, even if the land had a thin soil, it being by the sea.

"We will take it," the dominie said, "for we have nowhere to go except to the colonies beyond the sea. And we have no money for that. And who knows if it is not a worse wilderness there, and men with harder hearts."

5

THE HARVEST OF
THE WEED

The black knobbles of the weed were better cut below the sea water.
The dried bladders of kelp thrown up by the tides on the rocks did
not have the sap in them that was needed for the burning out of the
extract in the kilns, to be sent down south for the making of the glass
and the soap. The brine stung the grazes on Hamish Jamie's legs as
he stood waist-deep in a cleft in the cliffs, hacking at the tough plants
and dragging the slimy tendrils out of the swell and throwing them up
to Angus and Bain on the rocks to spread for drying in the wind and
the sun. Hannah was also wading in the sea on a shelving inlet, cutting
the kelp with a sickle and lobbing the indigo strands back to Katie
and Rachel on the shore. This was the promise, the harvest from the
fields of the sea. But it was wet work that tore the hands and bent the
back and wounded the legs. It was not work fit for a farming family
of the glen.

Mary had the cuddy by the dried patches of kelp. She was packing
the creels on either side of the donkey's back with the crop of the sea,
so that she could lead the animal up the path of stones and slippery
shale to the kilns at the top, where Hamish and Iain were labouring
at the burning of this tillage from the deep. There had been no place
for them in the black boats, for there were too many displaced men
on them, learning the craft, while the catches of herrings were less
each year. Even the riches of the boundless ocean would not stretch
to the needs of the new folk now come to furrow it. There were places
at the kelping and the lime-burning, but at poor wages, where all the
family must labour to earn less than a living, but enough for broth
and potatoes. But then, the potatoes – it was not a lie that the Islanders
had told. The new crop was diseased and smelled of corpses in the
ground. The very earth was sick, as if the rottenness of the ways of
men above it had infected the roots below.

In the circular holes of the kilns, Iain put the dried kelp on top of the smouldering peat. With his clatt, he spread the weed evenly over the heat of the dried bog earth, using his long iron poker to stir the seaweed and render it into a tarry mass. The smoke and fumes made him cough and wheeze as if his lungs were old bellows. Soot coated his red face in a highwayman's mask. His bare feet were singed and corroded by flying embers. To his father Hamish, the young man seemed like an ogre in the legends, one of the miners of the underground who smelted metal for the gods of the north. But in the kilns they were smelting an alkaline residue, which cooled into thick crusts of brittle blue. Powdered and mixed in the southern factories, this dust became invisible in window panes or washtub suds – the evanescent gift of the sea.

The hot reek of the kilns tasted more sour than disgust in Hamish's mouth. He tapped his son on the shoulder and nodded towards the low door.

"This is no work for a man, Iain. We'll away."

"Wait."

Iain raked the glue and knit of the surface of the weeds with his clatt, then turned to follow his father out of the kiln shed. They stood at the door, looking to the path up from the beach, along which Mary was leading her donkey, loaded with the creels of dried kelp.

"Muckle more," Hamish said.

"For aye," Iain said. "Muckle more work, muckle less pay for it."

"That's the truth, lad. Give Mary a hand the now."

Iain took down the creels from the cuddy's back and emptied the kelp into piles by the kiln door.

"Da," Mary said. "Da, they say the ox is in the pound. There was black cattle straying from the top of the cliffs to Mackenzie's field, and his man has catched them all. And they will not give back our ox until the paying of a fine. Four shilling."

"Four shilling." Hamish gave a dry snort that might be a laugh. "We barely earn four shilling from Gavin Macdonald for four days at the kelping. And if an ox recks there is greener grass than the muck of the common land, how shall the poor beastie know more?"

"Mackenzie says our ox should not be in his field."

"And tell me, if Mr Mighty Mackenzie cannot build a wee fence to keep out my ox, then how the devil –"

"Don't you, Da –"

"Sorry I am, Mary, but how does Mr Mackenzie expect my ox to stay out of his open field?"

"It's in his pound now with a great fence about it, and not a thing to eat. Da, you must get it back."

"I will," Iain said. "I will say a word to that fine Mr Mackenzie."

"No, Iain," his father said. "I will say the word. You would say it with your fist."

"And if I did –"

"Mr Mackenzie is a friend of the sheriff and the constables. I will say a word to Mr Mackenzie, and it is not the last word he shall hear from me."

So Hamish Sinclair set off to free his ox from the pound. And as he walked past the crofts by the sea, where sometimes an upended black boat was the roof, with mosses on its keel where barnacles had been, he thought how queer it was the now, the coming to the sea, eating the limpets and the mussels and the crabs, not the berries and the nuts and the eggs, the salt in the taste of the silver herrings that were not sweet and taut as the red salmon or the brown trout. But the oatmeal and the potatoes were still the same, the porridge and the broth, and these gifts of the ground were the true living of men, that came so hard from the sea.

As he passed the graveyard by the kirk, Hamish saw the red earth heaped over two narrow graves, slashing the darkling green of the sod and the stone crosses, weathered by time in memory. These were the Mackay twins, never a hope for them when the storm blew up sudden from Barra, their boat caught like a mussel-shell in an eddy and them whirled under, mermaid-deep, so that they might only come back again as seals and dreams, a warning to other farmers never to trust to the waves. Hamish never would. He was a man of the moor and the brae, he could not swim, he hated water beyond his depth. You could not take a man from his natural ground and put him on a treacherous element and call that his own.

"God be with you," Hamish said to the new graves, "but do not go out on the great waters."

A scarlet man was coming down the road, bright red in face and jacket, ruddy of bonnet and knees, only his kilt in green and black and blue denying the general bloodiness of him. Hamish had been hearing of his coming, the recruiting sergeant, giving a guinea to every lad who would leave his home for the service of Her Foreign Majesty.

"And good day to you," the recruiting sergeant said. "And to your family. What would be the name?"

"Sinclair," Hamish said.

"You're new to these parts? Sinclairs here are rare as eagles."

"We're new the now."

"And your sons, they will be working at the kelp?"

"How else? There's not a thing but that."

"And what age will they be? Bonny and braw I have no doubt."

"They are not for you, Sergeant. Not for the foreign wars."

"Foreign, is it? If seeing the world is foreign, why then it is, and good it is." The sergeant put his finger along his nose. "There's gold in it for you, man. And the Ninety-third Highlanders, why, it's the finest regiment that ever fought for God and the Queen, God bless Her."

"Aye," Hamish said, "and where do all your fine lads live now? In the far lands and over the seas. When do your lads come home, if they come home and stay not under the ground? After twenty years of service to a land that is not their land. Once we served our laird, and he gave us land that we held was our land. Now we serve your Queen –"

"Our Queen Victoria, God bless Her."

"And Her laws take the land that was our own."

"You have Her pay, Her glory, Her honour –"

"Her land that was our land, we do not have. Go away with you, Sergeant. My Iain and my Hamish Jamie you shall not have."

So Hamish went away towards the pound to look for his ox, while the recruiting sergeant went to look for his Iain and his Hamish Jamie, named so unwisely by their father. And Hamish heard the lowing of the black cattle and the bleating of the sheep that were penned inside the pound of Mr Mackenzie. And there was a queer stench as if a beast had died and rotted, but more harsh to the nose. And there was the gentleman himself, as if the title would cover such a stout and shifty fellow in tight breeches of yellow pigskin.

"And it's good day to you, Mr Mackenzie," Hamish said, polite as you please and murder in his soul.

"And it's good day to you, Hamish," Mr Mackenzie said, always trying to be the superior.

"Not such a good day," Hamish said. "I hear you have my ox."

"With my grass inside him. He is a great ox to eat of my grass."

"You have grass growing out of your ears," Hamish said, "if you cannot hear the ox complaining he has no grass inside him the now."

"Will you pay the fine for him," Mr Mackenzie said, "or he will eat no grass until you do."

"I will take him with me the now," Hamish said.

"When you pay me four shilling."

"When I pay you four shilling, Mr Mackenzie, for a swatch of grass, it will not be before Judgement Day."

"That will be the next assizes, if you do not pay me four shilling."

"Out of my way, man," Hamish said. "You will not make suffer my ox."

"Do not enter the pound," Mr Mackenzie said, "or you will suffer worse than the ox."

"Ach, away with you."

Hamish put a hand on Mr Mackenzie's shoulder and thrust him to one side. Then he opened the gate of the pound and walked inside among the cattle and the sheep. His ox knew him and came towards him and rubbed his face with the slobber on its nose. And Hamish threw his arm over the ox's neck and walked him back to the gate into the pound, which he found closed against him with Mr Mackenzie on the other side. Only Mr Mackenzie now held a fowling-piece in his hands with his factor stood behind him.

"On payment of four shilling," Mr Mackenzie said, "you may leave with your ox."

"And if I cannot pay."

"You cannot leave with your ox."

"And if I will not pay."

"You will not leave with your ox."

"I am leaving with my ox."

But when Hamish put his hand to the gate, he saw it was locked with a padlock, and he had no way out.

"I have not the money," Hamish said, "and I will have the ox."

"Then you must bide with the ox in there," Mr Mackenzie said, "until you have the money."

Behind Mr Mackenzie and his fowling-piece, Hamish could see a column of black smoke rising from the cliffs by the sea.

"That is the kilns," Hamish said. "For drying the kelp."

Mr Mackenzie turned to look behind him.

"Where you work with your sons?"

"There is muckle smoke," Hamish said. "The kilns will be on fire. I must go and see."

"Not without paying four shilling."

"Don't be daft, man. I must go."

"Pay me four shilling. And take your ox."

"I have not four shilling."

Hamish glared so intently through the gate at Mr Mackenzie that he raised his fowling-piece and levelled it at Hamish.

"Give me my four shilling."

"I do not have it, you daft bugger."

"And you are a man of God, Hamish. And would you swear so?"

"There is muckle worse to say of you."

Hamish began to climb the bars of the gate, while Mr Mackenzie followed him with the barrel of his shotgun. When Hamish reached the top of the gate, he looked down on Mr Mackenzie.

35

"Shoot," he said. "Who dares to meddle with me?"

He jumped down off the gate, staggered and righted himself like a boat after a gust.

"When I have settled the fire at the kilns, I will come back with my sons for the ox."

"You are the daft bugger," Mr Mackenzie said. "Too many of you Sinclairs, too many. Can you not see? Muckle too many. So you must go over the seas or in the army regiments. What else can a Sinclair do?"

"I have a cousin Archibald," Hamish said, "and he went over the sea to fight for General Oglethorpe against the Indians. And now he has land there in a place called Georgia. And many a Sinclair has gone over the sea to fight in Sweden and in France, and in Ireland and in Canada, and they have land there the now. But we will not go."

"You will go," Mr Mackenzie said. "Starve you or emigrate. You will go."

"We will not go."

"You will. Have you not seen the blight?" He pointed to a swill bin at the corner of the pound. Now Hamish could smell the reek that came out of it, the stench of putrefaction and decay. "The cattle will not have them, nor men either. Potatoes. All rotten, all foul."

"I do not believe you."

"Go to your fire. And look at that swill on the way."

So it was that Hamish saw the slimy and liquid tubers, their skins black and tattered as the seaweed, in a bin that heaved and belched with bubbles of fuel gas. And he hurried away towards the black smoke, his heart heavy within him.

Hamish met his two elder bairns on the road from the kilns, the giant Iain leading the cuddy with Mary on its back and still holding the long clatt in his hand. The black smoke was now a pillar in the sky, but Iain looked not back on the evidence of the burning behind him, no more than Lot looked back on the fire and the brimstone that fell upon Sodom and Gomorrah.

"The kilns are burning, son. What is with you?"

"Let the kilns burn and the weed, Father."

"You should be asking what is with Gavin Macdonald, Da," Mary said from the back of the donkey.

"I reck nothing with Gavin Macdonald," Hamish said, "but that he would sooner lose his heart, if he has a heart, than a shilling from his pocket, and he would sooner see us starve than pay us wages for the kelp."

"He was lifting Mary's kirtle, Father –"

"Hush, Iain, now –"

"I hit him with my clatt. Look, there's the hair and blood on it."

"God help us, Iain," his father said.

"And he fell down, and I was that mad with us chaving like slave folk for that swick and cheat that I put the peat to the timbers of the kiln shed, and I am taking Mary away home."

"Is he dead?"

"If the devil will have him –"

"And what will you do the now, Iain?"

"Enlist. They do not reck if a soldier is a murderer. And if he is a murderer, he is the better the soldier."

"Never," Hamish said. "Come away to Canada with us."

"The sheriff will find me. But if I take the guinea from the recruiting sergeant –"

"You've met with the red devil?"

"Aye. He's not so bad."

"His clothes," Mary said. "The kilt on him. All the lassies love –"

"Hush," Hamish said. "And if you are a soldier, and if we go to Canada on the ship and find us a home and land, then you can leave the army and come to us, where none shall know you –"

"I will not go to Canada," Mary said. She slipped down from the donkey's back. "I will stay in Scotland."

"And who will see to you?" Hamish asked.

"The laird," Mary said. "I will go to the castle with the dominie. He has written a petition. From the people of the glen. Give us back our land. The laird, he does not know what is done in his name."

"He does," Iain said and spat. "Damn the laird. You ken what he calls his castle? Dunrobin. Because he has never done robbin' his own folk."

"Hush," Hamish said. "Never say that of our laird."

"I'll take the Queen's guinea," Iain said. "And my chances."

"And who'll be after caring for your mother and me?" Hamish said. "Who will care the now?"

"You have Hamish Jamie, Father. Only he wants to be taken for a soldier more than me."

"He never will."

"You cannot stop a son, Father, any more than your father could stop you. If he must go."

"No son of mine will fight for a foreign queen and another country."

"A fight's a fight," Iain said. "It's only a better fight if it's for the right." He swung his clatt round and round, making the iron whistle in the air. "It is the blood, Father. We like to fight. It is the motto of the clan. Fight."

"What will you tell your own mother?"

"You tell her, Father. I will be gone the now. Or they will have me for the murdering of that mean man."

The pillar of black smoke had spread sideways until it was a broad toadstool between earth and heaven. At the top of the cliffs, Hamish could see people running towards the base of the smoke. Among them would be his wife and his children, all of them except this one, who was lost to them.

"You will not tell her. You will be a soldier, and you will not face your own mother." A prickle hurt Hamish's eyes. He would not cry. No Sinclair cried. "You break the family. Ach, you will not do that, my son."

"I must," Iain said. "You will tell Mother. Father –" Iain shivered, the huge man that he was, as a fir in the wind. "I cannot. You tell her. I must go, or I –"

"Aye," Hamish said. A tear was now running down his cheek, but he did not brush it away or hide it. "You must go. Or you may be hangit. And it was for your sister."

"Give me your blessing, Father."

"God be with you, my son," Hamish said. "Never forget. Your home is always where we will be."

"I will never forget that." Iain bent and kissed his father on the brow, then turned and swung Mary round off the ground with his free arm.

"Don't you go and wed the duke," he said, "though a countess you are, even the now." He kissed her and dropped her head down and twirled his clatt so fast that it made a dark circle in the air, which seemed to draw him away.

"Fight," Iain said, "and I will do that."

6

THE CASTLE AND
ITS KIND

"Scones," said the duchess, "there is nothing better than scones.
They're almost worth coming to Scotland for."

"And butter," said the duke, spreading plenty on his hot tea-cake.
"But those bloody builders. They will never finish this castle. Sometimes I think they are building one of those new railway stations. They
all look like castles too."

"Oh, we do not want trains here," the duchess said. "Or passengers.
Because that is all guests are. They move through. And all that smoke.
It would ruin things. Like the blight."

"I am sorry about that," the duke said. "They say there is a famine.
But there cannot be. They have the fish now and the sea. My mother
moved them there in time. It was providence. Somebody had to compel
our backward peasants – and do not call them Highlanders, for
they are peasants – into modern existence. My mother was a great
improver."

"And you," the duchess said. "The model fishing villages you made.
Port Gower and Golspie and Helmsdale."

"And the emigration. I have spent tens of thousands of pounds, my
dear, to assist the poor unfortunates to make a better life in a new
land, perhaps more suited to their peculiar talents, in order for them
to earn a living."

"You are so good. That is why they come to you with their petitions."

"Oh, not *another* one," the duke said, blowing out a froth of crumbs
from his cake. "Just as we were taking our tea."

"Shall we receive them?" the duchess said. "Or it will hang over
us." She picked up a small silver bell and rang it in tiny chimes that
dropped through the air like breaking china. "I cannot bear something
hanging over one like poor people complaining. It takes away the
appetite. Ah, Mackay –" She addressed the footman who came into

39

the tea-room. "Please clear away. And bring in those poor people who wish to complain about their good fortune."

"Really, my dear," the duke said, "you do not have to trouble yourself –"

"I am your wife," the duchess said, "and I wish to know all that concerns you. It is my duty and my desire."

The footman brought in a tall and cadaverous dominie in black and a bonny young woman in a plaid skirt and shawl. The man ducked his head in a quick nod, and the girl bobbed up and down like a float struck by a fish on the hook. But there was no bow, there was no curtsy. Abrupt Highland manners, or downright rude.

"If it please you, sir –" the man said in English. "And lady–"

The duke shook his head.

"Where did you learn to address people of quality?" he asked.

"I am a teacher, sir –"

"That is why you are not taught," the duke said triumphantly. "Is this your daughter?"

"No," the man said. "Her name is Mary Sinclair. She is of the petitioners."

"Come over here," the duchess said. And when Mary did not move, she added sharply, "You do understand plain English?"

"An it please you, lady," Mary said in English, the alien words harsh on her tongue. But she still did not move.

"You're not deaf, but you are wilful," the duchess said. "Come here, girl."

Mary moved forward slowly and stood near the duchess, sitting in the floral chintz that Queen Victoria was making popular because she wanted her Scots castle to look homely.

"Turn around," the duchess said.

Mary slowly turned around, her head low, her hands clasped before her, trying to hide her rough fingers. She felt like a heifer at the fair.

"You'll do," the duchess said. "After a scrub and a change. Report to the housekeeper, Mrs Rogers."

"An it please you, lady –"

"It does not, if you repeat yourself."

"I was not thinking . . . a position –"

"I know it is too good to be true," the duchess said, "and I know you people find it hard to be grateful, but I do wish to *do* something for you – and it so happens a position is vacant." Then very brightly, "And here you are!"

Mary was silent, wondering how to refuse, when her dominie spoke. "If you wish to do something for us, lady, then you will hear our petition."

"Give it to the duke. It is for him to hear."

"Where is it, man?" The duke held out a hand, on which his polished nails glittered as brightly as his signet ring. "I can read English."

"Pray, may I hear it?" the duchess said.

"You may," her husband said. "Although it may not be to your taste." And he read this:

That the land of your Petitioners was laid waste under your Mother the Countess by the sheepfarming system, in consequence of which your Petitioners were removed to other parts under leases. That these leases now being ended, your Petitioners were removed again to the sea, already overcrowded with a surplus population. That your Petitioners formerly paid their rents by rearing Cattle and by fishing, but now that ten families occupy the place formerly inhabited by one, the rearing of Cattle was rendered unpracticable, and the fishing which at all times is precarious has this year in a great measure failed. That your Petitioners are prevented from improving the little land they Cultivate, not only by not having leases on it, but above all being prohibited from using the sea ware on the coast for manure. For that ware must be made into extract for the kelp factories, and moreover, the potatoes have been utterly ruined by the blight. That, in consequence of these hardships there are not in this parish nine families which can be supported for nine months by the produce of their lands, that the young men of the parish, though much attached to their superiors and to their country, are compelled by their grievances to emigrate to Foreign lands, but before they reluctantly leave their native soil they deem it their duty to make their case known to Your Grace.

The duke put down the petition. He said nothing for a time, then he looked at the man in black.

"At least you know what to call me," he said, "when you write. Is this true?"

"It is all true."

"We cleared these Sinclairs originally?"

"Yes. And they have moved on. And now they have no food and nowhere to go."

"I will give you more money, damn it," the duke said without grace. "Another ten thousand pounds to assist their passages to Canada or the colonies or where they will."

"They do not wish to go over the seas," the dominie said. "They wish to remain in Scotland. This is their home – their land."

"My land," the duke said, "which can no longer support them with

41

their idle ways. The hand of God struck down the potato crop, not my hand. Is that not so, teacher?"

"It is so."

"Then tell them that. It was for their sins – in opposing me, and others in authority."

"I cannot tell them that."

"Really?" The duke considered the dominie. "You make it difficult for me."

"They do not wish to leave their own land."

"They must go. I will assist them."

"Aye," the dominie said. "The sight of our folk gone – and gone for aye – it will not offend the view from the castle."

The duke was silent, but the duchess spoke out.

"The view is beautiful now. A garden down to the sea. Sheep in their pastures. A panorama – purple moors, far hills, the noble stags – and no huts."

"No huts, lady, no huts. And no folk either."

"You will take the money and go to Canada," the duke said. "The land cannot support you. You have no option. Or else you will starve."

"If we must, we must go," the dominie said. "But do not fear yourself, we will return." He gave a bob of the head to the duke. "I will tell them that I gave you the petition and you said, 'Get you away to Canada.'"

"That is putting rather a strong construction on my words."

"You did not say that?"

"In so many words –"

"In so many words." The dominie turned to Mary, who had stood mutely by the duchess all the while. "Are you coming away with me?"

"She is staying here," the duchess said. "I am offering her a place here in my service."

"Her place is with her own folk," the dominie said. "Not in your service."

Mary flushed. The words that came out of her mouth almost surprised her. "We have no place, dominie. So how can you say my place is with my own folk? They have no place. There is a place here – and it is in Scotland – and I will stay here."

The dominie paused.

"What will I tell Hamish and Hannah?" he asked.

"I will find them when they have a place to call their own. It is not our fault that we have to leave. It is your fault, their fault. We have no home."

"You shall honour your father and your mother."

"I do – but I cannot live with them because they have no home for us."

The dominie shook his head and turned to the duchess.

"She will bide with you, lady. Care well for her."

"I trust she will care well for me."

The dominie turned to face the duke. "We will take your money as we have nothing else to take. We will leave the land as you have taken it when it was also our land. But when we return, this land will be as it has always been, the land of God and his children, and never will you take it from us again."

7

THE CROSSING

"There's no decency," Hannah said.

"We be buried," Bain said.

"It is only for the crossing," Hamish said. "Bear with it the now."

They were viewing their berths below the decks of the *Hopeful June*. These were low boxes, one on top of the other, six feet wide and six feet long and two feet one inch high. Just enough for one person or a closely married pair, but these were for four people, and devil a matter if they were of opposite sexes, a place in a berth was a mess of pottage, you took what you could get next to you, a bairn or a lassie or a Herod.

"In here," Hannah said, "there will go Katie and Rachel and Angus with me. And below will go Hamish and Bain and whatever shamelessness the Good Lord inflicts upon them. And Hamish Jamie, if –"

"Mother," Bain said, "you know he's gone for the army and to keep a good eye on Iain there."

"Aye, he loves his brother," Hannah said, "but he will not leave us."

"He will be back," Hamish said. "Just as soon as we have our farm in Canada. Iain will be back, and Hamish Jamie will be back, and we will be one family again."

The emigrants' quarters in the *Hopeful June* were a catacomb in wood. In the thick and fetid air, hutch was piled upon hutch for the thousand souls that were to endure the crossing. Cattle have their byres, horses their stables, even cut corn has its cribs – but the emigrants had their berths as the slaves from Africa had their berths. Human beings were packed as tight as tripe in the bowels of the ship. There was not room to swing a cat, for there was not even room for a cat at all. Bedding, boxes, bundles, shoes, shawls, petticoats, waistcoats, bonnets, hats, pipes, curling-tongs, cut-throat razors, flat irons, corsets male and female, fiddles, swaddling-clothes, nostrums and remedies for all ills filled every crack and cranny and crevice below decks. The one universal was Holloway's Pills, the Greatest Sale of Any Medicine in the Globe. They were guaranteed to cure any ailment including sea-sickness, scrofula, venereal diseases, tumours, the whites and the King's Evil.

"Help me with this, Bain," Hannah said, driving hairpins into a plaid over the wooden hole into her berth. She would be private. "I'll not be such a sight for the likes of these."

The likes of these were the other poor folk on the boat, assisted to emigrate beyond the seas. Most of them were young men in their only pair of breeks with a dirty shirt and an old coat of rents and patches, their boots open at the toes. They smoked clay pipes with anything they could stuff into them, shavings, old tea-leaves, wool and coarse tobacco. Their lips were black with swearing. Their red eyes had the look of beaten puppies. They had lost the strut of the cocks of the walk for the crouch of curs.

There were some young women with red raw hands, scarred from the gutting of herring or the lime-burning or the power-looms. Big Kirsty MacNeice, wide at the shoulder as any man, had only the one hand, for the other had been severed at the wrist by a spinning-machine. "Ach, they give me a week's pay and a Certificate for Good Conduct. It was not my fault. So I tore the certificate into wee pieces with the fingers still on me – good and slow – and I threw their certificate in their good faces. Give me back my hand, I said. And do they? They do not, they cannot. Only another poor lassie works the same machine."

They had all to fight for their food, and the weakest did not eat. If eating you could call it. The rations, when they were doled out, were never what the book said – a cupful of flour, mouldy rice and oatmeal, biscuit harder than a whetstone, tea and molasses, and salt pork so tough and acrid you might have been eating the kelp itself. The mates swore without drawing breath, "I'll break your bastard head in, God damn your soul." You had to fight with the other passengers to get near the mates giving out the stores, and then fight harder to get near the six stoves serving the thousand wretches. And as for getting to the cook without a bribe of money or brandy, or to the ship's doctor, who was only an upstart drunken apothecary, you might as well be climbing Jacob's ladder to heaven, and come tumbling down like the bad angel to hell.

If you could not live like that, you could die like that. The dying started on the fourth day of the crossing, when a child would keep nothing down and lay in her mess with nothing to be done about it. And the doctor said it was dysentery and muttered of cholera and typhus under his port-wine breath. And the captain swore he had not a cloth or canvas to spare to sew up the little body inside. So she was thrown into the waters of the deep without even the benefit of a prayer, for there was no priest aboard. There were only the sailors pulling at the ropes with their song, which was no hymn of praise:

Haul in the bowling, the Black Star bowling
Haul in the bowling, the bowling haul –

In the darkness below, the air was thick as brose or milky porridge. Its stenches and smells coated the nose. The candles ran out, and the wicks in the whale-oil in the single lamps guttered and burned black. There was always a battle for supper and the slops. And after the unspeakable visit to the privies at the stern, with the sailors leering through the cracks in the boards, Hannah would retire with her children while there were still the lines of evening light. She would huddle in her wooden tomb until the coming of dawn, having to suck in the foul air only to blow it out fouler, praying for the crossing to be over in just one more day.

But the crossing was never over, and the dying and the sickness went on. There was an old shepherd, Stewart MacPhee, who stood at the bows of the *Hopeful June* as still as a figurehead. He would not be moved. He looked for the land. The agent had said twenty days for the crossing, but it was twenty-four days now, and there had only been the false hope of the sighting of Northern Ireland to the lee. But Stewart MacPhee stood wrapped in his plaid in the bows, watching for that Newfoundland to come out of the squalls and the mist, watching as he had for his sheep in Benbecula, before he and his people had been driven out by the wolfhounds sent by the black Gordon of Cluny, the buyer of the Hebrides. It was not as if the Good Lord gave any man the right to buy islands and make them into the desolation of the wilderness.

"Yes," old MacPhee sang in his rant to Hamish Sinclair, who often stood with him on watch for the Newfoundland, "many a thing have I seen in my own day and generation. Many a thing, O Mary Mother of the black sorrow! I have seen the townships swept, and the big holdings being made of them, the people being driven out of the countryside to the streets of Glasgow and to the wilds of Canada. And many of them died of hunger and plague and smallpox while going across the ocean. I have seen the women putting the children in the carts which were being sent from Barra and Benbecula and the Iochdar to Loch Boisdale, while their husbands lay bound in the pen and were weeping beside the women, crying aloud, and their little children wailing like to break their hearts. I have seen the big strong men, the champions of the countryside, the stalwarts of the world, being bound

46

on Loch Boisdale quay and cast into the ship as would be done to a batch of horses or cattle in the boat. The bailiffs and the ground-officers and the constables and the policemen were gathered behind them. The God of life only knows all the loathsome work of men on that day."

Hamish took the old MacPhee into his berth with Angus, and the three of them held it against any other intruder. Hannah and the three bairns above shifted and knocked, listening to the moanings and the laments of the sick and the dying, the snorings and the cursings of the weak and the living. For the cholera and the typhus had come among them. The illness began with shivering and the grip of the claws inside the forehead, then swelling in the face and muck in the nose and in the throat, then the blood in the eyes and the muscles squirming beneath the skin, then the stupid stare of the idiot to show the brain was dull and half dead. The pulse in the wrist sometimes raced in a fever and sometimes slowed to a plod. Then the skin became dark as if burned by the sun.

The name for it was *fiabhras dubh*, the black fever. On the fourth day, sores afflicted the body in large boils. The fever was now a loosening of the limbs, so that the sufferer could no longer move to crush the lice on his berth. Yet if he would live to the seventh day, a sweat might come from him and a smell as from the byre, and he might rise from the black fever weak as a lamb that is born, but in rejoicing. The remedy on the *Hopeful June*, at the cost of one shilling, was a dose of Epsom salts and castor oil. And at the cost of two shillings, thirty-five drops of laudanum were given, and then the face was rubbed with vinegar.

The cures did no good. There were twenty dead on the thirtieth day of the voyage, and forty-one dead on the forty-first day, which was a coincidence, but hardly a blessing, except to the dead, who were out of the suffering. By now, there was no water for the poor folk below, but only from the stinking bilges. The salt pork was cooked in water from the sea, making the thirst from drinking the bilge-water even more terrible. So hardly a man or a woman or a child alive was not gripped by spasms of vomiting and running discharge from the bowels. They groped in the darkness of their berths, they fouled their resting-places, they crawled on the decks to breathe some kind of life from the winds that stretched the sails overhead, bringing them to the promised Newfoundland, which never came to them.

And when it did come, it came as ice in the night. The *Hopeful June* struck the berg off Nova Scotia. Her rotten timbers were breached. The sea water came as a cold wall into the quarters below decks. The screaming of the awakened was drowned by the roar of the flood. Hamish clutched Angus and struggled down to the planks of the floor, the sea rising to his knees. He was struck from behind, nearly thrown over, but held upright. He reached above to bring down Hannah, and Angus reached for Katie and Rachel and Bain.

"Hold fast," Hamish shouted. "Hold tight."

And there was the shrieking and the keening and the cursing of the damned. The weight of the waters pushed the trapped against each other, stirred them into cold porridge in a wooden pot. They clung to each other in the grip of life, which would be the death grip also. And above them now a flicker of red light jumped through the cracks on the decks, a sound of crackling, a whiff of sharp smoke.

"Oh dear God," Hamish said, "fire."

Two men fought up the companion way, banging at the hatch above. But none could open it. They were penned below to die between the roaring deep, the ice to the side, the fire above. They surged against each other, shouted, implored. And there was a sudden mercy. The blade of an axe splintered the boarding between the steering and the forequarters of the ship. Kirsty MacNeice threw her one hand forward to clench at the splinters and wrench out more wood to widen the gap. And she nearly lost her other hand, with the axe driven through again and again to clear a way of escape for the damned souls below.

The waters were waist deep now, as the emigrants struggled through the hole in the boarding. Three more sick bairns died now, two crushed and drowned among the desperate press of the people, and one small boy broken by a tier of berths collapsing on his shivering body. But the rest of the people struggled out and up the ladders and the steps to the hell above, where the way from the chill salt waters led to the masts of fire and the cables of flame, casting weird shadows and the shapes of devils and imps on the cracked whiteness of the great iceberg, which had stove in the hull of the *Hopeful June*.

Sailors were lowering the two boats that still hung clear on the lee side. But already the ship was tilting with the weight of the inrush of the waters and the shifting ballast and cargo of pig-iron. Hamish and Hannah and the children found themselves scrambling up the slope of the decks, bombarded by loose boxes and lashed by broken cables from the wreckage. And now burning fragments of canvas were fiery birds settling on the screeching mob below. Three kneeling figures by the poop were singing a hymn, but they were enveloped by the flames, as a rush of fire ran down and split the rigging and brought it down on their heads in a burning shroud. The stays above shed sparks and ropes were alight, the fibres falling in fireflies on to the shoulders of the men and women, who screamed as they tore off the scorching embers. And old MacPhee slid down the decks to the rail and fell overboard on to the berg, where he hung by his hands until the

48

chillness loosened his grasp, and he vanished in the crack between the ship and the wall of ice.

One boat was lowered and was swamped, the other lurched down the tilt of the ship's side and bobbed on to the waters. Sailors and passengers slithered down ropes into the single boat, until it was loaded to the gunwhales and cast off. For the rest of the abandoned, they scrabbled up the shelving decks and clung to the lee rail or to the masts or to lashed boxes or to coils of rope. Hamish struggled with his wife and children forward to the end of the jib, which was already crowded with others, clinging for dear life to the spar. Their hands held on to boom or arm or leg. And down on them rained the torches of the burning sails, charring their skins already shivering from the cold of the blast and the sea and the ice.

Now Hamish heard a fearsome cracking and crashing. And he looked back to see the fiery foremast falling towards the berg, carrying with it the fastenings of the jib. And those who were holding the spar were lifted into the air and shook down on to the tilted decks or dropped into the waters between the keeling vessel and the walls of ice or thrown on to the harsh whiteness of the immense berg. But Hamish and his own were still clinging to the remains of the hanging jib, where it had broken from its cables. None of them was hoisted and swept away.

Now Kirsty MacNeice came to their salvation. Her red hair black and singed, naked and scorched to the waist, she held the sailor's axe which had broken down the partition below. She was wedged against the smouldering stump of the foremast, chopping at a lashed coop of hens, mostly dead, but with two birds squawking and thrashing their wings.

"Get you over here," she shouted. "The good ship *Hopeful Mac-Neice*."

First Angus let go of the battered jib and slithered across the decks to catch at the coop. Then came Katie and Rachel and Bain. Then Hannah, rolling over and over as the ship lurched sideways ready for its deep plunge down. Then Hamish pitched forward to grasp at the coop as Kirsty's axe split the last of the lashings. Fire fell on them, burning their hair and hands, but they did not let go. And with a mighty groan and wrenching and rush of great waters, the *Hopeful June* split apart, shrugging the coop and its human cargo into the ocean by the cliff of ice. In that terrible cold slap, the breaths stopped in all the survivors. In the suck of the going under of the ship, they were drowned in the tomb of the deep that squeezed their lungs flat and choked them in black brine.

Then God spat them up from the grave of the drowned. He threw

49

them up upon the mercy of His waves that had no mercy. The coop and its human limpets were driven against the ice. Only at the last, the wind blew up a spray that sheered the frail craft past the jag of the berg to the sea beyond. And by the grace of heaven, the cutter *Ahoy!*, out of Quebec City, saw the wreck and wretches in the water and took them aboard, Kirsty MacNeice and the six Sinclairs and twenty-seven others of the thousand and more who were drowned in the splitting and the sinking of the *Hopeful June*. And they were set ashore at Grosse Isle with only sailors' clothes from the slop chest on their backs. Katie and Rachel were hot and shivering with the black fever, although a cold coming to Canada they had of it.

8

THE BURSTING AT
GROSSE ISLE

Doctor George Douglas had served as the medical superintendent of
Grosse Isle for ten years. Here the ships had to dock as they sailed
down the St Lawrence River on their way to Quebec City and Montreal
and Toronto, and here Doctor Douglas inspected the passengers. If
he did not like the looks of them, he took them off to the tents and
shacks and sheds on the island for a period of quarantine. But naturally
they had to be ill, very ill, before Doctor Douglas would take them
off their ships. Feeling under the weather was good enough to be
passed on down the great river into Canada. Feeling at death's door
was just about enough to be landed at Grosse Isle.

It was the sultry late summer that was called an Indian summer,
although the Indians did not bring it with them or leave it behind
them in their forcing to the west. The tens of thousands of poor folk
flung from Scotland and Ireland were bringing the fever heat with
them. It was typhus and dysentery, and the contagion was spreading
with the lice and the flies and the mosquitoes that bred on the swampy
ground of Grosse Isle which never seemed to dry out, even in the sun
that conjured pestilence out of the dank earth, not purgations or
curatives.

Once Doctor Douglas had only three people to help him on the
quarantine island, Tom Fitch the steward, old Johnson the orderly,
and the gap-toothed tyrant Meg Halloran of the black tongue and the
healing hand. But this summer there had been more than twenty
doctors on Grosse Isle. Whatever their lack of qualifications, they were
trying to deal with the plague of the mass contagion, the sick lying on
bare boards in their bunks in the fever sheds or on straw in the
bell-tents. And the doctors were dying as fast as the patients, ten of
them expired and five more sick of the typhus, and only six grave-
diggers to bury in the sodden shallow graves over the rock the hundreds

of bodies that Doctor Douglas discovered day by day, dead on the open ground or in the huddle of loose stones or under old sail-canvas or stiff in their berths in the fever sheds that were worse than the steerage holds from which he had plucked them into this hot fate.

Oh God, dear God, he could not go on, he must go on, he would go on. He would write to his superiors in Quebec City, but they would do little but send him one or two more doctors with their mother's milk still wet upon their lips to die here. The poor folk from the isles off England were not really the concern of the people of Canada, who were now learning to hold dominion over themselves. And so Doctor Douglas went to his quarters in the plague camp, and he penned a letter to the authorities who would ignore it down the river.

Grosse Isle, Tuesday, 9 a.m.
Out of the four thousand or five thousand emigrants that have left this island since Sunday, at least two thousand will fall sick somewhere before three weeks are over. They ought to have accommodation for two thousand sick at least in Montreal and Quebec, as all the Greenock and Liverpool passengers are half dead from starvation and want before embarking; and the least bowel complaint, which is sure to come with a change of food, finishes them without a struggle. I never saw people so indifferent to life; they would continue in the same berth with a dead person until the seaman or captain dragged out the corpse with boat-hooks. Good God! what evils will befall the cities wherever they alight. And as for the typhus and the black fever, they no more resist it than a lover's kiss. This hot weather will increase the evil. Now give the authorities of Quebec and Montreal fair warning from me. And send me, for the love of God, all the doctors and orderlies and nurses and grave-diggers you may provide to undertake service on this pest-island. Take these from the gaols if need be, for I have need of all servants here in this extremity. I have not time to write at length, or should feel it in my duty to do so. Public safety requires it . . .

There was a large, thick-set man standing in the room, his awkward boots making the pine-boards creak and groan as a wind in the original branches. Doctor Douglas had not noticed him enter, but there he was, freckled and burly as if he were planted there.
"And what would you be wanting?" Doctor Douglas asked.
"A life," Hamish Sinclair said.
Doctor Douglas snorted and shook his head.
"That is the last thing and the least thing you will find here."
"Yet that is what I will have," Hamish said. "This life."

And then he moved as though uprooted. He weighed heavily on the pine-boards with his boots and left the room and was gone but a moment and returned with the body of a child in his arms. Her long fair hair splashed from her lolling head on to his knees. Her mouth was fixed in a gape, her eyes stared wide and blind.

"But she is dead," Doctor Douglas said.

"I will have the life of my Rachel."

Douglas rose and walked round the trestle table where he worked and put his hand on the chill cheek of the child in the man's arms.

"I am no sorcerer or resurrectionist," he said. "I cannot make the living from the dead."

"Her life," Hamish said, "I must have her back."

"Come with me," Douglas said, speaking before he knew what he was saying. "We will find a place fit for her."

The doctor and the man carrying the dead child emerged from the pine-board shack and walked past two large sweltering sheds and five rough tents, pitched to shelter the sick and the dying. The torrid air hung in an invisible sheet, damp with the effluvia of fever. One voice was crying out, "No, no, no . . .", then fell away. Some bull-frogs croaked from a marsh as if gasping for air.

"We will walk to my farm," Douglas said. "It is over there, by the trees."

"I cannot leave my wife and bairns for muckle time," Hamish said.

"I will show you a place where your Rachel may rest, and then you may bring your family to her."

The farm, which Douglas had on the island, was the only farm. It was his solace and his refuge. Near some maple trees, he had built a cottage out of stone, with a barn for cattle nearby. He had half a dozen cows and an old bull, and there was a vegetable patch at the back of the house. To Hamish, carrying his dead daughter, the farm seemed to be the dream which he had crossed the ocean to find.

"I did not think," Hamish said, "in this isle – where we are cast like dung into a pit . . ."

"I have to live here," Douglas said. "But I like to think I have made a farm like a farm in Scotland."

"If I had that farm in Scotland," Hamish said, "we would never have crossed the water."

Douglas led the way to the maple trees, their leaves already beginning to show the blood in them. Between the trees, a small grave had already been dug, or what seemed to be one.

"We use it for storing the jars of maple syrup," Douglas said, "when we tap the trees. Perhaps Rachel might rest there, and we might say the prayers to wish her good night."

Hamish stood with his small daughter above the grave. Although he was weeping, the tears did not show among the many beads of sweat on his face. Walking was swimming through the hot clamminess of the atmosphere. At last, he brought himself to speak.

"She was a one for the trees," he said. "She will be lying quiet here."

Hamish straddled the gash in the earth and lowered his daughter's body into the pit. Now it lay below ground, enclosed by the earth, it might have been uncovered, as a man might dig up some marble statue of a sprite or an angel of time past.

"She is a beautiful girl," Douglas said. "She will rest easy there. Will you go and find your wife and your children and bring them here? I will be fetching a Bible from my house."

Hamish turned to him and wiped his eyes and his cheeks with the back of his hand.

"Why should you be after caring for us, Doctor Douglas?"

"Death is random," Douglas said. "Thousands are dying. I cannot care for them all. I am failing in my duty. People even say I have a farm on Grosse Isle to sell the produce to the sick in my care. And I do that."

"I was a farmer," Hamish said. "I will be a farmer. We must sell the things we grow."

"I can only care for the people one by one," Douglas said, looking down at the body of Rachel lying so whitely in the earth. "This one I care for. Do not ask me why."

Now Hamish also looked down at the body of his daughter, and he raged and cursed and spoke the blasphemy that he had never spoken, not even when Hannah had lost their firstborn son.

"You care!" he shouted. "And God does not care! Why did God give me Rachel and take her from me? He does not care! God does not care!"

Douglas put his hand on the shaking and drenched shoulder of Hamish Sinclair.

"Hold your peace," he said. "God makes me care. For this one, your Rachel, His Rachel. And for you. Do you see that farm? There is no one to work it. All are sick or dead. And I have too much to do and may be sick or dead soon. Go you there with your wife and your children. You are a farmer. Look after the cattle, grow the vegetables. I will teach you how to take syrup from the maple trees that watch over your daughter."

His eyes red with rage and grief, Hamish stared at the doctor.

"I cannot take that from you."

"Take it," Douglas said. "I can only offer it to one. And it is you."

"I cannot thank you –"

"Thank God, not me."

"I am not in the way of thinking to thank God."

"Thank Him."

"Aye."

Hamish turned and looked down again at the body of Rachel in the little pit. She was so small, but she seemed to trust the lap of the earth with the arms of the soil about her.

"Thank God," he said, "for saving her sister Katie from the black fever. Thank God for preserving us from the sinking of the ship in the ice. Thank God for bringing us to this good man, when I was thinking that there was no good in any man, no, no good at all."

"I am not a good man," Douglas said. "I do not know why you are the one. I simply do not know."

So Doctor Douglas sent away Hamish Sinclair to find the rest of his family and bring them to the burial and to the farm to dwell there. And as he walked towards his small stone house, the only cool place on all the island in this Indian summer and sultry fall, he did not know why he had displaced himself for this one poor family among the thousands of families of the displaced, for this one distraught mourner, for this one dead child. He had seen the babies dying and the fathers weeping and the mothers in agony in their tens of thousands in the ships that lined the bay, waiting for him to go out and inspect them before they sailed on to discharge the human wreckage from them. And for some reason that was beyond his understanding, he chose to save this father and his unknown wife and children. Because Rachel had died, because her father had brought her body to him, because he could not live with his guilt at doing so little for so many, because he could do no more, because all we may do on this earth is to save one another one by one by one. God only knew.

9

A FOREIGN EDUCATION

Iain would never have thought it of the army, but the Sutherland Highlanders which the British had put their number on as the Ninety-third, were like a parish in musket and bonnet and boots. The men formed themselves into a congregation, they chose their own elders, and they paid for a minister in Edinburgh to preach to them on Sundays. It was a queer thing, the soldiers being that way, but most of them came from parishes that were not cleared as the Sinclairs had been, and the worst of the punishments for them was not a flogging of five hundred lashes with the cat o'nine tails, but the threat to post a notice on the door of their kirk at home telling of their disgrace, so that when they did go back to their clachan, why, all would know their shame and none would bear with them for it. For they had taken the guinea and were bound to be a good soldier for their terms of years, even though there was not a tack of land at the end of it now, only the honour of the clan that was not the honour of the regiment, whoever heard of a thing like that?

These were men that matched Iain himself in size and spirit. Willie McBean was that big, he could look down on Iain and call him a wee man. And when they came to it with the wrestling of hands, Iain could only hold Willie for forty minutes with the blood squeezing out of the tips of his fingers, before Willie put Iain's hand gently down on the scrubbed deal and said, "Toots, wee man, you'll make a tussle of it when you grow." But Tam Ogilvie was a bantam cock with a kick like a cuddy; Iain saw him put four big fellows on their hams with his head butt and his fists in two blinks of the eye. There were hard knocks in little packets, and Tam Ogilvie was the very devil when the blood ran up, for all the pint bottle he was.

When Hamish Jamie came to Edinburgh, it was not to the Sutherlands, for he would have none of them, but only to the regiment from Ross where they had been cleared before the family were shipped to Canada. His was Fraser's Highlanders or the Seaforths, also the

Seventy-eighth, but they were a wild lot at the grogshops and the flogging-post as often as not. The meeting of the brothers in the barracks was not easy, but it was done, and Iain heard of the loss of the ship to Canada and the dying of his sister Rachel of the fever and the family in the farm at home, but they had moved west now into the woods to clear their own farm, and not a word from them the while.

"We were in Montreal," Iain said, "and we only came back the now. And we will be in Canada again and see them all."

"If you have the luck, Iain," Hamish Jamie said. "The Seaforths have been in India for years, and they have been dying of the cholera, and that is why they need me out there, more oats for the illness. They say it is as bad as the potatoes, you swell and go black and stink like an old fish. And I want the fighting."

"You'll have that," Iain said. "When we last shipped to America, we were at a big river, they say the Mississippi. And the idiot officers, they walked us into the American long muskets of the men of the woods – and good Scotsmen all of them, Bowies and such. And every man of them could hit a squirrel in the eye at two hundred paces. So we were soon dead or wounded, though I heard tell it was better in garrison in Montreal, where we took the curling and the bowling. Fine it is to play them."

"I want the fighting."

"Have the playing while you can," Iain said. "The fighting will come surely."

And so it would with the Russian bear striking his claws south to Constantinople, which was halfway to India, where the Russians were also at the Himalayas and wanted to come in. And there was the balloting for the soldiers' wives and the children, "To Go" or "Not To Go" with their husbands to the front. Would they exchange one dark room for a worse wet tent, one scrubbing tub for another, one sick bairn for a sicker one? But if the paper was "Not To Go", it meant a separation for ten years or more. They were not paid a pension, they had to be paupers on the parish. Even a shack or rotten canvas for their cover on half rations was better than the workhouse at home. The marrying of the uniform, that was the proud day in a lassie's life. But following the flag was slow dying and shame.

Before his posting, Iain had a letter from Mary, telling him that she was with the duchess in her grand house in London. He was given a leave of embarkation, and since he had no parish and no family in Scotland, he was after taking the new steam train to London to see the great city and his sister there. But Hamish Jamie did not tell his brother of his own troubles with the flesh, how one of the soldier's wives, Meg Robertson, who did his washing and pipe-clayed his straps and leggings, had the eye for him and taught him the things the Bible said were not to do and yet were so sweet to do. And on a foul mattress off the market, where rooms were at rent for twopence an hour, Hamish Jamie learned of love or what was called love. After the thrashing and the cries of pain and the release, there was a time of peace and joy when the lines of labour and sorrow on Meg's face were soothed soft as curds, and she spoke as honey, "My one, my own Hamish," and the smile on her lips was the smile of sixteen, and that was the wonder of it for Hamish Jamie, how the desperate coming together made such a calm and a child out of her weariness. There could be no sin in it, but there surely was, and never did Hamish Jamie meet the eye of Robertson in the mess. And when one night Meg's husband asked harshly for the loan of his kettle and never did give it back, Hamish Jamie never did ask for it, reckoning Meg was worth more than a piece of old tin, even if her man did not.

There was no end to their fifth winter in the woods, although it would be the end of all of them if the spring came not soon. But it did not come, and the chores of staying alive made every day a chill labour with skin cracking in the frost, and fingers and toes turning blue through fur mittens and boots, and the very breath of a man changed to steam in the still air or to crystal if he spat to the snow. There was wood enough for the chopping, in truth there were too many trees. For the forest staked their log cabin round in a bristle of giant fence on fence on fence, as if God Almighty had tossed ten thousand cabers from the sky in some High Heaven Games.

Ice had to be chopped from the spring too, when water was needed, and it froze in the pail as old Hamish toted it back to the cabin door. Inside the smoky and small space, the holes between the log walls plugged with dry mud clotted with twig and reed, Hannah was the abiding miracle of herself. It was sore hard with the penned spirits of the children, Bain and Angus and Katie, fretting at their long confinement, longing to run out over the white wild that at first fall had been snowballs and sliding and laughing, and now was a pale shroud laid across the world.

Yet Hannah tended to the iron stove that the waggon and the ponies had taken with them, giving them less each day of the sour lumps of dough called flapjacks, which were the cold porridge cakes of Canada. The only sweetening was some drops of maple sugar gone into the boiling water until there was a thin syrup with a faint taste of far joy as a love remembered. They were at the bottom of the sack of dried apples and plums, and their teeth were loose in their black gums, while their lips were as white as linen. They thirsted like the moose

58

and the bear and the snowshoe rabbits for the berries and the grasses of spring to make them whole again.

Angus was the first to despair. They had prayed before the meal, a simple Grace and God be thanked for His mercies, and it was an occasion, the last of the bear's bacon, even if it was more rind than lean. But Angus kicked the table on the sudden and fell back on the big bed he shared with Bain and said, "Rachel's lying sweeter than we are in those trees on the island. Why did you bring us to die in the snow, Father? For we will."

"God will provide," Hannah said, "but until He does, we must."

"We have the land now," Hamish said. "Thirty acres. Did we have that ever to call our own?"

"Thirty acres of trees," Angus said. "And what do we grow on trees? Nuts and bears?"

"We will bring the trees down," Hamish said. "And there will be a town in these woods, with a kirk and a mill and a store and a school-house. And we will be the making of this new land, for that we were unmade in our own Scotland."

"We had a farm by the river and the sea at Grosse Isle –"

"It was not our farm. It was the farm of the good Doctor –"

"And he gave you the money to come west, and the ministers and the relief. And it was not for the saving of us, but for the ridding of us."

"Hush, Angus," Hamish said. "They were good folk. We should not be here as we are if they –"

"We should not be here as we are." Angus coughed into the smoke that blew back from the stove and could not escape from under the low ridgepole and planks piled with stones and sod that was their roof. "There's no place wants the Sinclairs the now. We are the outcasts – that goat in the Good Book."

"The scapegoat," Hamish said. "Aye, Angus, you are right in what you say. There was no sin in us for what we had to suffer –"

"Talk of himself," Hannah said, "that he does. That's for you to say, Hamish. And how do we know the now what the Lord saw in us that we did not do right?"

"When the snow's gone . . ." Katie said.

"If it is ever gone," Bain said.

"Can I have a new dress at the store?"

Hannah's heart bled to see her daughter wrapped in a grey wool blanket with a robe of stitched beaver- and wolf-skins thrown over her to keep her warm. Dear God, were the woods making them the savages that even the braes and the mountains of Scotland never made them be?

"You'll have a fine woollen dress of the red and the white," Hannah said, "an the men catch enough skins for Rafferty at the store. And you will have them, Hamish, will you not?"

Hamish and the boys spent the winter months in the making of the traps that were their living until they could clear the land. They already knew the art of the snare and the noose and the deadfall and the wooden cages, for the skins of beaver and otter and wolf and mink and fox and coon only sold without a ball-mark in them. And they were down to the last of the powder for the old smooth-bore and muzzle-loader with a flint-lock that was almost as old as Hamish himself. They had to use their knives to kill and flay the furred beasts of the forests, which God had given for their clothing and their trading. And now the pelts were pegged on their stretchers under the roof in black flags, waiting for the thaw that did not come.

"There's game enough," Hamish said, "for every man. But it takes a pile of skins for Rafferty to cut a dress out of it – if a dress he has at all."

Rafferty's store was a walk through the trees, away to the river, where the canoes brought in the goods – new lead bars laid over the barrels of gunpowder, muskets never shot off before, bolts of cloth in all the colours of the rainbow and blankets brighter than lightning, beads and ribbons and bells and rings for the Indian finery; and the knives for hunting with the horn handles, and the axes and the tomahawks, and the iron rails and hammers and steel saws for the cutting down of the trees and the building of the cabins. And the keg in the corner with its spigot and tap, spilling out the sour sharp smell of the whiskey that pinched the nose, while the Indian braves sat by, trading their furs for tin mugs of the spirit that made them wilder than the natures God gave them in His mysterious way.

"Rafferty will have cloth for a dress," Hannah said, "if you don't spend all the tally for the skins on knives and blacksmith's traps and whiskey –"

"And when did I ever spend on the whiskey what was for the family?"

Hannah heard the hurt in the voice of Hamish that was also his defence against a weakness so rare it should be forgot. But she never forgot a weakness.

"It is not that you never, Hamish," she said. "It is that you will not now. And we will have yeast so we will have good Christian bread again with the meal, and we will have that dried fruit paste you cannot tell from chewing leather for the good of our sore mouths – and cloth for Katie's dress. For to look at her, you will think she was a squaw

60

and worse, for they have fine beads and bells on their leggings, while Katie has no shift or shirt to call her own."

She took the last of the flapjacks off the skillet with the flat fork and put it on the plate of Angus.

"Eat," she said. "You will live. We will clear the trees. There will be a fine farm house, but builded in wood, not the stone. But we will have a stone hearth for the winter to come, and another room for the boys, so we do not have to sleep like cuddies in the barn, and we will plant potatoes and corn on the land which God has given us."

"Listen to your mother," Hamish said. "And we will bide this winter."

And the very next morning, there was a noise as of a volley of rifles, and it was the daggers of ice splitting from the rims of the roof and the frozen water cracking on the top of the spring and the frost breaking open at the coming of a warm wind that sang of the hope of the ending of the winter without end.

"Lord, and you think working for the duchess in London was better than being in the army, Iain? But men, they ken only what they do, and they think they have the worst of it. If you think privates and corporals and sergeants and captains and majors and generals are anything to *our* household, you have many thinks a-coming. You no ken what we have to do and every missie keep her place, or it's out on the street, bag and baggage, if there's any you have.

"Work your way up, Herself says, and when they say work, it is *work*. I was starting as a second dairy maid, and out with the cows at the milking before it was light. And then it was under-laundry maid, Iain, and never you saw so much bleach and starch, for they soil their linens and their chemmies just as bad as anyone, for all their ladies' airs that nothing but Paris perfume ever come under their noses."

Mary swept back a strand of her hair which had worked loose on her forehead. She had to tell her soldier big brother all that had happened to her. That's what brothers were for. They had to listen.

"After upper-laundry maid, I was promoted to under-housemaid, and glad I was to keep out of the kitchen, for cook calls himself chef, and the only thing he had out of France was his sauce, not his sauces, and a temper worse than red pepper. But chambermaid was not so grand, up at dawn to light the kitchen fire and clean the other grates, dust off the night before and prepare the morning after, sweep the hall and stairs, and all before breakfast, and the seeing to the ladies in their bedrooms, their fires and their hot water, and waiting for their rising and their dressing by their lady's maids, so their rooms be aired and their mattresses turned and their sheets put on fresh as daisies every day. And so on until the afternoon, when all is done backwards, for the hours are sixteen every day, and hardly a holy day of rest.

"But the *rank* of it, Iain, and keeping your place, and where you may sit in the parlour and in the kitchen for your dinner, it is worse than the army, even if you and Hamish Jamie say it is not. I no ken if His Grace – and he has not a grace in him – the duke is worse than His Mr Menzies and the Lord High Butler. You would think the moon shone out of his westkit buttons, for bulging they are, and he is worse than the Duke of Wellington to the footmen. And he would tell off the housekeeper, Mrs Rogers, only he is scared she will rap his knuckles with her great bunch of keys, so it is Her Holy Cow who has the minding of us parlourmaids and nursemaids and skivvies and such. And she says to me, 'Mary Sinclair, if you took it upon yourself to be educated instead of remaining as thick as porridge, why, I might recommend Her Grace that you be her lady's maid, after Céline goes back to that God-forsaken country where she was born.' But you have to be French to be a lady's maid."

Mary could see her brother smiling and shaking his head at her, not disapproving, but enjoying the story of her life below stairs. And she could not stop the telling of it.

"We eat in the kitchen, while Mr Menzies and Mrs Rogers eat in their parlour, and we wait on them there. And breakfast for them, Iain, it is what we had for a whole day in Scotland, and better – hot rolls and dry toast and a fancy bread loaf and a common loaf and a pound of butter and a red-hot iron in an urn of boiling water for the making of their tea and a thick coffee that is more of a chocolate really. And all of us below the stairs take lunch at one in the kitchen and dinner at six, and if you saw the spread of it, Iain – cold cuts and soles fried with saws, a leg of mutton and a dish of ox, pullets and potatoes, rice and rhubarb tart. It would feed an army, that it would.

"And this silk dress I am wearing! I might be the grand lady, for off the back of Her Grace it is. Céline was clever, she was. Pleats and flounces, Her Grace wants them right and neat every time like the guards on parade, and I do them for Céline, I am a dab hand at the ironing. But this silk dress Céline did, and she burned it and stitched it up poorly and put it on Her Grace and said, 'Oh la la, ma'am, it eez not 'vair good, eez bad stitches, look ze dress-maker, kell horror!' So Her Grace give Céline the dress and Céline give it me and I stitch it so it is good as new. And I am the lady now – on my day off, if I get one.

"I got one to see you, Iain, and I got one to see the Great Exhibition. Albert took me, the footman, very saucy, but he's a cockney, and London's like a brae to him, and there were so many folk in the park we never did get inside, but there was this crystal palace shining in the sun like a dream big as our mountain, but all glass with trees *inside*, and it is all took away the now and the trees still in the park, but it was the wonder of the world, and I saw it. But you are took away over the sea to Russia, and you will not come back. Iain, oh Iain, must you go?"

"I must," Iain said.

He had been listening to his sister Mary talk of her life for an hour or more, as they sat in a tavern off the Seven Dials. His tartan forage cap was set on the table before him by his mug of porter, but there was bare room enough to squeeze his knees under the wood, while Mary billowed out in her green silk like a wave over the sawdust. She was bonny now with the oval face of the Sinclair women, and she surely had found her tongue. Talk, talk, talk, it was longer than a sermon, though more lively for all that.

Outside by the Seven Dials, they could hear the ballad-seller shouting, "Awful catastrophe! Awful catastrophe! Only a ha'penny!" And Mary rose in a surge of silk and held out her hand and pulled him up and said, "Come and buy a ballad! Albert takes me here, when he can – and they are an education! I ken they are not holy, but they have a tidy moral. And if a good murder is the subject, why, Iain, there is murder enough in the Good Book – Saul slew in his thousands and David in his tens of thousands –"

"There is killing and killing," Iain said, "and some of it is legal and some of it is not, but for the dead man, he does not care, for he is too dead to care at all."

They went out among the costers at their barrows, crying, "Mussels, a penny a quart! Live eels, three pound a shilling! All large and alive – O, new sprats, O, a penny a plate! Cherry ripe, twopence a pound!" And Iain bought Mary a pound of cherries, which she sucked into her mouth till her lips were stained black with the juices of them, while she stored the pips in her cheek till she could slip them into her glove and drop them while no one was looking. For they were all gawking at the red-faced ballad-seller in his black hat and coat of pearl buttons, talking of a dreadful murder at the Seven Dials, a father killing his pretty little boy, the sadness and the badness of it.

"No, my friends, here you have, just printed and published half-an-hour ago, a full, true and particular account of the life, trial, character, confession, behaviour, sentence, repentance, and execution of that horrible malefactor, J. F. Jeffery, who was executed and hanged after on Monday last, for the small charge of one ha'penny – and for the dreadful and wicked murder of his only son Arthur, pretty and tender and handsome. You have here every particular, that which he done, and that which he didn't. Ain't this just a dodgy country? We loves birds and dogs and flowers, treat them right we do – and we puts our sons and daughters down the mines and up the chimbleys, 'Sweep, sweep, chimbley-sweep!' and we does away with them most unnatural – and for only a ha'penny!"

"I never heard of such a thing," Iain spoke down to Mary from his tartan cap that perched above the crowd as high as the faces of the Seven Dials. "Murdering your own boy!"

"Did I not say it was an education?"

And the patterer went on, as a boy walked round the crowd, offering the pink sheets of the ballad.

"Yes, my customers, to this is added a copy of serene and beautiful werses, pious and immoral, what he wrote with his own blood and skewer the night after – I means the night before his execution. It is addressed to young men and women of all sexes – I beg pardon, but I mean classes – my friends, it is nothing to laugh at, for I can tell you the werses make three of the hardest-heartist things weep – a bailiff, a banker and a copper. And look at that soldier lad, down from bonny Scotland and tall as the gallows what they hanged the horrible murderer on, he'll have this dreadful tale what is tidy moral and highly educational – for the small charge of only a ha'penny!"

And as the boy with the ballads put a pink sheet in Iain's hand while he fumbled in his sporran for a copper with his other hand, the patterer began to sing in a voice like a gurgle in a drainpipe:

> *You kindest fathers, tender mothers,*
> *Listen to this sad tale awhile,*
> *Listen, listen, listen brothers,*
> *To murder in the Seven Dials.*
> *In Earl Street lived a wretch named Jeffery,*
> *His trade a tailor I am told,*
> *His little boy called Richard Arthur*
> *Was a tot of six years old –*

"Toots, man." Ian shouted, "if this is the best you can do in your great city, the ship to Russia can no come too soon."

"Hush, Iain," Mary spoke up to him. "We will away, then."

And as they pushed through the crowd at the Seven Dials among the crying voices of the costers, they could hear the boy joining the patterer at the end of his song, his piping answering the deep voice of his master.

> *The villain took him to a cellar,*
> *Resolved his offspring to destroy,*

Tied his little hands behind him,
Hanged the pretty smiling boy.
"Now upon the drop you see me,
Guilty and heart-broken here!
Who in Heaven will forgive me?"
"I forgive you, Daddy dear!"

"If that is what you call entertainment – *theatre* in London –"

"Others there are – The Vic!" Mary said.

"I will never see the theatre again," Iain said. "And if there is to be killing, I will be killing Russian bears and not wee boys. Mary, Mary, how can you bide in a schlorich and a slummock like London?"

10

THE MOUNTAINS AND
THE STONES

"All officers are daft," Iain Sinclair said, "for anyone must be daft to buy in to be an officer, but only one of them has a brain to put beside the next –"

"He'll be Sir Colin Campbell," Tam Ogilvie said, running his whetstone along the edge of his bayonet. "Put all the brains of all the officers' mess in the army in one skillypan, and boil 'em, and Sir Colin would have 'em for breakfast, and who'd know the lack of nothing?"

"He must have asked for us," Iain said, "and that's the pity. A river to cross and then a mountain to climb into the Russian guns. So Sir Colin says, 'Send you for the Highlanders. They're fools and they're goats. They're fools enough to fight head on climbing a mountain, but they're goats enough to climb it.'

"More'n *they* can!" Iain said. He nodded his head towards where the battalions of the Brigade of Guards were waiting in scarlet coats with brass buttons bright enough to blind an eye on. "Them Grenadiers and Coldstreamers, they'll fight on the flat –"

"With the cannon behind them."

"But on the hills . . ." Iain laughed. "Why, if they won't fall over their big boots on a wee scree of stones!"

The Highland Brigade was in the second line with the Guardsmen under the heights of Alma. They could clearly see how bad the fight would be. If ever there was a battle lost in advance, this was it. A river to cross, bare scraped slopes to mount towards two great and lesser redoubts, hairy like a sporran with cannon, then cliffs with dozens of grey Russian battalions waiting on top. The only good thing was that the Highlanders were not in the front line. That was for the Light Infantry, they that had won so many hard battles for the old Duke of Wellington in the Peninsula against Boney's armies and now were cussing at the pounding from the long Russian guns, lying and waiting for the order to attack until the afternoon. So when it came and they had to struggle across the river, they stopped to drink for their terrible thirst, even though some of them were drinking blood, as the grapeshot and canister cut them down.

Now the Russian guns were reaching them and they were told to lie down too, and Iain felt his own berserker blood surge into his head, as he watched the Light Infantry stumble up the barren slope towards the great redoubt, with the smoke obscuring them from the brushwood fires lit by the Russian scouts. But on they climbed with more and more laying on the slopes, but then, far and away, a hunting cry, "Stole away! Stole away!" And daft it was, the Russian guns, all limbering up and drawing away behind the horses, and the beaten men of the Light Infantry going over the earthworks on to the heights, all because the Russians had stole away.

"Forward, forward," Iain muttered to himself, as he squinted from the ground along the lying lines to where the royal Duke of Cambridge sat on his grey. But the duke did not budge, he did not speak, he might have already been the statue or the pub sign that would surely become of him. There was no word of forward or backward from him, but the silence of stay where you are, stay where you'll always be, down and out of it. And looking forward again, Iain could already see the grey Russian battalions come in wedges towards the great redoubt to push back the Light Infantry. So it would all have to be done again, as it always had to be done many a time and dead men too many.

And done again it was against the mountains and the odds. Crossing the river was not so bad, although the weight of the water on his kilt dragged Iain down at the knees and the fur fringe of his big bonnet fell in his eyes. And it was luck that hardly a Russian long gun was firing as they picked their way up the left of the slope among the dead and the dying of the Light Infantry, moaning and piteous as curlews on the moor over the sea-shore. The Highlanders were ragged, but faster up the hill, for they were surely used to that. But the Guardsmen, they were a sight for the drill sergeant, their two thin red ranks advancing as if to the pacestick, thirty inches between each pace, and eighteen inches from shoulder to shoulder, how could they keep that order and that perfect distance? And when the round-shot and the musket balls hit a Guardsman and threw him over in a crumpled scarlet shroud, why, the rank closed up from the left, you'd have thought an invisible bar was keeping them straight and an unseen wire was pulling them together, as they marched over the bodies of the Light Infantry and their own. And now it must be over, for four columns of grey Russians, each thick as a man o'war, came over the hill to ram the thin red ranks and sink them utterly.

67

But now the red ranks halted, and the Minié rifles were raised thicker than the prickles on a hedgehog, and the command came, "Fire!" and the smoke and the crackle came from the muzzles of the Guardsmen, and then they slipped in another cartridge through the muzzle beneath the bayonet and rammed it home and marched on this devil's parade. The Russians coming down from the heights had stopped, the rear ranks pushing forward, the front ranks stepping back from the wall of their dead comrades lying as heaps of spent kelp before them.

Looking forward, Iain saw two more columns facing the Highlanders in two bulwarks and piers of grey stone. They also fired a volley, but the firing of the volley was not the way of Sir Colin Campbell and the mountain men in the attack, and there was a shout that might be for a charge, but it was lost in the yelling and the wild outcry of the pipes, and Iain was shouting and running up the scree, swinging his rifle and bayonet to the fore, his kilt clapping and sticking at his bare legs. Then the shock as he stabbed home the point of his bayonet into the grey cloth of a man under a shako, and the twist into the wound, and the kick forward on the falling shape to jerk out the bayonet, and the swinging of the butt in a club, and the cheeks and noses breaking open in spurts of red and then slipping down.

Now he was slipping down himself, and then he was rising at the lunge, and another body was writhing on the bayonet and taking him down so he had to pull it out with a boot on the bloody cheek of the other, then swing the butt, swing and strike, and strike home. All the while, the red mist was in his eyes and the war cry was breaking out of his throat wilder than bulls at the mating, till the white faces in front were grey backs on the sudden, and the bulwark was a broken sea wall, with the kilts and the bonnets streaming through, and the Russians in dull waves on the slipstream away.

And as Iain reached the heights of Alma to see the broken battalions of the Russians in one great ebb tide sweeping back towards the true walls of Sebastopol, he heard the hurrahs and the shout of triumph to the right, and he looked across to see the earthworks of the great redoubt fringed in the scarlet of tunic and ensign, and he knew that the battle of the Alma was won, if a battle is ever won, for it is lost for some, the wounded and the dying and the dead. And even the terrible Duke of Wellington, was it not he that said, "Next to a battle lost, there is nothing so dreadful as a battle won."

But there is always another battle to lose. And so it looked outside Balaclava, where the generals had got it wrong as they always did, and it was left to Sir Colin Campbell and the Highlanders to save the day, as they always did. There were only five hundred and fifty of them not dead or wounded now, and another hundred sick, and some Turks who were better off at the running than the shooting, for they had poured down from the lost redoubts in front, shouting, "Ship! Ship!" How to get out seemed the only Christian word they knew. And seeing the Russians coming down from the taken redoubts above the valley leading to the port, Sir Colin ordered his men to lie down on their faces in two ranks like Guardsmen on the far side of the hillock that was their position.

So Iain lay down with murder in his heart to take the pounding and the shot of the Russian horse-guns lobbing their shells over the crest. The lying down and the taking it was the bitter part and the British part that was called the discipline, while the real pounding was the blood in his temples redder than his coat and telling him to rise and charge, yelling, forward. And what was that? From the corner of his eye, Iain could see the distant glitter of the Light Horse Brigade to the side, waiting to take the enemy on the flank, but they were wheeling now and going about and leaving the Sutherland Highlanders in the lurch. But what could a Scotsman expect from a bunch of Sassenach dolls on fancy gee-gees who might have been riding on a merry-go-round at the fair for all they knew of war?

Now the Turks were running over the hillock, shouting "Ship! Ship! Ship!" again, and they were scampering like rats in a grain barge back to Balaclava. And it must be the sight of the Russians, and so it was, for the cannon had stopped, and there was the sound of horses in a far trotting that rose to a near clatter, and Sir Colin shouted, "Rise! Take your aim! Fire!" and they were just like the bloody Guardsmen in their two thin red lines raising their Minié rifles with the bayonets tipping them with steel and taking aim at the four squadrons of horsemen that had halted down the hill, surprised at the sudden view of them.

When they fired their volley at the Russians, the men came down like skittles, the horses like broken stools in a wild whinnying. The rest of the horsemen rode on, but when another cartridge was rammed in, and the order came again to aim and fire, the second volley took the guts and the wind out of them, and they staggered as in the gust of a gale. And Iain started forward with half the Highlanders, but he heard Sir Colin shouting the British number of their regiment, "Ninety-third! Ninety-third! Damn all that eagerness!" And Iain steadied with his line, and he put another cartridge in the muzzle, and he pushed it home and he aimed and he fired on the order, and the third volley broke the Russian cavalry, which wheeled and rode away from the downed and heaving carpet of their own. And a yell split the air over the valley. The Sutherland Highlanders had saved Balaclava, and the fancy dolls on their fairground gee-gees had the devil to do

69

with it as usual. It was the two thin red lines, and didn't Sir Colin say, "I did not think it worthwhile to form them even four deep."

For Iain Sinclair, that day was the last he had of the fighting in the Crimea. He did not see, he did not know of the charge of the Heavy Brigade against the Russian massed horse and their breaking of the bears with six legs, and he did not see, he did not know of the foolishness of the charge of the Light Brigade into the cannon to the left of them and cannon to the right of them and cannon to the front of them that volleyed and thundered. For it was sure that no poet was to write of the foolishness of him getting his wound, bending over a fallen Russian hussar to strip the helmet off his head as a keepsake for Mary, and a dead man rising up behind as a solid ghost and shooting him with a horsepistol through the back, before Iain in his falling dropped him dead at last with a giant fist as heavy as a hammer on his bare skull.

Iain tried to stop the blood coming out of the hole in his chest with his spread hand, but it was no good. He felt his veins pumping out his life through his back, and he could not walk away. And Tom and Willie McBean came, and they plugged the holes in the front and the rear of Iain with wadding and lint for the cleaning of their rifles, and they bound it tight with a sling round his chest, until the red flow of his veins was stoppit, and they made a cat's cradle of their hands, and so it was that they carried him with his arms round their shoulders all the way to the ships at Balaclava. For if Sir Colin Campbell expected his men to die for him, he also wanted them to live for him, and after the fighting, he was the man of all of them to see after that.

The woman, who sat writing in the lamp-light was dressed in white. But her face was not angelic. It was practical and almost dour. She pinched her lips as she wrote to her friend, Doctor Bowman, in England, which seemed at the far end of this world.

> On Thursday last (November 8th), we had 1715 sick and wounded in the Hospital (among whom 120 cholera patients), and 650 severely wounded in the other building called the General Hospital, of which we also have charge, when a message came to me to prepare for 510 wounded on our side of the Hospital, who were arriving from Balaclava.

A moaning rose from below in the Barrack Hospital at Scutari that was not the moaning of the Black Sea. It was more like a moaning from a purgatory below. The woman in white was still writing, but now she wrote about herself.

I always expected to end my days as a Hospital Matron, but I never expected to be a Barrack Mistress. We had but half an hour's notice before they began landing the wounded. Between 1 and 9 o'clock we had mattresses stuffed, sewn up, laid down, alas! only upon matting on the floor. We have had such a sea in the Bosphorus and the Turks, the very men for whom we are fighting, carry in our wounded so cruelly, that they arrive in a state of agony.

This time she did put aside her pen. How could she write it all? And should she write that the army was killing its own soldiers by its inefficiency and cruelty? The truth pointed itself in phrases through her head, as her lips spoke what she must write.

Twenty-four cases died in the day of landing . . .

We now have four miles of beds, and not eighteen inches apart . . .

The wounded are now lying up to our very doors, and we are landing 540 more from the Andes . . .

And there are two more ships loading at the Crimea with the wounded . . .

We have erysipelas, fever and gangrene, and the Russian wounded are the worst . . .

I am getting a screen now for the amputations, for when one poor fellow, who is to be amputated tomorrow, sees his comrade today die under the knife, it makes impression and diminishes his chance . . .

In all our corridor I think we have not an average of three limbs per man . . .

Her pen did not go on writing. She would finish the letter later. The wounded were waiting for her, and the dying. It was a ritual now. "The lady with the lamp", she was called that. But sometimes she felt of no more use than the lamp, casting a light here and a shadow there indifferently, and the wick going out from time to time, which she was never allowed to do.

Walking along the miles of the mattresses, hands were stretched out to her – when there were hands to stretch, and not stumps. It was gangrene, and the only remedy was whatever sawbones there were, for the surgeons did not relish army pay and stayed in England. There must be a better remedy for gangrene than draining the green matter and all the hygiene that could be managed; but when the wounded came in from the Crimea, their wounds were already infected. And the nurses they sent her, some of them downed as much *arak* and rum as the male orderlies, who were mostly dead of cholera or *delirium tremens*, and the poor devils got blind drunk before they lost a limb or two, tied down on the blood bench.

There was Mrs Roberts, worth her weight in gold, and Mrs Drake, who was a treasure. And that extraordinary Lady Alicia Blackwood, but what about the baggage she had to dismiss all because of the caps she made the nurses wear to show they were also in uniform. "I came out, ma'am, prepared to submit to everything," the hoyden said, "but there was the caps, ma'am, that suits one face, and some that suits another. And if I'd known about the caps I wouldn't have come to the Scutari."

Well, she was gone, and good riddance, to put wearing caps above caring for dying men. Four in ten had been dying when she came, and now it was down to two in ten, but two in a hundred would still be too many. But down below in the cellars, those were the worst, where she had sent Lady Alicia Blackwood to cope with the remains of it all, the sewers and the soldiers' wives and the children that the army forgot even more than its men. The rats did better there than the people, but Lady Alicia would have to manage. It would be about time that she learned about life downstairs, Miss Nightingale thought. She herself was needed above.

She passed along the lying men, heaving up to her, mumbling and muttering, shrieking and calling to her or somebody quite beyond her. Only as she came by, she could hear the cursing stop, the foul words end. Armies lived on their swearing, she knew that – not on their bellies or on their boots, as books would have it. But as her lamp threw ahead its little swinging path along the great corridor with its mattresses of the wounded fresh from Balaclava, she only heard "Gi' us . . . Tell me . . . I'll live then . . . Write me mam . . . They'll no have my leg . . . Water, for the love of God . . . I canna bear the pain . . . God ha' mercy . . . mercy, then . . . mercy."

And she repeated her litany in passing, the words they wished to hear, the things she could not do for them.

"Brave lads, we'll look after you . . . you will get better . . . you're in good hands now . . . God has sent you to us . . . only have faith . . . we are doing all we can . . . all we can for you . . . God bless you . . ."

Why one Scotsman caught her eye rather than hundreds of others in the corridor, Miss Nightingale did not know. It must have been the size of him, for he was a giant, with his bare feet protruding from the end of the mattress. He had shaken off the sheet and showed above a draggled kilt a naked chest bound by a bandage, black with his old blood and red with the new. The bullet must have missed heart and lungs, for he spoke to her with the rough lilt that the Queen herself loved so much in her Highland servant, John Brown.

"Will you be writing me a letter, Miss Nightingale? For as it is, I am sore hurt and no can hold a pen, and I have no pen to hold."

Miss Nightingale stopped and cast her lamplight on the strong, sunken face of Iain Sinclair, his ruddiness drained down into his bleeding bandages.

"If I write for you, I must write for all."

"Write for me," the giant said. "To my sister Mary Sinclair. She is with the duke, and his mother, the countess, she was the laird of our clan. But we are scattered now to the four corners of the earth . . ."

"Your mother and your father?"

"Gone to Canada, and the devil alone knows where."

"God knows," Miss Nightingale said. "Have they not written to tell you where they are?"

Iain Sinclair shook his head and winced at the pain of it from his smashed rib bones.

"We are not a writing nation," he said. "But we are a fighting nation."

Miss Nightingale smiled. It was her first smile of the day and the night, and in the lamplight Iain saw a trace of sweetness that could hardly be shown.

"I have read your Sir Walter Scott," she said. "Is his name wrong?"

"We are not a reading nation neither," Iain said. "That is for them as has the time for it."

"I will write to your sister Mary Sinclair, but tell me, what shall I say?"

"Tell her . . ." The giant paused, but the fever in his eyes struck two sparks from the candlelight falling from the lamp in the lady's hand. "Tell her – she'll be seeing her Iain again in London. An she will wait, I shall be home again. It is but a wee hole in my ribs and a touch of the heat in my head . . ."

The fever, it might come down. The holes in his chest and back, they might not be infected with gangrene. His smashed ribs might mend. He might not catch any of the hospital diseases that spread from bed to bed. He had survived the dreadful crossing from the Crimea to Turkey. He must be as strong as an ox to do that. And perhaps the glint in his eyes was hope as well as fever.

"I will write that you will return," Miss Nightingale said. "And which duke does your sister serve?"

"Serve?" The giant's loud laugh turned into a cough. "Och, I'll not laugh – it hurts. But no Sinclair serves another. It is all one clan except some do forget it with English ways. I am in the Sutherland Highlanders – and surely that is the duke's name."

"And his address?"

73

"Is there not a House of Lords in London big enough to house them all? And find them?"

Miss Nightingale knew she should reprove the wounded giant for his resentment, but she felt a secret pleasure in his words. What were the battle orders of the Duke of Cambridge and the Lords Raglan and Lucan and Cardigan, which had sent him to Scutari in such a sorry state? As if she herself had not suffered from the pig-headed peers who ran the army worse than a slaughter house –

"I will send your letter to your sister Mary Sinclair," she said, "and I will find the duke. But now, I must go on. And you *will* be well."

"Aye," Iain Sinclair said. "I will be well now."

And a strange certainty possessed Miss Nightingale that he would be well, not another maimed hope. She found the rest of her rounds less burdensome than she had dared to expect. She even looked forward to seeing Lady Alicia in her office. Whatever complaints there might be from the worse hell of the women and children below, she would send Lady Alicia back to her place and the duty which her class so often preached and so rarely practised.

All the same, she found it hard to answer what Lady Alicia told her. A dead baby had been wedged in a sewer-pipe to stop the muck flowing into the cellars. Was it not too much to bear? How could heaven above allow such a crime?

"I would advise the three Ps," Miss Nightingale finally said. "Practicality, a parson and a plumber. Take the baby out, give it a Christian burial and divert the sewage. Do not think about it, Lady Alicia, just do something. I am afraid that we must work now and pray later. God helps those who help themselves – and God help us if we don't!"

God made the world, old Hamish Sinclair thought, but it was certain He put too many trees and stones in it. As if cutting the trees for the clearing of the pasture was not bad enough, the lifting of the great rocks and drawing them aside with the oxen was a worse work. A tree had a use in it, but a lump of stone did not, except as a boundary mark. Hannah had her hearth now builded of the wee stones, and under it was a turnspit for the meat, a large kettle and a small kettle on their hooks, an iron skillet and a Dutch oven for the bread baking. And she had a broom of dry brush, tied with rawhide strips to a pole. And the fire was always banked now, if it was not burning, for the phosphorous matches from the store were sore dear, and there was no need for the fire ever to die. And Hannah had moulds for the deer tallow now, melting it in a saucepan and pouring it round the wicks that spanned the shaping. And if there was a blaze of light needed when the buckskins were drawn tight over the window at night, why, pitchpine would flare on the fire or a twist of rag would flame if it floated in a pie-plate full of bear's grease.

Other women papered their walls with pages from the newspapers and magazines that sometimes reached the store. Then they read the walls. But Hannah would have none of that. The reading in the house was the Bible, and that was good enough, and Hamish had learned to read and write the English when he had served in the army, and now he taught the reading and the writing of the English to Bain and Angus and Katie, for other schooling there was none. Except they learned some of the French down along at the store, because the trappers went up and down river, and many of them only spoke a sort of French and said they were longer in Canada than the Scots were.

But Hannah was feared as she watched her man and her young man working at the trees and the stones, for Hamish was bending now as an old pine bends to the sea wind, and if Bain loved the land that was at last their own, Angus did not, he was restless for the learning and the wide world beyond the prison palings of the trees. And Hannah knew in her heart that she would not keep him, no more than she had kept her Iain and her Hamish Jamie, gone to Russia and to India in the service of Queen Victoria.

In the fall when the leaves on the trees and down on the ground were yellow as broom and scarlet as blood and bright as cramaisee, Hamish was so wearied that he could not put a spoon to his broth at dinner, and he slouched at the table like a pricked bag of meal. And Hannah spoke her mind, for she could not live without that great bent body near her in the dark.

"If the clearing of the trees and the moving of the stones is more than a body can bear," she said, "we can go west again. They say there are plains there and grass as far as the edge of the sky. It is good for cattle."

"For cattle and men," Bain said. "But bad for women and wood."

"This home is not to your liking," Hamish muttered so low that Hannah could hardly hear him.

"Eat your broth," she said. "This is a fine home. It is not that. I ask you, where are the other homes?"

"The Mackenzies are here –" Bain said.

"More than a mile away."

"And the store –"

"Three miles to the river. And there is no minister, no church. That store, you ken, Hamish, a woman cannot go in alone, for those drunken Indians and naked children playing with the dogs, and those old squaws liking a dram of whiskey as much as the braves."

"But why will we go on west?" Angus asked. "Back east, I say, where there is schooling and opportunity. That is the answer they all speak. Why did you come from over the sea? Opportunity." He threw out his hands to encompass the log and mud walls of the cabin. "This is slavery. Worse than the black men in the South. Slavery. Chained in here all winter. Eaten by black flies all summer while we break our backs on the trees and the stones."

"It is our land now," Hamish said, sitting upright. "And here we bide, until –"

"I want dresses," Katie said. "And the dancing. And who shall I meet in the woods? A big brave and I am his squaw and wear leggings with beads and bells, and never a skirt again."

"Hush that foolishness," Hannah said. There was no keeping children in their growing except they were as her Bain, patient as the ox they hired from the store for the rooting out of the stumps and the stones. "All things come if you wait for them. There will be folks here – our own folk –"

"When I am an old maid fit to knit stockings for the bairns of the neighbours –"

"Soon, Katie, soon. More will come down the river."

"How long, O Lord," Hamish said. "How long?"

"Too long for me," Angus said. "I will go, when I am able, back down the river. To learn. And to America, it may be. They say that opportunity there –"

"You will bide with us," Hamish said. "Two of your brothers are already gone far away to India, and your sister Mary in London –"

"I will bide here," Angus said, "only as long as I must."

Hamish took a spoon of broth and spoke. "Angus is right, Hannah," he said. "This is no life for a lad who must make his way in the world. The land is for one man, and Bain is the older."

"But others will come. There will be more land to clear."

"In time. In a long time. In too long a time. Have you not seen how it is for the Scots? We never live in our time but in the time of our children. We go out in the world to make the way for others, and not even for our own children." Hamish's voice was powerful now as a surge of white water along a stream. "We do not labour for ourselves but for what will be. Iain and Hamish Jamie, they spread the red empire over the four corners of the earth, and their blood is not counted. Look at them, gone to India for the Mutiny of folk who do not want us there. Mary works in the service of our duke and duchess, who do not reckon her, and who sent us away to a wilderness where they have forgot us. We break our bones clearing these trees and these stones for they who will follow us and feast on the fat of the land. It is never the time for the Sinclairs, only a time to work for them who will inherit the earth the Sinclairs have made for them."

Hannah's heart was proud with love for what her husband had said. It was true, but a woman expected that, raising bairns for their sake, not her own. But for a man to reckon that he worked always for other folk, and never for his own . . .

"You are right, Hamish," she said. "But you would still be a Scots family, for all that."

"I would be what we are," Hamish said, "and nothing else. But as for the way the world is, I would it were other."

"The world is other," Angus said, "if you will go and find it in other places."

"Hush," Hannah said, "you will bide here."

"As long as I must," Angus said.

"You must," Hannah said. "Your mother and your father and your sister Katie have need of you."

"He will go if he must," Hamish said. "But not before it is the time."

II

THE SERVICE OF THE
FOREIGN QUEEN

"Trust," Hamish Jamie said. "No trust at all."

He had been trying to catch a rat for days, now the rat seemed to be inside his belly, gnawing him to death. It was not so much to bear for him, for he was used to hunger as a child in Scotland, and even in the army in India, on the long marches to nowhere from the cantonments across the plains where the red dust stood up in a brick wall, advancing pace by pace, surrounded by the artillery of the storm, flashing with lightning and belching black clouds and thundering louder than a victory salvo. Then they had been buffeted and soaked and starved for days and nights until the tempests passed, and the soldiers spread-eagled on the ground might resume their weary plod to the ends of the earth.

Now the cannon were manned, the twenty-four- and eighteen-pounders that the Sepoys had captured, and the big guns volleyed and blasted the mud walls of the entrenchment at Cawnpore, they took the heads off men with roundshot or broke both arms of Mrs White carrying her babies, so that she lay on her back in the main-guard, a twin suckling on each of her breasts, and her hands unable to cradle them. Hamish Jamie had been on the sally when they had spiked the Sepoy guns and bayoneted the sleeping gunners, but more had been brought up, you could not stop the thunder of the pandies from killing you.

"But they're sending us elephants," Missie said. "They'll take us to the boats on the river."

Hamish Jamie looked at the scarecrow on his left, who still chirped and hopped after him, lean and moulting in her torn and dirty dress, her yellow hair streaked white with dust powder. It was an odd attachment. Her father and mother had been killed when a blazing bolt had struck the thatched roof of the second barrack and incinerated those who were inside. Missie had run out into the resistance to the mass assault, and had hung on to Hamish's bare left leg under his kilt, while he bit off the tops of the greased cartridges stinking of the cow-fat that had started the Mutiny, and he loaded his Enfield rifle with them, and he fired it time and again until the oil spurted out of the stock and burned his hands and the gun barrel glowed in the dark with the Sepoys falling in front of them like herds of sleeping Jacob's sheep for the vultures and the adjutant-birds to consume in the light of the morning.

"If we get to the river, Missie," Hamish Jamie said. "If we get on down to the river."

"I'm thirsty."

"We all are that. Here."

Hamish Jamie pulled the last button off his tunic, gashed and burst on his blackened chest.

"Suck it," he said. "It helps."

Missie popped the button in her mouth and began to suck, while Hamish Jamie peered across the dust and rubble to where the Sepoys ringed them with their tens of thousands and their guns. They had given up the attacks, they would starve them out, dry them out – for one of the wells only provided moist grit, and the other well was full of two hundred and fifty dead from the siege. The defenders had endured for twenty-one days and nights, and now they were to surrender to the Nana. How trust a man with a name like the bogies of the fairy tales, how trust the millions of his pandies that were trying to put an end to the Raj, all because of some cow-fat on the cartridges, and the false tale that every Hindu or Moslem should be massacred or converted by force to Christianity, as if anyone wanted the pandies in the kirks anyway?

"Will you come with me in the boat to Allahabad?"

"I'll not be leaving you, Missie," Hamish Jamie said. "Did I tell you I had a sister like you – Rachel?"

"Tell me again."

"She passed away in Canada, but I have another sister called Katie, she will be grown the now, and she lives in a log cabin in the woods in Canada."

Missie took the button from her mouth and looked at it to see why it had not melted and put it back in her mouth again.

"What's Canada?"

"It's a country full of bears and Indians and trees, lots of trees."

"I like trees. They're shady."

"They don't like trees in Canada. They have too many stones and too many trees. They have to clear them, pull out the stumps, before they can make a field to grow food."

"I want to go down the river now. I want to go with you to Allahabad."

A musket shot pinged in the entrenchment. It was the heat which caused it, nearly one hundred and forty degrees, the ferocious sun exploding the cap on a musket, the molten barrel sizzling off the round. But the enemy believed it to be the end of the cease-fire. Bullets and grapeshot whistled round their heads, throwing splinters of wood and chips of brick and scraps of iron about them. Hamish Jamie threw himself on Missie and held her under his body, feeling her scraggy shape quivering and boiling beneath him.

"It will be well," he soothed her.

And it was. For the firing stopped, and the evacuation was set for the morning. There was no more horse soup now, but double rations of *dahl* and *chapattis*, like the Indian cakes that had appeared just before the Great Mutiny as a signal of the revolt to come. No more lump, thump, whack of slaughtered cow chucked into the stewpot, causing howls at blasphemy from the Sepoys as they saw the holy stew bolted down in sacred chunks. But if they had done such sins and transgressions to the gods of the Hindus, how should they be given safe passage to Allahabad? The Christian scriptures were more unforgiving. Did they not say that stripes shall be meted out according to faults, and death for abominations?

In the morning, sixteen elephants and eighty palanquins drawn by bullocks appeared in front of the battered entrenchment. The Sepoys came out from their emplacements and talked to their old masters. They could not understand how so few had held out against so many, they feared the white devils who had become as burned black as they were with dirt and cordite and dried blood. They said there was a safe passage to Allahabad, that forty roofed country boats stood at the river waiting for their transport. They mourned the deaths of their old officers and carried the little relics that the garrison sought to take with them, Bibles and heirlooms, knick-knacks and photographs and one feathered hat. But Hamish Jamie slung himself with bandoliers of ammunition until he was weighed down like a loaded donkey, and he walked beside the elephant on which Missie Gordon was now hoisted proudly in state.

The river boats were moored in the shallows and sunk down flat on the sand-banks with all the load put on them. For the rains had not yet come to settle the dust and fill the flood, and the Ganges was running low. But as the soldiers tried to push off the boats, all the Indian sailors jumped off and began wading to the banks. Smoke now rose from burning charcoal hidden in the thatch of the roofing of the craft, and as Hamish Jamie brought up his rifle to fire, he saw the barrels of guns appearing from the buildings and ghauts by the landing-place. The mounted troopers who had escorted the elephants and palanquins down to the river now opened fire with their carbines, and Hamish Jamie shot two of them, dropping them from their saddles, careful to spare the horses, which were worth more.

"Push the boat!" Missie shrieked beside him. "Push it!"

Hamish Jamie leapt into the shallow water and began heaving at the loaded craft. Bullets and grapeshot were hornets at his ears and clipped the wooden rails. Every bush was spitting fire, while four nine-pounders were firing canister into the massacre, raking them with shot. The boats burst aflame, all the passengers jumped into the shallows and waded out until only their heads were showing as marks for the fusillade.

One boat alone floated free down the current, and Hamish Jamie plunged towards it. And as he surged on, he looked up to see Missie's body falling down to him. In a vision against the sun, he thought that he was seeing Katie, her red hair flying in the wind. But it was a spray of blood, flung out from her face and chest, exploding in droplets over the air. And he caught her in her fall and held her with one arm and unbuckled his dragging bandoliers with his free hand and began to swim out in the slow dog-paddle that he had learned towards the sole boat escaping downstream. And soon he saw that Missie was dead, and he let her body drift down the holy river, let it redden the waters that receive the dead and take them to a Hindu heaven.

Bullets whipped the surface like jumping trout, serries of shots lashed the water into spume, but Hamish Jamie paddled on. Near him, two brothers swam, but one of them weakened and sank, and the other, Ensign Henderson, was struck in the hand by grapeshot. He put his wounded arm over Hamish's shoulder and swam beside him to the boat, which had stranded on a sand-bank close to the Oudh side of the river. And there they were pulled aboard, the few survivors of the slaughter, and they were still able to hear the far and piteous crying of the women and the children, who were being netted in the Ganges waters and brought to the bank, while the last of the living men were shouting or groaning in their death agonies. Even the blunt-nosed crocodiles shunned the carnage and sheered away. They would return for the corpses later to bury them in the bank for their future store.

Now the last boat swung free and wallowed down the current, slow, too slowly. It was a target until midnight came. The scuppers were filled with the wounded and the dying. A mother standing above her six-year-old boy was struck by a bullet and fell off the stern, and the small child came up to Hamish Jamie, saying, "Mama has fallen overboard. Oh, why are they firing upon us? Did they not promise to leave off?" But Hamish Jamie was firing back with the Enfield that was on the boat, and he did not look for the boy for another two hours, and then he never found the wee fellow again. He never knew how or why the child was gone.

They could have all died in the morning, but the rains came. Curtains of water turned the Ganges into a torrent, they wetted the powder of the Sepoy guns, they deluged the attackers who lined the banks on either side of the river. All the same, the dying went sluggishly on, four more officers killed and two women and Ensign Henderson, shot through the groin and begging Hamish Jamie to finish him, for God's sweet sake, a quick release from all the pain. But Hamish Jamie said, "No, no, I cannot. I have a brother Iain in the Sutherland Highlanders, and he is seeking for me even now with Sir Colin Campbell, and if I kill you, a brother who has lost a brother, I will not see my brother Iain again." But Ensign Henderson died towards the evening, his guts spilling out over his torn britches, and Hamish Jamie heaved him into the Ganges, which always takes the dead.

But the following morning, the matter was finished. The craft drifted into a backwater opposite Soorajpore. The Sepoys following along the banks discovered the boat through the downpour of the rains and moved upon it in their hordes. And the last surviving major, shot through both of his arms, ordered the final act of desperation. "Lieutenant Delfosse," he said, "and Sergeant Grady and Corporal Murphy" – for he called Hamish Jamie that in his pain – "and you ten privates of the Thirty-second and the Eighty-fourth, make your way ashore. Drive off the Sepoys. You thirteen men will rout their thousands."

And so they did, the thirteen against the thousands. They were mad, they were berserk, they charged and hacked and stabbed their way through walls of flesh with sword and bayonet and rifle-butt. Behind them, they could hear the screaming of their companions as they were butchered on the boat by the swarms of the enemy. But the thirteen ran on with a rabble of murder at their heels. Each quarter of an hour, they turned on their pursuers and dropped to their knees and fired one volley. It stopped the mob and left a few more corpses littering the retreat. So the flight and the chase progressed for three miles by the banks of the Ganges, until the British soldiers spied a temple set apart against a cliff and took refuge there. Sergeant Grady was shot through the head and expired instantly, Lieutenant Delfosse was crippled by a machete swung at his knees and was hacked to pieces. But the other eleven survivors made their way into the temple and turned about and fired volley after volley from the dark interior until they closed the open entrance with a wall of Indian bodies.

There was a hesitation then, then the crackling sound of faggots piled outside with the fire being put to them. Smoke bellied inside the dark chamber of heathen worship, then there was a mighty explosion as of the end of the world. A barrel of gunpowder had been put on the flames. Shreds and shrapnel of flesh, burning shards of firewood were blown into the faces of the eleven defenders, who were hurled to the ground. Then Hamish Jamie arose and gave the order, "Fire your last rounds. Then charge the enemy and make for the river." And there were only nine men to obey him, for one had died of a chip of stone that burst his eye, and they fired their final fusillade and charged with fixed bayonets over the burning wood and charred pieces of human remains, and they savaged and stabbed their path through the clawing mass in front of the temple, and three fell to be torn to pieces, but seven fought their way to the river, and one of them was Hamish Jamie.

As the seven men struck out for the meandering current, three were killed by the intermittent firing from the banks. Hamish Jamie and the three survivors paddled or stroked onwards through the waters for five miles through the night, and by the mercy of heaven, the crocodiles did not intrude upon their passing, as if the very reptiles were more merciful than men in preserving God's creation.

And on the coming of the next morning, exhausted on a mud-bank, naked and shivering, the four men were found by the washerwomen of Dirigbijah Singh, the rajah of Moorar Mhow, who was still the faithful subject of the Foreign Queen when all had risen in revolt around him. And the washerwomen were not ashamed at the nakedness of the four men, piebald with their blood and bloated skin, blistered with the sun and wrinkled with exposure to the Ganges. They took the men under their armpits, a woman on each side of each man, and supported them severally to their master, who had them bathed and treated and, within the fullness of a month, returned them on a steamer that General Havelock had sent upriver from Allahabad to reconnoitre the Cawnpore region.

What a meeting they had of it, although some of the soldiers were old comrades to Hamish Jamie, the Seaforth Highlanders who had left him at the depot at Cawnpore sick of the fever when they were shipped out to fight the Persian War, and now they had come back to put down the Mutiny, they called him Murphy again, because he looked a real Murphy in his turban and wide trousers from the Rajah.

"And Murphy I will always be," Hamish Jamie said. "For that a Sinclair never did give up the women and the children before, aye and it is a crying shame that I did it, and a Murphy I am to let it be done."

There was hardly a body who would believe the stories of their escape, how had so few hewed their way through so many? But there the four men were, they were alive, you could touch them or taste them, the proof of the haggis . . . "There's a thing the now," Hamish Jamie said, "and I cannot ken it – why thirteen can put to flight a thousand when we are serving the Foreign Queen and the English Empire, and why a thousand Highlanders are put to flight at black Culloden by the Foreign King and the English? Tell me the truth on that."

"They had the big guns," Murdo said. "They have the big guns."

"No," Hamish Jamie said, "Nana had the big guns at Cawnpore and along the Ganges. It is not that. What is it? Service – foreign service – for a German Queen and Her German husband – why do the Highlanders fight like devils out of hell?"

"Why," Murdo laughed, "isn't that the oath we take! For God and the Queen, which might be to say – for the devil and Her Own."

"You've a foul mouth in you, Murdo."

"You've a black asking head on you, Hamish Jamie."

As Havelock fought his way back to Cawnpore to save the captured women and the children, two hundred and ten of them confined in dark closets worse than the Black Hole of Calcutta, Hamish Jamie followed in the rearguard, watching the terrors of the retribution. Havelock had taken command from General Neill with his heart of flint and noose of vengeance in his hands. Neill hanged any suspect spy, any Sepoy, in figures of eight, nine men dangling in two circles, skinny and rotting as an example to nobody very much. The death of Missie still flew as a red angel in Hamish Jamie's mind, a haunting presence asking for blood and yet mercy, as he marched with his comrades back towards Cawnpore, the vultures coasting and the jackals crying and the pie-dogs yapping about their column, ready for the pickings of war.

Havelock would not let them rest in their work of rescue. In the full heat of July, he marched his Highlanders twenty-four miles in one day through the whirling dust, then made the attack on Nana's troops at Fattehpore. With the screech and the skirl of the bagpipes as wild as the furies, Hamish Jamie ran upon the Nana's guns, his legs buckling under him, his throat dry as a kelp kiln, his feet raw and bleeding in his boots, and he fired and skewered and swung at the pandies, who fell or were chased away and vanished, as nightmares leave at the break of day with the dreamer waking in fear and sweat and exhaustion.

There was no cease to it. Two days later, the Highlanders charged again at Pandoo Nuddy, and the enemy fled once more, leaving their guns and their corpses behind them. On the morrow, the bulk of

Nana's army stood before Cawnpore in their tens of thousands with Havelock's brace of regiments facing them. The attack of the Highlanders was as a sword entering a scabbard or a dirk making a wound which enclosed it. For the ranks of the enemy enveloped them utterly. They fought hand to hand and bayonet against tulwar for two hours, but Havelock had kept his reserve of irregular horse at the back, and he sent them to wheel round the right flank of the foe and rout them.

The Nana in his flight did as the British had done at Delhi, he blew the magazine so that Hamish Jamie, leaning on his rifle in trembling fatigue among the turbaned dead, as a corn stook shakes in the wind among the fallen sheaves, he felt a pluck at his bare knees as a blast of hot air streamed across the plain, then a banging of pans that seemed to split the burnished sky, then a tongue of fire towards Cawnpore, followed by a vast black balloon in the ascendant. The whole city appeared in conflagration, but when the Highlanders advanced inside the rubble and the destruction the following day, they found that the ruins and the houses and the palaces were still there, but all the white women and the children had been killed in the Beebeeghur.

Hamish Jamie could hardly bear the sight of it. The bodies were gone, thrown to the cleansing of the crocodiles in the Ganges. But the walls were dark with blood, and the ground was stained with blood, and strewn about were collars and caps and round children's hats and combs, locks of long hair and the torn pages of books. Hamish Jamie picked out one bloody Bible, which was inscribed in the fly-leaf, "For dearest mama, from her affectionate Louis, June, 1845." Pages had been ripped out of it, but from a coincidence that was none, the thin papers fell open at the blood-smeared Forty-seventh Psalm, and so Hamish Jamie read:

> *For the Lord most high is terrible;*
> *He is a great King over all the earth.*
> *He shall subdue the people under us,*
> *And the nations under our feet.*
> *He shall choose our inheritance for us*

Now blood obscured the text except for two more phrases:

> *God is gone up with a shout,*
> *The Lord with the sound of a trumpet*

and then:

> *God reigneth over the heathen*

It was no consolation. Missie Gordon and the departed Rachel seethed in Hamish Jamie's mind. He would kill and kill to settle their ghosts. Before the Highlanders were marched away once more to rescue the garrison that was still surviving in Lucknow, Hamish Jamie had heard tell of General Neill's verdict on the murderers at the Beebeeghur. "Severity at the first," Neill said, "is mercy at the end." Each pandie sentenced to death by hanging would be taken to the house of slaughter and forced to lick clean the stains of blood on the walls and the floor.

"For why?" Hamish Jamie said to Murdo. "The Ganges has taken their bodies. Can men's tongues wash away their blood? I do not see the sense in it. They will not come back again."

And there was a kind of recognition of true courage. For when the new Victoria Cross was given to the Seaforth regiment – a piece of copper worth a *lakh* of gold – it was given to the surgeon who had saved many lives under heavy fire. What was the killing after all beside the curing? And what was the fighting beside the needing to eat and drink at the siege of Cawnpore? And Hamish Jamie determined that he could not move to the curing, for he did not have the skill for it, but he could move to the commissariat, which saw to the feeding and the clothing of the men. Bullets and bayonets were all very fine, but he had had muckle of it. He would live in the provisioning of the weapons of war, not die in the using of them.

12

A VISIT TO MISS
NIGHTINGALE

When the duke or the duchess came down the staircase of the house in Belgrave Square, Mary Sinclair had to step into the broom-closet. She could not be visible to her employers. And to pass anybody on the stairs, particularly one of the two Graces, was great bad luck. "You must never be seen or heard," the housekeeper Mrs Rogers told Mary, "unless you are summoned by His or Her Grace. And then you may speak when spoken to, in the proper manner."

"But children can be seen," Mary said, "but not heard."

"You are not a child, Miss Sinclair," the housekeeper said, "even if I am not certain of that at all, by the way you behave."

Life was not bad in the basement and the attics where the servants saw and heard all about each other. There was the comradeship of close encounters with the dreaded quality, the times when one of them had dropped the tea-tray, stumbled over a curtsy, said "Disgrace" instead of "His Grace", frizzled the marchioness's hair with the curling-tongs, burst the laces of the marquis's corset, dropped the hot ash and cinders on the Turkish carpet to improve the pattern, aged the Gainsborough by cleaning it with a wet mop, put a hot iron through the seat of a lady's unmentionables, and generally made a terrible mess of something, without being caught or owning up. "Honesty," Mrs Rogers declared, "Her Grace insists on total honesty in all her staff," and then she would cover for everybody. Within her starched and virgin breast lay a heart of syllabub. She was strict only for show, and she knew which end of the social ladder was which, and she was not on the top of it.

Albert was the bane of Mary's life. He was the marquis's footman and cockney clever, wise off the streets of Blackfriars and Whitechapel, the sound of Bow Bells always ringing in his good ear, for one of his ears was deaf if he did not want to hear something that he did not want to hear. He was bonny enough in the sharp southern way, his nose as thin as the edge of a dirk, his eyes as washed-blue as the sky after rain, and the skin on his face too thin so that his skull shone through its surface, but his sandy moustache and his hot hands made him difficult to evade. He had acquired the arrogance of his masters without their courtesy. Impudence was his excellence. He courted a woman as if indelicacy were a compliment.

"Got yer," he said, as Mary slipped into the broom-cupboard on the sight of Her Grace descending the stairs.

"You've been waiting here, Albert!"

Mary felt Albert's hands crawling over her bodice, his hard stomach thrusting against her back.

"Whisht," he whispered, "or *she'll* hear you."

Mary wriggled under Albert's caresses in the dark closet, but she could not cry out or escape. Her Grace's heels were already outside on the stairway, clip-clop, tick-tock, as if time would never pass by. Mary drove her left elbow backwards and dug Albert sharply in the ribs.

"Wooh," Albert grunted, then changed the noise into a "Miaow."

The tick-tock stopped outside the closet. Her Grace was listening.

"George," she called, "there is a cat in the stairs cupboard."

"Instruct Mrs Rogers," His Grace called back, "to instruct Albert to put it out."

The tick-tock of the heels continued down the stairs. Mary breathed again.

"I'm the mouser," Albert said in Mary's ear. "And I'm going to put it in."

Mary felt her face redden in the dark, but Albert could not see her flush. She hacked back with the heel of her shoe and caught him on the shin.

"Strewth," he swore. "You bitch."

Mary shook herself loose and fell forward out of the closet on to the stairway. The light from the Regency windows shone on to the azure carpet by the curling ebony and ironwork banisters that seemed to direct a way to heaven up the stone steps.

"You, Albert, you –"

Albert emerged on to the stairs, limping and grinning.

"You like it, Mary," he said. "I knows you do. I knows women, I do."

"Some women do," Mary said, "and I wouldn't call them ladies. In there it was like that Cawnpore. My brothers, they'll kill you, Albert, when they come home. In Cawnpore, they locked the women and children in dark cupboards –"

"And what they didn't do to them," Albert said. "'Course, we're not the ones to know. They'll never say to the likes of us, never say. All women's now like Her Majesty, ain't they? Not bloody human. They ain't got anything to sit down on. Sort of lost under that bustle, only you're not really. You're a woman, Mary, and a right pink 'un."

"I've got to get the fires out." Mary began to hurry down the stairs, but Albert caught her by the arm and held her.

"Tonight," he said. "I'm going to the 'Orse and Groom. There's soldiers there, back from India. Perhaps, 'ow do you know, they knows yer brothers –"

"I'll not go to a drinking den with you, Albert Smith –"

"Don't know what yer miss, Miss." Albert grinned. "I'll fetch you at six."

Mary shook herself free.

"You'll be waiting," she said. "Just because you think you're God's gift to the lassies –"

As she fled down the stairs, Mary knew that she did feel for Albert. There was something in him, rotten and common, but lusty and a man for all that. But it was no good. A girl, a poor Scots girl, there was only one way to make a way in the world. To be a spinster and find a trade. And if marrying there was, it would be marrying a fine man who could give her a home, a house that did not move with the battens in the roof, for her and her bairns for aye. No more moving, no more starving, no more, whatever the hot blood in her said on the moment. Hold, Mary, hold you.

At six o'clock, it was the duchess who fetched Mary, not Albert Smith. Actually, it was Mrs Rogers who brought Mary to Her Grace, who was working at her *petit point*. She was stitching a cherub flying above a pink cloud. It was a finger-pricking task that she had inherited from her mother-in-law, who intended to fill the whole of the Scots castle with hand-embroidered cushions. Alas for the duchess, it did prove a kind of continuance in the family.

"Ah, there you are, Mary," she said, abandoning her delicate labours. "Well, what do you have to say for yourself? Too much, as usual."

"Begging your pardon, Your Grace – nothing – unless you say what I have to say."

"Impertinence!"

"Not intended," Mrs Rogers said. "Miss Sinclair was trying to say that she does not know what Your Grace wishes her to say."

"She addressed one of the guests. About India!"

"My brothers –"

"You are in service here, Mary. You do not address our guests about anything."

"My brothers –"

"Especially when our guest happens to be the Foreign Secretary. And you ask him about your brothers –"

"An he should know, Your Grace," Mary said, "if he be the Foreign Secretary, he knows of foreign things."

"My dear child," the duchess said, "your simplicity exceeds your modesty. Although the noble lord is responsible for our foreign affairs – and dreadfully he honours that responsibility – sending that abominable weakling 'Clemency' Canning out to pardon all those barbarians and murderers in India – he does not *personally* know the fate of your brothers, however valiantly they are fighting for their Queen and country in India."

"I am sure that Miss Sinclair meant no disrespect," Mrs Rogers said. "A natural concern and affection for her family –"

"Very laudable, no doubt," the duchess said, "but absolutely inadmissible in this household. Mary, I had been considering you as a possible personal maid, to look after my minor requirements . . . but now – I really despair at eradicating in you those wild antecedents. To think I plucked you from those unspeakable huts and bogs, and placed you in a position where every refinement of culture and society might instruct you – and then, I am repaid by a total lack of application, an unwillingness to learn!"

"I try to give satisfaction," Mary said, "to be sure I do."

"Trying is not good enough," the duchess said. "It is succeeding, Mary, it is succeeding that matters. You will *never* address any of our guests on personal business."

"And if he falls over dead drunk like that Lord Chalmers," Mary said. "And he near to breaks his leg and he's calling out for help. Can I not go to him and aid him as I did do? Is that not a personal business?"

"We are never drunk," the duchess said, "although we are occasionally ill. We imbibe always with discretion. If a guest may stumble and fall by mischance, you may go to his assistance. That is not personal, it is unfortunate. Mary, you are incorrigible. Uncouth."

"Is that all, Your Grace?"

"It is all. Mrs Rogers!"

"Yes, Your Grace?"

"Put Mary on night duty, perhaps reflection in the small hours . . ." Her voice trailed away in the implication.

"Yes, Your Grace."

"On personal business –" Mary said.

"Did I request you to speak, Mary?"

"Tomorrow I am to see Miss Nightingale."

The duchess sat upright in her chair as if Mary had thrust a hot rod down her spine. She rapped her hand on the stuffed arm-rest where she had stuck her *petit point* needle. Her thumb was pierced. She said, "Ouch, damn it," stuck her thumb in her mouth, sucked it and glared at Mary. Then she spoke, "Miss Nightingale? The *nurse!*"

"She sent me a letter, Your Grace. She wrote for my brother Iain, he that was wounded in Russia. Now she herself will see me."

The duchess shook her head. Her laugh was as brittle as rice-paper.

"Miss Mary Sinclair," she said, "you do have ideas above your station. Be careful that you not aspire to more than you may attain."

"It is hard, dirty and dangerous work," Miss Nightingale said. "It has no respect. You know how the nurse is seen in the novels of our time – as drunken, foul and immodest. And you will see sights of men's bodies that no woman –"

"I have brothers," Mary said. "We had a board between us in our croft. Ach, I know the men, how they are."

"I had many Highlanders at Scutari," Miss Nightingale said. "They fought like lions at Sebastopol. They carried the Russian city with a charge. There were many of them with terrible wounds – the grapeshot."

"My brother Iain was with you," Mary said simply. "In the Crimea, he was wounded and he was not lasting among the living. But you saved him."

"Your brother Iain Sinclair. A Highland regiment?"

"The Sutherlanders. They are in India now. Both my brothers are in India fighting the Mutiny."

"A terrible thing that." Miss Nightingale shivered. "There is no respect for women there, not even for nurses. I cannot organise there. It is too soon for the army. They are dying of cholera and typhus as well as gangrene. I have told them, cleanliness and lye soap. But will they listen?"

"Look," Mary said, "I have a letter from you."

She took out of her small handbag a piece of paper, folded into four and worn brown on the edges. She passed it to Miss Nightingale as if it were the Grail. Miss Nightingale unfolded it with great care and read it.

"Yes," she said, "I did write this."

"You wrote it for my brother. You said he would be well again. You had it sent to me in London. It is my treasure."

"I see. You work for a duke?"

"Hard, dirty and dangerous work, Miss Nightingale."

Miss Nightingale laughed.

"I remember your brother. He was a giant. And he made me laugh too. Why is it that you have this sense of humour?"

"We only say the truth," Mary said, "and the English are amused."

"Why is it so hard working for a duke?"

"The hours are sixteen a day, and some nights. The kitchens and cupboards are dirty beyond pigsties, and in the summer, the horse-flies fall off the candles on the chandeliers on to the ladies' bare shoulders like shawls – and we have to clear them away. And as for dangerous, if some young master does not try to put you on your back, his footman will."

Miss Nightingale smiled this time, a tight grin that looked like wincing.

"You are very plain spoken, Miss Sinclair."

"I was reared with the cattle on a farm. We see what is there."

"And what do you want of me?"

"I wish to leave service," Mary said. "I will take up your service. Your hard, dirty and dangerous work."

"And will you stick to it?"

"I will."

"For ever, if I train you?"

"Aye."

"And the men, a husband?" Miss Nightingale stared at the handsome young woman. "They will want to marry you."

"You have not said yes, Miss Nightingale."

Again Miss Nightingale laughed.

"And how do you know if they have asked me?"

"I would, an I be a man."

For the third time Miss Nightingale laughed.

"You are too blunt for me, Miss Sinclair. But not too blunt for our profession. For that is what it is. A dedication. A lifelong service."

"I will do that," Mary said. "You have my word."

"That is good enough for me. Give your notice. You may commence at the Westminster Hospital within the month."

"The training," Mary said. "I have my brothers in India. Would I be after going there and training there?"

"The service must come before your family," Miss Nightingale said. "You must know that."

"I do."

"Then I shall take you." Miss Nightingale stood upright and held out her hand to Mary, who also rose and took the offered hand in both of hers and held it and said in her gratitude: "I say yes only to you, Miss Nightingale."

13

BLOWN FROM THE GUNS

"Tell me the story one time more," Iain said. "The blowing from the guns. And her."

"I seen her when they were blowing the pandies from the guns," Leish said. "They'd tie the pandies to the muzzles of the howitzers, for an example as it might be. And before they put the match to the powder, why, she would ride out in front of the guns, all in white, mind you. An angel on horseback, as you might say. And as the guns fired, and they fired away the poor beggars sitting on the end of them, why, she rode across all that bright red rain, and the pieces of the pandies flying through the air like robin redbreasts, and she was all dripping with scarlet like a Lancer, and she would ride away the far side. And we never did say a word, and we never did know who she was. The scarlet lady of the sorrows, as you might say."

"You never did ken who she was," Iain said.

"We never did ken. I heard tell she had lost a mother and sister at Delhi, and they were bound naked to the wheel of a gun carriage, and there were things done, and she would have her vengeance, she would."

"When a woman wants a vengeance," Iain said, "it is worse than a man."

"That it is," Leish agreed.

"But I will have that woman," Iain said, "for my own. But first, we will find my brother."

This time the Highlanders were marching with the heavy guns, Peel's Naval Brigade and the horse artillery of Hope Grant. They would batter their entrance through the walls and towers of Lucknow to the besieged residency, where Hamish Jamie was caught for a second time like a rat in a trap. "That brother of mine," Iain grumbled, "he's no more sense in his head than porridge. You're caught once, that is bad luck. You're caught twice, that's daft."

"Those were the orders," said the huge Willie McBean.

93

"They always are," Iain said. "Once you follow the orders, you're caught for life."

Their commander, Sir Colin Campbell, was not of the hurrying kind. He proceeded slowly, trusting Havelock to hold out. The big guns were in the front, blasting the Sepoys away, and the Highlanders were fighting like the redcoats, wearing plumes in their bonnets and practising as if on parade, firing in file one by one, picking off the enemy. There was no charging yet. The final dash would come at the walls of Lucknow.

An Irishman came to them first, one Kavanagh, as absurd an apparition as only an Irishman can be. A green turban over his ginger hair, black lamp-oil on his ruddy face, in orange silk jacket and pyjama trousers, he bluffed his way through eight Sepoy pickets and reached the rescuers outside Lucknow. He worked for the Post Office, and it was the electric telegraph of the Post Office in the new code that had stopped the Mutiny in its tracks. The message was transmitted that saved the Punjab and allowed the British to disarm their Sepoy regiments before the *chapattis* and the news of the first mutiny at Meerut had reached them.

But Kavanagh had also served night after night in the Sappers' counter-mines under the Residency, as the Sepoys tunnelled away to plant their explosives beneath the walls, and when the earth crumbled and burrow met burrow, then Kavanagh had blasted the enemy with his pistol and stolen away their gunpowder from their caverns and galleries. Now, in unlikely disguise, he had breached the enemy lines and would lead Sir Colin Campbell back to Lucknow. His first act was to dress himself for his new part, and that is how Iain saw him, wearing a cotton quilted tunic, corduroy britches, jackboots and a pith helmet.

"Hello, *sahib*," Iain said. "You're very *pukka* for a Kavanagh."

"Only because I cannot borrow your kilt," Kavanagh said.

"You'll have it," Iain said, "when you take me to my brother in Lucknow."

At the Sikander Bagh, the Sepoys were valiant and took the pounding of the heavy artillery and were crushed beneath the broken walls, until the Highlanders stormed the breaches with their bayonets and strewed two thousand dead bodies as a red meadow in the gardens at the back of the fort. And at Shah Najaf Iain found the way to his brother. He crept forward to the walls, where the Sepoys could not fire down on him, and, circling them, he found a breach at the back. He shouted his war cry across to his comrades, the bagpipes shrieked their wild notes, and the Sutherlands poured into the fortress. There in the passages and the halls and the catacombs, they were butchers in a slaughter-house, they were berserkers in a delirium, they were killers of other men who meant no more than beasts to them.

When the red rage cleared from Iain's eyes, the sight and the reek of the blood sickened him, and he heaved and retched and stood, until an explosion outside brought him running to an embrasure, where he saw a black cloud over the Moti Mohal. Havelock was dying in the residency, but the other besieged general in Lucknow, Outram, had blown up the buildings between him and the rescuers and was fighting his way out. And Willie McBean was fighting his way alone into the Begum's palace. With bayonet and fist he killed eleven Sepoys as they came at him, his vast shape lunging and battering as thunder splits the sky, and ending by spitting a havildar swinging a sword as neat as a Christmas goose. He was to get the Victoria Cross for it, which he shrugged away, saying, "Toots, man, it did not take me twenty minutes."

And so the Sinclair brothers met in the fallen city. The troops looked more like pirates than soldiers, the Sikh cavalry in bedspreads and drapes, the English infantry in slate-grey powdered with red dust, the Highlanders in their torn kilts and rakish feathered bonnets, and the Ninth Lancers, still dandy in their white turbans wound round their forage caps. But Iain only had eyes for his brother, and when they saw each other, they fell into an embrace, crying and shouting without sense, their tears streaking the blood and burns on their faces.

"We have found the brandy," Hamish Jamie told Iain.

"And the gold?"

"And the gold for any man who will pick it up."

It was the looting and drinking now. After the slaughter, the plunder. Through the courtyards surrounded by stucco and gilt palaces, thrusting aside the green jalousies and venetian blinds closing off the pierced windows, smashing the carved door panels with rifle butt and musket ball, the invaders sought their reward. Here Leish was draping himself with a sari encrusted with rubies and emeralds, there Murdo was shattering a jade vase to look for gems within, then he gouged with his dirk a jewel from the stem of an ivory pipe. Their faces black with powder, their cross-belts splotched with blood, the Highlanders filled their tunics with jewel caskets and loose pearls, gold bangles and diamond rings. Hamish Jamie used his bayonet to lever open an iron box that was full of gold-encrusted pistols and muskets with barrels inlaid with silver. He threw aside the weapons in disgust, "No bloody good to fire," and found a bag of gold mohurs and a swathe of silver brocade. But Iain looked to the little things of great value and found a string of blackish pearls as big as quail's eggs, a butterfly brooch with opal and diamond wings, a ruby locket and an

95

emerald ring in a thick gold setting, the green stone as big as a drop scone with a dark flaw in it, like a hidden tale not yet told.

"The brandy the now," Hamish Jamie said. "To hell with the baubles."

On the spread of the silver brocade, Hamish Jamie and Iain began their drinking. And a deep draught they had of it, swig after swig from the black bottles that had been found in the cellars, and the bagpipers coming to join them and playing the old songs, the charge and the lament, the only two moods that the Highlanders knew, a time of fury and a time of tears. And the two brothers became merry, and then they became angry, and then they wept, and then they sang, and then they were foolish, and then they boasted, and then they shouted and wept again, and then Hamish Jamie fell over on his back and lay as if he were dead. And his brother Iain slapped him on the cheeks and blew into his mouth and yelled for a doctor, who was also drunk and the other side of Lucknow, then he fell to keening and wailing in the *coronach*, but Hamish Jamie suddenly sat up and said, "That is one devil of a shindy you are making, Iain," and the two brothers fell again into each other's arms and finished the last bottle of brandy and became insensible for twelve hours until a sergeant-major kicked them awake with the threat of a flogging. And that night, Hamish Jamie went in search of the native women in spite of Iain urging him against coupling with the heathen, but he did not prevail. So Iain was left polishing the emerald ring as large as a drop scone and wondering what woman would wear it for him.

They could not hold at Lucknow. The enemy in their millions still beset the city. Two relief columns had burst in, but now they must all evacuate under the protection of the wheeled guns. And so a stratagem was set for their retreat. First Havelock's old garrison marched out, breaking their step in case the measured beat drummed a signal to the enemy outside the walls. But Havelock was dead, and only Outram went with them. Then the rearguard followed, the gunners and the Highlanders, passing the Ballie Gate and leaving their camp-fires burning in the ruins of the residency until the embers would die down and tell the foe that Lucknow was again an Indian city.

Nearing Cawnpore once more, Iain was wounded sorely in a storm. The heat had been beyond all description, the sky was an upturned copper cauldron with men broiled within it. Then the tempest broke with the clattering hoofs of ten thousand cavalry horses. The hail beat them with ball-shot, the rain lashed more lustily than the cat o'nine tails. The lightning flashed in streaks, in belts of blazing light, in blue zigzags, in bolts of fire, in split-ended jets, which leapt from tree to tree or ran along the ground in crackers and cobras of fire. The army halted and took cover, and Iain found shelter under a baobab tree.

And there among the down-curving branches, a superb and tall Gwalior man stood, a spy on their progress. And Iain grappled with him, and they struggled as twin oaks might lash one another in the force and twists of a gale. And Iain threw the Gwalior man, who drew his tulwar on the ground and hacked at Iain's leg and hamstrung him, the muscles and sinews cut, so that Iain fell upon his opponent and strangled him to death, pressing the life out with the balls of his mighty thumbs. Then he shouted through the howling storm, "I die. For the love of God, I die."

His fellow-soldiers found Iain and they bound his leg in a tourniquet with a rifle-sling and they carried him to a litter. And there his brother Hamish Jamie found him and said, "Thank you for finding me at Lucknow. You will not die of this wound. You did not from the one in Russia."

And Iain said, "No, there will be a nurse for me as there was at Scutari. It is the same kind of a wound. It will have the same cure. Look you for yourself, you wee man. How can I be looking for you the now?"

For his recovery, Iain was sent to Nainital, seven thousand feet high by a lake in the foothills of the Himalayas. The Mutiny was dying now in its last throes, and dying with it were the mutineers by the tens of thousands and the collaborators in the Mutiny in their thousands, hanged by the neck or blown from the guns, flogged or sentenced to thirty years in chains. "Vengeance is mine!" the Bible proclaimed, but the frightened rulers, nearly swept off a continent, imposed their order again by noose and gunpowder and manacle. Yet in the thin air of Nainital, Iain sat in the garden of the hospital by the lake, where the nights were so cold that his spittle was an icicle on his pillow, and the days so calm and hot that the sweat tickled the bandage on his leg. And down the staircase of the low hospital building, where an old Babu sat in his office mixing the certificates of birth with the certificates of death because he believed that living and dying were the same stream of being, the woman in white would walk, the woman who was to be given Iain's gold ring with the emerald mounted on it.

Many things are chosen, others are fortunate, some are fated, occasional ones are prophecies. There had been an operation that afternoon; the leg of the Lancer had turned green and blue; it had to come off. Sister Anna Macmahon was in attendance. There was no laudanum; the Mutiny had cut the supplies. The screaming could be heard in the mud- and tin-roofed town below by the lake. When Sister Anna appeared, she was wan and had not changed. She walked out into the garden with the red blood still spotting her white dress. Iain saw her, for he was always looking for her.

"Sister Anna," he said, "did you hear tell of a woman in white who was riding out when they were blowing the pandies from the guns?"

Anna stopped short. Her face was as white as her dress, but on her cheekbones, two red spots flared.

"I heard of her."

"You have blood on your dress."

"I was her."

And looking at that pale face with its tiger's eyes and squashed mouth like a split plum, Iain knew that he had found the woman he was forever seeking.

"You lost your sister and your mother in Delhi."

"I lost them there."

"And you wish for vengeance."

"You can never find it." Anna looked over the silver lake below them, her chin and nose lifted as in a profile on a coin. "There is no vengeance. Only remembering."

"I have been looking for you," Iain said. "I have been looking for you for ever and aye."

Anna turned and smiled at him and came over to move the blanket across his leg that was stuck out on the stool in front of him.

"The men always say that," Anna said. "They all say they have always been looking for me, just because they are in my care."

"But I have been," Iain said. "And I bring this for you, as a pledge."

He looked in his pocket and brought out the emerald ring with the stone as big as a scone and the dark trace embedded in it as deep as a secret.

"I can't take that."

Yet Anna took the ring and examined the gold setting inscribed with Sanskrit writing and turned the green gem to the light to catch the sun in its lozenge.

"It is for you," Iain said. "I will not take it back."

"Then I will have to throw it in the lake."

"Throw it in the lake then."

"I will not!"

A flash of spirit that might have been covetousness made Anna speak sharply.

"You will be rid of it, Iain Sinclair?"

"I will."

"Waste not, want not. I'll keep it."

"It is for you."

"What is for you?"

"You."

"You speak your mind, Iain Sinclair. You know emeralds are not lucky."

"They are for you."

"You're a big man, Iain Sinclair, but why are you in the army? It is no life for a man – and not for his wife either."

It was she who talked of his wife, and Iain smiled.

"I did not wish it," he said. "It was the Highlands and the clearances. My own folk went to Canada. I joined the regiment."

"Yes," Anna said. "We did not wish it. My father, he was a doctor in the army. My mother and my sister and I . . . we went with him. We did not have the choice. Except to die out here."

"Anna Macmahon," Iain said, "if you will be with me, I will leave the army, but not India. For I have no place back in Scotland. But there are matters here – the tea, the forests, the railways. This is a great country, and we may make it."

"You are all the same," Anna said. "Wild Highlanders. Why should I listen to one word you say?"

"Because I was looking for you for ever and aye," Iain said. "And you were looking for me for ever and aye."

"You are a clown," Anna said, then she suddenly slipped the gold ring on to her index finger, where it fitted as if it were made for her.

"Look you," Iain said. "As if you did not already know."

"I must change my dress," Anna said. "How should I be talking to you with the blood all over me?"

"You'll be back."

"Perhaps I will," Anna said, "and perhaps I will not." But she was looking back at him as she left him.

She was the scarlet lady of the sorrows for whom Iain was looking. He had found her and he would not leave her. The time for vengeance was over. And if the Scots were best at revenge, they were better at one thing more. They did not forget. Memory was all. And the remembering of what would be, that was sure to be better than the revenging of what had been.

14

THE SEA OF THE TREES

They could not take the fires. Many of the fires they lit themselves in the big stumps, so that these burned away night and day, and did their clearing for them. These little fires went on month after month, the cracks in the cabin walls glowing red in the dark from the smouldering trunks outside. And they set on fire the cut branches and even the great oaks and walnut and maple trunks, because these could not be rolled to the river to float down to the saw-mill. But from the ashes, Hannah Sinclair knew how to boil the lye and then to make black salts out of the lye, and these were sold at the store against the axes and handspikes and saws needed for the cutting of the timber.

The fires they did not start drove them west. One forest burning would have been good, for it would have cleared the brush and made the work of hacking fields out of trees an easier one, as well as the ash being good for the feeding of the soil. But there were five fires that season, and none of the Sinclairs knew the cause of them. It might have been the summer lightning that frolicked in the night like crazy yellow goats. It might have been the Indians, careless with the China matches that they bought in rows at the store, and wanting the white men off their hunting grounds. It might have been the sun shining off a quartz rock and lighting the pine needles piled drier than tinder. But act of God or acts of man, five fires there were, and the last of them burned away the ripening oats and barley and charred the outer logs of the cabin itself. Fighting the flames turned the Sinclairs into blackamoors, the soot on their cheeks streaked with their tears, the dark powder of the smoke as bitter as defeat in their lungs.

"We will no longer bide here," Hamish said. "We will away to the west."

"Ach no, Father," Bain said. "After all this work and the land the first land to call our own, and the earth so black, never used except for the trees."

"And the fires," Angus said. "The next time we will wake to see the roof in a blaze and we will be like quails on a spit."

"Aye, like when that sheriff burned our home with the constables in Scotland." Hannah put a basin of water in front of her husband and her two sons for them to wash away the grime and the smoke-stains. "And when Iain burned the kiln and had to be taken for a soldier. And Hamish Jamie went with him; how could he do that to his mother? And you, Angus, if we go as your father says to the west because of the fires, you will be coming with us?"

"I will go east," Angus said. "The work on the land is not the work for me."

"But you are hardly grown –"

"Old enough to learn a trade, Mother. I know I am your wee boy, the youngest, but look" – stretching up to touch a beaverskin drying on a rack above him – "I am tall now."

"Let him go, Hannah," Hamish said, "an he will go. But we would have your help, Angus, on the waggon to the plains. It will be a hard journey."

"I would never come back," Angus said. "It is far enough from here to Montreal. Or to Boston or New York, for there I mean to go."

"Take me with you," Katie said. "I could see the dresses – and go to the theatre –"

"A Sinclair woman has never yet been to the theatre – a low and sinful entertainment," Hannah said.

"But Mary wrote from London that she went to the theatre – and saw a man who sang funny songs – and a man who swallowed a sword and a snake and blew out fire –"

"There –" Hannah said. "Sinful and corrupt. The theatre is an abomination."

"Hush, Hannah," her husband said, wiping his face clean on a strip of coarse red cloth. "You cannot judge the theatre, for you have never seen it."

"Nor never will."

"Mother, I will not go to the theatre," Angus said. "I will go to school and be an engineer. I will build the railways. Do you hear, Father, what they say in the store? In Canada, they will build a railway from the sea to the sea. Like in America."

"And you will build that?" Bain laughed. "You do have the big notions, little brother."

"And I do them, Bain. You will see."

"We will ride on them," Hamish said. "When we are out west on our fine ranch with all our black cattle –"

"Longhorns," Bain said. "Buffalo. Not black cattle."

"Angus will ride out to join us in his railway carriage, driving the steam engine –"

"He will be shovelling the coal," Bain said. "Blacker than he is even now."

"I will be designing the bridges," Angus said, "not shovelling coal or laying the tracks. I have a head on me –"

"And a tongue in your head," Hannah said, "that gabs nothing but foolishness. You will bide with us, Angus."

"I will not," Angus said. "If you go west, I go east."

"We will eat on it," Hannah said. "We have deer meat. And if it is not the red deer of Scotland –"

"It is good meat," Hamish said, "and we will say a grace for it."

When they had thanked the Lord for what they would eat and sat down to sup from the venison stew, thick with broth and corn flour, they found that it was seasoned with the soot that floated from outside. And the savoury smell of the meat did not fill their nostrils, for the sour stench of the burning fields fouled the air. They had only one thing to do. They must leave the trees for the plains or even the Rocky Mountains beyond the plains. There were droughts there – to hear tell – and blizzards, and twisting winds that sucked up men and animals and carried them howling through the sky, but there were also mountains larger than the mountains of Scotland, and Hamish found the forest almost as sad and encompassing as the sea. They were drowned in it as surely as set on fire. It enfolded them and roasted them. It wrapped them like babies in swaddling bands, then fired them like kindling in its oven. The trees and the sea were no places for the Sinclairs to trespass upon. It was the grass and the mountains for the ilk of them.

In spite of its name, Craigiebrae looked like a Swiss chalet. Perched on the hillside above the glen near Simla, it looked down through pines and fir trees and giant cedars to a wooded valley, which was as picturesque as the romantic dreams of Lord Byron or Mary Shelley. In the summer, all the ladies of Simla would ride out for picnics or Fancy Fairs. The glen was called Annandale, perhaps after the glen in the lowlands of Scotland, but Anna Macmahon said it was named after her, Anna's dale. For she was born in Craigiebrae when her father had built it for her mother, the first house outside Simla. And now her father was dead and her mother and sister too at Delhi, and she was the heiress of Annandale, and she had married Iain Sinclair that morning, in the stone church at Simla, and the ladies and officers and civil servants were riding out to Craigiebrae for the reception – those who would agree to come. Most people had accepted, even though they knew Iain was only a common soldier. At the last resort, even in a hill-station, curiosity was stronger than snobbery.

Standing in the hall in his full regimental costume, double-breasted doublet with white pouches, kilt and sporran, long stockings and white leggings, fur helmet with a cockade to the left, Iain knew it was the last time he would be wearing the colours of the Queen. Anna had bought him out. He was still limping and unfit for active service. But he had never wished to be a soldier. It was a rotten life. And though he was sorry to leave his friends in the ranks, especially Tam Ogilvie and Willie McBean, he was glad to be a farmer and forester again among Himalaya mountains wilder and grander than Scotland even could offer. "I do not regret it," he told Anna. "The army is not for me. It is the orders. I cannot take orders. A Sinclair cannot serve."

"And if I tell you to do something?" Anna said.

"That is not the same, Anna. I will do it with all my heart. That is love."

"Then I'll only ask you. I'll always say please. That is love."

Now they were waiting for their guests. Anna had been all round Simla leaving the cards at the bungalows and villas and chalets with their wooden balconies and porches. She had been carted from door to door in a jampan, which she hated, an upright lurching coffin, carried by four bearers who tripped over the toes of their huge slippers. The first guest, indeed, was being lugged up to Craigiebrae in a jampan, not on the back of the hill-ponies, which Anna could see picking their way up the slope between the trees behind. The jampan must have set off from Simla hours before, and the bearers looked dead on their feet, supporting the weight of the woman inside.

The litter was dumped before the door of Craigiebrae. A jampanee opened its door. Out waddled Mrs Dalgety in a billow of white lace, as if she was the bride herself at sixty, even though her corset could do no more than make a small dent in her voluminous waist.

"My dear Miss Macmahon," she said, "I beg your pardon, Mrs Sinclair. I do declare," and, appraising the huge height of the kilted Iain, "you have married Mount Jakko."

"I bet you would like to climb him," Anna said.

Iain laughed to see the pale round face of Mrs Dalgety suffused with sudden crimson. He loved Anna for her sharp tongue and true wit. She hated being patronised even more than he did. And as for a matron as formidable as Mrs Dalgety . . .

"Your visit to that army hospital seems to have done something to your manners, Mrs Sinclair. We all disapproved, but your poor dear father was not able to restrain you. I suppose that is where you picked up your language and your husband."

"I carried her away," Iain said. "When I could walk, that is."

"A private soldier, I see," Mrs Dalgety said. "Were you never promoted?"

"Too busy fighting," Iain said. "We leave promoting to the officers, they that can pay for their commission."

"Well, you have married money all right, Mr Sinclair. The only estate in Annandale. You should have been here for the *fete champeter* given by that dear Prince Waldemar of Prussia. Oh, the costumes and the gowns. And then he had to be killed watching the battle of Ferozshar."

"I have seen a few killed," Iain said, "but fighting."

"Watching is very dangerous," Anna said. "Particularly in Simla. You never know when you will be shot in the back by tittle-tattle. The ladies have tongues sharper than bayonets. Ah, Doctor Gillespie –"

Through the door stepped a portly, ruddy man in riding britches and bowler hat. He bobbed up to give Anna a kiss on the cheek.

"You brought back a prize from the wars," he said.

"First prize," she said. "Iain, meet the doctor. The best man north of the Ganges."

"Anna told me of you," Iain said. "You were always her inspiration."

"When there are women doctors," Gillespie said, "Anna should train to be the first. She's got more guts and sense than the surgeon-general. But tell me, Mr Sinclair, what are you going to do with the fine land at Annandale?"

"Grow potatoes," Iain said. "Or indigo. And cattle and horses, if I can."

Mrs Dalgety rounded on him. She was horrified.

"You *dare* to plant in Annandale? Why, we shall have a racecourse –"

"And we will have potatoes," Iain said.

"This is for recreation, for beauty –"

"Nothing is more beautiful," Anna said, "than a spud roasted in its jacket."

Doctor Gillespie laughed and took Mrs Dalgety by the elbow and steered her away, as other guests came through the door to greet Anna in her simple wedding-gown of white silk.

"Come, Mrs Dalgety, we mustn't monopolise the bride and groom. And certainly we mustn't give them advice. They've hardly had time even to get to know each other."

Now the officers in their forage caps and pantaloons were greeting Anna, but they did not know how to treat Iain, the Highland soldier. They hesitated and waited, as if expecting him to salute them. But

Iain put out his hand to grasp theirs and crushed their finger bones in his grip.

"It is good to greet you," he said, "off parade. And Craigiebrae, it beats any officers' mess in the land."

The rooms filled behind them with the officials and the officers and the summer ladies escaping from the heat of the plains. Some of Anna's twenty Gurkha servants moved among them, dressed in green jackets and leggings, serving sherbet and cake, white wine and fruit punch. The noise of conversation rose as the sound of artillery rises on an advance towards the guns, from a mutter to a chatter to a roar to a thunder. And then as the last of the guests passed by, Iain saw through the open door his brother Hamish Jamie enter in his full uniform of an assistant quartermaster of the Seaforths. And behind him followed an Indian woman, glittering in a sari of red and gold braid. She wore a thin black veil over her face.

"I am Hamish James Sinclair," Iain's brother said to Anna, "come all this way to tell you that you could do worse than marry my big brother Iain. And this is Lila Singh. I wanted her to meet the family."

Those near the door fell silent as they saw the veiled Indian woman by the bride. But Anna only smiled and said, "How very good of you both to come to our wedding. It is very good to meet a woman who has no time for all this silly *purdah* business."

"Ach, Lila did not wish to come," Hamish Jamie said, "but I said she must. To get to know you."

"You're a terrible man for breaking the rules," Iain said. "But you and Lila are most welcome here."

As Hamish Jamie and Lila passed through the crowded rooms, people parted in front of them, shrinking back as though they were contagious. Only Doctor Gillespie came up to them to greet them.

"You must be Iain Sinclair's brother," he said. "A race of giants. And you, madam –"

Lila stared at the doctor with black and glittering eyes above the veil.

"Lila Singh," she said in a low voice.

"I am Doctor Gillespie. I admire your courage in coming here."

"That is what Iain's wife said," Hamish Jamie interrupted. "It was my doing. Lila should get to know the family –"

"Why, if I may ask?"

"She is my family now," Hamish Jamie said.

"You are married, then?"

"The commanding officer would never give me permission," Hamish Jamie said. "What do they say? White is white and brown is brown and never the two will meet. But they do. Only nobody must see it."

"You think we are all hypocrites, Mr Sinclair?"

"It is the only way to rule India, it may be."

As Iain and Anna left their sentry posts by the door to join their guests, Mrs Dalgety rolled towards them in a monsoon.

"How can you let *that* woman in here?"

Anna smiled.

"As easily as I let you in, Mrs Dalgety."

"But she is an *Indian*."

"So are we all," Anna said. "I was born here as she was."

"But if you let them into our homes –"

"We already do," Anna said, taking a glass of fruit punch from the tray of the green-clad Gurkha servant. "They run our homes for us."

"But *socially*. It is perfectly unacceptable."

"Not to me," Anna said. "I am glad my brother-in-law has the courage to step over a few of these silly prejudices about colour and caste –"

Mrs Dalgety's face seemed to swell. Iain thought that if he tapped her cheek, it might puncture and pop like a balloon. "Nobody will ever – I repeat *ever* – receive you in Simla again, Mrs Sinclair."

"Not to worry," Anna said, putting her arm through her husband's. "Iain and I, we intend only to see each other for months and months now."

"Sociable," Iain said. "It is not in my nature at all."

When the last of the guests had gone with a new scandal to pass the time of night in Simla, Iain took Hamish Jamie and Lila outside to watch the sun set in pink and golden rays through the banked clouds that clustered above the white peaks of the Himalayas. The constellations seemed to be shining on the slopes of Annandale, wild geraniums and hill anemones, columbines and pheasant's eye. The wind sang in the tree-branches high and low in a skirl of bagpipes. The trees breathed out resin and pine as they stood to ragged attention down the sides of the mountains.

"You are a lucky man," Hamish Jamie said. "To come to all this."

"It was meant," Iain Sinclair said. "I feel I have come home."

"It is fairer than Scotland, Iain. And I never thought the day would come when I was saying that."

"Where we find mountains," Iain said, "we make Scotland again."

"You will not change these Himalayas. They are too big even for you."

"Who would change them? Look."

And the sunset sent down spikes of light through the clouds and the snow bonnets on the far mountains glittered with white gold and only the tune of the wind in the forest piped its soft airs.

"Hamish go to China," the veiled woman said. "He not tell you. He take me to you for you care for me."

"We have a boy," Hamish Jamie said. "Look after him and Lila. They are sending an expedition against the Chinese Emperor. I am a volunteer in the Commissariat."

"A boy?" Iain did not wonder at the news. "And what will become of him?"

"Not in my world," Lila said. "Not in your world. He has no life. But he is."

"When you need us," Iain said, "Anna and I, we will help you and your boy. And my brother will return from China. Now he is in the feeding game, not the fighting."

Anna appeared at the door of Craigiebrae, a silhouette against the light like the black cardboard outlines cut by nail-scissors for children.

"Dinner," she called.

"We must go," Hamish Jamie said. "It is your wedding night."

"Time enough for that," Iain said. "Every night shall be a wedding night for ever now. Come to dinner."

The East Indian Railway was both a dream and a nightmare. Mary Sinclair did not have the money for the first-class fare with sleeping-carriages and leather padded seats, but only for cane-bottomed and wooden-backed compartments in the second-class. To travel third class was out of question in the Raj, with a hundred and twenty Indians locked into their compartments for the length of the journey, and their numbers calculated by weight rather than by tickets sold, a black hell-hole worse than Calcutta on wheels.

Mary would have wanted to travel with them, for she had her wish to come to India after her training, to assist the Zenana Missionary Society in its work of looking after women in *purdah* who could not be seen by male doctors, but who were doomed to risk death by dirt and puerperal fever at every child-birth. Florence Nightingale had taken up India as her cause, and letters flew from South Street thicker than bombardments at the civil service and the army, demanding hospitals and sanitation, soap and water for the whole continent, with a woman's hand in it all. She had sent Mary out to work at the only place where women could work in the medical way, and to report back to her so that she could recharge her batteries for more cannonades at the male fortresses of imperial control.

But Mary was on the railway to Delhi to visit her brother Iain before she took up her duties in Amritsar. In her carriage were soldiers' wives and clerks in the Civil Service, with the train guards and servants pushing through, and the din of the sellers at the stations during the interminable journey on a vehicle that did not seem to go much faster than the bullock cart she had to take from Bombay. Among the scrum of passengers in *dhotis* trying to pack their way on to the jammed third-class carriages with baskets on their heads, the vendors would cry, *"Hindi pani, Musselman pani"*, because even the water was segregated here, and *"Tahsa char, garumi garum"* for the hot fresh tea that made the travel tolerable, and *"Pahn biri"* for the betel nuts that she could not chew because a lady could not spit. As for the child beggars clinging on to the train windows with the limbs that had not been cut off them, Mary had not learned to take them for granted yet and gave them a few annas, causing a riot and disapproval from the other travellers.

"It only encourages them," a soldier's wife said. "If you give them money and the market's good, they mutilate *more* children to beg, and it's worse."

"Supply and demand," a clerk said, lighting a huge cheroot. "The good old law of supply and demand. I hope you ladies do not mind if I smoke?"

"Good of you to ask," Mary said, but she did not dare to stop him puffing out more black smoke than the locomotive dragging the train along.

She began to talk to the soldier's wife, whose husband was a sergeant in the Seaforths. Yes, she had met Hamish Jamie Sinclair, whom they all called Murphy now after his escape from Cawnpore. He was doing well and had risen to assistant quartermaster. He was a wonderful organiser. The men had never had such good supplies and always on time. There was talk about him and some Indian woman, and when there was going to be this expedition to China and he applied for it, why, it was thought good he should go to get away from the woman.

"It doesn't do," the soldier's wife said. "I mean, it is bad enough, most of the soldiers having no woman even to speak to for a tour of duty that may be ten years. But if they go to the native women, even for their washing – with the temptation" – a small shudder shook her that was not the heat – "where will it end? A *khaki* continent."

"I am here to work in the *zenanas*," Mary said, "with the Indian women in *purdah*. Four out of ten mothers die having children. Dirt, disease, not able to see a doctor. And those midwives of theirs –"

"The *dais*. They're a caste on their own."

"What they are is dirty, pig-ignorant, superstitious and daft," Mary said. "They even give an English midwife a good name, for she is only gin-drunk and incapable."

The soldier's wife laughed and looked at Mary with admiration.

"Good luck to you. Are you going to your place now?"

"No. To see my other brother Iain. He has married and has a farm near Simla."

The soldier's wife was now impressed.

"And was he a soldier too?"

"He was. In the Sutherlands. He was wounded and married the woman who nursed him, although she was not trained, but helping."

"My husband says, if he is ever wounded, he would sooner die than let the medicals lay hands on him."

"It is getting better. And when they let women do the work too –"

"As you are –"

"As I will be, in the only place I can be." The carriage jolted and swayed and jerked forward as they left the station. "When will you go away from India? And where do the Seaforths go then?"

"To Canada, as I hear."

"To Canada? And Hamish Jamie off to China?" It was Mary's turn to give a laugh, which turned into a cough as she inhaled the smoke of the clerk's cheroot. "I beg your pardon – ugh." She cleared her throat. "My mother and father are in Canada. My brother is always in the wrong place at the wrong time."

"We all are," the soldier's wife said. "Soldiers always are. My name is Rose Campbell."

"Mary Sinclair," Mary said. "We will meet again. In the end."

The train gathered speed. A blast of hot air threw dust through the window and a gritty smoke layered them with dirt.

"But this journey will never end," Mary said. "So we will know each other, Rose, for ever."

The journey did end thirty-six hours beyond endurance, and then the question was how to find transport to Simla. There were coaches of sorts drawn by horses or camels or bullocks. And then by *tonga* up the steep and winding slopes of the cart track that bore the hopeful name of The Great Hindustan and Tibet Road.

The *tonga* had two wheels and was drawn by two ponies. Riding on it, Mary felt she was in a scull on a choppy sea, not a curricle on a road that was one bump after another up to the finish, past precipices and gorges deep enough to disappear down, never to be seen again. One way, Mary thought, to oblivion.

But Iain was waiting in Simla, wearing a plaid coat and trousers and boots now, taller by a head and chest than any of the hill-people with their flat faces and nose-rings in the *bazaar*. And he took her and her two bags out to Annandale on a pony-rig, then walked up to the house with the luggage, past new terraced fields among the tall trees. He trod heavily now, as a man does on his own ground, feeling the weight and the worth of his property.

As for Anna and Mary, it was communion at first sight. Sometimes at one looking of the eyes, there is a binding between two people. Sometimes the few words of a voice spell out a sentence for a lifetime. These two women knew that they had already met before they had. It was not Hindu doctrine of the transmigration of souls, the meeting in another life. It was this encounter in this life, an immediate understanding, a mutual recognition of each other. Instant and everlasting friends, they became so close and so quickly that Iain was quite left out of it. He had to stop himself becoming jealous about his sister over his wife.

"You are doing what I always meant to do," Anna said to Mary over the dinner, the candles on their silver stands making a dozen spear-points of light in the still air. "You are healing women."

"But you were healing men."

"Unofficially. I was not really allowed. I visited the hospital. But they had to use me. There was nobody else."

"Miss Nightingale will get women nurses into army hospitals. She has sworn to it. The day will come."

"It cannot come soon enough," Iain said.

"And women doctors," Anna said. "There is a female hospital in New York in America. The Blackwell sisters, who studied medicine in Paris and London, are in charge. And you here at Amritsar –"

"Miss Hewlett there studied nowhere but in books and by experience. It was the need of the Indian women that made her learn. It was so for Miss Nightingale and for us. The medical schools still will not admit us. So we must learn in the wards – from the sick and the needy. We may cure some of them, but the rest are our experiments – which do not always work."

Anna and Iain laughed. The Gurkha servants in their green tunics poured wine into the incised glasses, cut into diamonds and petals.

"Learning as you work," Iain said, "it is the best way."

"You learned to kill," Anna said.

"It was the best way to learn," Iain said. "I am planting now. Potatoes. And we have horses. But cattle, they will not last the winter here. And driving them down to the plains is too far. And there is so little water in the Punjab –"

"Water, clean water, that is Miss Nightingale's answer to everything," Mary said.

"She is right. If they would hold the water from the melting snows, if they would spread it across the plains, there would be a thousand villages, a hundred thousand farms, a million people where the dust is. Dams and irrigation, and the Punjab would bloom like the rose."

"If it isn't enough farming in Annandale . . ." Anna smiled.

"India gives people big notions," Iain said. "It is the size of the place – and the reason we are here."

"There's muckle to be done," Mary said. "That is what we were saying back in Scotland."

"Aye, muckle," Iain said. "Clean water, then, that's the secret?"

"For everything," Mary said.

"You do not like the wine? It was all the way from France."

"Once in a wee while. But water, that is the true stuff."

"It is," Anna said, "if you can get it where it is wanted."

15

THE WASTE OF IT

The high plains were called the inland sea. Hamish could see why. The red grasses moved in ripples and surges on the eager wind, they stretched to the horizon without end. But there was no peace on the journey because of the Red River cart. It shrieked like a banshee, it groaned as a soul in torment. The wheels were tree sections bound with shrunken rawhide, the axles were unpeeled poplar logs. There was no bear's grease in the hubs because the dust would have stuck to it and clotted the turning axles. The cart with its light hide cover was drawn by only one pony. It carried all the Sinclairs had in the world which they could take from their cabin – mainly traps, for the prairie before the Rockies was still hunting country and owned by the Hudson's Bay Company, not yet by Canada, edging its way towards self-government.

Hamish and Hannah and Bain walked with the pony, but Katie sometimes rode. For she had a kind of fever that Hannah said was young woman's fever, the longing for something she did not know, but knew she wanted. But Katie stayed curled in a ball in the jolting and screaming cart, rather than walk the wild grasses of the plains. Hannah tried all the known remedies from the medicine box on Katie, but none had any effect – not sulphur or powdered alum, castor oil or rhubarb, soda or sage tea. It was a growing pain, Hannah said. Katie would bounce out of it.

One day, a roaring ahead was louder than the howling of the cart. It might be a river, with the water cantering down in a clatter of currents and tossing white manes. It might be an angry mob of Indians with their drums, beating out some sinful ritual or portent against the coming of the new people. But the Sinclairs had hardly seen any of the savages on their horses in the long grasses, or dragging their summer camps behind their ponies on two long joined poles. The noise came from the buffalo they had travelled so far to find, the bulls roaring at their mating and at their dying, for that great reverberation over the wavering wasteland announced the presence of the herd and drew the hunters to it.

As the Red River cart plodded and jerked closer to the source of the sound, Hamish heard interruptions to the steady bellowing. There were cracks and yips – the sound of rifles and scavengers. Over the tide of grasses, shapes were moving as fast as the shadows of the clouds scudding on the breeze. Buffalo bulls charged out, showing only their tufted woollen heads and horns, then paused and snorted and rolled back to the herd behind. The bare and painted chests of Indian braves swept behind the living hobby-horses of their mounts, as they discharged arrows and musket-balls towards the vague mass of the surrounded buffalo. And now, ahead of the pony, Hamish saw timber wolves and prairie wolves yelp away, waiting to feed off the carcasses made by man.

"We could use some hides and meat," Bain said.

"What about them?" Hamish said of the Indians.

"There's muckle for all," Bain said and moved over to the cart and brought down the musket, already primed and loaded against the day. "They do not own that cattle more'n we do."

As the shrieking cart approached the hunt, the buffalo broke and stampeded across the plains. Some of the bulls did not budge, but stayed in a circle around their dead. The Indians on their horses rode away after the herd, yelling and firing. But still there was the steady crack of a rifle fired within the confines of the bulls, and one by one, their shaggy heads dropped below the red sea of the waving grasses.

As the pony and the cart approached, a buffalo bull charged towards them. The pony reared and whinnied, the bull lowered its huge head and stopped and pawed the ground which had cleared into the cropped mounds of a prairie dog town. Bain raised his musket and fired. It was a good shot. The lead ball hit the bull in the back of its lowered head, severing the spine. The great animal fell on its knees, flailing, then it toppled to the side, threshing the air. Bain yelled and ran forwards. Then he stopped at the sight in front of him, lifting his useless musket, before setting it aside. Hamish took the pony by its traces and pulled it forward while Katie got down from the cart to see the goings on.

Only two bulls stood now in the circus ring of slaughter beyond the clearing made by the prairie dogs. Aiming at one of them with his long rifle was a tall figure in a buckskin jacket and wide hat. He fired, and the bull dropped as if a spike had been driven into his heart. Standing untouched in the middle of the ring of dead or dying great beasts, the man seemed to be called among them for their massacre. He was invited for their ending, their chosen slayer, the angel of their deaths. Now he leaned on his rifle and watched the pony and cart come towards him, leaving the last bull to break and run after the herd that was leading the Indians away on their stampede towards safety.

"Easy there!" the buckskin man shouted. *"Gardez à vous!* Gopher! Dog-'oles!"

As he shouted, Hamish stumbled. His foot broke the surface dirt and plunged into a hole. There was a squawk of anger. A small burrowing owl fluttered out of its nest and hopped about in a rage of feathers, trying to get these intruders away from its nest. Hamish pulled his boot free and trod carefully forward with the pony picking its way between the holes. Hannah and Katie walked beside him round the hairy lumps of the dead buffalo, which Bain had already reached on his way to talk to the buckskin hunter.

"Henri Chatillon," the man was saying. "An' you?"

"Bain Sinclair. And my family. Hamish and Hannah, my father and my mother. And my sister Katie, the lassie with the red hair."

It was like one of the miracles in the Good Book. If it was not the raising of Lazarus, it was the casting out of devils. Katie was instantly well. Her blue eyes had the glint of the sun in them, although its light was at her back. Her face moved with thoughts and smiles more than the grasses.

"Why kill so many of the poor beasties?" she asked. "You cannot eat even the one."

"Bulls," Henri said. "Too many bulls. They fight for zee cows." He smiled, his teeth white under the shade of his hat, not black as were those of most of the *métis*. *"Les hommes* fight for you?"

"We are God-fearing people," Hannah said. "Hush, Katie," for Katie was laughing. "We are here for the land and for raising the black cattle."

It was Henri Chatillon's turn to laugh.

"What black cattle?" He threw a lazy hand towards the bleeding mounds of the dead buffalo. Already the wolves were moving towards the humans and the pony and the cart with its canopy of hide.

"Buffalo. All we 'ave. *Dans les montagnes*, sheeps *sauvages*. Big 'orns. *Boeufs sauvages*, sheeps *sauvages*. Maybe you come *trop tôt* – soon."

"We care not for the trees," Hamish said.

"We hear there is a railway coming," Hannah said.

"Is under Medicine Line," Henri said. "To river, Missouri River. *Mais il ne peut pas passer les montagnes.*" His hands followed his speech and swept up into the air. "Ver' up. Big, big. No *passer* railroad. *Jamais.*"

"It will be," Katie said. "You cannot stop the railway – railroad? I have not seen it, but my sister in London . . . my brothers, they have been on it. It will come here."

"*Jamais*," Henri said. "Buffalo. Red grass to zee red river. See –"

The blue sky was suddenly alive and grey. Startled by the stampede of the living buffalo, innumerable birds filled the air with rags and scraps of flying things – passenger pigeons and meadow larks, long-spurs and little grouse. The beating and twittering overhead of the birds in their hundreds of thousands was a small storm of hail in their eyes.

"'Ow many birds? You count zem? 'Ow many buffalo? An' bears. An' wolves? *Ici, dans les prairies, ce n'est pas l'homme qui compte.* No peoples. All zee *animaux.*"

"We come here to farm," Hamish said. "And we will bide here."

Henri Chatillon laughed and leaned on the muzzle of his rifle. "Is plenty room," he said. "You 'ave it all. And plenty lonely. *Les indiens* – Crow, Blackfeet, Utes – and *les métis*. I am *métis, ma mère*, she Crow. All we 'ave is no people, no people, so you *les bienvenus. Et le Bon Dieu vous protège.*"

"Where do you live?" Katie asked. "You must live somewhere."

"Where is buffalo, I live. Sometime I see *maman*. Sometime at post on Red River. Trade buffalo robe. Pemmican. Fur."

"So it is all grass country," Bain said. "But there are no cattle yet."

"Right," Henri said.

"And there will never be cattle?"

"*Jamais.*"

"There will be," Hamish said. "And wheat and oats. To there."

He pointed his arm now to the far horizon as a lone branch might stand out from a tree-stump on the plain while round him flies began to buzz the carcasses of the buffalo.

"I do not see so far," Henri said.

"My father," Katie said, "sees far too far. Past his children and his children's children. Somebody else will take it all."

"Hush, Katie," Hannah said. "If we work now, we will have the cattle."

Bain had taken out his skinning knife. He turned back towards the buffalo bull, which he had shot and killed.

"You 'ave two, three my bulls," Henri said. "You need zem. Is ten day to Red River. And zen, you swim. Take wheels away – 'e float, *la chose-là*," indicating the waggon. "Is post at *village*. But 'er," now opening the palms of his hands and smiling at Katie, "*elle est trop belle pour la frontière.* She too *belle pour les métis et les indiens.*"

Katie smiled at Henri's face under the shade of his hide hat.

"Will you not protect me, then?"

"We can do that," Hamish said.

"Our blessing on you for the meat," Hannah said.

"I 'elp you," Henri said. And while he stripped off the buffalo hides and cut off the choicest part of the meat and the fat and the insides, Katie stayed near to him. Even if his doing sickened her, she could not draw away from him. And when he offered her a small piece of raw liver on the point of his hunting knife, she took it and chewed it and swallowed it as if it was a sweetmeat from the hiring fair. It seemed to put the life back in her that had fluttered and ebbed in that last winter among the trees.

The cry of the baby gave a twist to Mary's heart. As she cleaned the little girl and swaddled her and put her in her mother Lila's arms, Mary felt her own loss of children. All this birthing she did for Indian women – and never giving birth herself. And this new little niece of sorts, for certainly she was the child of Hamish Jamie, what would become of her? Her mother's room off the bazaar was squalid enough in spite of the bright cloths hanging on the walls and the brass lamp and the little charcoal fire, where a kettle had been boiled at least for the purifying of the hot water. Through the single shutter, bars of light striped the bare boards of the stifling place. Little Seaforth Singh, called after the regiment perhaps in the hope that it would adopt him, was in the care of neighbours. The birth of his sister was no sight for him at the age of two. In fact, Mary thought, clearing away the last of the mess on the linen she had brought with her from the midwives' training centre, there should be a neater way of having babies. It was all just like an animal, and God did separate men and women from the beasts of the field. He really could have done a wee bit more about child-birth, even for Jesus. How Mary must have suffered in that stable.

"It was lucky I was here, Lila," she said. "Or you would have had one of our *dais*. And we can teach them all we can about hot water and clean linen, but they still have their superstitions – keeping the cord on and leaving it till it falls off, wrapping up the baby's head till the hole is gone, such foolishness, as my mother always did say."

"I not know you come," Lila said. Tears streaked her face as she lay on her mattress on the floor, looking at her infant.

"Of course I had to come," Mary said with the cheerful briskness that she had learned to use as her armour in this alien land. "*Another* nephew or niece – how could I stay away?"

"Hamish – he away in China. He not back here."

"Oh, he will be back the now," Mary said. "Scotsmen turn up like bad pennies. Now I will be cleaning you –"

"No. You will not –"

"That is the worst thing here," Mary said, stripping off the stained cover above Lila's body. "They say the mother is unclean for forty days after she has had her baby. Forty days lying there without being washed! We did not do that to a cow in our byre! It is not natural – and it smells!"

With a towel dipped in hot water, Mary began to wipe Lila's legs, gradually working her way up towards her stomach. At first, Lila shuddered and her flesh puckered, shrinking back from the touch of Mary's fingers through the wet towel. But slowly she relaxed and lay against her pillow, holding the baby.

"We are unclean," she said.

"Rubbish," Mary said. She rose and changed the stained towel for a clean one, over which she poured the last of the hot water from the kettle. "You are as clean as you wish to be. And certainly as clean as I can make you."

She came back with the fresh towel and continued wiping the brown skin of the Indian woman, who was the mother of Sinclair children, which she would not be, for it was already nearing the time when she would be past her time.

"When the husbands first let me into the zenanas," she said, "it was only because their wives were already dying. Some of the wives with *bairns* – scarce thirteen years of age. And their husbands old enough to be their grandfathers. Shocking and disgusting – left to die in a cell full of flies – no soap, no water – and if the wee babe was a *girl*, God help the mother, for no one else would, until Miss Hewlett and I came along, and we were graciously allowed to assist because we were *women* – despised women – so we did not break the rules of *purdah*."

Mary finished wiping the worst off Lila and threw aside the towel.

"And now," she said, "for the changing of the sheets. It is much more important than the changing of the guard. Shift you to the side, and I will change them. I carried clean sheets with me."

Lila slowly moved across the mattress inch by inch, holding her baby.

"You do too much, Miss Sinclair," she said.

"My brother does too little, that is sure," Mary said. She twitched the soiled undercover out and bundled it up and tossed it down. "But do you not worry. Hamish Jamie will be back from China and Iain is coming to visit us in Amritsar. He will see to you and your children. He has told me he will."

"We will go to the Himalayas?"

"No, you will wait here for Hamish Jamie to come back." Mary spread the clean sheet across the mattress that was stained as well, but she could not do anything about that. "Iain himself is coming down to the plain in the Punjab. To plan irrigation – bringing the water to the dry land. And the railway. There will be improvements, he said. We are here to *improve*."

Mary tucked in the corners of the sheet under the mattress, pleating them exactly so they made a triangle at each end. Bed-making, it was the first thing to be taught to nurse and soldier. If you were not squared off, there was no sense in your life.

"You are here to change us," Lila said, giving her breast to her baby for the first time. "And if we not want it, you still change us."

"Improvement must be," Mary said, finishing the tucking of the sheet at the top, forcing Lila to shift back with her baby across the clean linen. "My brother Angus, the now, he writes from New York City in America where he studies for to be a surveyor and an engineer. For he says, the rail roads as he calls them, they will come all over the world." And the sight of the red wrinkled face and tight-shut lids of the baby gasping as it drew back from the breast smote Mary's heart. "And babies too," she said.

"And babies too."

Lila gave her breast again to the baby. There was a sadness in her eyes as well as a sharpness.

"Your brother Iain, he has babies?"

"Two also," Mary said, squaring off the undersheet. "Hamish Macmahon and Hamilton. Two boys they are. But they have a fine mother."

"And I am not?"

Lila looked Mary full in the face. Dark eyes stared at blue eyes that looked away. Mary blushed, and she never did.

"It is not . . ." She paused to think. "It is not you are not a mother. It is . . . you are not the mother my mother Hannah would wish for the children of Hamish Jamie."

"You do not lie."

"Ach, plain speaking and plain living, that is all the Sinclairs are good for." Mary began to spread another clean sheet over Lila, who had plucked her loose cotton wrap below her knees.

"You not like me."

"I do. That I do. Why am I here, Lila?"

"Duty. That bad word you say."

"Duty?" Mary laughed, then she stopped laughing. "Aye, I am never off duty. There is no end to the women having babies in India and having not a good time of it."

"And you not having babies?"

A dagger went into Mary's heart. It was an assassin's thrust. She did not see the sharp point strike her. But it hurt, it hurt sore.

"It seems everyone is having babies," Mary said. "And someone must tend to them. If we all had babies, where would you find a woman to look for you?"

"You want babies," Lila said. She took up the infant and laid its head over her shoulder. "You want Sinclair babies. You say, why *this* woman? Why not me?"

The truth of it was too much. Mary felt a sudden pain in her womb. It was the time of the bleeding, and it was a time that would not go on for ever. The lives within her were draining away into the cloth between her legs. She crouched down and rocked and blew out her cheeks, panting. The heat was as an oven. The strips of light from the shutters divided the room into brightness and dark. The shouts from the *bazaar* were a nest of wasps. She looked at the brown woman with her baby's head as a lump on her shoulder, lying on the white sheets laid around her.

"Many have babies," she said. "Some of us do not. I give my life to other women. I do not give it to babies."

"But you will."

"I will not." Mary rose, feeling a cramp in her stomach, a dragging down. Then her temper rose. She would not show anything to this woman. "But do not think it is not for the want of the asking. Many men have tried . . ." Not many, to tell the truth, but some. So Mary went on, "But I said no. I said to Miss Nightingale, I will ever say no. I am here for the healing, not having babies."

Still with the dragging down inside her, Mary smiled a quick smile of false security, as she went over to Lila and touched her cheek.

"I have seen that the good milk will come to you," she said. "Also there will be rations from the barracks. The commanding officer knows you because I told of you. He says there will be no wedding –" Mary saw the pain upon Lila's face, as the baby began to whimper. "But I said – a mother is a mother is a mother, and this is the child of Hamish Jamie Sinclair, and she will eat, and her mother will eat."

"Thank you, Miss Sinclair." Lila hugged her baby to her. It was more in defiance of her, Mary thought, than in seeking consolation.

"I will bring your boy to you."

"No. My friend, she will do that."

"You need anything more?"

"You do too much."

"Yes," Mary said. "I do too much. That is the truth."

"And you like to say the truth. When it hurts."

Mary picked up her bonnet and a hatpin to pin it to the coil of hair on her head.

119

THE FAR CORNERS OF THE EARTH

"It may hurt or not," she said, jabbing the pin home, "but I like to say the truth."

As if the mention of it brought the man himself, Mary found another suitor pressing his hand on her in Amritsar. Erskine Montgomery was a captain in the Lancers, but not the sort who thought that pig-sticking and *chota pegs* before tiffin were the best things about army life. Lean to the point of emaciation with sunken cheeks and luminous black eyes, his mouth was full and unexpected in its lines of humour. Erskine had heard of Mary by reputation and from Rose Campbell, the soldier's wife encountered on the train. But when she met Captain Montgomery at one of the rare receptions she was obliged to attend, Mary found herself caught in the concentration of his gaze. He did not look at the other guests, but only at her. He seemed to be searching something out of her. He spoke as if he had known her for ever.

"Miss Sinclair," he said, "your remarkable work among the women here – what gives you the strength to do it?"

"Because you men who say you are strong," Mary laughed as she answered, "you soldiers – you cannot do it. So I must."

"Because the women will not let us near them."

"Nor will their husbands."

"You are not married –"

"I can look after myself, sir."

"What I see in you" – the captain's eyes pierced her own – "I see a woman who does not wish to be on her own. What woman does?"

"You do not know me."

"I have always known you. We merely have not met before." Erskine Montgomery was arrogant in his certainty. "But anyway, all women are the same. You – are you different?"

"All women are different, Captain. It is only the men are the same in the approach to the women."

Erskine Montgomery laughed. Mary had to admit that he looked devilish bonny when the mirth was in him. And he still gazed into her eyes as if nothing mattered in the world but herself, not the other officers in scarlet from the cantonment, not their few wives and the poor relations come out from England to marry abroad.

"I trust you will find the difference in me," he said. "I am not as other men are. And certainly not as other lancers are."

It turned out to be true. While his regiment was still quartered at Amritsar, Captain Montgomery became Mary's weekly companion. He would take her off riding on the quiet pony which he provided, and he would show her the ancient Indian temples and sacred caves ignored about the city. Flouting all conventions, he did not treat her as a Victorian woman, but as a comrade with a mind of her own. The erotic carvings in the caverns, the sexual or animal characteristics of the Hindu gods, these he explained to her as if they were natural. At first, she was shocked, but in the end, she took his confidence in her as a great trust. She began to depend on his Saturday appearance at the clinic as her only escape from her dedicated, enduring, frustrating work among the women. His telling her of their religious beliefs, his refusal to think there could only be one God and one way to Him, these began to liberate her from the certainty of her Scots faith and the teaching of the dominie that there was only a single true path to righteousness. And, frankly, Mary was falling in love with this elegant scarecrow with the smiling mouth and the intense, brilliant stare. For the first time, she wanted a man to ask her to marry him, to take her away from the blood and toil and tears of her nursing. But he said nothing, until one sultry Sunday, when he came to her to announce that he was posted to the north-west frontier with his regiment, and he must go.

"The only thing I cannot leave in Amritsar," he told her, "is you."

"Then –"

"I must."

"I have my work," Mary said. "I had it before you came here. How could I go?"

"Your sacrifice?" The smile on Erskine's lips for once made them thinner with mockery. "You would still nurse on and not come with me?"

Was Erskine asking her? Mary did not know. If it was a proposal, it was a queer one. He had hardly touched her on their long expeditions, except to help her down from her pony. Once she had slipped from her saddle into his embrace, but though he had held her to him for an instant, he had pushed her away with a strained joke, as though he had to deny himself. And was this really a proposal? Or only a test of her secret love for him?

"You have not asked me to come with you, Erskine."

"Not in so many words."

"So few. You never have."

Erskine smiled again with his mouth tight against himself or her.

"How I shall miss you," he said. "And you will never know –" He put out his hands and pressed her cheeks between his palms and burned his gaze into her eyes like a brand. Then he kissed her fiercely and briefly on the lips. And then he put her away.

"Erskine," she said. "What? What will I never know?"

"How I have stopped myself –" He shrugged, his thin shoulders hunched in despair. "I cannot. Yet I love you –"

"Ah," Mary said. "And if it is love, what is *cannot* to that? Love always *can*."

"I have a wife," Erskine said coldly. "She is insane. In a superior Bedlam in England. I cannot." Roughly, he took Mary by the shoulder. His fingers were iron claws digging to her bone. "Now you know." His eyes were sudden red with passion like the Indian actors Mary had seen who put crimson dye in their eyes to show anger. "You know now. And I will go." He turned and walked towards the door.

"Erskine," Mary said. "You men are all the same."

"Why?"

"You are always married."

Erskine's laugh was short and dry.

"What a woman you are, Mary. A joke, *now*."

"It is true. And you are always the same, because –"

"What?"

"*You* are hurt. You have control over yourself. Your pain. Your suffering. Your love of me." Mary was now staring at Erskine with her bright eyes. "What about mine? Did you think of that?"

"Mary, I never –" Erskine started forward. "I could never have hoped –"

"Get away with you, Erskine," Mary said. She had meant to sound cold, but her tone was fond enough. "You will never know. Never ken at all."

"Then you do love me." Erskine was suddenly happy. "And you might –"

"Get away with you, man. You will not know. How can you? You are a man like the rest of them."

At the end of the war in China, Hamish Jamie found himself at a plundering and burning worse than at Lucknow. In the Summer Palace at Peking, he burst in behind the French, who had draped silk robes and hangings over their epaulettes higher than their shakos, with gold and jade ornaments falling out of their knapsacks and pockets. There was so much more gold inlaid in the painted carvings which decorated the palace walls that it looked like brass. Hamish Jamie was prising out a strip of it, when he saw a young captain in the Royal Engineers with a blazing torch in his hand, setting fire to some silk hangings. Flickers of flame ran as red mice up the wall.

"Ach, you're burning gold, sir."

"It's brass."

"Look you."

Hamish Jamie handed over his strip of inlaid metal to the captain who bent it and whistled.

"Gold it is." Then watching the flame run up the silk to the ornate ceiling. "Too late now. But no matter. There are hundreds of other pavilions. And we are ordered to burn it all. They did torture our envoys. Ungodly swine."

"But we'll get the prize money."

"So our commander says. He's given his share back to us." The captain laughed. "Damn fool, but a good general. What's your name, Sergeant?"

"Hamish James Sinclair, sir. In the Commissariat."

"Charles George Gordon." He smiled briefly under his black curly hair, but his eyes remained filled with a hard blue light. "I have seen you on the carts. You did a fine job, bringing up the shells."

"I saw you on the pontoons at the Taku Fort. Engineers win wars."

"And transport. To hell with the glory boys. Glory is nine-tenths twaddle or ninety-nine per cent twaddle. Getting there is what matters."

The flames began to roast them and the smoke made them cough. They moved towards the door of the fiery pavilion.

"It's a damned shame burning this," Gordon said. "It's wretchedly demoralising work for an army."

"Aye," Hamish Jamie said. "The waste of it."

His prize money came to ten pounds. A private received four pounds, and Captain Gordon forty-eight pounds. The Summer Palace was burned to the ground, its ashes its only legacy. And though Peking proved as dirty a city as Cawnpore or Amritsar, Hamish Jamie found a consolation in it. It was filled with concubines and prostitutes, even more than those denounced by the old prophets in Babylon and Sodom and Gomorrah. There was no holding the troops.

Hamish Jamie chose a young woman called Wu, so slight and delicate that she lay in his arms as small as a thrush chick in a nest. Yet when she took the combs out of her hair, its black waterfall covered all of his body as if drowned in her tresses. He taught Wu to say one word, "Love", and she taught him a great gentleness in the touching of her skin. Tracing the line of her leg to her ankle with his thick fingers, he came to her crippled foot, bound to the size of a scone with the bones crushed inward. He stroked the foot and said, "How is it, Wu, the more people are wise, the more they cripple you sore?"

16

DANGER OF SURVEY

They were stuck in a hard sea. In the winter, their sod and timber hut was trapped like a small berg in ice. In the summer, it was becalmed among the blowing grasses. Too cold for most of the year, too hot for a part of it, and windy pretty much all the time. And what winds, when they wanted to make a breath of it! Turn the corner of the hut in winter, and you would bend double like a half-open jackknife, as the gust hit you in the vitals with the point of its sword. And in the summer, suddenly out of the plains, a tall black tower would rise as a black keep shredding at the edges, and out of it volleys of lightning would crackle or split it from top to bottom, with the thunder breaking your ear-drums with the clap of heavenly hands.

So it was to Bain, who wanted to master these new lands. They had three hundred and twenty acres for the taking, and that was an estate in Scotland, they would be the lairds there. But here, it was flying in the face of the ground. Because of the wind, they had to build their hut in a bottom, where the river ran – or did not run nine months of the year. It was not a burn, but a trickle over stones some of the time, a torrent for a month at the melting of the snows, and a dry rock bed for most of the year. And when they ploughed the grasses for the planting of the wheat and the barley, there was no keeping the crop or the soil. For they could not fence the field from the plain. There was not the wood for it nor the time nor the water for the hedges. So the living things came in to eat them out, the prairie dogs and the deer and the pigeon. And one summer with a beating of bronze wings, the plague of locusts came as foretold in the Good Book. They were called hoppers now, and they ate the grain and the grass and all that was green under the moving carpet of their clacking wings. And there was no riddance from them except the burning of them. And that left nothing but a black devastation.

"Was it good to come here?" Bain asked his father. "There is nothing the now. In the trees, there was the timber. And now –"

He spread his hands to the horizon half as far as time away. "We come to nothing. And nothing we have of it."

"There will be the day," Hamish said, "when there will be the wheat to the sky."

"But the buffalo –"

"They will be gone. We are killing them all."

It was truly said. Now that the Indians had rifles to fire from their horses, and now the railways were pushing across the American continent below the Missouri River, the workers had to be fed, and the buffalo hunters went on at their work of massacre as if the killing would never stop because the herds would always be there, which they would not. And Henri Chatillon was little now at the trading post, so that Katie was sore sick at the loss of the sight of him. Not that his courting of her was anything at all – or to his shame, Bain had to admit, Katie's courting of Henri. For she was fair throwing herself at this man. And him half a savage as well as half a Frenchman. And what did they say about the *métis*, the half-whites and half-red men? They took the worst out of both the races.

But even Bain would not say that about Henri. At the post, when the other men and women and children ever were drinking themselves into the forgetfulness of whiskey and rum that all craved – perhaps because the furs were being trapped out and the ploughs were beginning to turn the grasses – Henri stood back, leaning on his rifle, making his few comments, or sometimes telling the elaborate tales of the frontier that ended in one final soft joke. He never seemed to fall out of his detached concern. Only once had Bain found him passionate, when he was talking with the trapper Gerald Fitzgerald who had come up from Missouri over the Medicine Line, as sharp and intense as a flung knife.

"Then you will be with us," Fitzgerald was saying. "For he that is not with us is –"

"Not against you," Henri said and laughed. "But I am not for you."

"Only for yourself," Fitzgerald said.

"Is big country," Henri said. "*Ce beau pays est pour tout le monde. Eh*, Bain, you know Fitzgerald. 'E wish we join America."

"You'll no be a friend of the Queen of England," Fitzgerald said. He took a tin mug and held it under the tap of the whiskey keg and gave the drink to Bain.

"I am not," Bain said. "But I have two brothers fighting for Her in India."

Fitzgerald spat on the mud floor.

"Wearing the red," he said. "How could you do that? But the Scots are not our friends in Ireland."

"So my father says," Bain answered. "But I have nothing against you."

"In France," Henri said, "*on aime les Écossais*. Zee *Garde Royale* it was zee Scotsmen. Often, zee Scots fight for France. *La belle alliance*."

"Then it's time for another *belle alliance*," Ftizgerald said. "The Scots, the Irish, and the French."

"And my mother's people," Henri said.

"The redskins, why not?" Fitzgerald laughed. "One thing we have in common. We all hate the bloody redcoats."

"I was telling you," Bain said, "my two brothers, they wear that coat. Though Iain the now, he has a fine place of his own in India and he's out of it. But my mother and father, they will not have a word against the Queen."

"The more fool them," Fitzgerald said. "And all the murdering she has done in Ireland."

Henri stroked the muzzle of his rifle.

"A woman – a little woman – can she kill so many?"

"Not herself –"

"So she does not kill. So why we join America? Zey kill my brothers and sisters –"

"Redskins –"

"Zey not kill zem 'ere."

"You work for a British company?" Fitzgerald's lips were as sour as the whiskey in Bain's mouth. "You work for the Hudson's Bay Company? And you're French and redskin. They can't keep this Rupert's Land. Canada will have it if we don't."

"*Bon*," Henri said. "But zey look for my brothers and sisters. No wars wid Indians 'ere. Zat is for Americans."

"You will not be for the Fenians then?" Fitzgerald said. "Not for free men in a free country."

"I am free," Henri said, picking up his rifle, and then speaking with hardness. "And I kill zee man who say I am not free. We go, Bain, and see Katie."

Bain put down his tin mug on the rough wooden bar. It still had some of the whiskey in it.

"I would give you back all your whiskey, Fitzgerald," he said, "only the half of it is in my stomach."

"Where it will curdle," Fitzgerald said. "So stupid you are."

Henri seemed to know all the people in the hide tents pitched round the trading-post, the big squaws with a baby clung like a lump on their backs, the lounging braves braiding their hair, the naked children that clung to his leg, and even the thin dogs that did not cringe at his passing, but shivered towards a caress from his hand. Bain was almost

jealous at the trust and love that Henri seemed to inspire. But not in
him, not in Katie's brother.

"How is your" – Bain paused for the word – "squaw? Wife?"

"I not marry," Henri said. "She is Indian wife. We together ten
year. But no boy, no girl. *Et je pense* – is it zee end of Chatillons? *Pas
plus les* Chatillons? No –"

"So you think of Katie?"

Henri took Bain by the arm and stopped and turned towards him.

"Bain, you please me. But – Katie and me – is for us. Not for you.
I ask your father –"

"He will say no."

"Why? I am not – you say – Protestant?"

"What do you believe in?"

"God. Who else?" Henri smiled and walked on with Bain following.
"Crows, Blackfeet, Assiniboins, Sioux, we all believe God. He make
zee world. You believe God. He make zee world."

"We don't believe in the same God."

"Same world," Henri said.

"Not the same God," Bain said.

"If zee same world," Henri said, "and many Gods, or same God
wid many faces, we live in same world – and God show 'is face to each
of us as 'e wish."

"Sounds good," Bain said, "but it is not true."

"Why?"

"The minister says there is only one God . . ."

"And I say wid many faces."

You could not help liking Henri, and Bain saw Hamish and Hannah
fall under his spell, even though their wills were hard against the
buffalo hunter going with their daughter. Katie did all she could to
change minds and win hearts, but it was the stubborn bent of the
Sinclairs, that once they had set their thought, it was like hot lead in
a mould cooling into a bullet. The more she made Henri tell the tales
of his courage and cunning in the wilderness, his loyalty and humour
in adversity, the more she saw Hamish and Hannah were determined
not to let this man of the wild take their daughter as his own. She
knew why. He was a half-breed, and her parents would think that he
would make a squaw of her. As though being in a hide tent was worse
than in a sod hut, which was *all* dirt, if you came to think of it.

Henri took Hamish outside to ask for Katie's hand. It was the time
of the setting of the sun. The broad and turning globe of yellow light
was balanced on the rim of the land, and the shadows behind the men
were a hundred feet long, two giant spokes of blackness across the
stubble of the remaining crop that Hamish was able to harvest, barely

enough to last them for the winter. The soil was loose and powdery to their feet, and the toes of their boots scuffed up dust.

"I marry Katie," Henri said, "I give you dowry of five hundred beaver skin."

"You do not buy women here," Hamish said.

"I no buy," Henri said, his eyes yellow in the low light. "I *give*. I wish I give!"

"I will not take from you," Hamish said. "You will not take my daughter."

"She take me."

"She will not go against her father."

"She is of age. She take me."

"You do not fear God," Hamish said. "You will make a squaw of her. A wild woman."

"I build her a big *tipi*. And a cabin – timber for zee winter. She live as Queen – as Queen in England. I hunt for her. I die for her."

The passion of Henri startled Hamish, but he did not show it.

"I will not have it the now," he said. "Did you not hear me?"

"It is for her who say," Henri said. "Katie say – Henri, you are my man. I say, Katie – my woman. And you say – no?"

"I say no."

"She say yes. I say yes. And you, old man" – Henri stood over Hamish, so that their two shadows now made one black path away across the plains – "you will not stop us."

"I will," Hamish said. "My daughter will bide with us. We have need of her."

"I need her."

"Go back to your squaw," Hamish said. "That is your place. With the savages."

Hamish saw the stooping figure in front of him shaken as a sapling in a gale with a terrible anger. Then the man mastered his wrath and grew still.

"She come to me," Henri said. "I call and she come."

"The devil you do," Hamish said.

"She come."

And Henri Chatillon went on, loping over the plain, the rifle a third leg on him black against the sun, its face orange now and cut in half by the land. And Hamish went into the hut to tell Hannah and Bain and Katie that Henri would never come to the hut again. And for all her red hair and temper, Katie did not weep and storm. She was almost too calm, as if she knew what had to be. But she was only biding her time. For at the end of the winter, and come the spring, she was gone at the silent call of Henri Chatillon. And there was no trace of her, no tale of her. She was gone as the wild geese are gone and the wild duck are gone, migrating after their kind.

Angus never knew a survey could be that dangerous. He was the transit man with the axeman in front of him and the leveller behind. He had been slung on a rope with his theodolite in mid-air over the edge of a gorge to make his calculations. He had been swung on a log on chains over a roaring torrent. Now he was hanging by spikes clamped into his boots on an ice-slope with his fingers too frozen to turn the screws of the transit. His eyes were full of tears from the invisible spokes of cold that the wind drove at him. He could not see the angles of his theodolite, let alone record them for the leveller behind him. He blinked furiously and turned a screw and wrote in his mind eleven degrees. Then he jerked out his spikes, turning on to his back and cradling his instrument to his chest. So he slid down the slope to a ridge, where the leveller stood with his assistants and their graduated poles. He was lucky in his scramble down. No snag of rock tore through his clothes or between his legs. But a survey was a pig all right.

"It's murder up there," he said to Donovan, the leveller. "The wind's so sore you cannot see through your little telescope."

"You have the readings?"

"Aye." Angus put his mitten in the pocket of his jacket to pull out pencil and pad. "I have them."

Another railroad was being driven across the Appalachians to compete with the two that already ran to the plains. The market on Wall Street was well watered with stocks sold in tracks to the west that were not yet laid. When Angus had reached New York, he had found work at once as an assistant on a preliminary survey, holding the painted pole as the leveller adjusted his sight and made his reckonings. But the team was working against time and the wastage of men did not matter. The first leveller was lost to dysentery from dirty water, his replacement broke both his ankles slipping down a cliff of shale, while the transit man cracked his skull open when the axeman felled a tree that tumbled down backwards. The accidents were good for promotion, if you were quick to learn. It took Angus all of three days hanging around the instruments to study how to set a theodolite and even to level the tripod and turn its small telescope to sight upon the graduated poles. It was just a question of being careful, and some simple subtractions between the levels of the front-sight and the back-sight. As the poles were moved forward, fresh sums established a profile or a backbone line, showing the gradients. Contour lines were made at right angles to the central line, though plotting the path of

129

the railroad was a mazy way through the mountains, doubling back and forth and sideways, always along the easiest slope or through a natural pass, because tunnels and cuttings cost millions of dollars, and why not use God's cracks in nature to ease the path of the iron roads of man?

They were lucky to have an abandoned cabin as their base camp. A mountain family had moved on west in despair. They had hoisted an iron stove on to their pack-mules, so they had hot hash and corn bread for dinner, and the bitter black scalding coffee that made the wheels turn all over America. There was an uneasy respect among the team, different as they were. For they had to labour together, even if they did not like each other. And the work of each one meant the wages of them all.

"There's a better route," Donovan said. "The recce party, they are wrong to be sure."

"It is good," Mencken the axeman said. "Open land. No trees."

"Lazy bastard," Donovan said. "Never lift an axe, do you? Give me some coffee."

Angus poured the last of the tin pot into Donovan's mug.

"They must have their reasons," he said. "To want to go this way."

"Lawyers," Donovan said. "And all lawyers are crooks. They should be hanged, not the people they put on the rope's end. Thieves, every one of them. To be sure, they bought the land cheap that this road will run on, and they sold it back dear to the company."

"That is a fact," Thorvald said more as a statement than a question.

"That is a fact." Donovan mimicked Thorvald's thick accent. Thorvald held the front pole for him and could not answer back. "And there is politics too. Towns are built ahead in the hope the road runs there. Millions of acres are sold in the hope the road runs there. And if it runs another way – what?"

"Ruin," Angus said. "And the poor people moving again."

"We already moved to America," Donovan said. "We poor people."

"Aye," Angus said, "but there is no call to move again when we are here."

"This is a moving nation," Mencken said. "I move."

"You move." Donovan now mimicked Mencken's guttural sounds. "He, she, it moves. We move, you move, they move. Here, it is a declension of move. And what are we doing? We are putting the whole of this American nation on to iron wheels. And that is how they will stay – moving. Rolling up and down the length and the breadth of the land. Rolling like timber, rolling like the river, rolling, rolling till they roll off the Rockies into the ocean on the far edge of this all."

Angus admired the talk that Donovan had in him, although he did not admire the man.

"It's a mighty land," he said. "And do not the people move towards their opportunity?"

"No," Donovan said. Then he swallowed the last dregs of his coffee. "They did fail, and they fail again in this new land. They move from one failure to the next. And our job is to make them move faster. We grease the wheels of failure. We export it to the frontier and beyond."

There was a hush in the cabin. It was difficult not to believe Donovan, but none of the seven men wanted to believe him, for he suggested their failure too. Finally, little Cappeto, the other assistant on the back pole, dared to speak.

"We make opportunity. We build railroad. All go and make west."

"Baloney," Donovan said. "We are spreading the great mistake. Does the west want our rejects? And what will we do in that desert out there? It is fit for Indians, not for the likes of us, who cannot even make a go of it in a better country."

"My folks are out there," Angus said. "But I would not go. I said, here, come here for opportunity –"

"Then they had a smart one," Donovan said, "to be sure. Except for one matter, Angus Sinclair." He jerked his thumbs at the dank walls of the cold cabin, which had already wet the pile of their bedding rolls. "Do you say this is opportunity? Speaking for myself – and you know what a religious man I am – I would call it purgatory. We are here because it is nowhere – to remit our sins without a chance of a progress to the heavenly land. We may help to build the railroad, but only for people to pass through looking not to the left of them, and not to the right at this forgotten place where only fools would ever waste their time."

Mencken rose to his feet and stood over Donovan.

"It is work," he said. "Then I go home to Baltimore. Do you have home, Donovan? Your home is in your mouth, I think."

The men laughed at Donovan, and he did not like it.

"Your home is in your belly, Mencken," he said, trying to turn the joke. But his voice was too sharp to raise another laugh. "I speak the truth, but you do not want to hear it. The company – it will kill us or wear us out for a few dollars more. And when the railroad is laid, and all the moving nation – that's what you said, Mencken – when they are all moving upon it, they will never give any thought to them that made the railroad there. We will be dead and gone and forgotten – for a few dollars more. And devil a one will know of the men who made the iron road."

131

Angus rose now to stand beside Mencken and look down on the plausible Donovan.

"Do you not think, Donovan, that if we do our work, we may not live in that work? That work is ourselves – if we do it well."

"There speaks a canting Scot," Donovan said, and now he mimicked the burr of Angus. "By their work you shall know them."

"Aye," Angus said. "And by your mouth we know you."

The other men laughed again and rose. And now they stood around Donovan in an accusing circle, looking down on the voice which made them doubt what they did. But Donovan was not put out. He remained squatting and snarled out his disbelief.

"And how would they build a railroad at all without men with potatoes for brains?"

"You have potato in your head," Thorvald said. "Mashed potato."

"Go to bed," Donovan said. "Or you'll not be fit for the *work* in the morning."

"You are not fit for the work at all," Angus said. "For you do not mean to do it."

Now Donovan rose to his feet, lean and hooked forward at the shoulder.

"I mean to do my work," he said, "for a few dollars more. But do not ask me to give my mind to it. That is set on other matters. I tell you, there will be a change here and a war here. And all you slaves to the dollar, even you will be free – if you want it, and even if you do not."

The colonel's office in the barracks at Amritsar was hardly surprising, even if it was not expected. The desk had been brought from England, but it was a military travelling desk in pine and leather, on twin trestles. The paintings were horse pictures, but not the usual ones of ladies sidesaddle in pink hunting-coats. Here a tiger attacked a frightened charger, there a mare kicked a wolf attacking her foal. And Hamish Jamie liked the hoof on the colonel's desk that had been converted into an ink-stand. He had thought that they were foot-soldiers, the poor slogging infantry; but the colonel must have been in the cavalry before he had to get down on to his feet.

"Sinclair," he said, "you know why you are here. Everybody in this camp knows what I am going to do before I know myself."

"Well," Hamish Jamie said, denying what he knew, "you do not mean to make an officer of me."

"I do."

"The mess." Hamish Jamie came to the sticking point. "The officers' mess. How will they speak to me there?"

"As an officer," the colonel said, "and a gentleman." He paused. "Sinclair is a great name."

"There were Sinclairs fought at Bannockburn. And with the Heart of Bruce, the Sinclairs died fighting the Moors. And at Flodden Field. It is an old fighting clan."

"Your citations from China are excellent," the colonel said. "You are right about supplies. They are the backbone of the regiment. You will accept to be quartermaster. You will be gazetted as a captain."

"Aye," Hamish Jamie said. "That I will. But I will not pay for it, for I do not have the money."

"Buying commissions is on the way out, Sinclair. As for the quarter-master, you were always my personal employee. You had to make your mess bills on the sale of the supplies, but now the government will pay them and another thirty pounds a year, so you need not be a thief. I never liked buying pips. Nobody did. The rich do not always fight the best. Of course, if you are defending your wealth – the price you paid for your commission – you might fight like the devil to save your investment. But there are better reasons."

"Aye, sir. The regiment."

"And Queen and country." The colonel gave Hamish Jamie a long stare. Then he smiled, or Hamish Jamie would have sworn that he did, only the flicker on the thin lips under the grey moustache could have been a sneer or a grimace. "But as we are the Seaforth Highlanders, and as you are a Sinclair – and which side *were* you on at Culloden? – I think the regiment is a very good thing to fight for."

Now Hamish Jamie could not stop a grin that spread over his face, incorrigible.

"The regiment is a very good thing to fight for," he said. "For it is a very good regiment – the best of the regiments."

"Only because of the men in it," the colonel said. "Including you. But you must understand, Sinclair, there are your fellow officers who may not wish to include you."

"Ach, then I will not include them in the circle of my acquaintance."

The flicker passed across the colonel's tight mouth once more.

"And there is another matter – more serious even. I do not wish to mention it, but . . ." the colonel paused, "I believe you may know what it is."

"About me? My habits?"

"About your character. An Indian woman –"

"Ach." Hamish Jamie paused to think. He felt the blood in his cheeks and a dirk in his heart. He knew he would betray what he held most dear.

"I have heard tell of that."

133

"It has been mentioned to me," the colonel said, "that you and a certain lady – even that there are children. A boy, it is said, called *Seaforth –*"

"That would be impossible, sir."

"Impossible, Sinclair? Now I agree. No officer of this regiment could have a child by a native woman. And certainly not called by the name of this regiment. It is impossible. Therefore, Sinclair, as it is impossible, I presume that it is not possible."

Hamish Jamie looked the colonel in the eye with the straight blue stare of untruth. But he chose his words defensively. "As it is impossible, sir, it must not be true."

"I am glad to hear that, Sinclair. It would have been an insuperable impediment, however much we wished you to join us as an officer in this regiment. But as it is impossible, and you have told me it is impossible, I trust that I shall never hear of this impossible matter again."

"That you will not, sir."

The colonel rose from behind his desk. He walked over to Hamish Jamie and put his hand on the epaulette of the sergeant-quartermaster's tunic.

"I will take you to the mess myself," he said. "And I will introduce you. There will be no problems there, if you have courage enough, and I know that you have. And as for what is impossible, that never happened, because it is impossible. The army only has time for the practical, as you do."

Hamish Jamie dropped his eyes. His heart seemed to fall into his belly and drag it down. Yet he had been given all he wanted at the price of his word.

"You may trust me, sir," he said, "to do all that I must do as an officer of this regiment."

He went to Lila the following night, changing his pony-chaise to hide his tracks, in case somebody might be following him. When he came to the open stairway to her room in the *bazaar*, the market children shouted at him in the streets or begged, clinging on to his kilt or his arm until he shook them off and shooed them away. When he sweated up the steps to the wooden door to knock three times on it, he knew that she had already seen his coming. She always did. But then she was shy, and she would be huddled in a corner, fearful of the father of her son and daughter now.

The door opened. A small boy stood at it, so small that he reached only to the knee of Hamish Jamie, who bent and seized him and whirled him round in the air and put him down. Then he walked over to the bed where Lila sat, her purple shawl wrapped around her face, the baby absently crawling over the bedspread of brown and crimson stripes.

"I am here, Lila," he said.

"I think I not see you," she said.

"But here I am," he said. He looked round the dark white walls with their pitiful brightness, the painted woodcuts and the patterned cloths pinned on the plaster, and the shining dragon silk hanging he had brought from the spoils of Peking. "Seaforth –" He picked up the solemn small boy again and looked at him. "You like the mountains?"

The small boy made a face.

"He not know mountains."

Lila dropped her shawl and turned the black beam of her gaze on Hamish Jamie. "You send us to the mountains? To your brother? Why?"

"The air is good," Hamish Jamie swallowed on his lie, "for little children. Here there is dust, flies, illness. In the mountains it is clean –"

"Pah. You send us away."

"I do not." Then Hamish Jamie could not bear his own deceit and went over to Lila and kneeled before her and took her face between his two hands and spoke to her. "I do. My brother will look for you and the children. I am to be quartermaster – an officer. And the Seaforths must away to Canada. I will see my mother and father there. I love you, Lila, but – I must away. And you must away to the mountains."

Hamish Jamie felt the tears prickle at the corner of his eyes. The relief of confessing had provoked a weeping in him that he just held in check.

"So you will send us to Himalaya. You will go from us."

"I am a soldier. You always knew Hamish Jamie – a soldier."

"And liar," Lila said. "We cannot go back to Singhs. I am *pariah*, worse than dog to be with you. To have your boy and girl. And you send me to your brother. And I am dog to him."

"You are not." Hamish Jamie was indignant. "You met him and Anna. They loved you."

"They love you. Me they hate. But Seaforth –" The small boy came forward and stood within his mother's arm. "He is of you. Seaforth Sinclair. For him, they love me and they hate me."

"Do not make it hard, Lila," Hamish Jamie said. "I do what I must do. I do all I can for you."

"You make me a dog," Lila said. "You make Seaforth and Peg more than dogs. For who will want them?"

As Lila began to cry, the black *kohl* running down her cheeks, the small boy ran at Hamish Jamie. His head was as high as his father's bare knees under his kilt. He began drumming at the man's thighs with his tiny fists like hail on cloth walls. He was shrieking cries that Hamish Jamie could not understand, the sound of the mewing of gulls, so he picked up the little lad by the waist and let him wave his hands in the air and keep on screaming.

"Put him down," Lila said. "Give him me. He is not for you. He is for me."

So Hamish Jamie put him in his mother's arms, and she tried to hold his arms to his sides, but she could not. He flailed away and ran out and clutched his father's leg by the ankle of his white boot. He wound his father tight to him in a ball and chain. And Hamish Jamie stood foolish there, shackled in front of Lila. And now the baby girl began to cry, and her mother took her up and unbound her *sari* and gave her daughter the breast.

Hamish Jamie took money from his sporran in a pouch, and he threw it on to the bed.

"There is for you and Seaforth and the girl," he said. "It is more than enough until Iain and Anna come to find you –"

"Your sister Mary will come," Lila said. "She think you are bad."

"She is my sister yet," Hamish Jamie said. "And never think you or your kin will be between me and my kin. But Mary also will look for you until Iain comes. I will see to that."

"She will see to that – she is a woman."

"Aye," Hamish Jamie said, his leg pegged to the floor by Seaforth. "And I will come again if I can. But the colonel does not want –"

"You to be with an Indian wife."

"It is impossible, he says."

Lila gave a harsh laugh, the cracking of dry sticks in her voice.

"It was possible for you."

"I loved you, Lila," Hamish Jamie said. "And I still love you. You do not believe it, but I do. But I must go the now. The regiment –"

"Daddy," Seaforth called, holding harder on to the leg of his father.

It was the hardest going that Hamish Jamie had ever had of it. He could not shake off the small boy like a burr. This was his son. And bending and trying to prize him off was no good. The boy cleaved to him as to one flesh and blood. In the end, he had to break the child's grip by force and drop him yelling on his mother's lap as she fed the baby. And Hamish Jamie had to make a stumbling backwards run from the room, the most shaming retreat of his army life. He would rather have shrapnel and grapeshot whistling round his ears than the sounds of the sobbing. He would rather have been dead than having to walk back to barracks with his own living self, and knowing the wrongs he had done and the sort of man he was.

17

IRON ROAD
AND WAYWARD PATH

"He's drunk and he's slow and he's dumb," Sergeant Hockmeister said. "That's why he's the general."

"He knows where the railroads go," Angus said. "That's why he's the general."

Grant and his army were the wrong side of Vicksburg in 1863. His supply barges and steamers had to run past the Confederate batteries to carry his supplies down the Mississippi. His ammunition waggons were commandeered from the local plantations. They ranged from fancy carriages to cotton carts, pulled by mules and oxen with straw collars and rope lines for harnesses.

The armies of Dixie lay north and south and east of them, and the railroads converged at Jackson, from where trains could reinforce Vicksburg at will. The Union soldiers only had five days of rations, hard bread and coffee and salt. "What I do expect," Grant said grimly, "is to make the country furnish the balance."

The foraging parties were scavengers on the face of the earth. They stole the chickens and dug up the buried sacks of seed corn. Grant's subordinate, William Tecumseh Sherman, was driven to living off the land as Moses was, when taking his people from Egypt to Israel. For Sherman, his foragers were God's instruments of justice. He would make the South howl. He would squeeze the soil until it bled supplies for him. And he would burn the rest as an example. For he did not think he was fighting only soldiers, but a whole people, who had to feel the hard hand of war before they laid down their resistance. Devastation was the truest weapon.

Angus could not bear the sight of it. It was worse than his childish memories of the clearances. In the name of God and the right of the North, barns were fired, dirt yards jabbed with bayonets to find hidden plunder, cattle butchered, families beggared and turned from their blackened homes. His duty was with Grant's only pontoon train, which was needed to cross the rivers that flowed into the Mississippi. But he had little to do, while Grant struck at Jackson and took it in a downpour, leaving Sherman to destroy the railroad system there, and Sherman liked to destroy. Grant doubled back towards Vicksburg, driving the Confederates ahead of him to bottle them up in their city. They burned the bridge over the Big Black River, and Angus was called to bring his pontoons into action at Bridgeport. The iron and wood casings were slotted and bolted and roped into place, and Sherman's corps of pillagers crossed over the shaking and makeshift bridge to Walnut Hill, where they set up a base on dry high ground, which could be supplied by the navy from Haine's Bluff and the Mississippi. Vicksburg was doomed.

But if Grant cared that his men ate and their ammunition pouches were full, he cared less for their lives. He ordered two frontal assaults on the entrenchments before the enemy city. Angus had never seen such a shooting gallery or skittles game outside a country fair. As the masses of Federal troops ran forward with fixed bayonets, a deadly hush fell on the Confederate diggings. Then out of them rose lines of grey men aiming their muskets and rifles. Deliberately, they fired volley after volley into the advancing troops while another grey line appeared to shoot over their heads at the enemy. Grape and canister swirled like devil dust among the Union men in blue. They were struck down and shaken and whittled away until they fell back, only to be ordered into a second assault which mowed them to the earth as the sickle and the scythe might reap a tall harvest of blood. After such a brilliant preliminary strategy, this was the stubborn folly of mass murder. And Angus could not comprehend it.

Now Grant settled down to a siege. Where marching had prevailed and assault had failed, walls and starving would do the work. The foragers scattered as locusts over the land behind the earthworks, while the troops in the trenches watched the surrounded city that must give in, for there was no hope of relief. War was waiting, Angus knew that. It was very rarely fighting. And when General Sherman sent for him, he knew what to expect. It would be a plan to spread the war behind the rear of the enemy, to destroy the front lines by striking at the back country. A dirty business, but dependent on good communications.

The intensity of the general was almost biblical. There was a preacher in this soldier, and as a surveyor of things, Angus did not relish a sermon in his fighting.

"How mobile can you be, Sinclair?" Sherman asked, pacing up and down his tent as if sitting down were an expression of defeat. "Can you pull those pontoons over country roads thirty miles a day – forty even?"

"I doubt it, sir," Angus said. "You cannot depend there will always be mules. And axles break. Fifteen miles a day. No more."

"Too slow. We will have to swim, if they burn the bridges."

"A raid is it, sir?"

"That is my business. But I hear well of you. You raised that pontoon at Bridgeport in less than a day." His eyes radiated light at Angus. "Could you design for me a *light* pontoon – and quickly assembled – a new kind that could go with the cavalry?"

"Aye," Angus said. "I could. But it would take time."

"We do not have time. We have God's work to do, and it must be done quickly."

"Burning the houses of the innocents –"

Sherman scowled at Angus. "I am disappointed in you, Sinclair. I had thought you might have more imagination. And dedication. Do you not reckon? We are not only fighting hostile armies, but a hostile people. We must make old and young, rich and poor, feel our wrath. We can punish Georgia and South Carolina as they deserve. Did they not punish their slaves? And if they are given into the hand of destruction, we can repopulate them. The devastation of them and their roads and their houses and their crops will destroy their armies. For we cannot occupy the South, we do not have the men. So we will burn it. And without resources, their soldiers will perish on the vine." Sherman was influenced by his own dark vision. "So you will make me my light pontoon?"

"As I can," Angus said. "But in good time. And I do not think in good time for your black work. I come from a land cleared by the burning of the crofts –"

"But this is a just cause –"

"That is what the lairds said to us."

"God's will and work."

"There is fire from heaven," Angus said. "But it is better direct from the hand of God than from the matches of your men."

And indeed, waiting proved to be the best policy. For Vicksburg surrendered on the Fourth of July.

Angus was assigned to count some of the weapons of the Confederate soldiers as they stacked them in front of their conquerors. The heaps of rifles and swords and long bayonets looked like the horns of a thousand dead elk and stags, their prongs sticking out in futile aggression. The beaten soldiers even had to drape their regimental colours over the tops of the piles of weapons, draping their muzzles and points in a ragged bright blanket of defeat. Angus found the sight too sore for him, a last and unnecessary insult. But there it was. The war must be changing him, too. For he had precious little feeling for a flag and certainly not for the Stars and Stripes, and now he was feeling that the yielding of a piece of gaudy cloth was a true humiliation.

Later, when Angus was checking the roll of the thirty-one thousand prisoners who had been taken, he fell on the name Archibald Sinclair. And when he found the Confederate officer leaning against a wall, tracing a pattern in the dirt with the toe of his boot, he appeared a reflection of the face of Angus himself – the same long jaw with a cleft in the chin, the parallel sad hollows which ran down from cheekbone and nose, the projecting brow over the sunken blue eyes.

"Kinsman I see," Angus said and held out his hand, which the other man took.

"You are a Sinclair, then."

"Angus Sinclair. Hamish is my father. We were cleared and came to Canada. They are in the west there."

"We came with Oglethorpe to Georgia. We whipped the Spaniards and they never came back from Florida. And we were given fifty acres and five pounds and a year's rations to stay on as settlers. And we did, on Saint Simeon's Island, and we built a fine plantation there by the sea. And how it will be now, I dare not reckon."

Archibald Sinclair traced in the dirt with the point of his boot as if he were trying to draw a plan or a map, when there was only a prison camp ahead of him.

"Will your slaves take it now?"

"The *nigras*? No. They like us well. It is a Northern fiction they are not happy with us. Why, they need us. For they'd never look after themselves."

"That is what they said of us in the Highlands," Angus said. "We were too feckless to look after ourselves. Without the black cattle we were good for nothing." He looked at the piles of arms sticking out from under the Confederate flags. "We are good for something."

"To fight each other?" Archibald gave a sour laugh. "Brother against brother? It is not your war, even."

"I have two brothers fought for the Queen in India. I am a surveyor and an engineer. The wages are fair. I build pontoon bridges. I will not hold a gun."

"Would you have some whiskey, cousin?"

"I do not."

"If I did not carry a sword," Archibald said, "and I do not now, why, I would carry whiskey."

"It would do you more good," Angus said. "And I shall get you a dram."

"Spoken like a cousin and a gentleman," Archibald said. "You look like me, you know."

"I do not agree. You look like me."

Archibald laughed. "Do you always have to be in the right, as all the Sinclairs do? Or shall we say it is the same thing?"

"I am in the right," Angus said, "but it is the same thing."

"When the war is over, and I think it is nearly over now," Archibald said, "will you come visit me on my plantation? Saint Simeon's Island in Georgia. They know the name there."

"I will, but first the whiskey –"

So the prisoner and the surveyor began drinking together that night, and they became friends where they had been said to be enemies. But they were never true enemies, or so Angus and Archibald reckoned. They went out to do the bidding of their opposite sides, and to be paid or killed for it. All around them, the soldiers in grey were drinking with the soldiers in blue, and one thing was certain in the chatter of accents, the nasal and the throaty, the burr and the drawl, they were all Americans. And by the end of the second bottle of liquor that Angus had found, he also found himself drinking to the toast that Archibald proposed: "To a most civil war."

Henri Chatillon was not as the other men were. Katie knew he would not be, but so many men – or so she was always told by Hannah – reverted to brutes when they had what they wanted from a woman. Henri did teach her to be a man, or more like an Indian woman. He bought her buckskin leggings and a short skirt and put her astride a pony so that she could ride the tall grasses with him, avoiding the pitfalls of the prairie dog towns and a stumble on to the broken leg of a screaming horse. But in their life in the cabin which he built for her a mile from the fort, he taught her to be a woman, to reach for him in the night under the buffalo robe and make him cleave and cling to her, to be dry with desire as a thirst in the desert, to be soft with fulfilment as a calf in clover, to wait for his coming as for an annunciation and to weep for his going as for a burial. She was always probing into her man, wanting to know and possess all of him, for he eluded her, not holding back the heart of him, but the kernel that kept him solitary and strong. It would never be given to a woman, and she had to have it from him.

He spoke her language better now, for she was not good at learning his tongue, neither French nor Crow. He told her what the Indians called her, Flame Wind, for the red mane of her hair that floated behind her as she galloped across the plains. It was better, Henri joked, than being called Black Buffalo woman. She was the maiden who was causing all the trouble between the Oglala Sioux, because she went off with No Water, a warrior in Red Cloud's group of Bad Faces, and she met with Crazy Horse, the young raider against the Crows with his polished medicine stone behind his ear and a red-backed hawk in his hair.

"He dream dreams," Henri told Katie. "He see Sioux die if all white men not killed. He bring war."

Katie saw him once, when there had been fighting along the Platte River in Minnesota across the Medicine Line, and the United States cavalrymen had been drawn away into their own civil war, and the Sioux and the Cheyennes had taken their vengeance on the settlers and the miners, and now the militia were on them, and they were slaughtering and mutilating each other, children and women scalped and hacked to pieces among the men, and Crazy Horse riding north among the buffalo, which were fleeing the long guns as he was. And Katie saw him on the plains one day on his pony, charging along into nowhere, his long black hair flying out with his calf-skin cape that was spotted with the white hailstones of his angry vision.

After this sighting, Henri kept Katie in their cabin for a week. Crazy Horse and his band of Sioux hated the Crows and the whites. And there was other trouble, raiding American parties coming up to the Red River to compete for the skins and the hides, and to try and drag them into the war in the United States so that they would be incorporated into that land. Slowly, slowly, the British were giving the Canadians their own government, but it might well come too late. And the Medicine Line of the forty-ninth parallel, that artificial boundary splitting a continent in half, only existed in the mind and might never be drawn, and then Western Canada would be swallowed into the snare of America as the north of Mexico had been.

"We will send for my brother Angus," Katie said. "He is a surveyor. He will draw the Medicine Line, and we will be safe above it."

"I do not think you see your brother again."

It was true. When Katie ran on to the red plains to meet Henri and be taken to his *tipi* on his horse, she knew she would not go home again. Hamish had sworn to her that, if she left with Henri, he had no daughter. And Hannah had not winked at her or said soft words to her, but she had spoken as harshly as her father. "If you go in sin we cast you out for ever." And Henri did take her to a priest at the fort, a black father in the wrong religion, and there was a ceremony in the Latin and the French, but not a word of it did she understand, with drunken *métis* as the witnesses, shouting fond curses at Henri and trying to kiss the bride though Henri struck down one of them at the attempt. But it did not matter now, for all the love and need of him that overwhelmed her. Except when he left her alone for the hunting of the buffalo, and she had days and nights of thinking of the other folk dear to her, Hamish and Hannah and Bain and Angus, and the lost ones in India. And she wept bitterly until she found herself smiling in the memory of her new love, who would come back to her soon.

Her wild spirit now ran free. She had always chafed under the orders of Hannah, telling her what the Good Book told her to do, or not to do, which was more often. She would rather have the dirt of the life of a *métis* wife and the awful lack of privacy – the passing women round the fort pinching the freckles on her white skin, not believing they were real, or begging meal and salt buffalo tongues from her stores. She learned from them the brewing of bitter herbs and wild grasses for teas and purges, the softening of the buffalo robes by pounding and chewing, the stringing of the bright beads and the sticking of the patterns on the supple hides. She even learned to fight, giving better than she got with a squaw who snatched away her best silver spoon and left a handful of dark braid in Katie's hand to show her defeat. Katie loved riding the wind and sending up clouds of the pigeon and the quail with her pony's hoofs and hearing the buffalo bellow in a rumble to the west. Once she saw Bain plodding after the plough yoked behind his oxen in the river bottom, and she found her love for him drowned in a wash of pity. He was doing the wrong thing on the wrong ground, and she had escaped rightly from that sad toil.

When the baby kicked inside her, she put Henri's hand on the walls of her belly so that he could feel the tiny thumping. He smiled and waited with the palm of his hand for the next shifting of the child.

"He is very strong."

"She is, I hope."

"She is very strong. But she have red hair. Then I love her."

"One day my hair will be white."

"After I am gone." Henri rose to his feet and looked down, seeing her hair as embers glowing bright and dark in the firelight in the cabin. "I will go first. I am twenty years more. What you do then? Go back to your people?"

"They will not have me," Katie said. "I am a lost woman now." She laughed. "You don't know how glad I am to be lost, when it is you who found me."

"I worry," Henry said. "It is not good a woman *sans famille*. When baby come, a woman, her mother –"

"You have to be my mother and father now, Henri. I'll settle for being your woman."

"*Bien.*" Henri walked over to the hide hanging over the cabin door and twitched it aside to look out. There was a far noise from the fort of drunken voices, then a shout, then a silence.

"I do not like this war," Henri said. "It come here too. *Je n'aime pas.*"

"Come here." Katie held out her arms and waited until Henri lay down and put his head against the swell under her robe, the shape of the life to come. "Hold on. Keep this. And I will see the war never comes to us."

On other plains in the deserts of the Punjab, there was hunger. The five rivers of the Jhelum and the Chenab and the Ravi and the Beaz and the Sutlej hardly watered its barrenness. The wanderers and cattle-thieves who haunted its wastes were called the *janglis*, but even they could starve when there was no rain for years, and the land at the edge of the water bore corn parched in the husk. And there was hope now. The iron rails ran to the Punjab, and the British government no longer used starvation as a weapon to clear the land as it had at home in Scotland and Ireland. For where would the Indian people go, if they were driven from their poor soil? What country would receive such refugees?

Bags of grain filled the extended waggons on the train from Amritsar. Two steam engines pulled and pushed the increased load towards its destination. Packed as tight as the corn sacks in the box-cars, the passengers on the lower tier of the third-class carriages sweltered and suffered from the dust and black grit blowing through the compartment. Lila, shrouded in her shawl, had managed to make a kennel under her seat of wooden slats for Seaforth and his little sister Peg. But there was no way of her moving in the crush, no means of answering the calls of nature. So down below was a moist playground of rank smells, unfit for children. There was nothing else to do. They had to go to Simla this way, the only way for them.

Up the train, Mary lay on the top of her pull-down bunk, also prickling with the heat through her bodice and clammy from the touch of the padded wall of the compartment. Below her, the missionary wife, Mrs Dougal, asked for more tea, which was brewed on the train floor by a half-naked man with a top-knot and a saffron loin-cloth, who appeared between stations offering his scalding brew, the heavenly *char-wallah*. There was a theory that drinking boiling liquid in a temperature of more than a hundred degrees somehow cooled you off. Perhaps. But Mary did not see the logic of it. The tea seemed to pass out directly in drops through her skin, which only then cooled her off a bit.

She was making for the Punjab because disease had followed famine as it always did. Cholera and fever were bringing down the *jangli* women and children, as they had in the camps of the railway workers, and the *jangli* men would not let male doctors touch their sick families. But Mary also knew that Lila and her two children were travelling to join Iain and Anna at Simla as an *ayah* for their four children. She had tried to book Lila on the second class, but caste and expense were too much for her. So she had to settle for the inhuman double-decker flesh-trucks that were called carriages by the Amritsar and Multan Railways. These meat-waggons did not seem to be progress to her, but mere incubators for more contagion. Sauntering along at twenty miles an hour, the Indian trains were a slow route to heat-stroke and a quick exposure to disease. If the sun did not fell you, the filth would.

Entering the new Lahore Station was going into a medieval castle by a tunnel, not a drawbridge. Since the Mutiny, passenger stations were built to be defended. Turrets and bomb-proof towers dominated the outer walls, riddled with loop-holes for rifles, while iron sliding doors stood either side of the tracks, ready to close them off. Strategy was based on the railways now. The metal tracks were the wrought nerves and sinews of the Raj in India. There was not much need to talk the languages or to know the various peoples as long as communications were quick by rail or telegraph. Messages in English were all, and delivery of the goods to the right place in double time.

The howling of the vendors in the station, which seemed to be a roofed *caravanserai* of all the displaced of the south, nearly put Mary off her purpose. The windows of her compartment were blocked off against the maimed beggars, but she rolled down from her berth and bribed the *char-wallah* to fight his way ahead of her along the platform. She was hardened now to the plucking of little hands on her skirts and the strange bright things thrust into her face. She was carrying a wrapped bundle and she had to get through. And looking into the openings on the lower layer of the carriages, she saw a hand wave to her from a shawled woman, and she knew she had found Lila. She passed the bundle through the aperture, food and drink of sorts, *chapattis* and boiled water and limes and sugar.

"Where are they?" she shouted.

"Take them," Lila shouted behind her shawl. "They die here."

There was no choice in it. Mary took Seaforth in her arms, as his mother handed him down, and the *char-wallah* took the shrieking and damp Peg. And the two of them pushed their way back to her carriage. All Mary could think was that she was breaking all the rules, and the Raj ran only on the rules as the rails, and they had to be obeyed, because if the regulations were not followed to the letter, there would be another Mutiny and no Raj at all. Of course, the whole Empire would crumble if two half-caste tots got into a first-class carriage. But there you were. Since Mary had become a nurse, she had really found

145

caring more interesting than ruling. In fact, healing people meant breaking the rules. And Seaforth was even hugging her as if she could defend him against the press of the people and their push and bustle, and the welcome he would receive on the train.

Mrs Dougal took the intrusion of the children in fairly good part. After her first shocked surmise that they were Mary's own little mistakes, she began to warm to them. No question, Seaforth and Peg were a relief from the monotony of the journey. It was even fun finding them hiding-places from the guards and the ticket-collectors and making a game of it. "You go in there and keep very quiet until we say, 'Shoo,' then you come out and get a barley-sugar" – or a sweetmeat that did not appear too toxic.

"I will never tell a lie," Mrs Dougal confided, "but I do not mind a cloth over the truth when it is a matter of children."

And so they reached Multan and the changing of the railways. Mary had to transfer to trains for the Punjab, Lila to transport to the hills. There was no common railway gauge in India any more than there were common peoples. Divide and rule was the British principle, even in the width of iron tracks. Mary kissed Lila on her cheek through her shawl as they said goodbye. It was the first time she had done that, but she had fallen a little in love with the children. Lila trembled to her kiss on that public station, and Mary trembled too. It was a declaration of what could not be declared, and there might yet be a judgement from it. But there was no other way to go.

At Annandale, Lila was killed with kindness and stifled by diffidence. She could not get it right, because she could not do wrong. Her errors were condemned by silence, her mistakes were pointed out by talking of other things. She could never understand the invaders, or so she thought, because they included and rejected her at the same time. She was their servant, the *ayah* of their children, Hamilton and Hamish Macmahon, Margaret and May. And the children seemed to accept her little children, who were their cousins, that was the truth. But with Anna, for all her warmth and her feeling, there was the barrier, as strict as for the Untouchables of India. She was the lady of the household, and something in her past made her shrink from Lila, who could see Anna's mind fighting against the mutiny of her skin. Iain was easier, but more casual and brutal, the master of the place, even if he was the serf of his wife. For he seemed bound to her as though she were the chieftainess or maharanee of his clan, so great was her hold on him. Often Lila would see the huge man kissing the large flawed emerald on the gold ring on Anna's hand, and bowing before her.

Lila was outside the bedroom door, when she heard the talking that would send her and the children away, only she had nowhere else to go, and she could pretend that she never heard a word of it.

"They are my kin," Iain was saying. "There is nothing I can do about that."

"But people will see," Anna said. "And people will say."

"You welcomed her to Annandale. When Hamish Jamie brought her here for our wedding, you took her to everybody. You were proud that Simla would never ask us again. And now –"

"And now we have our children. And I am proud of them."

"And she is the *ayah* to our children, Anna. And our children play with her children."

"Yes. And that is what they say in Simla about us, Iain."

"And you care about it."

"I do." Behind the bedroom door there was a rustle and a soft slap that might have been a kiss.

"Darling, things change. The government, they think you have done wonders at Annandale. It is your use of the water, the small dams and the ditches. And now in Punjab, where there is a desert –"

"They want lilies." Lila could hear Iain laugh. "But what is the use of it?"

"Out of hunger, you will grow plenty. Out of sand, you will grow wheat. Out of the strong came forth sweetness."

"And out of Lila, we will grow servants?"

There was a silence, then again the sound of the kissing.

"Come to bed. We have taken her in, Iain, for the sake of your brother. But we must not take it too far. Believe me. I know."

Again Lila heard Iain's low laughter.

"One thing I ken from you, Anna. A man's place is always in the wrong."

There was the sound of Anna laughing now.

"Don't say that."

"I do."

"Then a woman's place is always in the right."

"It is."

As Lila stole away from the bedroom door, she knew one thing. Her place was where she would never be wanted.

18

A SORE WHILE

A letter from Hamish Jamie was rarer than a white Christmas in India. It almost made Mary weep to have the sealed envelope in her hands. She smiled as she saw her name spelt out by his hand in the careful letters that were not joined together so that they were the more readable. She had worried when he was posted to yet another absurd war in Africa because of his experience with the Commissariat. This time the tyrant Theodore, King of Abyssinia, had made hostages of the British consul, Captain Cameron, and of assorted German and French missionaries and adventurers. He tortured them from time to time, then proposed to exchange what was left of them for artillery and machinery for making explosives. He wanted the best of western technology in return for some of its representatives. Queen Victoria's government sent the machinery to Massawa in the Red Sea, but by the time it had arrived, King Theodore had lost control of his country and his senses. He threw the captives into the dungeons in his mountain fortress at Magdala. It was now a question of saving face as well as the lives of the hostages. They must be got out. And Hamish Jamie had gone to do it, although never were so many sent at greater cost to rescue so few.

Mary wanted to know how it was done, and the letter told her. Hamish Jamie wrote:

We have the prisoners but they say the whole thing will cost nine million pounds, which is about quarter of a million a head. Is it worth it? I think our heads were not worth that when we were in Scotland. Probably sixpence each.

We live rough, we have no sugar, no milk, no butter, no flour, no bread, no rum – nothing but water, we get char though, but not much. We eat biscuits, which are like dog biscuits broken up into hard bits, murder on the teeth. And tough beef killed just before being taken. When they brought our ration of it this morning, the muscles were still twitching. This sounds odd, but it is true. Alive, alive-O, like those cockles and mussels in London.

I am writing to say how good the hospitals and doctors are. No nurses yet, but they will come! There is a new stuff called carbolic, and they put it on wounds and scalpels and saws, and now there is not so much gangrene in the soldiers. It seems to kill the rotten stuff, I don't know how. But we will lose only about three hundred men, this is a record for an expedition like this.

You know what I want to ask. Did Lila and Seaforth and Peg get to Iain's house in Annandale? I know that you cannot let me know, but I want you to know that I do care, even if I do not seem to, because of coming to Abyssinia. But I come to Abyssinia because it is my duty. You know that. Please tell Lila when you see her that this is the only reason. Duty.

Sometimes I do not know what the Army is all about. Sometimes I am back in Scotland, and we are working at the kelp. I know that even my life now is better than the kelping, and your life helping the Indian women, and Iain is doing famously. But I wonder. What we are doing in Abyssinia when nobody wants it, not even the people here? I do not know. And as for our family in Canada – you know I could not find them on my tour of duty with my regiment in Montreal, for they were too far gone across to the west – are we condemned always to be wanderers, never with a home of our own (except for Iain, and that is Anna's)? Will we always work for others and never for us? Is this duty, and if it is, why do we believe in it?

I am only a soldier, my dearest Mary, but even a soldier may wonder just what he is doing. The rain beats down on my tent, the oil is low in the lamp. I must stop. My love to you and Lila and the children and Iain and Anna and theirs. But tell me when we meet again – why do we do what we feel we must do? There are so many other beautiful things to do . . .

Louis Riel was young, only twenty-five years old in 1869, but he could inspire and seemed able to lead. When he declared himself president of his Red River republic, he hauled down the Union Jack from Fort Garry and put up his own flag of the fleurs-de-lis and shamrocks. For he hoped the American–Irish would come over the Medicine Line to help the *métis* in their rebellion from the British Crown, which had just taken over Rupert's Land from the Hudson's Bay Company and incorporated it into the Dominion of Canada. And Gerald Fitzgerald was in the Fort, as Henri Chatillon knew he would be, and with him a man called Donovan, who said he knew Katie's brother Angus –

they had worked together surveying railroads to the west in America. Both Fitzgerald and Donovan boasted that they had been with the Fenians, when fifteen hundred veterans had invaded Canada after the Civil War and again the previous year, when they had been licked at Trout River.

"And if you not make your free republic two time in Canada," Henri asked, "why try now? Third time lucky, you say."

"The French and the Irish," Donovan said, "we're natural buddies."

"Maybe."

"We hate the Queen."

"Maybe."

"You don't want to be free?"

"We are free now," Henri said. "Sometime a Mountie come in red coat, *ça va*. Indians, *mes amis*, zey come 'ere because zey are free. No trouble, only south zee Medicine Line. Louis Riel, our *président* –"

Henri had to laugh at the thought, although the two Irishmen did not.

"He's not funny, Riel," Fitzgerald said. "He's a Napoleon."

"*Alors*, I am Marie Antoinette," Henri said. "I think 'e not fight. When army come from Montreal."

"They'll never get here."

"I think yes."

"We'll stop them in the woods," Donovan said. "Shoot 'em like bears. They can't make it. It's thirteen hundred miles to Toronto. And its murder all the way. I wouldn't even reckon I could survey it. Mosquitoes, black flies, swamp. They will never come this far. Impossible."

"My wife, 'er family, zey come 'ere. So will army."

"Then we will kill them," Fitzgerald said. "The French and the Irish, they're the best fighters in the world."

"I do not know," Henri said. "*Ça se voit*."

Sir Garnet Wolseley and his twelve hundred men were already on their way from Toronto to Georgian Bay by the railroad, by steamers along the Great Lakes, by waggons through the forests, and then by foot and portage over river and lake to Fort Garry. Not a man was lost, surprise was complete. Even Henri had not suspected their coming. Then there they were, in scarlet and in line, advancing on the wooden walls of the fort. Louis Riel ran, and Fitzgerald and Donovan. For reasons he did not know, perhaps because of shame, Henri picked up his rifle and fought with two other *métis*. He was not aiming to kill and he killed nobody; but a fusillade ripped through his buckskin jacket, shattering his ribs, shot from the Sneider and Henry rifles that were in the hands of the attackers. And so Henri died in a farce of an action which achieved nothing.

Katie and her child Marie were inconsolable. Her life was Henri, and with his death, she thought she must die too. But she did not. She wept twenty times a day, and she could not sleep for the missing of her man's body not beside her. She took his hunting knife in and out of its sheath, and she even cut her thumb deliberately on the edge of it, practising her killing of herself. But there was always Marie, who loved her and clung to her left ankle, as if she would never let her go. And her mother had to live on because of her, there was no alternative.

Katie found a task, washing for the garrison at Fort Garry, ignoring the scorn of the *métis*. She and her daughter had to live. She might have travelled the hundred miles west across the red plains to see whether Hamish and Hannah would take her back. But she could not. The terrible pride of her family was a hard fist inside her breast. If she went back, she would feel that she had betrayed Henri. And even if he were dead, the memory of him hardened her against her family, which had refused him although she had loved him with all of her nature.

There was always trouble in the west now below the Medicine Line, with the Crows and the Blackfeet and the Sioux moving north to safety across the invisible frontier, where the American cavalry had to rein up and watch their jeering adversaries ride away to safety. But the news was that the line which nobody could see was being at last made clear. From the east, the British were sending Royal Engineers and Canadian surveyors, while the Americans had commissioned their Corps of Engineers and a company of the Twentieth Infantry as an escort. By stone cairn and earth mound and hollow metal pole, a straight line would be delineated across an indifferent continent, and Canada would be defined above its powerful neighbour all the way to the Pacific Ocean.

Angus was in the Canadian party. It was the task of his dreams. Sometimes he would still wake in the night in a quagmire of sweat, struggling against his blanket and shouting, "No, no, I will not leave you, I will not go." His hope had always been to return to his family in proof of himself and in glory. It was worth his desertion of them in their need and his flight and his education in peace and war, his new job of mapping the haphazard soil into lines straighter and more rigid than furrows, into frontiers where the writ of one law ran and not another. Thomas Jefferson had decreed a grid map across the whole of the United States, stamping it in theory like a waffle-iron in three-mile squares to the Rockies. Now Angus Sinclair would draw the border for all time in the north of America, and all who crossed it would know he had done so. It impressed an order on nature, where none was.

The work was fearsome through winter and summer. At first, the Indian axemen worked in waist-deep swamp water, while the surveyors fell through the slime in the bogs up to their shoulders. One previous marker was found six feet deep in the area below the branches of the birch trees and the tamaracks. When the Indian summer was over, the temperature dropped to fifty degrees below zero. They mapped their frontier above the ice and snow, using dog sledges with brush shelters rather than the skin lodges of the hot season. Now mosquitoes and flies did not make their faces swell with their stinging venom, but frostbite and scurvy hurt their complexions. They could not turn the screw on the theodolite without their fingers sticking to the icy metal; ripping their prints free left blood behind, which froze at once. If an eyelid touched their telescopes, it held and had to be eased loose, leaving the lashes to fringe the eyepiece. But they drove the line on, by stake and chain and grit.

By spring, they had reached the Red River, by summer they were in the plains. Already they met the bleaching bones of the lower buffalo herds, hunted to near extinction, their old wallows stinking with their rotting hides. When the sun was high and burned away the clouds of flies, it was too hot to work at surveying because the air wavered and danced as it rose from the baking ground. And it was almost the fall again before they reached the highest plains near the Dakotas, and there it was that Angus learned of the two parts of his separated family, Katie and Marie at the fort, Hamish and Hannah and Bain still trying to plough the dry grasses.

On his scarecrow horse, ravaged by worm and bite, Angus found his sister in her cabin by the fort. She could not believe her eyes and wept with joy, pressing Marie into his arms, saying, "Uncle Angus, uncle, Marie! I said he would come, I said he would come." And Angus heard of the death of Henri, and he told of his own work in the Civil War and now on the laying of the Medicine Line, and then he asked Katie the hardest question of them all, knowing her answer, as she was also a Sinclair. But then he was a Sinclair too, and he was returning where he could never go again.

"I am off to see Hamish and Hannah and Bain," he said. "You must come, too, with Marie."

"I cannot. Never." Katie's eyes could not look at Angus, but they flickered in summer lightning. "They hated Henri. They drove me out. They said I must never come back."

"They did that to me," Angus said. "I deserted them, when they needed me. But God knows, Katie, they are our mother and father. We cannot change that."

"They drove us out."

"We will return."

"Never."

"That is what they say. Never. And if all we can say is never, we can never see each other again."

"Then we never can."

"The heart of a woman –" Angus said. "Hannah always said it was soft. But it is flint – or that new steel they make. You cannot forgive."

"I can. It is them. They cannot forgive."

"How do we know until we try them?"

After a night and a day of argument and fears, Angus persuaded Katie to come with him on a new pony he bought for her. It was this gift, perhaps, that persuaded her. Leaving him to hold Marie beside his lean horse, she galloped off across the red grasses, astride in her leather trousers and short skirt. Angus laughed. He had worked so much with the Indians now that he had come to admire the boldness and the freedom of their women, while the soft plump whiteness of the American city *belles* made him shiver with a slight repulsion. He saw why Henri had loved his sister, and he was proud of her.

As they approached the cabin in its bottom, the earth heaved and moved. On the grasses and the stubble of the crops, ten thousand thousand things with scales crawled and shook and beat their wings. The horse and the pony shuddered as their hoofs crunched the swarm of the insects. The locusts had descended to devastate the land.

"My God," Angus said to Katie, "our family – they never deserve it. Why does the Good Lord give them more than they can bear?"

They found Hamish and Hannah inside a barricaded post with planks nailed across the hide door. Perhaps it was the plague of insects, perhaps it was the fear of dying alone, perhaps it was the true love of their children, but they fell in each other's arms and spoke as if nothing had been said, there was nothing to forgive. Bain was away, looking for an exterminator for the locusts, but there was none, or none yet, only the news of some strange fence of wire that might keep out the buffalo from the crops, if there were any buffalo or crops left after the hunters and the locusts had had their fill. But that was forgotten. Now was the reunion and the coming together of people, who believed that they had parted for ever. The hard words were blown away like the dust on the plains, the streams of feeling flowed again in the spring thaw. Even the shy small Marie put her hand in her grandmother's as if she had always known her, always expected her to be there. In the trust of little children, Angus thought, we forgive all.

"You will not stay here now," Angus said. "You will move again."

"We have moved and moved," Hamish said. "We will not move again."

"But the locusts – the hoppers as they say across the Line –"

"They will not come every year."

"But if they do – and how will you live till then –"

"Hunting and trapping. There are still buffalo, very few – and wolfskins – and we will bide here."

Angus knew his old father was not to be changed. Too many calamities had at last fixed him where he had landed. Even the tumbleweed, blowing in the wind from thousands of miles across the dry plains, snagged in a bush and sent down its dry roots. Hannah was playing with Marie now, a game that Angus hardly remembered. Perhaps they used to play it with crabs on the beach, and now Hannah had crooked her old hand into the shape of a crab, and her fingers were crawling up the smock of little Marie, who was giggling with glee. And Hannah chanted.

> Tip tap taisie,
> The tide's comin' in –
> If you run a mile awa'
> The tide will take you in.

And as Marie squirmed away, her grandmother enfolded her in her arms and took her in. Then her old fingers were rain on Marie's hair, pattering down and combing it with her nails:

> Rainy rainy rattle stones
> Dinna rain on me
> Rain on Hamish Jamie
> Far over the sea –

Katie was laughing now, and she squatted by her mother, and she said, "I remember them. The old games you used to play with me."

"She's a darling," Hannah said. "Beautiful. You might have taken her to me before."

"It was because –" Katie caught her tongue, but decided to go on to the end. "I thought you would not want us. You would not want ever to see me again."

Hannah was indignant. "I never said the like. Not see my own daughter! I never said it. And this wee darling – Hamish! Tell her."

And Hamish looked at Hannah, and he knew it was no use telling her the truth of what she had said when Katie had run away with Henri Chatillon. She no longer believed she had said it and so she had not said it. If she believed she could never have banished her daughter for ever – for what mother could say that? – then she had never said such a thing. Anyway, at Hannah's age, it was useless telling her that she was wrong, or ever had been. She had the perfect gift of Scot's righteousness. However many times she changed her mind, she had only ever wanted to be steadfast, and that was the way that God approved. She was sure of Him, and so she was always right and always consistent.

"We were ever wishing to see you again. And Angus," Hamish added. "And now you are here, this is a day of rejoicing. And when Bain is home, we will have a feast of it though it only be pemmican and salt tongue and oatcake. And we will have the dancing and the singing – my fine daughter, my clever son, who have been away from us a sore while."

19

ALIEN LANDS

Advancing through the bush against King Koffee was not the sort of operation that Hamish Jamie had ever planned before. Sir Garnet Wolseley was an organiser above all. You could see that in his expedition to the Red River. To him, beating the Ashantis was another kind of routine, this time adapted for the jungle. His three thousand soldiers, spearheaded by the Highland Black Watch and the Royal Welch Fusiliers and the Rifle Brigade and Marines from the Naval Brigade would need three times that number of native carriers. Mules could not pass through the trees and the undergrowth. They were opposed by fifty thousand savages – or so Wolseley thought them – accustomed to draping the entrails of their mutilated prisoners round their ritual slaughterhouses in Kumasi. In his message to his troops, the commander had no doubt about victory against the odds. Technology and discipline would defeat raw courage and numbers.

> Each soldier must remember that, with his breech loader, he is equal to at least twenty Ashantis, wretchedly armed as they are with old flint muskets, firing slugs or pieces of stone, that do not hurt badly at more than forty or fifty yards range. They have neither guns nor rockets, and have a superstitious dread of those used by us.

Wolseley even had one of the new Gatling guns with him, the first of the machine guns, yet its murderous volleys would not be too effective as nobody could see more than a few yards ahead or sideways in the jungle. The real secret weapon was the superiority of the European over the African.

> A steady advance or a charge made with determination always means the retreat of the enemy. English soldiers and sailors are accustomed to fight against great odds in all parts of the world. It is scarcely necessary to remind them that when, in our battles beyond the Prah,

they find themselves surrounded on all sides by hordes of howling enemies, they must rely upon their own British courage and discipline. Be cool, fire low, and charge home.

That was the theory of it. The fact of it for Hamish Jamie was that he had been seconded to the expedition because of his experience in Abyssinia, as though Africa was one big similar continent, as far as the War Office was concerned. Actually, the bearers from the coast tribes whom the Ashantis regularly killed and enslaved, ran away as soon as they were paid or approached the enemy. Although the Royal Engineers were hacking a road of sorts towards Kumasi, the advancing troops had to slash their path through the bush and the creepers with swords and bayonets, if they could not follow the narrow ruts which ran between the hidden villages. It was an eerie business. From the tangled forest, the drums throbbed like a wound in the head and horns wailed as banshees and the thunder of the Ashanti muskets full of bad powder and chipped slugs cut swathes of twigs and leaves from the jungle canopy, a green rain on the advancing Highlanders. The whole terrain was a perfect ambush. On the sudden, these would be an onrush of black bodies, a pell-mell waving of spears, then up would go the line of Sneiders and Enfields, and a gust of lead would drop the Ashanti warriors, who would fall back into the recesses of the forest, leaving a few bodies and broken muskets behind. There would be a silence for a moment, then the bugles of the regiments would sound their whereabouts in brazen notes to each other, while the secret Ashantis would signal in bird-calls, followed by war-cries and whooping. Then hundreds of invisible voices would break into a chant that stopped the blood to hear. For even more than the bagpipes of the Black Watch, it foretold certain death.

The final battle took place before Kumasi, and Colonel McLeod led the Highlanders in short charge after charge, once rockets and canister shot and shell had cleared the way. Finally, the Ashantis fled, even their captains in their rams' horn helmets and plumes of eagle feathers. The wooden lodges of the Asantehene, called King Koffee, reeked of rotten flesh. Ancestral drums were hung with skulls and smeared with blood. Bodies were impaled on stakes or flayed or burned. Even the golden stool of the Asantehene was reddened with sacrifices. Wolseley was outraged. He seemed to have fallen upon the abomination and desolation of the Old Testament, and like a prophet, he ordered the city to be put to the cleansing flame. "*All ranks felt they had done a brilliant day's work,*" he wrote in his dispatch, "*and for our victory I am sure many fervent thanks went up to God that night.*"

Hamish Jamie thought that only God knew why they were in the

African jungle at all. It could not be of use to anybody except the Ashantis. As they fell back along the rough road they had cut to Kumasi and over the pontoon bridges across the rivers, they burned every village as an example. But it was all useless. The trees and the creepers, the thorns and the spines, encroached everywhere and overwhelmed them. They were irrelevant, a column of ants on an unnecessary continent. They proved nothing at all to the jungle set about them.

Hamish Jamie had soldiered for twenty-five years. He knew the cause of it, but not the reason why. Once he had believed that the orders which sent him to India and China and Canada and Abyssinia and West Africa had a sense, a policy behind them. But he did not think that now. He was helping in the slow spread of the red colour across the map of the world, which he had seen in his first school in Scotland, when the dominie had showed it to him. But this urge to kick and lunge into new territories seemed as aimless as the big centipede, which Hamish Jamie had turned on its back in his tent in the camp outside Cape Grant Castle, where he sat, waiting to organise the embarkation for England and a review by the little Queen at Windsor Castle. He had pinned the insect – nearly a foot long – by the point of his sword, and he watched its tiny legs strike out in a flurry of prickles, in a desperate greed for life. All that frenzy of action achieving nothing.

"Poor wee beastie," Hamish Jamie said and put his boot on the struggle of the centipede. If only it were that easy to end the fits and starts of the British Empire.

Lila only heard of Hamish Jamie now through her employers, Iain and Anna at Annandale. He never wrote to her, he had abandoned her to his brother's care. She had sunk from being a sort of poor relation into the position of a servant and an embarrassment. For the society of Simla had spread out to the Sinclair farm in the nearby glen. Where there had been woods and a few fields reaching down the slopes to a rustic valley, there were now formal gardens and a flat playground for polo and cricket matches, and a race course. Anna had told Iain not to stand out against the trend. Frankly, selling a few plots of land was worth ten years of crops of potatoes or indigo. And there was the pressure from Simla, both official and social. It was impossible to resist, with *aides-de-camp* in white uniforms calling from the viceroy himself, not to mention the imperatives delivered like broadsides from Mrs Dalgety and her kind, or rather unkind.

There was also a tacit understanding in a society where straight dealing would have been bad manners, and where the unspoken was an agreement. If some land was yielded at a reasonable price, then Iain's humble origins and the presence of his half-caste nephew and niece in his house would be ignored and the Sinclairs received into Simla society – to a degree. It was not that she cared, Anna insisted to Iain – and of course he did not care. But their four children had to go to good schools and make their own way in the world as it was. Hamilton and Hamish Macmahon, Margaret and May, they would not suffer for the sins of their parents or their uncle. It would not be fair on them. They were born innocent, not condemned.

So in the name of his children, Iain made a truce with the world as it was in India. It was true that the way for a boy to rise was through government service. And as for the girls, if they were to meet the right sort of young men . . . It was not that Anna had reverted to the position or the caste, from which she had rebelled when she became a pioneer nurse and met Iain in Nainital. It was that she was the best of mothers, and she wanted with a fierce and possessive pride the best for her children, particularly for the two boys she adored. If Iain sometimes thought of his own hard rearing, he did not mean to inflict that pain on his children, and he never ceased to bless the day of his marriage to Anna, who had brought him all he wanted – and if a little was unwanted such as having to be polite to the ladies of Simla, this was a small price to pay for the rest of it.

When they were small, Anna's four children had loved Lila as their *ayah* and second mother, and they had played with her children, Seaforth and Peg, with that blindness to any variation which most of the little ones have. If the two groups of children slept in different quarters or dressed in other clothes, their games and frolics were much the same in the flowering woods or on the bright snows. But this acceptance was changing now that Hamilton and Hamish Macmahon were youths and trying to grow moustaches, while Margaret and May were always trying to make their mother take them to the haberdashers in Simla for new dress materials and on to Jacob's shop, where he retailed wonders of turquoise and amber necklaces, green jade bangles and peacock-blue draperies, bought from the caravans which still crossed the passes of the Himalayas on the old trade routes to the far east.

In the shyness and doubt of growing up, Hamilton and Hamish Macmahon now avoided Seaforth and were relieved when he went to the missionary school in Simla, reserved for native Indians. Seaforth also began to avoid them, not from delicacy, but from sullenness. His sister Peg remained closer to Margaret and May, but she began to slip into the position of her mother, becoming a ladies' maid in their play and helping them to dress up in their new finery for the fêtes at

Annandale, where Peg was never asked and would not be. As for Lila, she knew that she would lose the love of Anna's children as they aged and needed her no more, and she fought to keep the bitterness of his exclusion from Seaforth and the awareness of a false inferiority from Peg. But Hamish Jamie never came back to protect her. She was becoming an alien in her own land, which was not this land of the hill people with their flat dark faces and strange dialect and stranger ways.

Lila also fought the pain when it came, because she would not admit to it. Seaforth and Peg had need of her. They could not live without her. She no longer trusted the members of the family of the father of her children. They did not seem to have the natural love of their own blood. The divisions put upon India had divided the human heart. Family was put asunder from family, kin set against kin, and it was called the Raj. So Lila waited for Mary to visit again, before she could confess to the disease that was wasting her, and when Anna said to her, "Lila, how good you look, so thin and majestic, I wish I could look like that too, but I am becoming a bit of a matron," Lila only said, "I eat less. I do not need it."

Yet when Mary did come at last to tell them all that she hoped to go back to London and study there to be a doctor, for Miss Nightingale had written to her that soon this would be possible, even in London, Lila waited for a week until the evening before Mary left to ask her to examine her. And Mary came to her room and helped her to unwind her *sari* and felt her with cold fingers and asked many questions and then helped her to dress again.

"Do you wish the truth, Lila?"

"I do."

"There is nothing that I may do. It is a wasting disease. It is not consumption, for that is in the lungs, and the air of these mountains would help it. It is the wasting disease that eats you from within, and there is no cure for it. I could say milk, eggs, meat – but you do not wish for food."

"I do not."

"But you do not wish to die?"

"I must live. For Peg and Seaforth. When Hamish Jamie come and take them –" Looking at Mary hanging her head, "He not come."

"His duty keeps him in Africa. He is a specialist now. In the Commissariat, in the military train. There is trouble now in the South. He must go there. It is his duty."

"His duty? And me. And Seaforth and Peg."

"That is his duty too. But it is not what he thinks. Lila, I tell you –" Looking at Lila with her blue stare, "I swear that I will see that

Seaforth and Peg are reared well. They will be a credit to you and their father. I swear that."

"But you not can. You are single woman. No family."

Mary smiled so quickly that it seemed a tremor on her face.

"I would rather be a single woman and spin my own yarn. Trust me. Though you have no reason. Trust me over your children."

Lila had no one else to trust. For her own people would never have her back nor her children. So she made a belief of necessity.

"I trust you," she said, and she believed that she meant her words.

Mary rose to her feet. "I will tell Iain and Anna that you are ill. You will do little. Look after Seaforth and Peg while you can. And I will arrange for their future care. Perhaps, Lila, perhaps Seaforth would wish to become a doctor, as I will be. Will you ask him? I will help him."

"I must ask him."

"And Lila –" Mary stooped and kissed Lila's cheek. For the first and last time, Lila put out her arms and held Hamish Jamie's sister by the neck with hands that trembled. "And, Lila – trust me. The children will do well."

"Why *you* do this for me?"

"I am a woman too." Mary took Lila's arms off her, laid them by Lila's side and moved away to the door. "And I am alone. In a world of men, I am a stranger. In a world of married folk – and mothers – I am single. And I am in India, not in my home. Do you not think, Lila, I may also feel apart? And not wanted. And out of place. As you are."

Hamish Jamie did not know what to write to Anna after the disaster. He had sworn to her to look after his namesake, her son Hamish Macmahon, scarcely twenty, a volunteer from India who was longing to get at the enemy and see his first action. It was not the boy's fault that Lord Chelmsford had left him behind in the camp at Isandhlwana in 1879, where he was surprised by a Zulu *impi* and stabbed to death along with fifteen hundred other men. It was not Hamish Jamie's fault that he was working in the supply lines for the army, as it moved on Zululand. He only reached the scene of the great defeat two days later on the ammunition waggons and he helped to bury the bodies, all disembowelled ritually, their right hands put where their hearts had been. What could he write of that? Senseless murder caused by a bad commander in a war provoked by an ambitious colonial governor, who wanted more and more.

Your son fought bravely to the end, Hamish Jamie wrote. *You can be proud of him. One of the few survivors, a gunner who got away on a horse, tells me Hamish Macmahon was shooting until he went down under a mass of enemies. His death was swift and merciful. He had a Christian burial. I know his last thought was of you.*

As Hamish Jamie penned these false and necessary words, he did not blame himself for the lies, given the real mutilation and the horror, the flies and the mass graves. The boy was dead. He had believed in what his uncle had never believed, glory and honour, a good cause and a just war and a certain victory. That is what his imperial schools in India had taught him.

But it was not like that at all. Yes, a handful of our men had won something back by mowing down a few hundred Zulus at Rorke's Drift in a frontal attack on their earthworks. But the truth was that the troops were so scared they fired at shadows as well as Zulus. At Fort Funk, the artillery fired into its own Royal Engineers and wounded five of them. They would have all been shelled to extinction if a bugle had not sounded the call. And Lord Chelmsford's response was as sickening as the sight of the dead at Isandhlwana. He brought up reinforcements and used the local South African mounted volunteers to search out and destroy all the Zulu kraals and stores of grain. All was looted, every Zulu woman and child turned out to starve on the *veldt*. It was exactly the same tactics as "Butcher" Cumberland had used after defeating the Highlanders at Culloden. It was not war, it was rational destruction by any means.

The final encounter outside King Cetshwayo's capital at Ulundi was surgical slaughter. The massed chest and two horns of the Zulu charge with the stabbing *assegais* were met by a hollow square of redcoats, behind which the Gatling guns and the seven-pounders and the rocket-tubes poured out a heavy annihilation. The Zulus could not get to close quarters because of the weight of fire. The canister tore through them like a harrow through black weeds. The rockets ravaged them with flaming zig-zags. The machine-gun bullets scythed them in swathes and laid them in the dust. And Hamish Jamie, supervising the passing of the ammunition from a chained waggon within the square that spat out lead and steel, again thought of his own Highland people in the past century, as they charged the Hanoverian guns with shield and claymore and were laid low by shot and shell on the moors of Culloden.

But the Sinclairs were not mountain savages now. They were the servants of the new machines of death, which had once divided the clans of Scotland into artificial shires on the English model, and were now dividing the tribes of Africa into provinces and territories and protectorates. It was a civilising mission, to be sure. There was no doubt of it. Hamish Jamie himself was educated now – a major and a

162

quartermaster, a man of dignity with a pension to come, able to write in English and think with the method and the order of Englishmen. And yet he was helping them at their greedy game of covering more of the globe with plots and patches of red. And Hamish Macmahon was dead of their grabbing, and his uncle had never finished that letter back to his mother Anna, trying to tell her that her son had died for something worth his blood sacrifice.

After another week, Hamish Jamie finished his letter to India:

We have won a famous victory and the Zulus are broken. They are a fine and fierce people, but they cannot stand our guns. As they advance at the run, they wave their painted, pointed long shields – black with white spots, white with red spots – white feathers and cow-tails and monkey-skins shake on their heads and shoulders and legs. It is like the waving of our kilts and bonnets, and I am sad to see it fall down. Hamish Macmahon died bravely for his Queen and Her Empire, and I weep with you for him – and for all the brave men who have fallen here. I am glad Hamilton means to be a naval engineer. We must have no more soldiers in our family. Tell Lila that Seaforth must not enlist. He is better as a clerk than a sergeant or a major like me. Better a live babu than a dead Zulu – for we are all somebody's son.

My love to you all.
HAMISH JAMIE

THE GREAT MOTHER

Before the Sioux fled to safety above the Medicine Line, they had their revenge, as the Zulus had before their breaking on steel and lead in South Africa. At the Little Big Horn, the Sioux wiped out Custer's men and seized their carbines and rifles and moved north, a whole Indian nation, driving the buffalo herds ahead of them with the American army and cavalry in pursuit, hardly believing in their defeat by mounted savages, who had taken the gun and the horse from them and now used bullet and hoof to halt their incessant advance. Now the Indians were pouring over the border, Ogdalas and Hunkpapas, Minnecoujous and Sans Arcs, Two Kettles and Tetons under Sitting Bull, but Crazy Horse stayed on with his hostiles in the Powder River country and the Black Hills of Dakota. He would not trust in a Medicine Line nor leave his hunting country.

Hamish and Hannah, Bain and Katie feared for their lives on the land by the river bottom. They could hardly believe the courage of the Mounties. It quite restored their faith in a scarlet jacket and a white helmet, even if they were worn by an Irishman, the tough and grizzled Walsh who built a log stockade in his own name with a powder magazine and blacksmith's forge, stables and bakery and quartermaster's store in the valley before the plains met the hills, bristling with jack-pine. Outside it, three hundred families of *métis* and Indians and a few Macleods lived in their log cabins and boasted a hotel as well as a pool hall and a restaurant and a barber's shop. This was civilisation, and the visiting Sinclairs riding in from their farm were right glad of it. And they watched with wonder and admiration as Walsh went out with his dozen men to settle the affairs of thousands of fleeing Indians, armed and angry, bluffing them into obeying the law that was so hardly there at all.

"I do not ken how you do it," Hamish told him over the long pipe they were sharing at Fort Walsh. Some of the Indian customs passed on. They were companionable. Smoking cheroots apart was not the same as drawing on a tobacco stem together.

"No more do I," Walsh said. "To tell you the truth of it —"

"What more is there to tell?"

"When I rode in to Wood Mountain, there were three thousand of them – and some scalps with yellow hair drying over the wood-smoke, maybe Custer himself – I did not reckon we would come out alive. My hair tingled on my head as if it were waiting to be lifted off."

Hamish laughed. He liked Walsh for never taking himself seriously although no man was more braw in all the west.

"They were all there, but not Crazy Horse. There was Spotted Eagle and Little Knife, Long Dog and Black Moon, and their hunting bands, all waiting to fire those fancy Martini-Henrys they took at Big Horn. But they said they had had enough of fighting the war, no food, no peace, no hunting. They wanted to stay in the Great Mother's country above the Medicine Line."

"Great Mother?" Hamish laughed again. "You reckon Queen Victoria would like that?"

"She would like it well," Walsh said. "For that is what she is to all these people in their manner of thinking. And it is the why I am alive. For I say to them, you must follow the law of the Great Mother, and this is the law. You will do no harm to any woman and any child and any man —"

"Thank God for that," Hamish said, sucking on the pipe that he had learned to love, the hot smoke cool in his lungs. "For there are muckle of them and few of us."

"You will steal nothing, not one horse nor one cow. You will not fight with the other Indian tribes, for they also love the Great Mother, and Her law is their law. And you will not hide north of the Medicine Line for the winter, and go south and raid in the Dakotas when it is dry. And you will not hunt beyond the Medicine Line, for the beasts of the Great Mother —"

"And she is the mother of the beasties," Hamish said. "I wish I had known the like in Scotland. The laird said they were his, not Hers."

"The beasts are American beasts. And anyway, all the buffalo are dead here, and you may only hurt their bones. And you will not send guns and bullets to Crazy Horse in the south, for he must fight his own war if he stays there. That is the law of the Great Mother, and you will obey it if you stay in Her land."

"And they obeyed it? How?"

"I do not know," Walsh said. "A dozen of us, and three thousand of them. And all they asked was bullets to hunt the buffalo, for now they could only kill them with lances and ropes. So I gave Jean Louis

Legaré the right to sell them bullets, for they must have the meat if they are to live."

"I do not ken," Hamish said. "They have the power to kill us all."

"I tell you," Walsh said. "If they believe a man will keep the faith, they will keep the faith. And they love this land, and they fear we will take this land from them. As we will, but not all of it."

"But enough for ourselves," Hamish said.

"But how many of ourselves will there be? Too many."

Crazy Horse did not cross the safety of the Medicine Line. He was told that he would be given the land of the Powder River country, and he believed in the word of General Crook. When he rode in with his eight hundred braves to give up his rifles, they wore paint and feathers and sang their songs of war. But it was all lies, the usual lies, with the broken promises whatever the pieces of paper said that the chiefs did not understand. And the Powder River was taken away and the Black Hills, and Crazy Horse brooded in his despair. He even offered to lend his warriors to fight against the last of the Nez Percés on their long flight east to the Medicine Line. But his word that he would fight till the Indian fighters were killed was said to be that he would fight until all the whites were killed. It was a time when only the reverse was true. So when he was brought in to be jailed, he fought, and a soldier of no repute stabbed him to death with a bayonet. And so the pride of the Sioux nation died and his followers were too broken and too jealous of him to follow his spirit, and the Indians of the plains remained humbly on their reservations on rations from the government that sometimes came and sometimes did not.

Angus was working on a railroad survey which would bring the iron tracks across the prairie to the west, and he asked one of his Sioux axemen why the warriors were not filling them with arrows and cutting their bodies into strips to mark out their boundaries. The Sioux told him about crabs, fresh water crabs. There was this Indian, the Sioux said, and this white man, and both had a pail of crabs. And as they walked along, the white man's crabs were always leaping out of his pail, while the Indian's crabs were quiet as could be. So the white man asked why the Indian's crabs were so damn quiet. And the Indian said: "They are Indian crabs. When one big one rise to top, all the other crabs, they pull him down."

North of the Medicine Line, Bain and Hamish were working to make a farm too soon on the high plains. There was no question but that Bain had more than horse sense in him, if horses could be said to have any sense at all, doing all they did for men. He heard of the Glidden wire, and he had the first rolls of it brought up by rail and steam and cart to Fort Walsh, and when the men were unloading it, why, François Dubois near ripped off his leg and lost a boot in its spikes, but on the day of the unrolling, most of the people of Fort Walsh came out to see the sight. And Bain and Hamish had set up the fence posts over a mile round the corner of their land, and they brought out the coils of barbed wire on the Red River waggon, and they put the end of the wire to the first post, and they drove on the ponies and the wire unrolled its spiky length behind them. And every two hundred feet, they stopped the waggon and they braced the wire to the posts. And when they came to the end of the spool, why, they jacked up the hind wheel of the waggon and wound the wire round the hub, and they turned the wheel until the wire was taut and trim. Then they hammered the wire to the posts by staples, and so the spiny barrier was put across the plains that tore into the hides of cattle and buffalo, men and horses, until they cursed the fierce barbs of the iron thing that kept living things in and living things out.

It was a sort of progress, and Bain believed in a sort of progress. When the wind began to blow away the thin soil of the prairies, he made his own invention, as if it had never been made before. It was a waterwheel with little dangling buckets. And if he harnessed a mule to the wheel, and it plodded round in circles several hundred times in a day, a rachet and a crank turned the great wooden wheel with the buckets upon it, and muddy water would be drawn out of the creek from the river, and some of it would fall into the crumbling ditches dug into the ground, and a little of the wetness would creep on to the edge of the fields, most of it lost on the way to the arid soil and the dry air. There was talk of sinking wells to find the water underground, and of making windmills to draw it up by the power of the breeze, but this was only talk, and Bain did not have the knowledge or the use of it.

Katie became a field-hand and a hand about the house. Hannah's joints were locking now. She would have to rise three times in the night, crawling out of bed, then levering herself upright, then cracking the bones of her knees and elbows loose, because if she set in one place too long, she set. Katie massaged her with bear's grease and put on hot herb poultices in wet bags to draw out the swelling and the pain, but it was no use. The knuckles of the bones came together again. Maybe the gristle between them was plumb wearing away, like living did to folks in little dribs and dabs. Working the land certain wore a woman away, the bending and the stooping, the weeding and the cropping, the threshing and the binding. The men couldn't do it alone, Hamish was too old for it, worse bent than a scrub-pine in the wind, and Bain was as dogged as an ox, but even he had a limit to him, and by the evening he plodded so slow anyone could see he was tuckered and fit to die.

The nights were the worst for Katie, when she thought of Henri and their love-making, and her skin was on fire and she felt prickly and scratchy with desire, and she had to hold her daughter to her, squeeze the breath out of her for the want of her man in her arms. There were other men at Fort Walsh, but none of them was a patch on Henri Chatillon, none with his grace and his smile and his holding of a woman, his making her feel that she was the only woman. There would be none other – even if there was.

"I will not settle for less," she was always telling Hannah, when she was asked to the dances at the Fort and did not go. "There was only the one of him."

The talk of the railroad was true talk. The Canadian Pacific was building west, and it might come to Fort Walsh. If it did, there would be a city there below the hills. If it did not, there would be a wilderness again. The problem of the tracks coming at all was the gradient of the hills and the swamp by Battle Creek, which was full of dead horses and buffalo and brought the fever and the typhoid down in the water, so it had to be boiled to be fit for drinking. And the Mounties were needed now to look after the railroad workers in their brawling camps, always fighting over the whiskey and the Indian women, and the Sioux and the Hunkpapas and the Tetons were moving back over the Medicine Line because the hunting was gone. There was talk of the Fort being pulled down, and one day it was true. All the old logs and posts and even the nails were hauled to Maple Creek and Medicine Hat to build stations for the railroad there. And the Mounties were to have a new fort at Pile O'Bones Creek on the main railroad line, and maybe there would be a city there to be called Regina, after the Great Mother Herself.

Angus came to visit at the valley bottom. Dust devils were swirling and scampering over the ploughed fields in little twists and capers. One of them struck Angus on his pony, and he coughed and spluttered and was nearly thrown as his mount snorted and reared and shook its head to clear the blinding dirt from its eyes. "Whoa, there!" Angus soothed the pony and patted its neck and took it on towards the low-lying cabin with its few shade-trees planted beside it to give a relief from the scoured plain. Even the barbed-wire fence had the look of a dried hedge, with the yellow weeds and humps of blown grass hanging on its prongs. This was no country to live, Angus reckoned. But it never was, wherever the Sinclairs wandered.

"I can do nothing about it," he told his father and mother. "I survey the routes the reconnaissance parties choose. And they choose the easiest way and the way the law says. If we can buy the land – and that isn't the problem in this wilderness – then we take the way that is firmest and has the least gradients and curves. Do you know what a cutting costs through granite? Or a tunnel? We've had parties in the Rockies and the Selkirks scouting for six years, and there have been hundreds of routes suggested. And it's not our final choice. Someone up there decides it, and that's that. And it's no good me crying, we've got to get the railroad to Fort Walsh because my mother and father, they live near there, and they want a town there. Think of the land values. The railroad bosses just say, what's the cheapest way, and what's the easiest way, and what's the best way for the fewest dollars. And in quick time."

"But we came here," Hamish said. "And as we are here, the rail must come."

"You go where the railroad goes," Angus said. "In Ohio, I tell you, there are a thousand ghost towns. And already over the American west. All because the railroad went to some other place. And here – the railroad won't come here now. It's too late. But it is expanding. Do you know the pace we lay the tracks? One day, in just one day, we laid six-and-a-half miles. That was sixteen thousand ties, more than two thousand lengths of rail and sixty thousand spikes hammered home. Call that track laying! I call it a miracle."

"Hush you," Hannah said. "Miracles are God's work. They are not the work of men who are playing with His work."

"But, Mother, you may go on the railroad where you wish. All the way to the Pacific Ocean, when we drive in the last spike."

"And will that be soon?" Katie asked.

"In two years. And then the one shore will reach the other shore, and we will have crossed a continent."

"We have crossed seas," Bain said. "And forests and plains. And the devil a bit of good it did us."

"Hush," Hannah said. "The Lord is with us."

"Some of the way," Bain said. "So we will be left in a backwater, Angus."

"Aye. There is no help for it."

"And what is the advice of the great engineer?" Bain could hear the sneer in his voice, but he could not help it. His young brother was right, he was the future, and Bain was getting nothing from being a slave to the dry land.

"Where the railroad goes, the dollars will go. Already the land near it increases in value – a hundred times if there will be a depot there. They are already building out through the Rockies and we will meet in two years. The opportunity –"

169

"That word of yours," Hamish said. "That word that was taking you from us."

"The opportunity is where the railroad goes. Father – Mother – and Katie – go west to the ocean. To Vancouver and Victoria. The land there is like Scotland. Hills and trees and the sea. It is a new Scotland. And there is not only the land, there is all the trade of the east. Go there."

"And who will pay?" Bain asked in bitterness. "Our land is here. You did not ask me."

"Because your land is here, brother," Angus said. "Because you always said you would bide with it. But for old folk – for a young mother like Katie – it is too hard here, too lonely. As an engineer on the railroad, I have a right to a plot of land. And I am taking it up in Columbia, in British Columbia, near the sea and the end of the line, where there will be a great city by Vancouver Sound."

"That is your land," Hamish said. "It is not our land."

"Honour thy father and thy mother," Angus said. "And shall I not honour you in your old age – and Katie, until she shall find another husband again?"

"That I never will," Katie said.

"There is another sort of man in Vancouver," Angus said. "With a head on him. Brains. Never in great supply near this creek."

"None of that," Bain said. "Brains are best in haggis or black pudding. You'll be taking the old folk and Katie and leave me alone here on the farm."

"Blowing away in the wind," Angus said. "It is already. You come too, Bain. You are wanted."

"I will bide. This is mine. I will find a woman. We will have sons. We will have a ranch here, a kingdom. Wheat and cattle."

"I will not have the family break again," Hannah said. "Now we have our Katie back."

"There is the railroad," Angus said. "To visit each other – over the Rockies – it will be a day and a night. It is not a season in a covered waggon. It is comfort in a coach."

"We will go," Katie said. "I want the best for Marie. A school. And her learning the piano and the violin."

"What nonsense," Hannah said. "As if the harmonium was not good enough for her!"

"She shall not always play church music," Katie said. "But I will go with you, Angus. And Hannah and Hamish will come, will you not?"

"I do not . . ." Hamish said and fell silent.

"The sea air, they say," Angus said, "is good for the bones. In places in Europe – they call them spas – they put old ladies in brine baths, and they come out skipping like lambs –"

"Get away with you," Hannah said, striking Angus's shoulder with her knuckle to show how pleased she was.

"And there are so many salmon in the river, a man has to put a fly through a bent pin, and he has a monster in his lap –"

"Who can hold a word of it?" Hamish said, smiling.

"Then it is a fact," Angus said. "In two years, when the last spike is driven, you will be taking the railroad to the Pacific, and I will see to it, a frame house is already waiting for you there."

"And if you have a bride –" Katie said.

"She will join us all." And seeing the glower on his brother's face, Angus added, "And Bain shall come every Christmas with his bonny family."

"You are like the dark man himself on Hogmanay," Bain said. "You come with muckle blessings. And they are all smoke up the chimney."

"Steam," Angus said. "From the railroad. It will take us anywhere it goes."

It was at St Thomas's Hospital where the new school for nurses was established that Mary Sinclair met Harry Lamb. She had a double reason to be there. She had to learn more herself and to teach about tropical diseases, for Miss Nightingale had recommended her most highly. And she had to arrange for the entrance of Seaforth Sinclair to the medical school, what with his mother Lila dead now, and her promise, and the need for him to leave Annandale and India as well, and for his own good.

The voyage home was shorter, but hotter, sweltering in the Red Sea on the steamship and passing through the new canal at Suez. There were the usual problems with Seaforth's accommodation, having to put him in a class below hers, and having to eat apart. He was as tall as any Sinclair, and his father's bones already made hollows in his dark cheeks, and the blue eyes under the jet hair were startling in their contrast and their contact with any inquiry. His politeness was dangerous. He seemed aware of living on a sabre's edge, watching for any slight so that he could strike back with an insidious flick. He put no one at their ease, for he was uneasy in his own skin. If he loved anyone, he loved Mary, and even she found him too self-aware for comfort.

"I was a poor maid," she told Seaforth in the hansom cab on their way to St Thomas's. "I was working for a duke with the manners of a coal-heaver, when Miss Nightingale gave me my chance. Don't think the English won't take every chance they can to patronise you and make you feel the size of a wee mouse. It is a trick of theirs. A trick of power. Making us feel the lower when we are not. We do their work and we are not thanked for it."

Seaforth smiled, his lips a black curve in the grey London light.

"Do not worry, Aunt Mary. You know I do not say what I feel. I know of the hardships of the Sinclairs. You are always telling me – the taking of the land, the clearing you away, the coming to India, the taking of our land –" He looked out at the carved and streaked stone of the newly-built Mother of Parliaments, as they rolled over Westminster Bridge to the hospital. "Losing your land, you take another's land. Or your brother does."

"And we take you back to learn here," Mary said. "You will be a doctor greater than Louis Pasteur. You will cure wounds, or heal the plagues –"

"Is that what I will learn here?" Through the side window of the cab, Seaforth could now look over the parapet of the bridge towards the five projecting little towers of St Thomas's Hospital on the far Thames bank. "Or will I learn how to take back our land and clear you once more?"

"You must not think like that, Seaforth. You must not speak like that. We are in London now."

"Naturally I will not," Seaforth said. "But you always told me to tell the truth, Aunt Mary. So only to you –" They had crossed the bridge and were turning towards the gates to the hospital. Through the rear window of the cab, they could hear Big Ben strike the hour of eleven as a repeated summons to the future. "I will not say or do anything to disturb. You know me."

"I do, Seaforth. And I worry. You are discreet. But inside you, I see sometimes – a new Mutiny."

Seaforth laughed.

"We must cure bodies first," he said. "Then we can change minds."

Too clever by half, Seaforth was; but that was not what Mary said when she recommended him for the medical school to Harry Lamb. She stressed the need for Indian doctors in India – the trust that the people would have in somebody more of their own kind. She also spoke of Seaforth's brilliance at his school in Simla, and she did not deny that she was his aunt. As for Doctor Lamb with his mop of white curls, he was more humane than his biblical namesake, and as fearless. He would lie down beside any British lion in perfect confidence that he would achieve his own soft purpose by his woolly persuasion.

"Miss Nightingale has spoken to me of you, Miss Sinclair. Of all the reports she receives from India, she praises yours the most – on the *zenana* mothers, on the military hospitals, on the famine in the

Punjab. Her regard for you is great enough to give you what you want. We will admit Seaforth Sinclair into the medical school, and his costs will be defrayed by one of those charitable foundations which are the hidden hand of mercy here to the unfortunate. As for you, you will see what we can do for training nurses now, and you will tell them what they can do in healing the diseases of the hot countries. And one more thing –"

"You are giving me too many things –"

"A personal application – or rather, an appreciation –"

"From you yourself, Doctor Lamb?"

"Admiration, really. Would you, Miss Sinclair, allow me to escort you to the opera? *Così fan tutte*, I believe, and cosy it will be. Some Italian warblers are gracing our shores and our ears. My sister will act as a chaperone."

Mary laughed and laughed. And when she had finished wiping her eyes, she said, "Do you ken, the last time I went to the theatre here, it was at the Seven Dials. It was a ballad-singer. He told the sad tale of a father who murdered his wee boy. My brother Iain was off to the Crimea, where he met Miss Nightingale at Scutari – lying down with a hole in him. I still have the ballad sheet – that poor dead wee boy."

"And you have never married?"

"I said to Miss Nightingale –"

"She said you had said. But she loses many nurses to matrimony."

"A word is a word."

"To you. Not to all. You do not regret – a boy not born to you –"

Mary was suddenly angry. "You are a prying man, Doctor Lamb. And who gave you the right? I am not under your medical examination."

"Forgive me, Miss Sinclair. Let me make amends at the opera."

"I have quite enough of children, and I prefer they belong to others. Seaforth, he is one of them. And why should I add to the many mouths of this world?"

"You should not. I only ask for your company with my sister as a chaperone."

Mary shook her head. "And if you think in India we have chaperones?" She stood up and looked down at the small and fleecy Doctor Lamb, smiling up at her in delight at her domination. "I have no need of your sister to protect me from *you*. I have been protecting myself a wee while the now. Unless, of course" – Mary towered over the shrinking doctor behind his desk – "you need your sister to protect you from me."

It was Doctor Lamb's turn to laugh.

"Miss Nightingale said you were a bold woman – but I did not know how bold."

"So you will not take me to the opera?"

"Twice over, if I may." Doctor Lamb now rose. His curly head only reached to Mary's shoulder, but his eyes were quick with sympathy and intelligence. "I don't need protection from you, Miss Sinclair. Only your company to shepherd me."

Mary was amused by the opera, although she did not understand a word of it, and she found women dressed as men getting away with it although they sang soprano as silly as fat tenors pretending to be lissom lovers. "To tell you the truth," she told Doctor Lamb, "it's all a great fuss over nothing, and I've heard linnets sing as sweet at no cost at all and hardly the weight of those warblers, as you call them."

That sort of talk made Doctor Lamb more attached to Mary. She could see that he might make a proposal to her, but he was so settled in his ways with his sister as his housekeeper, and how would she let another woman in the house to run the set affairs of Welbeck Street? And there were other troubles. Mary did not love Harry Lamb, as she called him now, although she liked him better than any man she had ever met. And she was past the age of having her own children. And surely that was the point of marrying, to create life and populate the earth, as if there were not enough people on it, anyway. Of course, there would be the comfort of him, and in their old age, the caring for each other, but there was so much to do in India, and the work was never done, as Miss Nightingale always said and did.

So when Harry Lamb managed to pop the question without popping all the buttons of his yellow waistcoat, on their evening at Nicols's new Café Royal, where the crown on the N stood for Napoleon and not for the proprietor, Mary had considered her answer. But all the same, she found herself blushing even redder than the two dabs of rouge she had put on her cheeks for the first time in her life. There was no question, being courted did turn a woman to a few vanities of her sex.

"I feel for you, Harry, and I would spend my life with you, but I must not. There is the work to do."

"You have done too much. You deserve happiness."

"Aye, I did think that once." Certainly the dust, the heat, the flies, the smells, hearing of pain, the utter fatigue which made her bones ache, she could do without that. It was, perhaps, her due to lie down with this lamb. But . . .

"But there is work to do yet."

"You are crazy, Mary. You will work yourself into a grave."

"Aye. I will."

"And what profit is that?"

"The grave's."

"Have you no heart in you?"

"Too much a heart. Oh, Harry, I would stop and care for you, but – if I do – what of all the years I worked? Why did I do it all? Why?"

For the first time Mary saw the sweetness of Harry Lamb's smile curdle into a pucker of his mouth.

"Sacrifice," he said. "Duty. Obedience. I would like to take those three words and hang them like the three gold balls outside a pawn-broker's and say, 'For you three liars, I pawned my life and my heart and my joy, and what did you give me back? A mean loan to keep me alive, and a ticket to happiness I could never redeem!'"

"Oh, Harry –" Mary took his hand across the table and noticed for the first time the scars on his fingers, where the chemicals of the experiments had burned him or the scalpel had slipped.

"I will only say no the now."

"You will give me hope, Mary, that last delusion."

"I mean to come back here for the Jubilee –"

"Three years away. How shall I live that long?"

"For my family have all sworn to come here from all the far corners of the earth. For the Jubilee. And then, if the work is done –"

"It is never done," Harry Lamb said. "My work, your work is never done. There is never a shortage of the sick. When they are better, there are more of them."

"But you will ask me again, Harry Lamb?"

"To hear you say no?"

"I will not say that I will say no," Mary said. "And I will not say that I will say yes. And that is the best answer you will have of me."

"It is both the most honest and false answer I have ever heard," Harry Lamb said. "It is saying no to yes, and yes to no."

"Well, that is what I mean," Mary said. "And you will have to take it or leave it. But I do agree with you, Harry Lamb. Sacrifice, duty, obedience – they are the three worst words ever said, and if they were all hanged, we would be well rid of the pack of them."

21

THE FAR FILAMENTS

They felled two forests to put up the Mountain Creek trestle bridge for the Canadian Pacific, more than one and a half million feet of timber to support the iron tracks. And when the gangs from the Pacific met the gangs from the Atlantic for the driving of the last spike, Angus was there. The portly director of the company, Sir Donald Alexander Smith, took the long hammer, and tried to play the smith at the forge in his frock coat, gasping at each blow on the spike, a slow and unsteady gong to signal the joining of the line. The head of the spike hardly seemed driven down at each flop of the hammer, but now it was nearly level on the top of the track. And Sir Donald Smith raised his thumping weapon for the last time, and the seams of his coat split like old bellows, and he brought down the hammer with a clang, and he drove the spike home. And the thousands of gangers and navvies, surveyors and engineers, train drivers and guards burst into a cheer that was lost in the prairie wind.

Over the hurrays and the hurrahs, a Scots voice was heard, "All aboard for the Pacific." And on that command, the watchers climbed on the carriages linked to the locomotive that stood on the eastern tracks, huffing and puffing at the boredom of the waiting, and the great iron wheels began to turn, and they rolled over the last spike, and the train steamed on to prove the link between the oceans. Canada was one bound land.

Only a month later, Angus took his mother and father and sister and little Marie to Vancouver Sound, where a frame house was already built on land that ran down beneath pine trees to a rocky beach. Bain would not come. His boots in a swirl of red dust, his hide hat in a cloud of flies, he said he would lick the land before it licked him. He was too young to retire or look for a city or a railway job or work on the docks. He was a farmer and he would beat the soil into shape.

Hamish and Hannah had not been settled for a year, running a small market garden to supplement the pension which Angus sent them, when they had a visit from a long-lost son. Hamish Jamie took the railway from his regimental depot in Canada to see the parents he had last left on the western shore of Scotland nearly forty years before. And now they were on the western shore of Canada. Truly, a great migration, a long separation.

In the middle of his fifties, Hamish Jamie was a fine sight, in his Number One Dress, with his white spats over his boots, and his sporran fronting the pleats of his kilt, and the new yellow facings on the tunics of the Highland units, for they were now the Seaforths without any British number imposed on their origins. Even with wearing his forage cap rather than a bearskin, he towered above his father and his mother, with the trim diagonal hollows that ran from eye to chinbone and from nostril to lip showing him to be the Sinclair that he was. At first, little Marie screamed to see him as if he were a bogeyman, but soon she was sitting in his lap and using his sporran as a muff for her hands, while he adored her as if she were a reincarnation of his unknown daughter Peg in India.

"I have not been a family man," he told Hannah.

"That is the truth of it, my son."

"All these wars, all these foreign places," he said. "And never a place any Christian would wish to be."

"You are not a family man," Hannah said, "and you have a family. And you are a Christian, and yet you did not marry."

"I cannot, Mother. The regiment, it did not let me."

"And poor Lila is dead, Lord rest her soul. She was a Christian."

Hamish Jamie shook his head. "She believed in her gods, Mother. And Seaforth and Peg, they are Christians. They went to missionary schools in Simla."

"Mary wrote to us that Seaforth is doing well in London. He will be a doctor. She wants that we come to London for the Jubilee of the Queen. It will be a fine show, she says, and all the family will be there. But –"

"Her bones," her husband said. "They do not move. I do not think as she can take the stairs. Even the steps into the railway train, we had to pluck her up."

"Go away with you," Hannah said. "A wee bit stiff in the morning. That is all, and at an age as mine, I have to be thankful."

The day before, she had dropped two of the best new china plates as her hands could not hold on to them while they were being washed. She was losing her grip, but she would not admit it. She knew she could do everything she had always done, although she could not.

"I want to go to London," Katie said.

"Me, me, me. Me too," Marie said.

"Of course you will," Hamish Jamie said, holding her. "I will tuck you in my sporran and carry you all the way, such a little thing you are. And you will meet your cousin Peg, for Mary wants her to train as a nurse in the new school that Miss Nightingale has started. Do you ken, Father, there are even army medical schools and hospitals the now, and the medical officers in the regiments are trained doctors, and they say army nurses will come one day, if Miss Nightingale has her way."

"Will Mary be at the Jubilee? And Iain and Anna and their four children? Then I will go," Hannah said, "if I have to break my bones to be there."

"Three children," Hamish Jamie said. "The eldest boy, he died in Zululand. I saw him buried. He was a fine lad."

"It is too hard," Hannah said. "The wars and the losing of the men. That Henri of yours –"

"He was the finest man," Katie said. "No one can take his place. No one –"

"No one?" Hamish was quizzical. "And what of Bob McDowell?"

"Ach, he's just a fancy bonnet and a watch-chain."

"A friend of Angus from the railway," Hamish told his son. "He has been visiting."

"He can visit till Kingdom Come," Katie said. "But there's not a word I will hear of it."

But she did hear of it. For Bob McDowell came to call while Hamish Jamie had not yet returned from his leave. And the Highlander had to admit that Bob was sporting a different sort of uniform. With the scarlet tunic and his ruddy cheeks, Hamish Jamie looked like a lobster after it was boiled, while in his blue train uniform, even with the gold braid on the shoulders and the cap, Bob looked like a lobster before it went into the pot. And the whistle that hung on his watch-chain on the other end of his hunter timepiece, why it was no dirk or grenade, but only a silly thing to blow to warn people you were coming. Bob was a chief guard on the Canadian Pacific, and he was too tight for his clothes, swelling into them with all the pride of his position. But there was a look in his eyes when he sighted Katie with her red hair spilling in long ringlets in the new fashion that made Hamish Jamie change his mind. Such humble longing, such a look of hurt from the past. His voice might boom, but his gaze was beaten. Life or a woman had given him a terrible whipping. Yet there was a buried charm in him that any clever woman might bring out, if she wanted.

So Hamish Jamie felt pity for Bob as Katie treated him cruelly, declaring herself not at all well on the evening he was to take her to the restaurant with the band by the sound. Hamish Jamie took him to a saloon instead and heard of a man who had barely lasted his time as a boy, and had no good to tell of it. Bob was an orphan, and he ran away at fourteen from his institution to be an engine-cleaner.

"We worked nights, two running, thirty hours at a stretch. They'd put us in the firebox of the boiler with the steam still in it, changing the burnt-out firebars, while the heat of the grate scorched our shoes, and the dust filled our lungs, and the black sweat ran off us in rivers. I had a mate got into the warm furnace of a dead engine to have a sleep, and a stoker put in a shovel of blazing coals not seeing him, and he died screaming. Then I got to be a lighter-up, starting up the furnace four hours before the engine was wanted. Then I got to the footplate, a passed cleaner – I could stoke the boiler of the train when it was moving. Then up to a red ink fireman and a black ink fireman, shovelling coal into that furnace till I swear the blood was near dried up in me, I was bone and not much skin left. Twenty years, and I never did get to be a passed fireman or a driver. So I took the ship over to Canada where the railways were starting up. And it was the best thing I ever did."

"You make the army sound like a love seat," Hamish Jamie said. "It is a terrible thing the railways are."

"And over here," Bob said, "I said, no more shovelling the coal into that firebox, I will march up the train and blow the whistle and do the stopping and the starting and I will grow back all that flesh and blood they have been working out of me ever since I was a boy. But look, I am not complaining. For I love the railway. There is nothing so grand as the engine getting up steam and pistons chump-chumping up and down and the hiss of the whistle and the horn blowing over those great plains and all the power under your feet, you can *feel* it rumble. I am a train man, although it was near the death of me."

"Have you never told this to Katie?"

"She would not care for it."

"She does not care for you," Hamish Jamie said, "because you never told of it."

Rob lifted his eleventh burning whiskey, and he said, "And what gives you the knowing of the women?"

"I had sisters, you did not."

"And you left your woman to be a soldier."

"You will leave yours. You will stay on the train."

"It always returns. It is the end of the line here."

"If you have a place to go."

"But why tell your sister of when I was poor and weak? Women, they love you strong –"

"Ach, they do not."

"Major Sinclair, if you took off that uniform –"

"I would be the same creature as I am." Hamish Jamie laughed. "You ken we wear nothing under our kilt. So why shall we pretend the sporran is the truth over it? We are no bigger than we are, for all that. And that is what the women wish to hear."

"I will tell her then –"

"That you are worse and better than a blue coat and a silver whistle –"

"That I was a poor lad –"

"And you still are –"

"That I love her –"

"Not that. There is much better." Hamish Jamie put his forefinger alongside his nose and squinted across it with one eye to make his point to Bob, and to prove he was still sober. "Tell her you need her."

"I need her?"

"You need her."

"But she needs me. To help her raise Marie."

"Yes, Bob. But that is not the logic of the women. For reasons only known to the Lord, their reason is all backwards. If they need you, you must say you need them. If they say they do not want you, you say you want them. And if they say, get away with you, you marry them in the morning." Hamish Jamie took away his forefinger from his nose and pointed it at Bob. "Do not say I did not tell you. I ken women."

"And you a soldier. You have passed all your life with men."

"I ken women. You need her. Tell her."

And so Bob did, not once, but many times. And soon Katie was smiling at him and allowing him to escort her and Marie to the park, where she would watch the ladies riding side-saddle and laugh to see them teeter so high and so uncomfortable. And kindly treated, Bob became playful and expansive. And when it came the time to take his train back to Montreal – and Hamish Jamie as a passenger back to his regiment – Katie in her best black silk dress took Marie looking like a church doll in white lace to the station to see Bob standing by the last carriage with its platform at the end, and blowing his silver whistle. And Hamish Jamie could have almost sworn he saw the light of pride in her eyes as he kissed her goodbye, and he said to Marie, "I have not forgot. Next time I see you, I will take you to London in my sporran," and Katie said, "Men will promise anything, but they never mean a thing," and then the whistle sounded for the last time, and Hamish Jamie scrambled on to the train, for the order of the guard was almost as final as the order of Sir Colin Campbell to advance on Lucknow, "All aboard for the Atlantic."

* * *

The Scots might have won all the charges and the battles once, but now they were manning the engines of the ships and the trains that steamed over sea and land, making a web of trade that bound all the world to Britain. Money followed the bayonet. These far filaments were serviced by millions of working hands and legs and heads in a dogged fury of connecting peaks to valleys, and deserts to saddle mountains.

Angus went to Peru now, to advise on the highest railway in the world which ran one hundred and forty miles on a switchback from Callao to Oraya and rose over fifteen thousand feet in the Andes. The project was a madness, but it was made to work on trestle bridges, on the edge of precipices, channelled through gorges and funnelled through mountains, wandering back and forth like a tipsy snail, leaving a whirligig trail behind. In one tunnel, there was even a reversing switch, so in the jet blackness, the engine came to a halt, before shuddering off in the opposite direction. It was worse than the slope on the Bhore Ghat outside Bombay, and they had to use special banking engines and put three cogs with double sets of pinion brakes on each loco-motive, each one able to stop the engine in ten inches on the steepest gradient. It made travel safe enough, bar a rock slide or an avalanche.

But was it worth it? Angus began to doubt it. Surrounded by the snow-bright peaks with cascades of howling silver torrents beating on the rocks, the eye falling sheer as the swoop of an eagle down cliff and crag, Angus found the work pitiful. The Inca roads were still there, the Royal Road with its wood bridges suspended on ropes and its rough paving stones. Mules and llamas were better beasts of burden than steaming engines and iron trucks inappropriate for such wild majesty. The fact that he met Isabella de Guadalluna because of her father Don Pedro's admiration for his feats of engineering did not make him think he was doing more than ornament the intractable. The line might last for a century or two and then it must revert into the Andes, irrelevant.

"You cannot really think we can conquer this," he said to Don Pedro, as they sat on the balcony of his town house on the square of Callao, looking past the church spires to the taller pinnacles of the mountains. "We are flying in the face of nature. We might live like the old Incas, behind great stone walls. Use natural things to build."

"But you *do* things," Don Pedro said. He nodded to Isabella to pour some more *coca* tea for their guest. "We, we live here – centuries, we do nothing. You have two words, iron and steam. We have two words, *nada* and *mañana*."

"Nothing and tomorrow," Angus said. "I've heard worse words if it is dealing with a landscape like this. Why try to change it?"

181

"We are trapped," Don Pedro said. "Eh, Isabella?"

Isabella glanced up at Angus, her black eyes huge and brilliant as wet coal against the pallor of her oval face.

"We are trapped," she said. "I learn English. We dream of London –"

"The fog, the grime, the dirt," Angus said. "You must be mad. It's a nightmare, they say. Read Charles Dickens –"

"No. Charles Darwin, Isambard Kingdom Brunel –" Don Pedro said in awe.

"The Royal Society, the Buckingham Palace –" Isabella breathed.

"I do not think the first has much to do with the second," Angus said. "The first dealing with the sciences royally, and the second with anything but. All the same, I suppose you will both be wanting to go to London for the Jubilee. Fifty years of Queen Victoria ruling, and it is quite remarkable. She has made – or rather they who work for her have made – of all the oceans an English lake. And of the Andes an excursion trip up the railway line."

"It is my dream," Isabella said. "It is my dream."

"And do you think dreams ever come true, Don Pedro?"

"Men make dreams true."

"And women?"

"They dream of men –"

"Who make the dreams come true?"

"Sometimes." Don Pedro clapped his hands, and a Peruvian servant came to collect the tea things. In his quilted hat and woollen tunic, his face flat and dark, he gave Angus a shock. He seemed exactly like the photographs of the hill people of the Himalayas, like those who served Iain and Anna at Annandale.

"Did your Indians walk here from India? They are the same as the hill people there."

"They were here when we came," Don Pedro said. "As your Indians."

"I have not been there," Angus said. "But my brother and sister are there. The Sinclairs have been on many of the continents."

"And God make you to come here," Isabella said.

"Or your dream," Angus said.

Isabella looked down quickly at her lap, then glanced up as if surprised and smiled. Her father was smiling too.

"I do not dream of men," she said.

"Not of men only."

Isabella looked down again. She allowed her father to reply.

"We dream of London," he said. "And he who will take us there. But we will not detain you, Señor Sinclair. You have your work, I know. But perhaps, if you have time to come again, to talk to those with *nada* and *mañana* in their mind –"

"I will come again," Angus said, rising. "You did not ask what my dream was. The next time, I may propose it."

The next time, he did propose it, formally to the father, but to Isabella on his knees, as he had read in the books. She did not seem surprised, saying, "I saw you in my dream. I have always known. What took you so long?"

Angus did not let his religion be an issue: to him, a priest was as good as a pastor. His job was to build tracks and bridges, not to pray. He married Isabella within three months, and they stayed at Don Pedro's *hacienda* in the valley among the corn and the *coca* plants and the horses. Angus was wild for her body as the stallions were for the mares, and she was fierce and pliant, for all the softness of her white skin that she always kept from the sun. The children were born every year, Hamish Charles and Arabella and Murdo. And when the railway was laid and the last bridge built and the work was done, then it was the year of the Jubilee. And Angus persuaded Isabella to live her dream, even at the price of abandoning her babies for a year to the nurses chosen by her father.

"This is the Jubilee," Angus said, "and every woman has a right to her dream."

Behind Brunel's behemoth, *The Great Eastern*, the cable unrolled and coiled into the depths of the ocean. On the sea bed it lay, the submarine snake that linked the outposts of the empire by the tapping of the operators, DOT DASH–DASH DOT – the Morse code that ran along the seven imperial serpents that girdled the bottoms of the seven seas. "Hush!" as Rudyard Kipling wrote. "Men talk today o'er the waste of the ultimate slime, and a new Word runs between: whispering, 'Let us be one!'"

From Craigiebrae in Annandale, Iain sent his Gurkha runner to the relay station in Simla, and there the message was clicked on the Morse keys by the cable workers, their little punctuations sounding their soft castanets in the night. And the stuttering points and strokes were picked up at Bombay, then sent along the third cable to England through Aden and Suez and Alexandria and Malta and Gibraltar, because the two overland cables went through Persia and Turkey, or through Russia and Germany, and who knew who was listening to what secret? It was safer to stick to the undersea, where the British navy patrolled above, Hamilton Sinclair in the engine-room of HMS *Repulse*, surveying the oceans and all that sailed upon them.

Mary was already in London for the Jubilee. She had left India early on the P. and O., the good old "dear and slow" which treated its passengers as though it were a favour to allow them aboard. She never confessed to herself that she might have come home a trifle soon, because she wanted to be there to see Harry Lamb before the rest of her family arrived for their reunion, whether she said yes or no to him this time. But she was none too early, because the cable was already waiting for her at Morley's Hotel on Trafalgar Square, where Harry had insisted that all the family must stay. It was translated from code into letters, and it ran:

ALL COMING TO JUBILEE
ANNA IAIN MARGARET MAY HAMILTON OFF SHIP

It said enough. A word in a cable cost money, and a Sinclair never wasted either one.

22

COMING HOME

The day of the Golden Jubilee of 1887 brought the Queen's weather. Brilliant sunshine bathed the crowds in the streets in yellow light. Her Majesty had turned down a glass coach. She would show herself to Her people in Her open gilt landau drawn by six cream horses. And She would not wear Her crown and robes of state. Her ministers might say that everybody wanted gilding for their money, or that a sovereign should be grand, or that the Empire should be ruled by a sceptre and not a bonnet. But She would wear Her bonnet, and quite a bonnet it was, all diamonds and white lace. On the way to the thanksgiving service in Westminster Abbey, Her eldest daughter Vicky sat in the landau with Alix, the Princess of Wales, while twelve Indian officers rode in front alongside Her three sons and five sons-in-law, nine grandsons and grandsons-in-law. Her family was on display as well as Herself, and all the gleaming cohorts of Her global realm.

One of them was an apparition on his white charger, the crown prince of Prussia, in the white uniform of the Pomeranian Hussars. His helmet with its eagle crest and his silvered breastplate glittered in the sunshine, setting off the sash of the Order of the Garter and the sky-blue of his marshal's baton. Around him rode the princes of Europe and the whole world, the Hussars and Horse Guards. But he was the spectre at the feast of Empire. He was Vicky's husband, but he was dying of cancer of the throat. The Queen knew this and also knew that her grandson William would then become the kaiser of Germany. He blamed his withered arm on incompetent English doctors called by his mother to assist at his birth, as he would blame his father's death on the same foreign meddlers. He was envious of England. He wanted Germany to do better on the seas and overseas. His dreams were the nightmares of the British Empire, while his father rode, a glorious white ghost, at the Golden Jubilee of the Queen and Empress.

Watching the procession from the balcony arranged by Harry Lamb, the Sinclairs were in London on their first and last time of coming together. In the streets, all the squadrons and the regiments were parading from all the red quarters of the globe. Those who had been thrust out from Britain when the Queen was young were gathered again to honour Her after fifty years of Her reign. The Sinclairs had been split like quicksilver and had rolled apart, but now they were drawn together again in one mass for this celebration of the ageing Queen.

As she passed below, so dwarfish in the splendour around her, it seemed incredible to Iain that such a dumpy old grandmother could command the allegiance of armies and navies and the respect of the world. It was all a fiction, but a necessary masterstitch for the patchwork of dominions and colonies across the earth. He was told that she had built Buckingham Palace in a series of small rooms, so that reaching her was a period of waiting times in one antechamber after another until the final interview did not disappoint the expectation of it, for she was raised on a dais and spoke down graciously to a suitor. In Westminster Abbey, where the gilt coach was heading, she would sit high on the coronation chair above the stolen Stone of Scone, elevated in her littleness to the majesty she did not possess. Such was pageant, making a glory of the insignificant.

The troopers and the horses passed, the mounted bands and the walking pipers, the gaudy palettes of the uniforms and the brassy helmets and the tossing furs and fluttering plumes. And finally at the last tramp of feet, even the cheering stopped in the crowds below, leaving only the piles of dung gently steaming on the cobbles from the horses that had clopped away. And Iain turned and stooped to enter the room behind the balcony through the open French windows. There Harry Lamb had arranged for a feast of cold meats and syllabubs, iced wine and fruit punch. And there the Sinclairs had their reckonings to make.

Doctor Seaforth Sinclair looked at the uneasiness of his father, Hamish Jamie, and almost felt a sort of pity wash over his bitter mouth.

"Father," he said, "it has been so long I fear we do not remember each other."

To Hamish Jamie, meeting this thin and tall reproduction of himself was like that strange phrase in the Good Book, watching through a glass darkly, then face to face. But he would never excuse, never explain.

"I hear you have done well for yourself, very well. A qualified young doctor, working under Doctor Lamb."

"I have much to thank Aunt Mary for. But as for you –"

"I could not be at your mother's dying," Hamish Jamie said abruptly, preferring to charge before he was accused. "I was on duty."

"You always were," Seaforth said. "She hated that word from you. It was your excuse for not coming to us."

"You have your duty now. In the hospital. Your roster. Your calls. Do not tell me you fail in your duty, Seaforth."

"Oh, I do not." Seaforth smiled the quick wry smile that he seemed to imitate from his aunt. "I have been taught duty. The only question is – to whom do I owe it?"

"To your patients."

"True. I have no family – yet."

"You have us."

"Some of you."

"We are all Sinclairs."

"I am not sure," Seaforth said, "that all of you recognise that. Have some wine." As he passed a glass to his father, he looked across to the far side of the room to where Margaret and May were ranged beside their mother Anna, as though they were defending their corner of silk and lace and parasol against all comers. Mary was talking to them with an unusual animation, hoping to disguise her nervousness. For once, she appeared out of self-control. Harry Lamb had not spoken to the family yet about their plans, although he had given them all their fruit punch, and now was taking Peg across to her father.

"Peg," he said, "she is a jewel in our crown at St Thomas's. I do not doubt she will do more for India than even her splendid Aunt Mary has done."

"Peg –" Hamish Jamie stood awkwardly, looking down at the elongated oval of his daughter's face, her dark hair off-setting the triangle of the white nurse's cap pinned on it. He put out one arm, then dropped it in a sort of shrug of despair. But then Peg came forward, her dark lips seeking upward from the shield of her nurse's cloak, and she kissed him on the cheek. He stepped back, as if he was stung by her forgiveness.

"It is good to see you, Father," Peg said. "A major – and what a beautiful uniform. You look – alight in that scarlet."

"Yours is better than mine," Hamish Jamie said. "And it does more good."

"True," Peg said. "But not many soldiers would say that."

"Oh, Father's very good at compliments," Seaforth said. "Mother always knew that. It is his way of avoiding responsibility."

"Seaforth!" Peg was angry and turned to Hamish Jamie. "Don't listen to my brother! He's always had a knife where his tongue is."

"He has cause," Hamish Jamie said. "As far as I am concerned."

"Saying you're sorry," Seaforth said, "is no excuse. The British are always saying they are sorry in India – but they still keep it."

"Shut up, Seaforth," Peg said and took Hamish Jamie by the arm and aside. "You have a whole life to tell me, so tell me. Don't listen to my brother. He won't ever forgive you for being his father – that's natural. But he forgets – without you as his father, he would not be here. And I neither."

The light from the French windows showed that Marie already had an extraordinary quality at the age of ten. The lithe speed of her movements, the slant of her cheekbones throwing up her wild red hair, the narrow green glitter of her eyes promised a fierce beauty. Iain was entranced with her as Hamish Jamie had been, and he told Katie that he had never seen a child as enchanting. "Like one of the wild faeries Hannah told us of. Born of the mountain dew and the salmon's leap. You must be very proud of her."

"Bob is also," Katie said, looking at her new husband, who stood stoutly in his check suit, looking ready to burst with pleasure and satisfaction. "I think he loves Marie more than me. Or his train engine, which is saying something."

"You'll not say that to me," Bob said, liking the teasing.

"Personally," Iain said, "I prefer an engine to a woman. More reliable."

Katie laughed. "Less fun."

"Don't be sure of that," Iain said. "Talk to Hamilton when he comes. He cannot see a lassie for all the cogs and pistons of Her Majesty's Royal Navy revolving before his eyes. But, Katie, they would not come?"

"They could not come. Hannah's bones – you almost have to crack them in the morning to make them move. And Hamish, his blood, it is so slow –"

"In India, they say the chewing of the raw garlic, it works wonders –"

Katie did laugh now, and Bob with her.

"Hamish reeking of the garlic –"

"Like an Italian waiter," Bob said. "We have one on the train. But I said, none of that heathen smell. Keep it for your pestilential *pasta*. For me plum duff and bread-and-butter pudding."

Iain looked at Bob's girth under his waistcoat. "I can see that. A fine diet. But now garlic, it does speed the blood. But, Katie, our mother and father, they are not in real pain."

"If they were, how would they tell me?" Katie smiled. "You know a Sinclair. If he's hurt, it is a wee nothing. And if he was in hellfire, he would say, 'More coal, more coal, please. I cannot feel it.'"

"If anyone was ever to go to heaven," Bob said, "your parents would."

"For putting up with me?" Katie gave her husband a mischievous smile. "Oh, I know you do, but that's what husbands are *for*. Putting up with their wives. Do you know, the last time I had a wee fever – nothing at all – Hannah was up in the middle of the night to bring me a bowl of brose. 'Feed a fever,' she said, 'feed a fever,' when eating is the last thing you can do. Then Hamish came in with what he calls a wee drop of something. 'Not to tell the wife, please, but there's something in there will chase away the chills.' And there was – enough whisky to fill a distillery! I love them both, Iain, and they are as well as might be at their age."

Now Iain looked across the room, hoping to see his son enter, but all he saw was his wife Anna being introduced by Angus to Isabella, dressed in lace flounces even more extravagant than Margaret and May were wearing, and with her hair piled on her head like the pyramid of Cheops. The ladies seemed to recognise each other instantly, friends in their social understanding against the lumpen menfolk in the room.

"Coming to London has been my dream," Isabella was saying. "And to see the Queen in that beautiful hat. It was a miracle."

"A good hatter is no miracle," Anna said sharply. "Doubtless She can afford it. Most of those diamonds come from India." And looking at the silken pink confection perched on Isabella's head, "And your hatter, he must be very dear."

"He is very dear to me," Isabella said, not understanding why Angus laughed. "But your daughters, they are so pretty. Which is Margaret and which May?"

"This is Margaret," Anna said, introducing the taller girl in her green silk gown with only a small bustle – thank the Lord the crinoline had rolled its last hoops away. "She is to marry somebody in the Indian government on our return. Douglas Jardine. Very well thought of by the viceroy himself."

"Oh, Mother," Margaret said, "Douglas has more than the viceroy's good opinion. He has mine."

"I don't know," May said, shorter than her sister in lilac with her buttercup ringlets almost violent to the eye. "You could do better. I shall."

"Those two sisters," Anna confided in Isabella. "They truly love each other, though you would never believe it to hear them speak. But it is only play."

"Girls, girls," Isabella said. "I was fortunate. I was an only child –"

"So was I –" Anna said. "You will inherit everything?"

"My father loves Angus. And our three babies – they are with him."

"Angus, I do declare" – Anna looked her brother-in-law straight in the eye – "you are as shrewd as your brother. You have married an heiress."

"Oh, she married me," Angus said. Then saw his wife blush and he added, "Or rather, her father married us two. He loves Charles Darwin and Isambard Kingdom Brunel, the great scientist and the great engineer. He has the wrong opinion that I know about both of those masters."

"And you do," Isabella said. "But if you say you did not marry *me*" – she turned on Anna – "Why, on his *knees*, he asked me –"

It was Angus's time to turn red, while the women laughed.

"I must say," Anna said with that dry humour that seemed to grow on her with age, "Iain asked me on his back with his leg up. Very romantic."

Isabella laughed and blushed.

"But – how could he?"

"Easily. He was wounded. But Angus tells me, you also have Indians in Peru."

"We do."

"We have Indians, of course, it being India. I love them, you know" – her gaze wandered across the room and fixed on Seaforth – "but I will never trust them. Not after the Mutiny. They killed my family."

Anna would have said more, but Hamilton came into the room, resplendent in his naval uniform. And Anna fell upon him, the blue apple of her eye. When he could disengage himself from his mother and his sisters and had shaken hands with his father, he found himself set upon by Angus and Bob with the technical questions and the mechanical talk so dear to that breed of men who live for their work. Hearing them gab about cantilevers and crankshafts, cog wheels and pressure gauges, Hamish Jamie could only bless the one thing his new position as an army officer had taught him – no shop in the mess.

Harry Lamb brought them all to attention by rapping with a silver ladle on the embossed bowl which held the fruit punch. "I have an announcement to make," he said, his voice tinny and sharp with an odd strain in it. Then he coughed and brought it down to his usual reasonable tone. "And it will be to my new family, whom I welcome here. Mary." He signalled to her to come to stand beside him, and she came forward with reluctance, her face gaunt in its preserve and power with the grey hair scraped back from her forehead to a bun behind. "Mary – she has accepted to become my wife. I have long waited for her to feel that she has done enough for others, but never for herself. And I have persuaded her that her work now lies here – she will be teaching the nurses at St Thomas's – and also that she needs care herself, and love – mine." Now Harry seemed to conjure out of his hand a yellow apple as if by illusion or magic. "And I will show you how Mary and I will always be. I call it the Platonic Apple. It must be cut in a certain way – most delicately. With a scalpel, with a surgeon's knowledge –" And now Harry brought up his other hand to hold the apple, and lo, the complete orb parted into two serrated segments. And then Harry put the pair of them together again, and held up one perfect pippin.

"What Plato said was this. Before we are born, there are two parts of us, one male soul and one female soul. They are severed before birth, born to different mothers. They spend all their lives looking for each other desperately. Only if they find each other will they become whole again – a circle – a oneness – a communion. I call it the Platonic Apple, and that is us."

He gave the yellow fruit to Mary, who looked at it dubiously, not knowing if she was meant to bite it. But then Harry gave her a ring, aglow with red light and blue light and white stardust, the ruby and sapphire and diamonds of the Empire. "And this too, a ring, which will bind us in the Platonic way."

"Platonic?" Iain growled to Anna. "I am not a man for the books, but does that not signify that he will not touch her at all, but he will love her from far away?"

"It was a sweet speech," Anna said, "and the dear doctor did not mean that at all. He said he had been looking for Mary all his life, and now she would make him complete. And it is a better asking than the asking you did for me, Iain Sinclair!"

The smile on Mary's face flickered on and off, brilliant, and then closed. She was full of joy and fear. "I don't know," she said, as Harry put the engagement ring on her finger. "I don't know –" And then she burst into hysterical weeping and then she kissed Harry full on the mouth among her tears. The women all hurried around her, leaving Hamish Jamie again with his son, who was smiling almost scornfully at the aunt he claimed to love.

"She should not have done it. Doctor Lamb, he is not for her. Not for any woman –"

"What do you mean, Seaforth?"

"Nothing," Seaforth said. "Nothing of any consequence. Certainly, he needs a good wife, and Mary will be that. It will even –" He paused and stared at Hamish Jamie. "Where will you go now? Back to your damned *duty*?"

"To Scotland," Hamish Jamie said. "Iain wishes to go there and see how the land is now. And my regiment, they say . . . If I go for the recruiting –"

"Recruiting? More cannon fodder for the Empire?"

"My pay," Hamish Jamie said. "It has been keeping you and Peg. I always send the main part of it to Mary. You know that."

"I thank you," Seaforth said. "It is the least a father can do, and you do it. But you were cleared from the Highlands. Will you go back to your shame?"

"It is still our country. And *your* country –"

"India is my country."

"And Scotland."

"India is my only country. And it is only for Indians."

"Ach, so you will have your father out of you." Hamish Jamie smiled. "You cannot, and you ken that. You cannot do it. I will always be the half of you. Like that yellow apple."

"Do not be too sure, Father. But Peg, she wishes it. You saw that."

"You are my only son."

"And I do not have a father."

The two men looked at each other, and then Hamish Jamie looked aside. "You will change your thinking."

"I will not."

"The Sinclairs are awful stubborn – but they can change their thinking, if their heads are beaten enough."

"What do you expect to find in Scotland, Father? More empty land and broken roofs? Desolation."

"I hear Mr Gladstone has passed a Crofters Act. They have been given the right to their land at a fair rent, and to give it on to their sons. Perhaps I shall have a croft again with my pension – and you, my son –"

Seaforth grimaced in that sudden quick smile of his aunt. "Burning *ghats*," he said, "are more for me. They only passed that act because there were troubles in Scotland. The Battle of the Braes on Skye . . ."

"I heard that," Hamish Jamie said. "So they sent Lord Napier over from India, and he said the crofters will have their land at last."

"There will be more troubles. There have always been troubles in that sad land you come from."

"There are always troubles everywhere." Hamish Jamie looked across the room to where the bright ring of women was breaking about Mary, who now leaned against Harry Lamb, and he put his soft hand round her shoulder and whispered in her ear. "That is why I am a soldier. I stop troubles. But you do not. There are no troubles here."

"Don't be too sure," Seaforth said. "There will be, and there will be soon."

★　　★　　★

Never had there been such a feast as when the crofters of Lewis stormed the deer park in that year of the Jubilee and shot the red beasts with their rifles and roasted their carcasses slung over wood fires or boiled the venison in great pots over the hearthstones under the broken roofs of the black houses of Stromas. Iain was welcome among the visitors, and even Hamish Jamie in his regimental uniform was forgiven for the wearing of it. For he had not come to take them. He found the whole affair most paradoxical. For the Earl of Seaforth himself had cleared the crofts for the game park, providing room for the deer as well as men for his regiment. But he had sold it, and now Lewis was in the hands of the widow Matheson, whose late husband had been a partner in the great China firm of Jardine Matheson, with its profits from the opium trade protected by the raid on Peking. The money was lavished on the surviving islanders, who were now biting the hand that did not feed them enough by the taking of the red deer, so sweet in the mouth.

"And you will not be punished for this?" Iain asked an old man from Morvig.

"For taking what the Lord provideth?" the old man said. "There is no jury in Scotland will convict on that."

"That is what I thought and I did when I was a lad," Iain said. "I took the salmon and I blessed God for it."

"And we have blessed God for this deer and said our Grace to Him," the old man said. He pointed to where a pile of blackened stones and mossy rubble showed a building once had been. "And we will build the Church there again at Stromas."

"Will you now?"

The smell of the roasting meat was suddenly harsh in the air, as sour as the rankness of the kelp charring in the kilns or the burning of the imperial palace in China. It was not the scent of plenty, it was the smoke of useless defiance, and Hamish Jamie had to question it.

"And how many now are there in Sutherland and Ross and Caithness? Are they not nearly all gone? A fair rent on the crofts, it is being given too late, for they are broken in and fallen down, and we are all gone away across the earth, and we will not come home again. There are thousands now, where there were tens of thousands, and how shall we fill the land again?"

There was the piping that night, and the fiddling, and wild laments sounded from the western island. And on their tour of the Highlands, Iain and Hamish Jamie found a terrible beauty, the brae and moors given back to heather and stag, the sheep close-cropping the grasses of the glens to a stubble unfit to eat, and a wilderness growing where the black houses had been and were laid down. Often as the two

Sinclairs gazed over loch and mountain, they seemed lost in their own company, as if no men had set foot there before, and no men would tread there again.

"We do more in Egypt and the Punjab," Iain said. "Where there are deserts, we make the water flow for other peoples. We irrigate the sand and plant colonies there. And here –" He flung out his arm to describe the sweep of the saucer of hills that cradled the loch below. "We have water that makes nothing grow. A few men take the fish from it and the deer drink of it and foul it. We grow gardens and granaries over the seas, and here there is wilderness and game parks –"

"We, Iain? *We?*"

"They. But we serve them."

"You always said a Sinclair does not serve."

"We do their bidding now. They bid us, and we do it."

Doctor Seaforth Sinclair was also right about other trouble in that golden year of Jubilee. It took place in the heart of the Empire under Nelson's Column. There beside the four bronze lions that lounged imperturbable at the base of the column, the vagrants and the unemployed had made their home, and there the socialists and the Irish reunited the core of their mobs of protest. On that Bloody Sunday in November, the people had been called in from South London, from Deptford and Battersea and Bermondsey, and they surged over Westminster Bridge, wearing their red armbands and their green sashes, and singing the "Marseillaise" or "Starving for Old England". A detachment from the five thousand constables called up especially for the occasion blocked the bridge and defended the Houses of Parliament. And under Big Ben, a battle was fought.

St Thomas's Hospital took in twenty-six of the wounded, and Seaforth had to treat them for cuts and contusions, bruises and broken arms. Worried about the Sinclairs who were still staying at Morley's Hotel, he took the horse-bus to Trafalgar Square. From its top deck, he looked down at the milling crowds as the charge of the socialists, carrying their banner, *Disobedience to tyrants is a duty to God*, met with the cordons of police surrounding the Square. The truncheons rose and flailed and struck home sickeningly, but the wedge of the protestors drove through. Some of the crowd were knocking off police helmets like coconuts on a shy with flung cobbles, while others were using little twitches on the police horses, which were backing and rearing and bounding and upending the high constables.

But now the Horse Guards appeared at the end of the Square, and they began to walk their mounts round the space. And from the north, the Grenadier Guards came on with fixed bayonets. The troopers quickened their pace to a trot and then to a canter. The booing and the shrieking of the crowd was an assault on the heavens. And now the Guardsmen began to charge, and the people split and ran, screaming in their panic. The horse-bus rocked with the pressure and the rush pell-mell of the fleeing mob. Below him, Seaforth saw the flying hair and waving beard of the radical speaker George Bernard Shaw skedaddling all the way to Hampstead. It was a disgraceful defeat of the many by the few. Only Seaforth hoped that when his day came in India, the masses would sweep aside the military as poppies before the scythe.

He found Mary safe in Morley's Hotel, while Anna and Margaret and May were on an excursion to the country. "I never thought to see," he said to his aunt, "such scenes in the capital of Empire. I don't know how you can send so many soldiers abroad when obviously you need them at home to keep down your poor."

"Seaforth, Seaforth," Mary said. "This is a most unusual Sunday. Most of us are at church, not in the streets."

"Tell me, Mary," Seaforth said, "how long do *you* think before India gets its independence? After Ireland?"

"Only when you can run it yourselves," Mary said with some asperity. "And when we are tired of running it for you."

"And an independent Scotland?" Seaforth smiled his thin smile.

"Now why should we need independence," Mary said, "when we Scots already run England and the Empire for the English? You will note, Seaforth, that where you go, it is a Scots person you will meet – doctor and nurse, engineer and guard."

"But not a minister –"

"Ach, we have had kings here – and ministers. But it is not they that matter. It is the Scots that run the real thing – the ships and the trains and the hospitals. And train you –"

"To make yourself unnecessary." Seaforth smiled again. "How *very* unselfish of you, Aunt Mary. But I will never understand – I can never understand – why after the clearances you still worked for the English."

"It was our own folk did that wicked thing," Mary said. "And we had to earn our bread. I am not ungrateful. Nursing, it is better than the kelping or being a skivvy. And you, Seaforth, are you not working for the English?"

"I am learning how to get rid of them, Aunt Mary. And they are kindly teaching me."

"And are you not grateful for that, you wicked boy?"

Seaforth laughed at his aunt's fond approval, and he took each of her cheeks between the palm of his hands, and he kissed her lightly on the nose.

"As grateful as the crocodile is to the fat sheep between his jaws."

Now he held his aunt's face firmly between his hands, so that she could not look away.

"Do not marry Doctor Lamb, Mary –"

"Do not tell me that. It is too late. In three weeks the now –"

"Men who marry late have their reasons –"

"He never met *me* before."

"He is a man who has always had to do with men. His life is very private."

"He helps with the nurses in the hospital."

"He loves women – at a distance. Platonic – you remember the apple. And I have seen him in the dissection of a woman – I would say a repugnance, an *aversion*."

"But she was a *dead* woman. I am alive. It is natural to feel averse to a *body* –"

"Not for a surgeon."

"But you know nothing *definite*, Seaforth."

"Nothing. Doctor Lamb is discretion itself. It is a feeling – as I have for some of our British civil servants. All smiles on the surface, and unspeakable beneath."

"And you say that of the man who has helped you so much!"

Two bright spots of rage or concern flared on Mary's pale cheeks.

"It is because I love you," Seaforth said, "and I do not want you to make a mistake."

"You are jealous of him," Mary said. "You fear to lose me."

"Let us say that," Seaforth said. "But never say I did not warn you."

He walked over to the windows of Morley's Hotel. Under Nelson's Column, only a few policemen patrolled lazily in the empty square. It was as though no battle had taken place. There were no casualties, only an eerie lack of evidence of what he himself had seen.

"Perhaps nothing will happen," Seaforth said. "Perhaps you will be very happy. I can never believe my own eyes."

23

REVIEW

He was too old to serve, and yet his regiment could not serve in Africa without him. Hamish Jamie sometimes thought he had been serving the army for nine lives, not just the one the Good Lord had given him; and yet the Seaforths had called him back from his retirement, when he had left the new Army Service Corps after nearly fifty years with the colours. But he could not refuse, he would not refuse to be the quartermaster of his regiment in Egypt and the Sudan. He had a personal reason to join Kitchener's expedition. He had not forgotten the martyred General Gordon from their meeting at the sack of the imperial palace at Peking. Indeed, when Hamish Jamie had heard of Gordon's killing by the Mahdi at Khartoum, he had not been surprised. That man would never evacuate. He could not retreat. He would stay to the bloody end, even if Sir Garnet Wolseley took two days too long to relieve him, struggling up river only to find a headless corpse.

On his belated imperial revenge, Kitchener was even slower at advancing up the Nile against the khalifa and his dervishes from the Sudan. Method was all. Cataract after cataract, he drove his forces forward. When they reached the khalifa's mud capital at Omdurman, they entrenched themselves and waited to be attacked. And when the assault started with the dawn, it looked as if the whole of Africa was coming at them staring through the spines of the *zareba* at first light.

Hamish Jamie saw the great sand plain in front of Omdurman covered with dervishes in their white *jibbas* with patchwork colours, their flying turban tails and black and blue and green flags, and the khalifa's guards with their red tunics – a parody of the foe they faced. They waved their long swords and struck them against their round shields and ran forward to the beating drums, shouting, "Allah! Allah! Allah!" But it was deadly work to watch.

From the corners of the brigades lined up in sections beyond the *zareba*, the guns opened up, pumping out the heavy lyddite shells, while the Maxim guns swung on a slow traverse, cutting down the dervishes methodically, left to right, then right to left, as a machete cuts the dry undergrowth, swinging from side to side. Then Hamish Jamie saw the Highlanders fix their bayonets and rise and fire section volleys, not a dozen times, but three short of a hundred volleys from their Lee-Metford magazine rifles, pulling the bolts and changing the magazines like workers at the new lathes at the government factory in Enfield turning out the rifled barrels and ejection mechanisms of the new standard rifles. Precision had replaced courage, pigeon-shooting was now the charge.

When the order came to take Omdurman, the Highlanders walked over a multitudinous sea incarnadine of bodies, making the dun sand red, with white torn *jibbas* breaking over the billows of the dying. The Maxims had been so effective that Hamish Jamie could count five or six crimson holes in each fallen dervish, while the two heroes who had held up the khalifa's black flag until the last were split blood puddings. There was no joy in this for Hamish Jamie, just the sight of the black flies clouding the wounded and the dead and the reek of the mud huts of Omdurman, where the troops in their looting could only find one silver snuff-box, and precious little else.

Hamish Jamie's only fortune or misfortune that night was to meet a young officer of the Lancers, his square face flushed with some sort of triumph, too young in his brash arrogance to see a hollow victory. He was a war correspondent as much as a cavalry officer, and he wanted evidence of how the battle looked from the Seaforths' point of view. He said his name was Winston Churchill – he was chiefly famous so far for breaking down the barrier in the Empire in Leicester Square between the bar and the stage. But Hamish Jamie did not take to him. It was his voice, which descended like the slow flick of a lash.

"You Highlanders, you hardly had a thing to do. Stay behind your prickles, pot them like snipe, then walk into town. We had a charge, a cavalry charge. It may be the last cavalry charge ever in the British Army!"

"Why do you say that, Mr Churchill? And you in the cavalry too!"

"It is the Maxims. When we fight our own kind, how are we going to charge machine guns? With armour on? The bullets will smack straight through. And look at you, firing cool as cucumbers, knocking down ten thousand of them, and losing a dozen or two."

"It was cool work," Hamish Jamie agreed. "But you had hot work in the Lancers."

"Indeed we did. There were only three squadrons of us – perhaps three thousand of the enemy. And we went straight through them. They did not break. They had these swords and spears – hamstrung the horses, hacked their bellies, cut them with backhanders. Hardly sporting, and when we rode on, they fired their Remingtons at our back, so we had to gallop back. I killed a few, a pistol shot in their faces, and the Lancers, they were giving them a good poke. You know what one of them said to me?"

"And I do not."

"It is nice to put a sword or a lance through a man. They are just like old hens. They say *Quar!*"

Churchill laughed, but Hamish Jamie did not join in his pleasure. He looked at the bulging blue stare of the young man.

"And what is it all about, now we have the Sudan?"

"We shall have the Cairo to the Cape railway. We shall have all Africa, even if we have to whip the Dutchmen in the Cape to get it."

"I have soldiered in Africa, east and west and north now," Hamish Jamie said. "And if my regiment goes to the south – I will look like an old compass. But God help me if I know which direction we are pointing in. I have never understood why we came to Africa at all."

"The route to India. The Cape. The Suez Canal. You must see that."

"We are a wee way from that up the Nile."

"Germany, France, Italy, even Belgium, they are seizing parts of Africa –"

"Let them have it," Hamish Jamie said. "I tell you, Mr Churchill, I do not doubt that Africa will see them out."

"Are you a Little Englander, man? Would you stay in our crowded island?"

"Aye," Hamish Jamie said, "but we were cleared from it, and we cannot go back the now. All that concerns me, Mr Churchill, with your grand *strategy*, where will you send me before I have my pension? And where will my old bones lie in the end? On what godforsaken shore?"

After the royal review of the one hundred and seventy-three ships-of-the-line of the Home Fleet off Spithead, some of the Sinclairs met at a waterfront hotel in Portsmouth in the Victoria Lounge. The chamber orchestra was playing Elgar and Strauss very prettily, and the aspidistras were almost as well-groomed as the ladies. May was very much the *grande dame*, as only those can be who are to the manner unborn. She queened it over the waiters, protested that the music was vulgar, and dropped the names of great acquaintances like sprinkling pepper. She used the nick-names of friends known only to her and her husband, Charles Seymour-Scudabright, as if not to know them were to be in *purdah*. It was all too much for Mary.

"Pom-pom," she said. "Is that not a tassle on a bonnet? And Dee-dee – ach, that's baby-talk."

"Dee-dee Devonshire," May said in reproach, "is one of the sweetest, kindest creatures –"

"I was not referring to her character," Mary said, "but to her nick-name." Then turning on Charles, ablaze in the white uniform and gold braid of an officer on the battleship *Majestic*, "You don't have time for tittle-tattle, do you?"

"My ship keeps me busy, ma'am." Malice sharpened Charles's eye. "But not so busy I had not heard – may we hope to see your husband?"

"Doctor Lamb is extremely busy," Mary said, but she could not help but flush. "His work at the hospital – it detains him night and day."

"At night," Charles said, "I heard that he sometimes roams the streets of London. As Mr Gladstone used to do, rescuing fallen women, I believe. Or not *rescuing* them . . ."

"Has that lie, that scandal, reached you?" Mary swung on May, who looked away in a flutter. "It must have been *you*, May!"

"I have never said a word –"

"Oh no?"

"Except that Doctor Lamb was not really interested in women. Not even in *you*, Mary. Seaforth told me about it. That word he used – an *aversion* to women."

"He is a good and kind husband," Mary said, red in the face. Water prickled in her eyes. How could her own family betray her? The Sinclairs had always stuck together. What was their life doing to them? And marriage with this superior sort of person, the same sort who had driven them out to wander the earth.

"Your doctor – he may be not much under the sheets, ma'am," Charles said, "if you'll forgive the plain words of a sailor. Yet in a surgery, cutting up people, a sawbones –"

"Then you do credit the lie?"

"Nobody will ever *catch* Jack the Ripper, ma'am. He was far too clever for that. Too good a *doctor* to leave any traces."

"I cannot believe this." Mary found herself on her feet with the tears running down her face. She tried to speak down to her niece and the insinuating Charles. "Do you know, there is not a single surgeon in London – not one – who has not been accused of being the Ripper? Just because the bodies were dismembered by somebody with a knowledge of anatomy. It could have been a butcher . . . a medical student. There are even other lies – the King of Belgium, a member of our royal family –"

"It had to be a surgeon," Charles said.

"Then why pick on my Harry Lamb?"

"An odd character," Charles said, "a very odd character. Who does not make my May's aunt happy."

"I have never said that," Mary protested. "I am extremely happy. Harry is so kind, so thoughtful –"

"So damned peculiar he never touches you, ma'am," Charles said. "And how do you explain that?"

"It is not for you to ask, sir. And I will certainly not reply. I came here to see the family – if family they are. But I will not stay to hear the gossip, the scandal, that rules this country. There's not a word of truth in it. Tongues wag, click, click, click. He did that, she didn't do that – all lies. You'd all rather tell lies and bring people down than . . . Hamilton!"

Through the lounge Hamilton rolled. He had not found his shore legs because he treated the steady Axminster carpets of the hotel like a pitching sea. Making his way carefully towards the family table, he trod as delicately as Agag of the Bible. He was wearing blue service dress, and when Charles rose and put on his braided cap, Hamilton had to salute him, although he made this gesture more of a throwaway of his right hand.

"Hello, Charles," he said. "Hello, May. You didn't have to get up to greet me, Aunt Mary. You weren't going?"

"Of course she was not," May said. "She was so glad to see you come in."

"I certainly was," Mary said. "You stopped me from going." She was trembling with agitation and horror. "I have heard such things. I cannot –"

"What's this?" Hamilton said. "Aunt Mary –"

"It's nothing," May said. "An idle rumour. Quite untrue. It has been a long day, watching the fleet. Do sit down, Aunt Mary. And compose yourself."

Still shaking, Mary found herself sitting down on May's command, while Hamilton enthused to Charles.

"Did you see our ship?" he asked. "The *Turbinia*. Didn't she run? What a lick!"

"I prefer sail," Charles said, seating himself and taking off his cap. "Steam – it's so noisy. I don't know how you *hear* down there."

"What we hear," Hamilton said, also sitting beside his shaken aunt, "is only the engine going wrong. Nothing else. It's all very well for you up on the bridge speaking down the tube, 'Full steam ahead', 'Hard astern'. Do you know what it's like down there, following those commands?"

"No, I do not," Charles said. "And I do not intend to know. Engine rooms are not for gentlemen. Steam, as far as I am concerned, is a necessary evil, and best left to them that understand it."

"Ship's engineers," Hamilton said smiling. "The lowest of the low. But then, you can't do without them." He hailed a waiter. "Rum, grog – whatever you call it. And don't say you don't have it – this is Portsmouth. Navy ground."

"It was wonderful, your ship," Mary said. "I saw it pass in the distance. It swallowed up the sea."

"Thirty-four knots," Hamilton said. "Put that in our new destroyers – with torpedoes and the new gyroscopes – and it will knock every battleship out of the water."

"Oh, I think," Charles said, his thought the wisdom of Solomon, "our big guns will smash you to matchsticks before you get near us."

"You're too slow," Hamilton said, "and too old, and you still think you can fight like Nelson, broadsides and all that bosh. I have news for you. Nelson is dead! And Sir Charles Parsons has invented the turbine engine." He turned to Mary. "Where's Seaforth? I wanted to see him. He does something *useful* like I do – being a doctor."

"Have you not heard?" Mary watched as the waiter set down a glass of rum in front of Hamilton as gingerly as if it were an explosive. "Seaforth has gone to South Africa. To Cape Town. I really am worried for him. It may be the wrong choice."

"Why?"

"Well . . ." Mary was embarrassed, which she rarely was. "He says – his colour . . . there are many Indians there . . . and he will call himself an Indian. He has very strong views. And they have very strong views against the Indians there."

"They call them Coloureds," Charles said. "I have been to the naval base at Simonstown. The Coloureds are a step up from being Kaffirs, though there are those who say they are a mixture of the worst of both races –"

"Or the best of both," Mary said. "As Seaforth certainly is."

"You always loved him too much," May said. "As if he were a son – because you don't have –"

Mary reddened again. "You go too far, May."

"A wee bit more love in the family," Hamilton said, "would go a long way."

Yet was it love, Mary thought, that had made Seaforth first warn her against Harry Lamb? Or was it jealousy about losing her love? Or both?

"Seaforth said he had more opportunity in South Africa." Mary was still flushed in her defence of her favourite. "There is a sizeable Indian colony –"

"They imported coolies to build the railways," Charles said.

"An influential Indian group," Mary said. "So he has gone there. I think, in a way, Iain was quite relieved. Seaforth and Peg were always a *reminder* in India – and it is such a caste society, the Hindus and Us are equally bad, I don't know which is the worst. Peg has gone back, of course, and she is doing very well in the hospital in Bombay. But I don't have to tell you, Hamilton. Your father must keep in touch with you."

"Hardly at all," Hamilton said, "except to tell me of his mighty irrigation work in the Punjab. Have you heard from Mother, May?"

"She does not write much," May said. "Everybody is well. Annandale is more of a courtesy club for Simla than a home now. Because Margaret's husband is an *aide* to the viceroy, and there are the two children, Ruby and Wallace. There is a good deal of entertainment – although not quite on the English level."

"And poor Iain," Mary said, "is banished to his culverts and his drainpipes in the Punjab. He never could stand the Simla ladies."

"I am sure making drains for Indians," Charles said, "is very worthy work."

"Actually it is," Hamilton said. "More worthy than a review of the Home Fleet."

"Are you suggesting, sir, that the British Navy is not the foundation of the Empire?"

"Only the policeman," Hamilton said, "on his beat. The foundation of the Empire is those who make it tick. Like my father."

As Charles glared at Hamilton, Mary intervened. She had fought down her agitation to a form of control. When there was too much to say, it was best to talk about little.

"And, May, how are your three? Gordon and Graham and little Ruth. In the pink, are they not?"

"Yes. The boys are down for Eton, but Ruth, we shall keep her with us at home. I feel that education quite spoils a girl's femininity."

"Oh," Mary said. "You think I am a male, then? It is the masculine in me which appeals to poor Harry Lamb."

"You have said it, not I." Charles could not restrain his smile. "Before you came, Hamilton, we were saying how sorry we were that Doctor Lamb felt that he had to carry on his work in London through the Jubilee, whatever that work is –"

Again the insinuations. Could Charles not be quiet? Mary found herself saying coldly, "They think my husband may be Jack the Ripper."

"No," Hamilton said. "That gentle man? Impossible."

"Indeed," May said quickly. "I am sure my husband doesn't

mean . . ." She stared so hard at Charles that it was now he who was flushing.

"No," he mumbled. "No offence meant, ma'am." But he had offended, even if he had called Mary "ma'am" as if she was the Queen Herself.

"Forget it then," Hamilton said. "A misunderstanding. But there is bad news. I suppose you have heard, the Queen – she is not well. She may not see in the next century."

"God forbid," Charles said. "I thought the problem was the Prince of Wales. His leg –"

"She receives daily bulletins about that at Osborne from his yacht. Signor Marconi's new invention – ship-to-shore wireless, he calls it. He hangs up electric wires on kites and masts, and you may now communicate from vessel to vessel or to port."

"Another one of your damned inventions," Charles said. "Semaphore is good enough for me. What you can't say with flags shouldn't be said at all."

Hamilton finished his rum in a gulp and signalled the waiter for some more.

"I don't know," he said. "No more turning blind eyes or deaf ears like Nelson. The right orders will go straight through to every ship's captain –"

"And where's the initiative, sir? That is the tradition of the navy."

"Communications," Hamilton said, "are more important."

Mary intervened again. "There is something I have to tell you all," she said. "That is the real reason I came down here. I have heard from Katie in Vancouver – only what we expect. Hannah is sore ill – and Hamish grieves for her. I think he will follow her. We must be ready to go to Canada, as many as can, the next year. For they will not see the next century, even if the Queen does."

"They will," May said. "They will always be with us."

"No," Mary said. And now other tears were falling from her eyes. But this was the weeping of pure grief, not of anger. "They were always with us, even though they took us away or left us. We would not be here if they were not always here. But soon –" She gave a sob. "We must go to them."

"We cannot go," May said quickly. "Even to see grandfather and grandmother. Charles has his duty, and I have the children."

"And your life here," Mary said. "But I will go."

"Perhaps your husband can spare you," Charles said.

"He will come with me," Mary said, "if his duty allows him."

"I will move heaven and earth to be with them," Hamilton said, "but I may be transferred. They say there's trouble at the Cape. They have need for ship's engineers to carry our troops to South Africa."

"I wish there was trouble in Canada," Mary said. "Then you could carry me there." Then she caught herself at her own words. "Of course, I do not wish that. Thank God, Canada is at peace. But we must be with them." She dabbed at her eyes with her handkerchief, then blew her nose to clear it in her forthright way. "Let us get there. All of us. However far we are scattered over the earth."

24

ALL THE CORNERS OF
THE EARTH

"Lord, Thou hast been our refuge: from one generation to another. Before the mountains were brought forth, or ever the earth and the world were made . . ."

Mary stood by the open grave in the churchyard, looking down at the coffin, in which her father was hidden. The pit was dug by another grave, covered with roses, the grave of his wife, Hannah. He had not lived a week after her death. Something was broken in him. Mary had sat with him as he lingered, and now he was laid to rest, with the clergyman reading over his body from the Order for the Burial of the Dead.

"For a thousand years in Thy sight are but as yesterday: seeing that is past as a watch in the night. As soon as Thou scatterest them, they are even as a sleep: and fade away suddenly like the grass. In the morning it is green, and groweth: but in the evening it is cut down, dried up and withered."

It was so. How long since they had moved from the glen to the shore and the kelping, how long since they came over the oceans to the shipwreck and the fever island and the forest and the great plains and on to the western shore of Canada? And she – how long a dairy maid in the castle at Dunrobin, how long a parlour maid in the mansion at London, how long a nurse in the *zenanas* and in the famine in the Punjab? Now she had lost both the men she had loved, Erskine Montgomery and Harry Lamb. They had never loved her back. Her yearning for them, her passion and desperation for their touch – they had withheld themselves from her. Erskine because of his mad wife, and Harry because he was like that, fearful of women, something killed within him in his fearsome trade, and now dead of a broken faith inside him, ripped open by the knives and scalpels of the tongues of London, accusing him of crimes he never had done and never could do. Yes, he had not loved to touch women, but he loved one woman – herself. Mary Sinclair, the widow Lamb, knew that. Not even his death would take the love of him away from her.

"Man that is born of a woman hath but a short time to live, and is full of misery. He cometh up, and is cut down, like a flower; he fleeth as it were a shadow, and never continueth in one stay. In the midst of life we are in death . . ."

It was true, it was so true. All that nursing of the dying. Mary had spent her life by the beds of sufferers, and yet – *Man that is born of a woman hath but a short time to live.* No man was born of this woman Mary, but of Hannah, how many had been born and how many were still living, how few were cut down, like a flower. And she had no child, not a one. It was her right, and she had given it away in serving others all her life. A useless sacrifice for a barren womb. What was it for? Who was grateful? Not the sick. When they were well again, who remembered? Not the married brothers and sisters, nieces and nephews, who looked at their old aunt and pitied her, the widow who had never had a proper man and never a child, condemned to be single now and an old woman. Even her father Hamish, who had been given so little from his long life had his Hannah until his last few days. And she had been given nothing but a bleak age. She was not pitying herself, she was telling herself the truth, and it was making her angry. And at her father's funeral, too . . .

It was time to cast the earth down on the coffin. Mary picked up some loose clods and dropped them over the grave's edge. They thudded on the wooden lid. So did the lumps of soil thrown down by Angus and Isabella, by Bain and his wife that had been Julia Mac-Kenzie. None of their children had been able to make the journey – indeed, Angus's eldest son was already in South Africa, serving in the Seaforths with his uncle. But Katie was at the grave side, sobbing below her black veil and clinging on to Marie, who only wore a small black cap like a pennant of death flying on her mass of red hair, her blazing beauty as shocking as lightning at this scene of grief.

When the rattle of earth on the coffin had ended like a volley of shots at a military funeral, Mary heard the voice of the priest read on from the service: "We therefore commit his body to the ground; earth to earth, ashes to ashes, dust to dust; in sure and certain hope of the Resurrection to eternal life, through Our Lord Jesus Christ; Who shall change our vile body . . ."

Tears prickled in Mary's eyes, so that she could no longer see. A roaring was in her ears, and she swayed and felt Angus's hand under her elbow to keep her steady. She was blind, she was deaf to the end of the service. But when it was over, Angus took her away to the carriage covered with *crêpe* which would pull her behind black horses to the house by Vancouver Sound.

"They had nothing to leave us," Angus told the rest of the family, assembled over tea and cakes, which nobody ate. "Their old Bible in Gaelic – which none of us can read now – and a few trinkets. This house is in my name, as I built it for them. It was theirs as long as they lived . . ."

"And now?" Mary said.

"If any of you should wish to bide here still. Mary, you have been here since Harry's death, helping to look after them. Will you stay on?"

"For a while," Mary said. "Then I must get my courage back, and go to the work in London. At St Thomas's Hospital, where Harry was and did so much. Miss Nightingale still expects, though God knows why she should." Her resentment suddenly spilled out of her. "What have I got from it all? She always expected too much."

"Too much," Angus said. "Isabella and I and the family will not be needing the house while my railway work is still in South America. But we may retire here yet. And you, Katie, and Marie . . ."

"I am going to London," Marie said. "The theatre there –"

"It is rubbish," Mary said. "Gaiety Girls. And the actresses who are *not* at the Empire –"

"The theatre there," Marie said, "is excellent. Mr Wilde and Mr Shaw and Mrs Campbell. Here, I can only sing and dance. There is no *acting*."

"How can you speak of that?" Bain was flushed with anger. "Your wickedness – it drove them to their graves! Flaunting yourself in the theatre – the music-hall!"

"She is the toast of Vancouver," Katie said. "I know Mother disapproved – but if you are as beautiful as my daughter . . ."

"Vanity saith the preacher." Bain's wife Julia had little to be vain about, except for her strength. She was built like a plough. "There is some as have no time to prettify –"

"Or reason," Katie said.

"Julia helps me on the farm," Bain said. "And the boys, young as they are, Rob and Gillon. You're never too young to get eggs or muck out. You would not know the place, Mary. It is the barbed wire. It keeps out the beasts and the Indians."

"Your trouble always was," Mary said to Bain, "keeping people out. You have always kept the family out of the land you got from Father."

"I have made it," Bain said. "There is wheat now, as far as the eye can see."

208

"It will blow away," Angus said, "the soil. Unless you engineer the ground – plant it with trees."

"Build your bridges," Bain said. "And your railways. Leave farming to the likes of us. You left us – all of you left us, even Hamish and Hannah – you left me alone till Julia came, and now, the land is mine – ours, I mean." He put an arm round the shoulder of his wife. They looked hewn together.

"You would keep out my grandmother, Uncle Bain," Marie said. "She was a Crow, and I am so proud of her. My father Henri was. He always said I got my looks from my Indian grandmother and my brains from Katie."

Certainly, that was Marie's special beauty, the upflung cheek-bones under her green eyes, the bronze tint to her skin under her flaming hair, the spring to her taut body. To Katie, she was lovelier than sin or even the memory of her husband.

"If you have my brains," she said, "you will bide here and not gallivant off to London to try your luck on the stage."

"You will help me, Aunt Mary?" Marie pleaded. "You will –"

"Acting is not my profession," Mary said. "Nursing is." Marie was too striking for her own good – or anybody else's. She would have everything that Mary had never had. Men would give it to her, and they had given Mary nothing. A stab of jealousy pierced the side of the older woman, and then she was ashamed of it. Marie was her kin. Marie was asking for her help. "I will see what I can do *if* you come to London. But I promise nothing. You should heed your mother and stay."

"Oh, thank you." Marie impetuously threw herself on her aunt and hugged her and kissed her, not on the cheek, but on the mouth.

"Get away with you, girl," Mary said and pushed her niece away, but she was smiling as she shook her head. Ach, the energy of the young. But it was good to be needed. "I do not promise, but I will try to help you."

"My mother says you can do anything and everything," Marie said, "if you only want to."

"That I cannot, Katie," Mary said, but she was smiling now at the recognition. "Everything I cannot do. But when I put my mind to it –"

"Angus says the same," Isabella said. "Now it is you who will hold the family together. In a family, there must be *one* –"

"But Iain," Bain said.

"Is he here?"

"And Hamish Jamie."

"Is he here? No." Isabella smiled at Mary. "It is you, Mary, who will be our Hamish and our Hannah."

A kind of peace began to steal over Mary. Yes, Hamish and Harry Lamb were laid to rest. But she would go on. Childless she might be, but there were all her parents' children, and their children's children to new generations. If Isabella was right, they would come to her. Because she was single, she would be fair or try to be. She would give her love equally, although her special Seaforth . . . Mary smiled at her weakness for him, but she would be the judge and jury and court of appeal of them all.

Now she was given her rôle, she would use it. She walked over to the table and took up the tea-pot to go round the room in the ritual pouring that was the quiet wake at this funeral. None of the Gaelic fiddling and the drinking. It was the sober ceremony of a family that had gone a long way, and still had a long way to go.

"Thank you all for coming to this burying," Mary said. "It was a sore journey to come here – but not so sore as it was for Hannah and Hamish. But they are at last at rest. They have found peace."

She began to pour from the pot into Julia's cup. "More tea?"

In London, another aged woman was fulfilling Her rôle after sixty years of doing it. From Her wheel-chair, Queen Victoria pressed an electric button in Buckingham Palace before She rode in Her open landau pulled now by eight cream horses to St Paul's in 1897 for Her Diamond Jubilee. It had been a hot night. The Queen Empress was restless. She was not sure that She could support the occasion, driving six miles through the cheering crowds and listening to a short service from the steps of the cathedral. "No!" one of Her German friends had complained. "After sixty years reign, to thank God in the street!" But She was too lame to climb stairs, and Her people wanted to thank God for Her reign in the streets. And so She would go. Already the beacons had blazed all across the Highlands of Scotland from Ben Nevis to Her beloved Balmoral. And the signal on the button was using the telephone to send a message to every last corner of Her empire. "From my heart I thank my beloved people. May God bless them!"

It was still the Queen's weather, as at the Golden Jubilee. When the first salvo of guns in Hyde Park announced that She had left the palace, the sun burst out from the grey skies and blazed down all day. Triumphal arches spanned the route, picked out in tributes: OUR HEARTS THY THRONE or SHE WROUGHT HER PEOPLE LASTING GOOD. Tiny gas-jets flared and the new electric-light bulbs glistened like constellations fallen from the heavens. And with the Queen in the carriage sat Alix, Princess of Wales, in lilac, and a favourite daughter Lenchen. Her two elder sons rode on either side of the landau, Her youngest Arthur to the rear. The commander-in-chief, Lord Garnet

Wolseley, rode in front, while the tallest man in the British Army, Captain Ames of the Life Guards, headed the whole procession. All the imperial forces which were not guarding Her domains marched or rode past, Bengal Lancers and Ghurkas, the West African Rifles and the Black Watch from Canada. The shouting and the hurrahs from millions of throats quite deafened Her Majesty who was already hard of hearing.

"No one ever, I believe, has met with such an ovation," She recorded that night. "The crowds were quite indescribable, and their enthusiasm truly marvellous and deeply touching."

Hamish Jamie thought it was stupid from the beginning. Advancing into the jaws of a dragon. Hills to the left of them, kopjes to the right of them, and a strong scarp to the front. You couldn't see the Boers, of course, they were too sly for that, hidden under their slouch hats with their repeating Mausers that gave out more rapid fire than the Lee-Metfords, and even better artillery: Creusot Long Toms and Krupp field-pieces and Vickers-Maxim Pom-Poms lobbing their little one-pound shells in bursts of twenty and blowing up gun crews and crowded infantry in clusters of explosions. The Boers had been clever. They had used their gold to arm in good time. They had better weapons than the British, and they fought from the ground like ferrets or wildcats. Hamish Jamie did not like the Highland Brigade going at dawn into the jaws of death in four massed columns, soaked to the skin after the deluge of the night. And he did not like going in himself. The quartermaster led from the rear.

Yet if General Wauchope was himself leading the Black Watch, with the Seaforths, along with the Argyll and Sutherland Highlanders on the flank backed by the Highland Light Infantry in reserve, Hamish Jamie felt he would have to join the action, even if it were his last action. Also, Angus's son Hamish Charles was in the regiment. The young fool had volunteered fresh from Harrow, following the footsteps of that other young fool at Omdurman, Winston Churchill, who had also come to beat the Boers. Hamish Jamie felt he had to keep an eye on another nephew. He had already lost one in South Africa.

Nobody knew the Boer trenches were at the foot of the ridges instead of on the top of them, where they should have been. Having no military experience, the Boers did better than those who knew how things should be done. For they did the unexpected, and it worked. They sprang their trap and surprise that dawn at Magersfontein from their bolt-holes behind barbed-wire fences hung with tin cans. The night advance of the Highland Brigade in its columns, linked with ropes to keep their masses perfectly aligned so they might suffer the worst from the Boer Mausers, blundered into the trip-wires. A hailstorm of bullets and Pom-Poms killed five hundred men in ten minutes.

"Fix bayonets! Charge!" Hamish Jamie heard the hopeless orders yelled in the gloom. Then at the back, another shout, "Retire!" And round him men in kilts stumbling forward, standing still, retreating – and all the time dropping and bending and falling, hurled down by the relentless fusillade to their front. He saw a few men reach the barbed wire and collapse, spread-eagled, on that final metal barrier, sieved with blood and bullet-holes. Ahead of him, General Wauchope was hit, a red spray gushing from his mouth. And Hamish Jamie found himself cradling his dying commander in his arms, hearing the cough and froth of the last words, "Goodbye, men. Fight for yourselves. It's man to man now."

It was not. It was repeating rifles and barbed wire that stopped any man to man. As Hamish Jamie laid down the body of Wauchope and rose to stagger forward at the impossible charge, he saw for the first time the broken Highlanders retreat or take cover behind the ant-hills from the murdering storm of the Boer volleys. He knew he was as good as dead. Where his nephew and namesake, Hamish Charles, was in this massacre at dawn, Hamish Jamie did not know. But he knew he must move forward. And when the bullet hit him in the chest and knocked him to the ground, it was almost a relief. The blow was like a pardon. He had done his duty. He could not go on. He could only lie on his back, watching the sun rise over the kopjes, and feeling his life gasp away from his shattered ribs and pierced lung. He sensed a dry smile on his face, then his lips moved to say, "After all that – and you will not have to pay my pension the now."

The rest of the Highlanders were staked out on the dry plain without food or water for the whole broiling day to follow, unable to raise their heads or move, stranded and sweating and beaten down before the enemy, overseeing their humiliation. Hamish Charles's dreams of glory were lowered to the red dust he inhaled from the ant-heap that was his only cover. The insects were active in the full sun, crawling over his bare knees and stinging him into movement, which unleashed a whirr of bullets worse than swarming bees. All around him were the cries and moans of the wounded, the dreadful sing-song of defeat. His own throat was too parched to cry, and by the afternoon there was stillness except for the Lyddite shells of the British guns and the running explosion of the Boer Pom-Poms in their intermittent arguments.

War shouldn't be like this, Hamish Charles thought. We always charge. We always win. We're fighting a bunch of Dutch dirt farmers. What bloody fool sent us into this death-trap? Someone had blundered.

And then someone else was singing, "Over the Sea to Skye". And a lad from the Seaforths had gone mad in the sun and was wandering towards the barbed-wire and the hidden Mausers, singing the old lament for the Stuart kings:

> Speed, bonny boat, like a bird on the wing,
> Onward the sailors cry,
> Speed for the man who was born to be king
> Over the sea –

A crackle and a thudding and a scream stopped the song, and Hamish Charles kept his head down until evening, until he could stumble back to the rear, over the corpses of the Highlanders that made mounds of flesh and tartan across the plain. He did not find the body of his uncle, who had died towards noon, and glad of it, in the end.

The news of the defeat of Magersfontein and the death of Hamish Jamie and the survival of his cousin reached Hamilton at Simonstown in the lee of the wild tableland of the Cape of Good Hope itself. He immediately sent a runner to find Seaforth and bring him to the naval base to tell him of his father's death. While he was waiting for him, Hamilton supervised the coaling of his new frigate, for the power of the British navy now depended on pyramids of best Welsh coal and coke, shipped out to dozens of dockyards and bases and stations across the world. Simonstown itself was like a home base with its pretty cottages and villas and whitewashed sailors' barracks and naval stores and a church with a steeple and the Admiral's House with its rose-gardens leading to a quay, where the flagship and the squadron lay. Wherever the Empire went, Hamilton had observed, the British took their surroundings with them. Even at the tip of Africa, he stood on a piece of England.

Seaforth was not moved by the news of his father's death at Magersfontein. "He was too old for it," he told Hamilton. "He should never have joined the attack. His job was getting the supplies up, not getting killed. That is for fools like Hamish Charles – and he survived."

"Stopping a bullet has nothing to do with justice," Hamilton said. He signalled the mess waiter for another drink of lemonade for Seaforth, whose frock coat and black bow-tie made him look like a visiting ambassador to the all-white officers of the Fleet.

"Stopping bullets has a lot to do with medicine," Seaforth replied. "I am dealing with your casualties all the time. Horrible wounds – dum-dums, explosive bullets, lacerations from barbed wire. Although the army medical corps is better now, they can't cope with all your wounded – and they have to call on me. I must say, you *are* taking a beating from the Boers."

"And which side are you on?" Hamilton said, all too conscious of a senior captain cocking an ear from the next armchair. He might be hung from the yard-arm for treason.

"Not the Boers. I find their attitude to people they called Coloured even more extreme than yours."

"Whose, Seaforth?"

"Not you personally, Hamilton. But you see, my father –"

"Your dead father –"

"Dying with the Seaforths at the hands of other white men – not Indians, because he survived the Mutiny. Killed by the latest techniques of western war. Myself, patching up the badly wounded – their lives in these hands" – turning up the pale palms of his dark hands to Hamilton – "begging *me* to save their lives . . . You must see, Hamilton, it is quite a reversal."

"I do see," Hamilton said. "But Aunt Mary, she saw you trained as a doctor."

"Yes. A wonderful woman. And now Peg is a fully-qualified woman doctor in Bombay. It is remarkable what British women have done for the Empire. But as for the men, I am not so sure."

"Are you staying on here, Seaforth?"

"I am doing well. But if the Boers win their independence . . ."

"They will not."

"I will go back to India and see what I may do about ours."

"We will never let India go. It is the jewel – the Koh-i-noor."

"I know that. It just makes our independence more difficult. I always wonder why the Scots are taking so long to ask for their independence back."

"We are a United Kingdom."

"Really? Ireland too?"

"You go for the sore spots, Seaforth."

Seaforth smiled his thin black smile.

"That is why I am a doctor." He rose. "I must go back to your wounded, Hamilton. Thank you for telling me about Father's death – I shall probably miss him more than I think. He did have qualities –"

"You seem to have his independence," Hamilton said drily.

"Fair enough. My regards to that idiot Hamish Charles and tell him to stay out of the line of fire. The Boers are very good shots. And if you do see Aunt Mary when you go back to England –"

"Yes, I will."

"Tell her, I love her still. She kept her promise to my mother about Peg and me. And she will be proud of us yet."

"She is to head the nurses' school at St Thomas's . . ."

"If you have the gift of self-sacrifice," Seaforth said, "I am afraid you will lose yourself and only be left with the sacrifice. Who is Mary herself? She is all given to us."

A thousand wax candles made a flickering firmament under the high arches and vaultings and aisles of the abbey. On this matins of the new century, the great and good, or at least the famous and the invited, were giving their thanks in Westminster Abbey to the Lord of Hosts. The Almighty had led the nation to become almighty upon the waters He had made, and upon a quarter of the dry lands He had also made to push back the waters. Standing beneath the marble images of previous rulers, so Roman and imperial in their still statues and busts over her, Mary Sinclair had moved to join in this paean of praise that appeared to be for the glory of God. Yet given the fervour of the singing, it might be in praise of the British people themselves. Strange it was, that the small population of two inconsiderable islands off Europe had spread themselves so thin and wide across the globe and had webbed and netted the seven seas. There might be a divine purpose in it, there must be a heavenly intervention. For the achievement was against all the odds. As it had been for the daughters and sons of Hamish and Hannah Sinclair, a scattering and a fulfilling.

And now the massed congregation were singing the *Venite*, "Come and Let Us Sing Unto the Lord". And the strains swept up past the stone images and the monuments with their swords and crowns and emblems to the roof of ancient England, Norman and Tudor and Stuart and Hanoverian, and now the Britain of the aged Queen Victoria at the apogee of Her empire.

"For the Lord is a great God," they sang, "and a great king above gods. In His hands are all the corners of the earth . . ."

Yes, they were, and in the hands of the British. And the Scots and the Sinclairs were flung to the corners to hold them.

"And the strength of the hills is His also . . ."

For the Scots and the Sinclairs would endure where they were posted. The strength of the hills was theirs, that was the gift of the Lord.

"The sea is His, and He made it: and His hands prepared the dry land."

Hamilton was on the steam ships, and the ships held together the seas and the seas brought them from one far land to another shore.

"For He is the Lord our God: and we are the people of His pasture, and the sheep of His land."

There would be a homecoming for all of them hurled to the far corners of the earth. If not for their children, then for the children of their children. And the sheep which had made for their clearing would now be cleared as all beasts were cleared. And the humans who were the true sheep of His land would be restored to His pasture of the Highlands.

"Forty years long was I grieved with this generation, and said: It is a people that do err in their hearts, for they have not known My ways."

What were His ways? What were their errors? They had been banished for forty years and more to the edges of the earth. But they were already coming home. Perhaps they had loved their high places too much, perhaps they had been cast down and cast away for their pride. There was no answer in it, but there seemed a kind of forgiveness, for the new generations at the least.

And now Mary sang in full voice with the choirs and the believers in the Abbey of Westminster.

"As it was in the beginning, is now and ever shall be. World without end. Amen."